THE
SERPENT
SWORD

MATTHEW HARFFY grew up in
Northumberland where the rugged
terrain, ruined castles and rocky
coastline had a huge impact on him.
He now lives in Wiltshire, England,
with his wife and their two daughters.

ALSO BY MATTHEW HARFFY

The Bernicia Chronicles

THE
SERPENT
SWORD

THE BERNICIA CHRONICLES: I

MATTHEW
HARFFY

ⓐ

First published as an ebook by Aria, an imprint of Head of Zeus, in 2016

First published in print in the UK by Aria in 2017
This paperback edition published by Aria in 2017

9 7 5 3 1 2 4 6 8

A catalogue record for this book is available from
the British Library.

ISBN (PB): 9781786693105
ISBN (E): 9781784978822

Typeset by Adrian McLaughlin

Printed and bound in Germany by CPI Books GmbH

Head of Zeus Ltd
First Floor East
5–8 Hardwick Street
London ECIR 4RG

WWW.HEADOFZEUS.COM

For Maite, Elora and Iona

Place Names

Place names in Dark Ages Britain vary according to time, language, dialect and the scribe who was writing. I have not followed a strict convention when choosing what spelling to use for a given place. In most cases, I have chosen the name I believe to be the closest to that used in the early seventh century, but like the scribes of all those centuries ago, I have taken artistic licence at times, and merely selected the one I liked most.

Albion	Great Britain
Bebbanburg	Bamburgh
Bernicia	Northern kingdom of Northumbria, running approximately from the Tyne to the Firth of Forth
Cantware	Kent
Cantwareburh	Canterbury
Dál Riata	Gaelic overkingdom, roughly encompassing modern-day Argyll and Bute and Lochaber in Scotland and also County Antrim in Northern Ireland

Deira	Southern kingdom of Northumbria, running approximately from the Humber to the Tyne
Elmet	Native Briton kingdom, approximately equal to the West Riding of Yorkshire
Engelmynster	Fictional location in Deira
Eoferwic	York
Frankia	France
Gefrin	Yeavering
Gwynedd	Gwynedd, North Wales
Hibernia	Ireland
Hii	Iona
Hithe	Hythe, Kent
Northumbria	Modern-day Yorkshire, Northumberland and south-east Scotland
Pocel's Hall	Pocklington

DÁL RIATA

Hii

HIBERNIA

N

IRISH SEA

ALBION
AD 633

PICTLAND

DÁL RIATA

BERNICIA ○ Bebbanburg

DEIRA
○ Eoferwic

ELMET

GWYNEDD

HIBERNIA

MERCIA

WEST SAXONS
CANTWARE ○ Hithe
Cantwareburh

FRANKIA

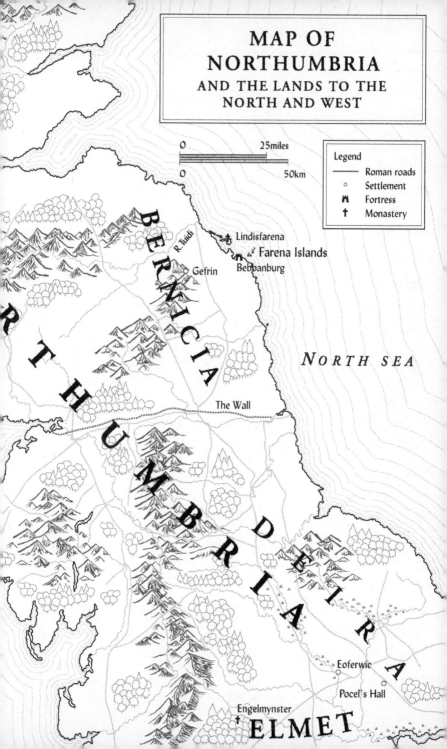

MAP OF NORTHUMBRIA

AND THE LANDS TO THE NORTH AND WEST

0 —— 25 miles
0 —— 50 km

Legend
—— Roman roads
∘ Settlement
Ⅿ Fortress
✝ Monastery

BERNICIA

R. Tuidi
Lindisfarena
Farena Islands
Gefrin
Bebbanburg

NORTH SEA

NORTHUMBRIA

The Wall

DEIRA

Eoferwic
Pocel's Hall

Engelmynster

ELMET

ANNO DOMINI NOSTRI IESU CHRISTI
IN THE YEAR OF OUR LORD JESUS CHRIST
633

"Infaustus ille annus et omnibus bonis exosus
usque hodie permanet"
Historia ecclesiastica gentis Anglorum
—BEDA VENERABILIS

*"This year is looked upon by all good men as
despicable and shameful"*
A History of the English Church and People
—THE VENERABLE BEDE

Prologue

The man stood in the shadows preparing for murder. He pulled his cloak about him, stretching muscles that had grown stiff from inactivity. It was cold and his breath steamed in the autumn night air. It was uncomfortable, but he would wait. His mind was made up.

His suspicions had been aroused before, but now he knew the truth of it. He had followed them here, had seen them go inside together.

Soft sounds of a woman's laughter drifted from the stable. His jaw clenched. His hand gripped the antler hilt of his seax. Holding the knife reassured him. But he would not use it tonight. No. There would be no fight. No clash of metal. No battle-glory.

No deeds for the scops to sing of.

Warriors' acts were recounted by the bards in the flickering light of mead hall fires. There was no light here. It would be a secret death. In the darkness.

What he must do was clear. But none could ever know of what happened here tonight. His life would be forfeit should he be discovered.

Somewhere, off to the land-facing, westward side of the fortress, a dog barked, then all was still again. From the east, he could hear the distant rumble of waves hitting rocks far below.

On the palisade, some distance away, he could just make out the silhouette of a guard.

A cloud scudded in front of the moon. The all-seeing eye of Woden, father of the gods, was closed. On such a night the gods slept and a man's actions could bend his wyrd to his own ends. A great man could seize what was rightfully his. His mother had once told him he would be a man to dethrone kings and topple kingdoms. Great men were not governed by common laws.

Clinging to that thought, he girded himself for what he was about to do.

He shivered and convinced himself it was because of the chill. He moved further into the shadows.

From the building came a new sound. The rhythmic gasps and cries of coupling. He recognised the sound of Elda in those guttural moans.

How could she be so fickle? He had offered her everything. By Woden, he would have made her his wife! To think she had spurned him and then opened her legs to that young upstart. The anger he felt at her rejection bubbled up inside him like bile.

And him! Octa. The man Elda was rutting with inside the stable. Octa had all a warrior could want. A ring-giving lord who looked upon him with favour. He had land and treasures. And of course, the sword. The sword that should never have been his. The blade was named Hrunting and had been a gift from their lord, King Edwin. He had bestowed it on the man he thought had saved his life in battle. But he had given it to the wrong man. The battle had been confused, the shieldwall had broken and the king had been surrounded by enemies. It appeared all was lost until one of the king's warriors, one of his thegns, had rallied the men and turned the tide of the battle.

Afterwards, Edwin had given Hrunting to Octa. It was a sword fit for a king. The blade forged from twisted rods of iron. The metal shone with the pattern of rippling water, or the slick skin of a snake. The hilt was inlaid with fine bone and intricate carvings. All who had seen the weapon coveted it.

But the man who waited in the shadows knew it should have been his. It was he who had smitten the leader of their enemies. He who had led the men in the charge that brought victory.

He who was destined for greatness.

It was with disbelief that he had seen the fabulous sword given to his rival. It was as if the king was bewitched. Ever since Octa had arrived in Bernicia, he could do no wrong.

His rage at Elda was nothing when compared to the ire he felt at his enemy's rise to prominence.

He fingered the hammer amulet of Thunor that hung on a leather thong round his neck. The priest of the soft new god, the Christ, preached forgiveness. The old gods would not expect forgiveness. They called for vengeance. Swift and terrible. The old gods would have their tribute of blood soon.

The door to the stable opened slowly and the object of his hate stepped into the night. The watcher held his breath. Starlight shone on Octa's golden hair, making it shimmer like burnished iron. He was broad and tall and moved with effortless grace. He looked like a hero from legend. Loathing and jealousy washed over the man who lurked in the gloom.

The blond giant moved between two storehouses, where the darkness was absolute. The shadowy figure followed him. He wore only kirtle and breeches underneath his cloak, nothing that would give away the noise of his movements. His hand gripped a stout stave of oak.

Stealthily, he moved close behind Octa. They could not be seen here from any of the palisades or the open ground between the buildings. He raised the club and took the last quick steps. Some instinct alerted his prey, who paused, turning back.

But the sense of danger had come too late to Octa. There should have been nothing to fear here. He was safe behind stout walls in the fortress. The warm passion of Elda was still fresh in his mind and body and he was languid with the glow of remembered pleasures.

Thus it was that Octa turned too slowly. He hardly glimpsed the dark figure surging towards him from the night. The club landed a solid blow on his temple with a sickening thud. He staggered back, hands flailing. He tried to pull Hrunting free of its scabbard, but he was dazed and his hand refused to grip.

The dark shape leapt in close to him and delivered another stunning blow to his head. Octa strove valiantly to defend himself, but his vision was blurred and he wasn't sure what had happened. He was in danger, but his body wouldn't obey him. Light flashed in his mind as another thundering strike hit his skull. He let out a grunt and sagged onto one knee.

Octa tried to rise, to face his foe on his feet. He struggled to stand but a frenzy of blows hammered his face and shoulders and he collapsed, unable to do any more to defend himself.

Soon, he lay still. His face a slick, glistening blackness. His attacker, panting from the exertion, breathed through his mouth and listened. If anyone had heard the struggle, he would be as good as dead. He waited until his breathing slowed. Nobody came running. No alarm was sounded.

He quickly pulled Hrunting from its wool-lined scabbard. The blade gleamed, lambent and deadly in the dim light of stars and moon. For a moment he turned the sword this way and that, marvelling at its balance, rejoicing in its heft. It was truly a thing of wonder. A great weapon for a great man. He wanted to gaze at the blade, but he must act quickly. There would be time for admiration later. He found a hiding place for it in the rubbish and weeds growing at the base of one of the buildings.

Once he was satisfied it was well hidden, he turned his attention to the prostrate form of his adversary. Octa was a tall man, muscular and heavy, but so was he. It would not be easy, but he would be able to lift him. He bent down and gripped Octa's wrist. The hand flopped limply, as if beckoning. He shuddered, but told himself the man's spirit had already fled. He pulled him into a sitting position and then, using a mixture of brute strength and his own body weight, he wrestled the corpse onto his shoulder. He heaved himself upright. By the gods, but the whoreson was heavy!

He had planned the route he must now take. He could get all the way to the southernmost part of the eastern palisade without being seen. If the Wyrd sisters, who spun the threads of destiny, smiled on him.

Cautiously, but with haste, he moved between stables and storehouses, past the kitchens and the alehouse, where the ever-present scent of brewing hung in the air. His path kept him far from sentries and torches, but should anyone step from a building to relieve themselves of tonight's mead and ale, he would be undone.

Reaching the foot of the ladder to the palisade, he cast a look along the wall and saw the guard at the far end. The wall ward was standing by a brazier, the light of which would make it difficult to see clearly into the darkness. Octa's slayer grasped the rung of the ladder and made his way up, one laborious step after another. Despite the cool air, he was drenched in sweat and his back and arms ached with the effort of carrying his grisly burden. He could feel his strength waning. He would need to be rid of the body soon, or he would drop him.

A grim smile played over his lips at the thought. He reached the palisade's platform. Below, waves crashed against rocks. White foam glowed in the darkness, like ghosts. Without pausing, keen to be rid of the heavy burden and the evidence of his crime, he hoisted the body from his shoulder and let it drop over the wall to the sea below. He watched as Octa fell, a dark shape against the swirling of the waves. He leaned against the palisade and drew in deep breaths. His pounding heart slowed and his sweat cooled. The guard at the end of the palisade was still hunched over his small fire.

In the morning, the body would be found, if the sea did not drag it away into its murky embrace. People would ask why a warrior who had everything would take his own life in this way, for surely he must have jumped to his death.

The clouds parted and the light from the moon gilded the fortress once more. Woden looked down again. Did he search for Octa? Or was he already in the All-Father's hall, feted and loved as he had been by King Edwin? Octa's murderer shuddered. This was the night in which he took control of his wyrd, but he did not wish to be judged by the gods. He turned his face from the moon.

Edwin should have recognised who amongst his thegns was most worthy. Instead he had chosen to elevate Octa. His blindness would lead to his downfall. Events were in motion that would see his destruction. Edwin would be dethroned and his kingdom would fall.

The killer smiled in the darkness. Before he fulfilled his mother's prophecy there was something else he must do. He descended the ladder and retraced his steps back towards the stable.

He hoped Elda was still there. She would soon regret her betrayal.

PART ONE
THE FORGING

1

Beobrand wiped the sweat from his brow. Pulling the long ship up onto the beach was tiring work. His legs felt weak, his stomach woozy. His body missed the constant motion of the sea beneath the keel; the continuous rolling of the waves which had been so unfamiliar to him only a few days before. He looked up at the fortress on the rock above. The mighty Bebbanburg, home of the royal family of Bernicia.

Guillemots and gulls careened in the grey, windswept sky, silhouetted against the brooding storm clouds that spoke of more bad weather to come.

"You'll have plenty of time to look, boy. Once we get the ship safely under that slope." Hrothgar's voice was rough, his throat hoarse from shouting at the hands on deck. "Now get pushing with the rest of us!"

Beobrand leaned once more into the side of the ship and heaved. They only had a little way to go before the ship was in line with the other two that were already beached beyond the high tide line.

He recognised the closer of the two ships as that of Swidhelm. He had seen the ship twice before and remembered the smooth line of its prow and the serpent figurehead carved there. Swidhelm must have missed the storm they had encountered the day before to be able to arrive before them. Hrothgar often said that Swidhelm was not only a fine seaman, but had the luck of the gods too. Fine praise from the taciturn sailor.

The other ship Beobrand did not know. He knew little of ships, but it was larger than any he had ever seen, almost a third longer than the other two. He wondered at the power of the owner of such a vessel. Could it belong to the king of this northern kingdom? How many men must he have in his warband? The figurehead was of a strange beast, long tongue protruding from fanged maws. It was painted red, like fresh blood.

"Alright, lassies," shouted Hrothgar. "That's far enough!"

There was a moment's murmured thanks from the weary men, who stopped and stretched tired muscles.

Beobrand was stiff from rowing and his hands were raw from pulling on the coarse ropes. He was no sailor and had struggled at first, but Hrothgar and the older men had humoured him. He learnt fast and was hard-working. He had little more to offer than his strength by way of payment for the passage. He suspected that Hrothgar hadn't needed an extra hand, but his story was well known, so the surly captain had taken him on board. Most likely out of pity.

He had seen pity on many faces in recent weeks. His was not the only family affected by the pestilence, but few were hit harder by the sickness. The first to succumb had been Edita. She had gone from sprightly, giggling girl, to pallid, shivering wraith overnight. Death had come to her rapidly, like darkness before a thunderstorm. And after that...

"Let's get on with the unloading or do you want to be out here when the rains come again?" said Hrothgar.

Beobrand and some of the younger crew members groaned, but the more seasoned hands began manhandling the bales and barrels off of the ship and onto the sand, ready for the climb up the steep steps to the fortress.

It was some time later when they reached the top of the cliff with the last of the ship's stores. The light had gone from the sky and it had started to rain. The chill autumn wind blew their cloaks about them, driving the rain into their faces. Beobrand followed the others through the archway at the top of the cliff steps and into a courtyard surrounded by large buildings. Across the open area, the welcome light of the main hall's entrance beckoned. The hubbub of voices and laughter reached them when the wind abated briefly.

A tall thin man, with a long moustache, ushered Beobrand towards a building. "Come on. Leave that sack on the right with the others." The man seemed impatient, probably wanting to be back in the warmth of the hall with a horn of mead. He pulled his fine woollen cloak more tightly around him and looked to see if any more men were coming through the arch.

"You the last one?" he asked Beobrand. His accent was thick and strange to Beobrand's ear, but he could make out the words easily enough.

"Aye. Those still down there are to guard the ships." Beobrand stepped into the storeroom and looked for the pile of sacks the man had mentioned. In the gloom he could see that the large barn was full of provisions.

When he emerged, the man closed the door, then turned toward the hall. Beobrand followed him.

5

As he walked into the smoky building, all the noise of talking and eating ceased. For an instant Beobrand felt conspicuous. Out of place. Sure that all eyes were on him. That for some reason he was the cause of the sudden hush. Then, just as quickly he realised that the men and women sitting at the tables were all looking at a tall man who was standing at the head of the hall. His bearing was that of one who commands. In his hand he held a finely-wrought sword. His long brown moustache was sprinkled with white as if with salt after a sea voyage. His bald head shone in the light of the blazing hearth.

"Word has come to me that Penda of Mercia, may God blast his bones, has joined with the Waelisc king, Cadwallon of Gwynedd, as we feared. At this moment they are camped with a warband in the land of Elmet." His voice rang clearly throughout the hall. "This alliance must be broken. Penda has gone too far if he believes he can invade the lands of Edwin, son of Aella. We march south in two days. I have sent riders out to summon the fyrd. The men of the land will do their duty and take up arms with me. Together our fury will smite them in the field, for that is where we shall meet. I am done with diplomacy. Penda is vermin. He must be killed as such. He has defiled my land and raised arms against my people. See now, I have drawn my sword," he lifted the finely-made broadsword above his head, the wave-patterned blade shimmered in the firelight, "and it shall not be sheathed till its thirst is quenched with the blood of our enemies!" With this last shout, he spun the sword downward, plunging it into the oaken board of the table in front of him. A wooden cup toppled over with the impact and fell to the floor, spilling its contents.

Nobody heard the cup clatter onto the wooden floor, for before Edwin's voice had finished reverberating around the

6

room, the crowd of thegns in the hall began to cheer. They stood and downed the contents of mugs and horns, shouting praises for their king and spitting curses on their enemies.

The noise and heat of the hall engulfed Beobrand. That is how a king speaks. He suddenly felt he could grow to love this place and this king. As his brother had. Beobrand scanned the occupants of the tables, searching for Octa's familiar blond hair. Octa had joined Edwin's warband three summers before. From what little news had reached Beobrand back home in Hithe in Cantware, he had done well in the service of his new lord.

Beobrand could not find Octa in the crowds of warriors gathered in the hall. He was probably on guard or perhaps he was tending to his own land, if the king had seen fit to bestow such riches on him. Well, Octa could wait. It had been an arduous, tiring day and the smell of the boar roasting on a spit over the fire reminded him of how long it had been since his last meal.

The hall was grander than his lord Folca's back in Hithe, but the layout, with benches and boards arrayed along the length, and the fire on the hearthstone in the centre was familiar to him. He did not often frequent his lord's hall, but the festive atmosphere reminded him of the Thrimilci feasts when all the freemen were invited to celebrate the bounty of the land. At such times copious amounts of drink were consumed, along with vast quantities of all manner of food. But in the feasts in Folca's hall there were many fewer thegns present. And their blades were less exquisite. Beobrand's eyes flicked to the sword, still quivering in the wood of the high table. Octa and he had always dreamt of owning such a sword. Perhaps Octa had fulfilled that dream, as he had succeeded in becoming a thegn.

He looked for a place on one of the benches. All the others who had arrived on the ship with him had found places and were being served mead, ale and food. The thin man from the storeroom had sat down at a place near the king. Beobrand was left in the doorway, feeling awkward. The atmosphere in the hall was buoyant now. The men were set on eating their fill and drinking to their exploits, both past and future. For soon they would march to battle, and battle is what these warriors lived for.

Beobrand envied them.

For as long as he could remember, he had wanted to be a warrior. Their father's brother, Selwyn, had fought in a warband, travelling far in his youth before returning to Hithe where he had filled his nephews' heads with tales of battle-play and adventure. Octa had left in search of the destiny he felt was his, to follow in the footsteps of his uncle and find glory in the service of a great lord.

He had left Beobrand behind. Beobrand had been too young to leave with him, so had stayed to tend their father's land and to look after their sisters and mother.

Now there was nothing holding him in Cantware.

A young man with a straggly beard saw Beobrand standing on his own and beckoned to a place at his side. Beobrand accepted, thankful to be able to sit after the long climb up from the beach.

"My name is Tondberct," the young man said, having to raise his voice to make himself heard over the noise. "You must have come on one of the ships from Cantware."

Beobrand nodded and his face must have betrayed his feelings because Tondberct, following his gaze, reached for a horn of mead and passed it to him. "You must be tired after the voyage."

"Yes," Beobrand replied after taking a long draught of the sweet drink. "And hungry," he added. "This is my first journey out of the lands of my lord, King Eadbald."

Tondberct waved to a comely slave who was carving meat from the pig. She made her way over to them with some choice cuts on a trencher. The thrall smiled at the two young men and returned to the fireplace. Beobrand picked up a piece of the meat and, although the hot grease burnt his fingers, he took a large bite.

Tondberct poured some more mead from a large earthen jug. He seemed to have no qualms about talking to a stranger and Beobrand was happy to listen while he ate.

"The day after tomorrow I will march with the warriors for the first time. My father gave me a new spear and shield last summer. Now I shall have a chance to test them." His eyes glistened in the firelight. Beobrand could understand his excitement.

Beobrand looked at the warriors in the hall while Tondberct talked about his new weapons and what he would do with them in the forthcoming battle. There were at least fifty able-bodied warriors at the tables. A veritable host. If Edwin could raise more from surrounding villages and farms, he would have a force worth reckoning with. He wondered how many, like Octa, were not present at this feast.

He finished a mouthful of bread that he had soaked in meat juices and washed it down with more mead. The warmth and the drink were relaxing him. He could feel the tensions of the voyage easing from his muscles.

Unbidden, his mind turned to the events of the last months. He frequently found himself reliving Edita's death.

Then burying Rheda and their mother on the same day. The three of them gone within a week. All the while, his father had remained hale and strong. Beobrand had wondered for a long time whether he had been cursed.

He frowned and stared at the fire. Trying to burn the memories from his mind. He did not want to think of the past. Of what had happened.

Of what he had done.

He had come north in search of a future.

He turned to Tondberct who was in the middle of a story about one of the king's sons, Osfrid. Apparently, Osfrid was a great huntsman, and that summer had single-handedly killed a bear. Tondberct's incessant talking was becoming tedious, so he interrupted him with a question.

"Do you know where my brother is?"

Tondberct looked puzzled, trying to make sense of the question with regard to the story he was recounting.

"I suppose that depends on who your brother is," he answered eventually with a smile, not appearing to be insulted by the interruption.

"Octa. He's a bit taller than me. His hair is so blond it's almost white."

Tondberct opened his mouth as if to reply, but then thought better of it and closed it again. He looked down at his hands, then took a swig from his horn of mead. Beobrand thought that something very bad would be needed to leave the talkative Tondberct speechless.

"What is it?" he asked.

Tondberct looked as though he wouldn't answer. But then, after a few moments, he blurted out, "He's dead!"

The words didn't make sense. "What? No, he can't be... I..." Beobrand stammered.

But the look on Tondberct's face told him this was no mistake. His face was ashen, aghast at what he had revealed to Beobrand.

"I'm sorry," Tondberct said. He took another gulp of mead, looking acutely uncomfortable.

"How?" Beobrand choked the word out around the lump in his throat.

Tondberct cast his gaze down.

"How did he die?" Beobrand repeated the question, raising his voice.

Tondberct stared into Beobrand's blue eyes. For a moment, Beobrand thought Tondberct would flee the hall rather than face his intense glare. But, after a moment the young man drew in a deep breath and said in a small voice, "He took his own life."

His words were inaudible over the din of the room. Around them, the hall celebrated. They were an island of stillness in the turmoil. Like a cloud shadow passing over a field of barley on a windy summer's day.

"What?"

Tondberct swallowed hard. "He took his own life," he repeated, louder this time.

"How? Why?"

Tondberct swallowed again. He cleared his throat. Beobrand was staring at him, waiting to hear his reply. Waiting to hear why the brother he had travelled the length of Albion to see was dead. Eventually, seemingly resigned to his role of bearer of bad tidings, Tondberct spoke again.

"He jumped from the wall. To the rocks."

Beobrand's mind reeled. He could not pin down his

thoughts. They were like leaves caught in a gale. None of it made sense. Edita, Rheda and his mother had all been consumed by the pestilence. His father was gone too. And now Octa. "Why?" He blurted out the word again, not sure whether he was asking Tondberct or the gods.

"His lover was found slain. It seems he…" Tondberct's voice trailed off.

Beobrand did not want to hear. He stood up quickly, suddenly feeling sick, the half-chewed piece of meat in his mouth made him gag. Wells of inconsolable pain built up from deep within him. Tears burnt behind his eyes. He did not want these strangers to see him cry.

Tondberct stood also, but he said nothing more.

Beobrand could no longer speak. His throat tightened. His breath came in gasps. The room began to blur, as his eyes filled with tears. He had to get out of this place. He turned, almost tripping over the bench and stumbled out of the hall.

The cold wind and rain slapped his face as he fled into the darkness.

Dead! All dead!

As he moved further from the hall, the darkness engulfed him. He could see torches guttering on the palisade where guards were posted, but he wanted to be far away from prying eyes. Alone with his grief. He headed for a large building that was completely shrouded in darkness, like the inside of a burial mound. It was the stables. He opened the gate and made his way inside.

He smelt and heard the horses more than saw them as he moved inside the building, feeling his way along the wall. He found a bale of hay and threw himself onto it. He hadn't allowed himself to grieve for his sisters or his mother. At first, all of his time had been spent caring for them. Later, he had pushed his pain deep down inside, where it had forged into the steel-hard blade of hate he had wielded at his father. His father who would never again raise his hand against him or anyone else.

With all of them dead, he had set himself the task of reaching Octa with the news of their deaths. Now Octa was gone too.

Octa. Quick-witted, cheerful and passionate Octa. His memories of him were as he had last seen him three years before. A tall, strong man of twenty, standing and laughing on the deck of the ship that would carry him northward. Blond hair whipping in the wind as Beobrand ran along the cliff top waving and shouting goodbye. He remembered the feeling of abandonment. They had been the closest of allies. They had worked the land together and trained with weapons under Uncle Selwyn's tutelage. And Octa had always defended them from their father's outbursts of violence.

Beobrand had never fully forgiven Octa for leaving that day.

He would never see that laughing face again now, or hear the warm, melodious voice. He had focused on finding his brother, and now he didn't know what he could do. He was truly alone for the first time in his life.

With this realisation, the tears finally came. They came in floods, all the tears he had held back, waiting to mourn for his family with Octa. Sobs racked his body. Small, animal noises came from his throat. Grief and self-pity consumed him.

He lay like that, face buried in the hay for a long time until his tears dried. He tried to compose himself. He imagined what his father would have said to see him crying like a baby, when he was a full-grown man. He would have cuffed him round the ear and told him that crying was for women and children. As weeping would accomplish nothing, there was no use in it. "Actions are what you need, son, not whining and tears." How many times had he heard those words from his father? A hundred? A thousand?

In the end he had taken his father's advice.

"Why were you crying?" A small voice spoke from the darkness, startling him.

"Men aren't supposed to cry. Father says so." The voice continued. It was very close. Beobrand sat up and wiped the sleeve of his kirtle across his face.

"Who are you?" he asked. His heart thumped in his chest.

"Eanflæd. What's your name?"

The voice belonged to a little girl. What was she doing in a stable in the dark?

"Beobrand," he answered.

"Are you from Cantware?" Eanflæd asked. "You talk strange."

"Yes, I am. What do you mean I talk strange?"

"You sound different," she replied, then repeated her original question. "Why were you crying?"

Beobrand did not want to talk about his loss, his overwhelming grief, especially not with a precocious little girl. So he asked, "What are you doing here? Do your parents know where you are?"

Eanflæd's voice took on a wistful tone. "I like sitting with the horses. Nobody knows I'm here. They are too busy feasting. My father is Edwin." She paused, and then, as if explaining something to a rather slow child, "He's the king".

Beobrand staggered quickly to his feet, bumping into one of the stalls behind him. If he were found here with this young princess, alone in the dark, it would be more than difficult to explain what they had been doing. A horse whinnied and stamped a hoof at this disturbance.

"Shhh, boy, that's it, calm now," he soothed the horse, using the soft voice he always used with nervous animals back on the farm. The horse quietened.

"Eanflæd, I don't think it's a good idea for you to be here. I think you should go to your bed now."

He heard her rise.

He hoped she would do as he suggested and that nobody would see her leave; he didn't want to have to explain this situation to anyone.

"Alright," she said in a very meek voice. "It is late, I suppose. Goodnight, Beobrand from Cantware."

"Goodnight, Eanflæd, Edwin's daughter," he murmured.

The sounds of her moving quickly and surely back towards the door came to him and the door creaked open slightly, letting in a gust of wind and rain. Then he was in the dark again, alone with the horses.

He sat there, listening to the storm buffeting the walls of the stable. The encounter with the princess had served to focus his mind, but he felt hollow inside. As if the bout of crying had emptied him of emotion. What could he do now? He could not travel back south with Hrothgar. There were too many ghosts there. Perhaps he could stay in this northern land. But how? He had nothing to offer.

He couldn't bring himself to care about his own fate. Nothing seemed important anymore. Whatever his wyrd had in store for him, he would face it as it came.

After a short time he thought he should go back to the great hall and get some food before the feast was over. Maybe that would help to fill the empty hole inside him. He got up and carefully made his way out of the stable. The wind was dying down and the rain had lessened. He closed the stable door gently behind him and walked slowly back towards the hall. Nobody called out to him and there was no sign of the girl.

Back inside the warmth and noise of the long hall he cast around for somewhere to sit. He didn't want to have to endure the prattling of the talkative Tondberct, but there was little room on the benches. As he was contemplating sitting with some of the younger men on the floor near the fire, he realised that the hall had gone strangely quiet, just as it had when he had first entered at the beginning of the feast. Imagining that the king was going to speak again, he turned towards the head of the table, where the fine sword still protruded from the oak board, and looked straight into the eyes of King Edwin. He was gazing directly at him. Beobrand's heart missed a beat. He saw a young girl sitting at Edwin's feet, stroking a grey wolfhound. He had not seen Eanflæd in the dark of the stable, but he was sure that this slim, flaxen-haired girl was the king's daughter. Perhaps the fact that she had also failed to see his face would save him. But this hope was quickly dashed when the king spoke. He raised his voice to be heard by all those present in the hall.

"You there. Are you known as Beobrand?"

Beobrand could not bring himself to speak, so merely nodded.

"Come here, where I can see you."

Beobrand slowly walked the length of the hall, acutely aware of all the eyes following him. And the whispers. People wondered what was afoot. As he walked past his countrymen, Hrothgar rasped close to him, "What have you done, boy?"

Beobrand didn't answer. He was caught in the stare of the king, like a lamb looks at the eyes of the priests before a sacrifice.

He came to a halt a few paces before the lord of the hall. Unsure what to do, he knelt before him and lowered his head.

"Well, Beobrand, Eanflæd here tells me you were in the stables, in the dark. What were you doing there?"

Beobrand did not even contemplate lying.

"Grieving for the loss of my brother, sisters and parents, sire," he said, his voice breaking. "I did not want to cry in front of everyone."

The hall now was completely silent, save for the crackling of the fire and the sound of the dogs crunching bones under the tables. Everyone was straining to hear what was said.

"Who was your father, and who was your brother?" Edwin asked, a softness entering his voice.

"I am son of Grimgundi and brother of Octa, my lord."

A murmur ran through the hall. The name of his brother was known to them.

"Your brother's death was a tragedy. He was much loved here, a valiant thegn whose deeds will be sung at our table for many a year." A shadow passed over his face. "Crying at the loss of loved ones does not belittle you, young warrior."

"I am no warrior, lord."

"Oh, but I see iron in your eye and flint in your heart, Beobrand. You may not yet know it, but I say you are a warrior. I see much of Octa in you. You will be great one day, I'll wager."

Beobrand was taken aback. He had expected retribution for some supposed misconduct with the king's daughter. Instead the king was telling him that he could follow Octa's path. A compliment indeed from such a powerful king in the presence of his battle host. Being a warrior was something he had only dreamt of. A secret dream. Like a shiny trinket to be brought out and played with for comfort when life was tough. He used to imagine what it would be like to don battle-harness and stand in the shieldwall. Shoulder to shoulder with heroes. The glory of battle. The songs of victory. The rings given by a lord.

He looked up into Edwin's eyes. He did not see humour there, only sadness and benevolence.

All of a sudden, kneeling there, with all the eyes in the room on him, he knew what he must do. What would come next he did not know, but with a sudden clarity he was certain that all the events of the last months had been leading him to this moment. His wyrd had driven him forward through death and despair to this. He could not turn back. It was as if a beacon had been lit in his mind, shedding light into dark corners where he had never looked before. Without contemplating fully the consequences of his actions, before the light in his mind went out, allowing the shadows to come rushing back, Beobrand spoke.

"If you think I will make a warrior, my lord Edwin," he said, in a strong steady voice that surprised everyone, including himself, "let me carry your shield into battle. Let me bear arms against your enemies and seek glory for you in all my endeavours. Let me serve you, as my brother served. What say you, lord, would you take me as your warrior?"

Even the crackling of the fire seemed to still. The hounds appeared to pause in the gnawing of their scraps.

Uncle Selwyn had recounted the oath sworn by warriors to lords, but Beobrand was unsure of the exact words. He continued as best he could, speaking into the silence. "I will to you be true and faithful. I will love what you love and shun what you shun and never displease you through deed or word."

The audacity of what he had done suddenly struck Beobrand. Seventeen-year-old farmers didn't walk up to kings and ask them to make them shield bearers in their warbands. The wrath of the king for such an affront would be terrible. He closed his eyes, cursing himself for a fool.

After a moment he chanced a look at the king and saw that Edwin had thrown his head back and raised both his fists high in the air.

He was going to smash those fists into him. He tensed, readying himself for the blow.

Then he heard Edwin's deep laughter. The lord rocked back on his heels and guffawed. A few of the men in the hall laughed too, now that they saw the king's reaction.

"By the bones of Christ, but you will be great one day!" Edwin tried to stifle his mirth. "You've got the bravery of a boar, Beobrand, son of Grimgundi. You make your father proud, and you are clearly Octa's kin. Aye, I'll have you in my warband. I need all the stout hearts I can get! Now eat and drink, for you'll be needing all your strength soon."

The hall was engulfed in a cacophony of cheering and laughter. The king sat down, placing his hand on his daughter's head. Eanflæd smiled at Beobrand. He rose shakily to his feet and walked back towards Hrothgar and the other Cantware men. Warriors he had never met slapped him on the back and shouted praise of his mettle as he walked by. He hardly knew what he was doing, his body was lighter than it should be. When he got to his countrymen, they made room for him and he sat down heavily, still in a daze at the turn of events.

"Well, laddies," Hrothgar shouted over the din in the hall, "looks like young Beobrand here is going to be a great warrior!"

Beobrand's countrymen cheered and raised their drinks towards him. He had been elevated to the status of hero and they would revel in telling this tale when they returned to Cantware.

For his part, Beobrand had no idea what to do, so he simply picked up a horn of mead and quaffed down its contents in three large gulps. Then, looking back at his friends, he forced a smile onto his lips.

Inside, the empty feeling had been replaced with the cold, coiling-eel sensation of fear, and Beobrand felt like crying again.

2

The next morning, Beobrand awoke with a pain in his head to rival that of his heart. The night was a blur to him. He recalled warrior after warrior coming up to toast his bravery and to give their condolences for his loss. Each man offered him mead or ale, so Beobrand drank more than many men twice his age could stomach. In the end he knew little of what was happening in the hall. Eventually, he had slouched in the corner, one of the dogs resting against his leg, and allowed the noise and warmth to smother him.

The drink, while blunting his senses to the outside world, did little to assuage the terrible feeling of loneliness and despair that engulfed him. As the night drew on people began to leave him alone. Although he didn't weep again, his soul was ravaged by a pain he could hardly endure. All he could do was drink more, hoping that he would finally be able to forget where he was. Or perhaps even who he was.

He vaguely remembered a bard singing of a great man who had killed a demon. Beobrand had tried to follow the story, to take his mind from his dejection. But in his addled state he couldn't focus. The intricate melodies the singer wove with his harp and beautiful voice became like the lilting sound of a flute, devoid of intelligible words. He never found out what became of the warrior in the song, because he fell into a fitful sleep.

He sat up gingerly and looked around him. There was a slight chill in the air, the door to the hall had been opened to let in some light and freshen the place before the men broke their fast. The sun was already up and several slave women were sweeping the floor of the hall and readying the boards for the morning meal. There were a few other men sleeping under furs, blankets or cloaks in other parts of the hall, but most must already be up.

Beobrand stood and noticed that some kind person had covered him with a blanket in the night. He rolled it up and set it on a bench and then decided that he had better get out of the hall quickly. The women would not welcome having to clean his dinner off of the floor.

He hurried outside, feeling his gorge rise. His head spinning, he dashed round the side of the hall and leaned against the wall, retches racking his body.

"Looks like you enjoyed a little too much of our lord Edwin's mead, lad!" a jovial voice spoke from behind him. "A nice bit of porridge will do you good. Are you finished yet? Looks as if you're going to puke your own puddings out!"

When he was able to stand straight once more, Beobrand turned and looked at the man who had spoken. He was a giant of a man, with a full brown beard and receding hair. A long scar puckered the skin over his left eye.

"You don't remember me, do you, lad?" the huge man asked. "I spoke to you last night, but I suppose you were in no state to pay attention. The name's Bassus. I was a friend of your brother's."

The fresh air and the fact that he had vomited up the contents of his stomach were making Beobrand feel a little better. His head still throbbed, but he thought he could walk without either puking or fainting.

"You're a quiet one, I'll give you that," continued Bassus. "Come on, let's get some warm food in you, you're as pale as lamb's wool. You need to get your strength up if I'm going to make a fighting man out of you by sundown!"

With this last disconcerting comment, Bassus placed a large hand on Beobrand's shoulder and steered him back into the hall where men were now gathering for the first meal of the day.

The beach was pristine, washed clean by the storm the night before. A brisk wind came off of the sea, but the white banks of cloud on the horizon did not look like they carried more rain.

Beobrand and Bassus walked down the steps from the fortress on the cliff and made their way towards the ships that were resting on their keels on the sand. There was a great amount of activity going on readying the two Cantware ships. Hrothgar and Swidhelm had both decided to take advantage of the fair weather and set out this morning. This announcement had caused the men from Cantware to curse and even now many complaints could be heard, as the men manhandled provisions and tied ropes, preparing the ships for sea. Despite the reticence of some of the crew members, who would have liked a few more days on shore before putting out to sea again, the work seemed to be proceeding at a fair pace.

Beobrand walked in silence next to the massive warrior, thinking about his future and the decisions he had made.

His life had changed in ways he could never have imagined only days before. His mind was clearer now. He had eaten some hot porridge and now, in the sunshine, with the cool breeze on his face, life didn't seem quite as terrible as it had the night before. There was still an ache deep down that threatened to surface at any moment, but he ignored it, casting his attention to problems at hand. His father would have been proud.

Bassus in turn surveyed Beobrand. By the gods, he looked like his brother. Beobrand was not quite as fair-haired, not quite as tall and was less heavily-muscled than Octa. But a few months of training would soon see him beef up and turn into a real fighter, just like his older brother. He had that same easy gait and the piercing stare. He could see why Edwin had thought he would be a great warrior one day. To a thegn's eye, it was clear that this young farm boy had the makings of a killer within him. Bassus just hoped he could teach him enough to get him through the battle they would fight only days from now.

He still couldn't quite believe that Octa was gone. From the moment they had first met they had become firm friends, despite Bassus being Octa's senior by some ten years. It was as if they were brothers. They had often joked about how similar their tastes were and frequently found themselves finishing each other's thoughts. Now, with Octa dead, he felt as if he had lost a real brother.

Over the morning meal, Beobrand had asked Bassus for more details of Octa's death.

"It is as you heard," Bassus had replied, his face sombre. "He was found by fishermen on the rocks below the palisade."

Octa's death had been an utter shock. Bassus could still see his body, smashed and broken by the fall from the lofty crag of Bebbanburg.

"But why would he do something like that?" asked Beobrand. He couldn't imagine his brother falling into such despair. But then, what did he know of his brother's life? Three years was a long time.

"He loved a girl called Elda," Bassus had gazed into the freshly rekindled fire, lost in memory. "Her body was found after Octa. She had been killed. A savage murder."

He had not told the boy how she had been slashed and hacked into a mangled hunk of meat. As brutal a slaying as anyone had ever seen or heard of.

"He killed her?" Beobrand had asked.

"That is what people believe. That he killed her, and then killed himself."

"But you don't?"

Bassus had been silent for a long time. Elda and Octa had been lovers. Everyone knew this and so, with nothing to indicate otherwise, the obvious conclusion had been drawn – Octa had killed Elda and then leapt to his death.

But none of that rang true. Octa had been passionate about Elda. They had courted for months. They were happy. They had talked of marriage. Even if Elda had committed some act of infidelity, Bassus knew that Octa would never have killed her. In battle he had been formidable, but he would not raise a hand against a woman.

Edwin felt the same way, but with no witnesses and no evidence to the contrary, the obvious was the only explanation. He wondered whether they would ever find the truth of what had happened that night. Should wyrd bring answers, Bassus hoped that he would be there to avenge his friend's death.

"No, I do not," he answered at last, "I think he was murdered. By the same man who killed Elda. But who that could be, or why, I do not know."

Beobrand clung to those words like a drowning man clutches to a piece of driftwood. He could not believe his brother was a murderer who had taken his own life. Better to believe he had been murdered.

Who could his killer be? Beobrand looked over his shoulder, up at the fortress. Was he there? In Bebbanburg? Had he been in the hall last night? Had he spoken to him? He did not know who had slain Octa. No weregild would be paid for his death. If Beobrand found his brother's killer, there was only one payment he would take.

They were nearing the boats now and Bassus dropped the two shields he had slung over his back and thrust the two spears he was carrying into the sand. Beobrand turned to the huge warrior and spoke for the first time since they had left the hall.

"I won't be long. I just want to say goodbye."

Bassus nodded. He sat down on the sand and looked out at the grey-blue sea.

Beobrand walked the short distance to the ships. Before he could shout a greeting to the Cantware men, several of them hailed him. A few stopped their chores to come to him and say their farewells. Most of the men were older than him and were rough and ready at the best of times, but there was a tenderness to them now that touched Beobrand. He was one of their own. They were leaving him behind to an uncertain fate and they were worried for him. They knew of his personal tragedies and hoped that he would find happiness in this northern kingdom. A few of the men gave him something to remember them by – a small leather purse from Anna, a bone-handled knife from Immin, and Hrothgar even gave him a whale tooth pendant, carved into the shape of Thunor's hammer, that he had always worn round his neck.

"May this bring you luck, young warrior," he said, gruffly, and then, clearly not wishing to show too much emotion, he turned quickly and began to shout at the men who had stopped work. "Come on, you maggots. We haven't got all day and the tide waits for no man!"

Some of the men waved to Beobrand and then went back to their tasks on the ships. Beobrand walked to Bassus. The massive thegn looked like a boulder on the beach. The two spears quivering in the sand beside him made Beobrand wonder how much he could learn about their use in only one day. He had said as much after they had eaten. In response to his doubts Bassus had replied, "Better to learn something, than nothing, lad!" Beobrand thought that advice could have been uttered by his father. In its pragmatism there was no argument to refute it.

Beobrand had often practised weapon-play with Selwyn, but he had always favoured the sword. Ever since his uncle had taken them to see a smith forging a blade in Cantwareburh. The smith knew Selwyn and had been happy enough to explain to the boys what was required to forge a strong blade. He showed them how twisted rods of iron were heated until they glowed like the setting sun and then beaten together, until they became one. This process was repeated over and over, giving the blade its shimmering patterns and also its inner strength and flexibility. The more strands of iron welded together in this way, and the more different twists each rod had, the stronger and more beautiful the final blade.

"Like the different stories that make up a man's life. The more twists in each story, and the more stories that are beaten together by life's adversities, the stronger the man," Uncle Selwyn said. Beobrand had never forgotten that.

Ever since that moment he had longed to own a sword like that. The blade had called to him.

His uncle had not allowed him to use his own fine sword, but he had crafted wooden practice weapons for his nephews, which they had used whenever they could get away from their duties. The spear seemed unwieldy and slow in comparison, and had never captured Beobrand's imagination in the way that the long blade of the sword had.

But he had no sword, and the shieldwall stood strong as a forest of spears. Now, with battle so close at hand, Beobrand wished he had devoted more time to learning the use of the ash-hafted spear.

So, when Bassus raised his considerable bulk from the sand and threw a spear to him, Beobrand caught it and made himself ready to learn as much as he possibly could.

This was the life he had chosen for himself. Battle-glory and death. Spear and shield.

The next day they would march south with the fyrd, the host called upon to defend the land. In battle, he would have to kill. That was something that Bassus could not teach. Beobrand thought fleetingly of his father. He was sure he could kill.

With thoughts of killing his mind returned to the man who had murdered Octa. He vowed silently that he would find him. And when he did, he would be ready. Ready to take payment.

They spent the rest of the day practising the techniques needed by a warrior. Bassus concentrated on those skills that would best serve Beobrand in the shieldwall. He showed him how to hold a shield so that it would protect him and be easily brought to bear on different types of attack. Beobrand also learnt how to thrust with a spear effectively.

"Don't try to poke their eyes out, go for the legs and feet. A man will not be much trouble after he has a spear in his foot!"

Bassus also showed him how to use a spear to pull a shield away from an enemy's body.

"You have to know what you're doing, mind, and trust that your shield mate will help you, or else you leave yourself exposed."

It wasn't long before Beobrand began to feel the strain. Muscles that he didn't even know he had in his arms and shoulders started to burn. His forearms began to ache from the constant repetition of lunges with the spear, and his back hurt from hefting the weight of the shield. Worse than the aching muscles was the throbbing in his head from the excesses of the night before. He soon began to feel queasy again.

Bassus was a hard master. He didn't let him rest until he was satisfied that he had picked up the basics.

He could see Beobrand's strength was failing and the boy was pale, but he didn't let him stop.

"You can relax after the battle, not before. You should have thought about this when you offered to carry weapons for Edwin."

Beobrand groaned. When he had practised with Selwyn, his uncle had always allowed him to rest when he was weary. He had been playing at war then, Selwyn humouring his young nephew. There was no urgency to it then.

"I can see you have been taught something of fighting before, but your stance is all wrong and you know nothing of spear use. Lunge again, let me see you put your weight behind it!"

Beobrand gritted his teeth and persevered as best he could. His stomach churned. He feared he would vomit again if he did not stop soon.

"I know you are tired and regretting the mead from last night, but there is barely any time before we must fight. I've already lost one son of Grimgundi. I will not lose another. You will be ready for battle."

When they finally stopped for a brief meal sweat was pouring from them both. Beobrand flopped down onto the sand and lay panting. Bassus pulled out some cold meat, bread and cheese from a leather bag. Beobrand felt terrible. His muscles were quivering and his head throbbed as if a smith was hammering his brains flat. He swallowed a dry piece of bread and washed it down with some water from a leather flask.

"What was done with Octa's body?" he asked.

"He was buried, in the way of the Christ god's followers. His grave is close by. I can show you later."

"I would like that. Thank you." He thought of Octa in the dark, smothered under earth. His fair hair mired and matted.

Beobrand's eyes filled with tears. Bassus discreetly looked out to sea, at the ships pulling away from the shore.

The one good thing about practising so intensely was that he had no time to think about his situation. Or his loss. So, before he could start contemplating things in earnest, he forced himself to his feet and readied himself for more gruelling exercise. Bassus looked surprised at his eagerness, but made no comment.

He stood up and they continued where they had left off.

They were both exhausted and stiff when Bassus called a halt to the training. They picked up their gear and Bassus led the way south, through the dunes and marram grass towards the burial place of Bebbanburg.

"If you keep on training on the march south, you might survive the battle," he said.

"What will it be like?" asked Beobrand.

"The battle? It will be over before you really know it has started, and by then we'll know whether you've remembered anything of what I've taught you. And whether the gods have smiled on you. If wyrd wills it, you will live."

Beobrand hawked and spat. "The gods don't seem to favour me at the moment."

Bassus replied in a serious tone, "You can never tell who the gods will choose to aid in battle, Beobrand. Men who you thought were lucky get cut down in an instant, while some of the wickedest men, with no weapons skill, survive countless wars and die old in their sleep. But one thing that is always true is that a warrior's first battle is like no other. Some men find they like the killing, others find that they have no stomach for it. Weak men often die quickly, or disgrace themselves by running away or surrendering. The first battle separates the chaff from the wheat." Bassus fixed him with a stern stare, as if measuring him against something. Octa perhaps.

Still within sight of the fortress crag they reached an open area. There were trees to the west. On the east, the land fell away down a small bluff to the sandy beach. The plot was dotted with long stone slabs marking where previous inhabitants of Bernicia had been buried. On the far western edge, near the trees were some larger, older barrows. They were certainly from many centuries before.

"This place has been used for burial since long before our ancestors travelled across the North Sea," said Bassus. "A fitting place for Octa to rest."

He threaded his way between the mounds and stone markers. Beobrand followed him. Both were subdued and quiet. They were careful not to tread on any of the tombs. It would not do to disturb the dead.

"This is where your brother lies." Bassus stopped before a mound of freshly-turned earth. "I saw that his body was properly prepared for burial. He had taken the Christ faith, as have we all, those who follow Edwin. But I made sure he was buried with a seax and a Thunor's hammer amulet. I thought it made sense to keep all the gods happy."

Beobrand nodded his thanks. He was staring at the earth. It was a long grave. Long enough to fit Octa's tall frame.

Bassus stepped back, giving the young man room. "I will wait for you back at the path. Say farewell, but don't be too long. I do not want to be here after dark."

Left alone, Beobrand sank to the ground. His fingers reached for the earth covering Octa's remains. It was cold, damp and hard. Dead. What had he expected? For there to be warmth coming from his brother's corpse?

No more tears came. He had cried them all the night before.

"Why did you leave me, brother?" he whispered. "You knew I couldn't follow you. I couldn't leave them alone with him."

Unbidden, his earliest memory came to him. He was four years old and their mother's screaming had woken him. He had crept from his cot at the back of the house to see what was happening. He had not been scared, merely curious to know what all the noise was about. Fear of his father came later.

The memory was dim and vague, but he clearly recalled Octa standing defiantly between their parents. Octa was some six years his senior, still a child. His slim body had yet to take on the bulk of adulthood that would make him a formidable warrior. Nevertheless he had stood there, hands on his hips and chin thrust forward.

"Don't you dare touch her again," Octa had said, his voice trembling.

Their mother had got to her feet and tried to placate their father, but he had found a new object for his anger and Octa's bird-thin, child's body was no match for Grimgundi's meaty weight. He had beaten Octa senseless that night. Beobrand had sobbed, begging him to stop. He had been terrified that he would kill him. He had seen lambs and pigs slaughtered and his brother's white-blond hair had been soaked with so much blood that he'd feared the worst.

He had cried and begged, but he had not stood up to their father. Not then. Not until many years later when Octa was no longer there to protect them.

A rustle made him look up. Had that been the sibilant susurrus of a spirit? He shivered. No, it was just the wind in the trees.

"I know why you left, Octa. You were scared you would kill him, weren't you? And I always thought you were the brave one. Now they will suffer no more at his hands. Nobody will."

The wind picked up, making the trees shake and rattle their branches angrily. A cloud blew in front of the sun and the burial ground was plunged into shadowy coolness. He shivered again.

"I don't know who killed you, but I swear on my life I will seek out your murderer. And when I find him, he will join our father."

A raven, the messenger of Woden, lifted up from the ground, flapping its huge wings against the stiff breeze. Cawing, it flew over Beobrand.

He stood quickly. He touched Hrothgar's hammer amulet at his throat and spat into the long grass to ward off evil. He wished to be away from this place. And the memories of the past.

"I will avenge you, Octa. As the gods are my witness, or I will die trying."

He turned and walked swiftly from the grave. Back towards Bassus, Bebbanburg and his future.

The next morning dawned crisp and cold. There was a light frost dusting everything. It made Beobrand feel as if he had woken up in a different place from the one where he had gone to sleep. It was an uncomfortable feeling, compounded by the fact that the preparations that were going on around him were like nothing he had ever been involved with before. He had never been a part of a warband and had no idea of what to expect. During the long hard days working the fields back in Cantware he had often dreamt about being a warrior, travelling to distant lands and smiting his enemies in glorious battle. After Octa had left, he had dared to hope that one day he might follow him. Selwyn encouraged him with his tales, but he had never really thought it would happen. Now that his dream was a reality he was not sure he had been wise to wish for this.

With the horses' breath clouding in the chill morning air and the sun just pushing over the horizon, Beobrand wondered whether he would measure up well to his brother. He didn't feel like a warrior. His arms and shoulders ached terribly from the day before and he could remember little of what Bassus had shown him. He didn't relish the prospect of physical activity, but seeing the men carrying supplies from the warehouse to the ox-drawn carts, he thought he should offer his help. It would be better than standing there feeling awkward and cold.

Some of the men acknowledged him with a nod, but there was a mood about them that did not invite talk. These thegns knew that many of them would not be standing a few days from now. In the frosty morning light the future seemed more sombre than in the hall with warm mead in their drinking horns. There was an almost ritualistic way in which they prepared the supplies and readied their weapons and armour for the battle. The young warrior, Tondberct, jokingly commented that all the men seemed still asleep. He received such stony looks that he was quickly quiet again. This was a serious moment, and the time for jesting had passed.

When the last of the supplies had been made secure on the carts and the warriors were gathered in front of the main hall, the doors to the king's abode opened and out strode Edwin. He was resplendent in a coat of burnished metal scales. He wore a helm that carried a golden boar emblem, the faceplate was raised, so that all the warriors and the onlooking women and children could see the countenance of their lord. At his side was strapped the beautifully-crafted, pattern-forged sword that he had wielded two nights previously. Beobrand noted that the blade was still unsheathed, just as the king had promised.

Next to Edwin stood his lady, the statuesque Ethelburga. Her face was lovely but stern, the set of her mouth told of a strength of character to rival that of any king. Also with the king and queen were their children. Their son, Osfrid, was as tall as his father and was also wearing the trappings of war. Next to Ethelburga, Beobrand noticed Eanflæd, her flaxen hair pulled back in a long plait. She turned towards him and their eyes met. She raised her hand slightly, as if to wave. Beobrand quickly looked away, embarrassed. Behind the royal family stood a tall, thin man in flowing black robes. A priest, Beobrand supposed.

Then the door behind the king was closed with a crash and the man who had slammed it walked around to face the gathered warriors. With a start, Beobrand recognised Bassus' bulk. He had wondered where his new friend and trainer was. Bassus was wearing a leather jerkin that was dotted with metal plates, he had a green cloak around his shoulders and a large shield strapped to his back. He carried a helm in his hand and a huge sword hung from his belt. He stopped before the royal retinue and faced the crowd of men gathered there. He looked each man briefly in the eye, giving no indication of friendship when he looked at Beobrand, and then he addressed the group in a resonant voice.

"Why are you gathered here today?" he asked.

"To fight!" the men replied in unison. Beobrand spoke the words slightly late and more quietly, so as not to draw attention to the fact he didn't know what he should say.

"Why do you wish to fight?"

"To protect our land," the throng replied.

"Who gave you your land?"

"Our king."

"Who is your king?"

"Edwin!" The men shouted this response, and Beobrand joined in, getting caught up in the men's enthusiasm.

Bassus waited for the noise to die down.

"So for whom do you fight?" he asked.

"For Edwin!" they screamed. If volume alone could win battles, they couldn't lose.

With the ritual thus concluded, Edwin and Osfrid strode

down to their awaiting horses and mounted. Edwin turned to his men and raised his hand.

"Come, my trusted warriors. My gesithas. To battle! Glory and riches await us on the field!" With this he wheeled his steed around and cantered out of the palisade gates, followed by his son and the few other thegns who were mounted.

The carts began to roll towards the gates. Beobrand joined the men who would travel on foot.

To battle. To death?

Beobrand squared his shoulders and matched his pace to that of the others. The hollow inside threatened to engulf him. He raised his eyes to the head of the column where Bassus rode on a massive brown steed next to Edwin.

He was not all alone. His brother had good friends here.

And enemies too. Enemies who needed repaying for his murder.

Beobrand didn't know what wyrd had in store for him, but he wasn't ready to die just yet.

3

Edwin was worried. They had been travelling for eight days. His scouts had spotted the enemy host camped in a shallow valley in the area called Elmet.

He sat astride his stallion and looked at the line of warriors marching up the hill to where he and the mounted thegns waited. The host he had raised was big, several hundred strong, as large as any he had ever commanded. Men had answered the call to defend the land as he knew they would. Ealdormen and thegns, accompanied by their gesithas, their retinues of warriors, had trickled in, swelling the numbers of the fyrd as it had marched south using the cracked and furrowed roads left by the Romans hundreds of years previously.

But looking at the warhost now, Edwin wasn't sure it would be enough. They were going to face the joint ranks of Penda and Cadwallon. Not one host, but two. And two of the most dangerous and capable leaders in Albion into the bargain.

Edwin felt the presence of Bassus looming behind him. For the other thegns and warriors, Edwin put on a show of bluff confidence, declaring that victory was their God-given right. But with Bassus, his champion, he didn't hide his true feelings. It would have been pointless anyway. The massive warrior could always tell his moods. It sometimes felt as if Bassus could see inside his head to what he was thinking.

"I have a bad feeling about this," Edwin said. "Do you think we have a chance?"

Bassus sat still on his chestnut mare for a time, thinking of his answer.

Years before they had conquered Elmet, easily wresting control from the native Waelisc tribe. They had been a dishevelled group of farmers, with very few real warriors and Edwin had crushed them in as long as it took to boil an egg. They would have more of a fight on their hands this time.

"There is always a chance, lord," he said at last.

Edwin smiled. He should have known that Bassus wouldn't feed his growing fears with his own concerns. That was not in his nature.

"What are your thoughts on the battle? How should we proceed?" Edwin asked.

It was late in the year and although the enemy would pose a much more serious threat than the Elmetii had, there was no time to play cat and mouse. The fyrd had few supplies and winter was setting in. So he had decided to march to where the enemy had chosen, rather than search for a more propitious location.

Bassus paused, thinking about the lie of the land in Elmet. "The place isn't the best, but it could be worse. If the scouts tell true, we will be fighting uphill, but the slope isn't too bad. We should try to attack at sun up, with the sun behind us. That will give us an edge."

"Will that be enough? Against Cadwallon and Penda?"

"We are strong and Paulinus has said that God is on our side."

Edwin sneered. "God. Will he bring us victory?"

The king's sombre mood was infectious. It was the presence of Cadwallon that unnerved Edwin above all else.

They had been like brothers once. Sent to King Cadfan's court during his exile, Edwin had befriended the young prince of Gwynedd and they had become inseparable.

How had Cadwallon changed from the youth he had hunted and played with in the mountains of Gwynedd, into the implacable warlord he now was? Edwin had no answer. Any frontier settlement taken by Cadwallon could expect only the harshest treatment. The men would be slain, and the women defiled and sold into slavery. Cadwallon would often butcher the children too, in an effort to eradicate the Angelfolc, the descendants of the invaders from across the North Sea, from the land he claimed rightly belonged to his people.

"Strong iron, stout hearts and hale warriors in the shield-wall will bring us victory."

"If only this unholy alliance had not held. Neither Cadwallon nor Penda would dare to face me alone."

"I think that is the point," Bassus said, raising an eyebrow sardonically. "Though with his hatred of our kind, I know not how Cadwallon allies himself with Penda."

"That is easy to answer," said Edwin. "His hatred for me is greater than his loathing of all Angelfolc. Penda would side with the devil himself if it would help him gain more land and riches."

They were silent a moment. Edwin's stallion swung its head suddenly, aiming a bite at Bassus' mare. The mare sidestepped quickly, almost unseating Bassus, who was not a skilled rider. Both men slapped the necks of their mounts at the same time.

They laughed. But the sound was jagged and forced.

"So? Have you a strategy in mind, old friend?" Edwin asked, once the horses had quietened.

"If their hosts can be split, then we should divide them. But I don't know whether we have enough men to cover two flanks." Bassus turned to Edwin, a smile on his lips and a glint in his eye. "Then again, the best strategy is simply to kill the bastards!"

Edwin returned the smile, but his unease did not abate.

That night they camped with the enemies' campfires in sight. The ever-swelling numbers of the fyrd had fallen into a routine at each evening camp, but this night was different. Where before the younger men had trained with spear and shield before sinking down beside the large fires to listen to the older warriors' tales of battle and glory, this night the men were nervous. The excitement had fled and they smothered their fears with drink. Mead and ale were consumed in huge quantities and many of the warriors were unconscious before midnight.

Beobrand drank sparingly. Early in the night, Bassus approached where he was sitting with Tondberct and some other young warriors and pulled him aside.

"Don't drink any more tonight, Beobrand. We fight at first light and the drunken men will be the first to die tomorrow. You need your wits about you."

"Pay no heed to that old worrier," jeered Tondberct, already well on his way to drunkenness. "Anyone would think he was your mother, the way he fusses over you." The others laughed.

Bassus gave them a stern look, then shook his head and left them to their youthful jests. Before he left, he patted Beobrand on the arm and said, "Seek me out in the morn. You will stand with me in the shieldwall."

"Come on, Beo," said Tondberct. "There is plenty of drink to go around." Tondberct passed him a flask and Beobrand drank, but sparingly. He heeded Bassus' words and would not let himself be goaded into drinking heavily, no matter how persuasive Tondberct could be. Gods, but it was hard to refuse him. He smiled and passed the mead back.

Tondberct had become his closest friend over the days they had trudged south. They had practised spear-play together in the evenings and both shared the common dream of becoming great warriors. Most of the other men had also been good to him, accepting him. They had talked and joked as they walked and sometimes he had even managed to keep his mind from picking at the scabs of the past for long stretches at a time.

He looked around at the men of the fyrd. They knew battle would be upon them with the dawn, yet they didn't seem to care. But Beobrand listened to Bassus and only sipped ale for a while until he decided to get some sleep. He found it very difficult. The noise from the men was distracting, but what really prevented him from sleeping was the growing feeling of fear. It had turned his stomach to water. But it was more than fear. It was excitement too.

What would the next day bring? Would they be victorious? Would he bring glory to his name?

Would he live up to Octa's memory?

He wrapped himself in his cloak against the chill of the night, but still shivered. One thought surfaced, pushing all others from his mind.

Perhaps the next day he would join Octa in the afterlife.

Bassus woke Beobrand the next day before dawn. Men were readying themselves all around them. Many were vomiting, leaving steaming puddles dotted throughout the encampment. Bassus handed him his spear and made sure he was holding his shield correctly. Bassus was wearing his full armour and in the dark he looked like a giant from a scop's tale.

"Here, take this." Bassus handed Beobrand a seax. It was short, not much more than a knife, with a simple bone handle. The single-edged blade shimmered with the patterns of finely-forged metal. "It doesn't look like much, but it is a good blade and holds its edge well. Once we are in close, you'll find it more use than the spear. Your brother gave it to me and it served me well. He would have wanted you to have it."

Beobrand thanked him and they walked together towards the edge of the camp. The shieldwall was forming there. Edwin had taken Bassus' advice and set up camp to the east of the Mercian and Waelisc host, so that when they attacked, the sun would be in the eyes of their enemies.

Nearing the centre of the line, Beobrand saw that Edwin and Osfrid were standing there, metal-garbed, battle-ready and proud, with their gesithas around them. They parted and allowed Bassus and Beobrand to take up places in their ranks.

Beobrand looked along the line. Spears bristled, held aloft, a deadly winter forest. Armour and weapons jingled. Somewhere a man laughed. A short, wiry man to his left drew a stone slowly along the length of his seax with a grinding rasp. Beobrand's whole body thrummed. He could feel his heart pounding in his chest.

Bassus said in a calm voice, "Easy now, Beobrand. This is your first battle and you will not be wanting to die in it, so listen to me." Bassus took off his helmet and Beobrand could just make out the scar running above his left eye. "Use what I have shown you. If you stick by me, you'll be alright. And remember, if I get one of their shields down, get in quick and skewer the bastard."

Beobrand nodded and turned his attention towards the enemy. Cadwallon's and Penda's hosts had seen the Northumbrians readying for battle and they were forming their own shieldwall. They stood in a ragged line at the top of a small rise, the sky behind them a dark purple. In between the land was flat and boggy. To the centre of the enemy line Beobrand made out a standard bearing a wolf's head and several wolves' tails. To the left of that he saw another banner, this one carried a human skull and a crossbeam from which dangled what appeared to be human scalps. The men below those standards were lifting up spears, and hefting shields. Preparing for battle. Preparing to kill.

Smoke billowed from the campfires behind them, mingling with the ground fog.

Would one of the men he could see in the dim pre-dawn light kill him soon? He felt sick all of a sudden and started breathing through his mouth in an effort to calm his stomach. He closed his eyes and leant his head against the ash haft of his spear.

Images from the last six months flooded his mind. Edita's tiny body, swaddled in a shroud being lowered into the ground. Rheda, sweet Rheda, her hollow eyes boring into his as he mopped her burning brow with a cool cloth. She tried to smile for him even then. His mother, shaking with fever, lying on the straw-stuffed mattress, soaked in sweat, reaching out to clench his hand in a grip that belied her frailty.

"Don't stay here, Beobrand!" she had hissed. "You have nothing to bind you here now. I know you wish to be gone, to seek out your brother. You were meant for greater things than tilling the land, my son." She had closed her eyes. Her breathing was so shallow he'd thought her spirit had left.

Then her eyes had opened again and she had spoken for the final time, summoning all her strength to say those last words.

"You... are... not... your... father's... son..."

What had she meant? He would never know. Her breath had left her with a sigh and his father's bones now lay in the charred remains of his house.

"Wake up, boy!" Bassus' gruff voice brought Beobrand back to the present. To the battle. To kill or be killed.

All of his dreams with Octa and Selwyn had come to this. He had taken heed of his mother's words and left Hithe. His father had confronted him for the last time. He was a farm boy no longer. He was a warrior in Edwin of Northumbria's warband.

He cast a glance at Bassus and the huge warrior flashed his teeth in a grin.

The sun was just beginning to peak out over the trees, shedding a pale light over the battlefield. The Northumbrian warriors cast long shadows in front of them.

"Come, my countrymen!" shouted Edwin. "The moment of truth is now upon us. You have answered my call to the fyrd and stand here shield to shield with your kinsmen in defence of the land that is ours by right of blood.

"I am Edwin, son of Aella, direct descendant of Woden. The blood of the old gods flows in my veins and the new God, the Christ, is on our side. Paulinus has blessed us in His name and I have promised to build Him a great church when he grants us victory.

"We cannot be defeated this day. Together we will send these pagans to hell where they belong.

"I will quench my sword's thirst in the blood of these Waelisc and Seaxon Mercians."

He flourished his fine battle-blade above his head. It glinted in the dim sunlight.

"Take up your weapons with me. Guide them with cunning and might.

"Kill them all! Attack them now and kill every one of them!"

"For Edwin!" came back the raucous response from the host, Beobrand's voice as loud as the next man's.

The shieldwall surged forward. Beobrand felt his shield bang against the man on his left as they ran. He tried to keep pace and to hold his shield in the right position. He could hardly believe what was happening; what had been a distant dream was now vivid reality. And then there was no more time for thinking. The men around him let fly their javelins with shouts of defiance. At the same time, the enemy threw theirs. Beobrand had no javelin but he watched as the light throwing spears were silhouetted against the sky. Those of each side mingled together at the apex of their flights, and then he could see the burnished point of one spear glinting as it fell straight towards him.

He raised his shield above his head and kept running. Something hit the rim of the shield, but he was not wounded. The man to his left screamed, tripped and fell. Beobrand caught a glimpse of a javelin piercing the man's right leg just above the knee. He looked away. The enemy were mere steps away.

The two shield lines crashed together like waves hitting a cliff. Beobrand's shield smashed against another. He pulled back, trying to get an opening at the warrior in front of him. As he did so, he realised it was a mistake. His opponent, a brutish, red-bearded Waelisc, wearing a leather helm, pushed hard as he stepped back. Beobrand lost his balance and fell sprawling to the muddy ground. The Waelisc warrior, smiling at how easily he had broken through the shieldwall, pulled back his spear for the killing blow. Beobrand tried to rise, but the Waelisc moved in too quickly for him to get to his feet.

But at the moment the spear point came hurtling towards Beobrand's exposed chest, Bassus turned and parried the blow with an over-arm swing of his barbed spear. He swung with such force that the warrior lost his grip. The spear fell harmlessly to the ground next to Beobrand.

With practised skill and uncanny agility, Bassus thrust his spear into the Waelisc's wooden shield. The barbs caught, and Bassus leant on the spear shaft, using his weight to pull the shield down.

"Now, boy!" Bassus shouted, struggling to hold on to his spear and avoid the cleaver-like blade the Waelisc had unsheathed. Beobrand scrambled to his feet. He snatched up his spear and, letting out a roar that was lost in the tumult of battle, thrust his spear at the Waelisc's midriff. The man attempted to parry, but was hampered by his trapped shield. He only succeeded in deflecting the spear upward towards his unprotected face. With all Beobrand's weight behind the thrust the point grazed over the man's right cheekbone and pierced his eye. He collapsed instantly and the sudden dead weight on his spear pulled Beobrand down. He stumbled, landing in a heap on the warrior's twitching corpse.

The anvil sound of metal on metal and the screams and grunts of warriors crashed around him. He struggled to free his spear from the eye socket of the warrior, but it was lodged fast. He pulled for a few heartbeats and then remembered the seax that Bassus had given him. He unsheathed it. It felt natural in his grip and with abandon, he threw himself into the rift in the shieldwall. He had killed an enemy and all his fear had vanished like morning dew in the light of the sun. The noise of battle subsided around him and an inner calm washed over him.

A snaggle-toothed man with blood-shot eyes peeked over a shield in front of him. Beobrand's seax flicked out over the shield and rammed down the man's throat. Bassus was screaming beside Beobrand, hacking and slashing with his sword, splinters from the enemies' shields making a dusty cloud about him. The Northumbrian line was moving forward. A fallen warrior clawed at Beobrand's leg, whether friend or foe, Beobrand neither knew nor cared. Battle lust was upon him and he had no time for the wounded. He stamped on the man's fingers, feeling them snap under his foot and pushed his shield forward to meet the next enemy.

The enemy shieldwall parted and a grey-haired man wearing a fine suit of scale mail stood before him. He was wielding a blood-drenched sword and there was a pile of corpses at his feet. Beobrand thought not of the danger. He saw a gap in the line and walked forward to fill it. The old warrior looked surprised and almost saddened as Beobrand, with no armour and only a splintered shield and short seax for protection, walked towards him.

Something in the warrior's grim features penetrated through the red mist that had descended on Beobrand. He looked around to see where Bassus and the other Northumbrians were, searching for aid against this mighty warrior. Too late he saw that he had become cut off from his shieldwall. The tide of the battle had shifted and the Mercians and Waelisc had outflanked the Northumbrians. Edwin's host had fallen back towards the encampment, leaving Beobrand stranded and surrounded by enemies.

4

Death surrounded him.
Screams of the dying mingled with the clash of weapons, creating a hellish cacophony.

The foetid bowel-stench of the slain hung over the battle-field, the miasma of defeat.

The calm that had made him formidable moments before had vanished as quickly as it had come.

Beobrand faced the grey-haired warrior. His legs were heavy. His stomach in turmoil. The warrior strode down the slope towards him. Beobrand struggled to lift his shield and seax in a menacing manner.

The grim warrior swung his sword, effortlessly swatting the seax from Beobrand's hand. Beobrand stepped backwards, vainly attempting to raise his shield. All strength had fled from his limbs. His right hand throbbed from the sword blow. The shield in his left was too heavy, as if being dragged down by unseen forces.

He knew then, looking into the dire, grey eyes of the warrior, that he was going to die. From deep within himself, a spark was rekindled. If his wyrd was for him to die this day, he would at least die fighting. Not cowed and mewling like a woman.

He scooped up a fallen spear and stood tall; straightening his back, squaring his shoulders. He would not die so easily. This old man would regret attacking Beobrand, son of Grimgundi.

Letting out a scream of defiance against all that the gods had taken from him, Beobrand charged towards his enemy. Too late, he saw the old warrior step nimbly to the side. The momentum of his headlong rush carried him forward. He stumbled, off balance. He tried to recover his balance, to bring his shield to bear. But it was hopeless. The linden-wood board was too heavy. He was too slow.

Before he could regain his footing, he was struck a jarring blow to the temple.

Dazed, he staggered and then fell back onto the corpse of the snaggle-toothed warrior.

He looked up at the sky, unable to move. Carrion crows circled, patiently awaiting the feast that the battle-play would provide. The noises of death and battle grew in his ears, became distorted. The grey clouds scudding in the sky turned crimson.

He fought to retain consciousness. His thoughts became addled. His sight faded. So, this is what it was to die. Beobrand's hold on middle earth slipped.

His mind turned to Octa. He would see him soon.

Beobrand came round to the sound of laughter. Voices, indistinct and distant, sang a bawdy song. Somewhere far off someone was screaming. He could feel cool water hitting his face. His head ached and there was a sharp pain in his

chest as he breathed. He tried to open his eyes but found that
the left one would not obey his command. With his right eye
he could see that the sky was darkening and the water that
hit his face was rain.

He couldn't move his arms. He lifted his head and
looked down to see what was impeding their movement.
He immediately saw what was causing the pain in his chest.
A warrior lay face down on top of him. The boss of his shield
was pressed into Beobrand's ribs, the man's weight on it.
The warrior's head had been smashed, a mess of dried blood,
bone and matted hair. The stench of death slowly pervaded
Beobrand's awareness.

He felt faint and let his head fall back. He twisted his head
towards the sound of voices and could just make out the
shadows of men, silhouetted in front of a large fire. Next to
the fire stood the wolf standard of Penda and the grisly skull
totem of Cadwallon. So, Edwin had lost the battle.

And Beobrand had survived. He should have given his life
with honour. It was the duty of a warrior to die with his lord.
But now the thought of death in battle seemed less noble than
it had that morning. He had seen it first-hand. He had killed
two men. Seen the life fade in their eyes. Heard the wails
of the wounded. Smelt the blood and shit of spilt innards.
And now here he lay, covered in cloying blood, both his
own and that of others. Gone were the dreams engendered
by Selwyn's tales on the mead benches. The truth of the
shieldwall would make poor songs. He was lucky to be alive,
he knew, and he would have to be careful if he wanted to
live through the night. If Penda and Cadwallon's men should
discover him, all would be lost.

From the way he was feeling Beobrand was certain that
he wouldn't be able to move very quickly, let alone fight.

He decided to wait till nightfall before attempting to get up. With luck, the men would be too busy celebrating their victory to search for survivors amongst the enemy fallen.

In preparation for making his escape he began to move his arms and legs slowly, flexing his muscles, working the long period of inactivity from them. The rain was falling harder now and within moments he was soaked.

By the time it was dark enough to stand without being seen from the camp, Beobrand was shivering uncontrollably. He carefully slid out from under the corpse that had partially shielded him from view. The pain in his ribs was much worse now and he bit his lip to avoid crying out. He lay there, beside the body, on the muddy ground, and willed himself to get up. He reached up to gingerly touch his left eye, thinking that it may have been stuck closed with dried blood. The side of his head throbbed and the eye was swollen and tender to the touch. It would not open. No wonder he had been left for dead. His face must look awful.

He sat up carefully. He felt dizzy at once and the jolt of pain in his chest made his vision blur. His breathing came in ragged gasps and he began to believe he wouldn't be able to stand.

If I don't get up, I'll be as good as dead.

He felt the hard wet shaft of a spear under his hand and grasped it. With its help he managed to finally haul himself upright, but the effort caused him a wave of nausea and dizziness. He stood for a few moments, panting in the dark, the rain driving down. He trembled and it was all he could do to keep his teeth from chattering. He had no idea where he could go on foot in his condition, but it was clear to him that the best way to begin would be away from his enemies' camp.

He was preparing to make a start when he heard voices raised in anger. They were very close by, only the dark and the rain had prevented him from being discovered. He stood still and tried not to breathe. The voices had been lowered and he could not make out where they had come from. Suddenly, seemingly right next to him, Beobrand heard the voices talking in loud whispers.

"I tell you I saw it first! And it was my idea to take it." The voice was gruff, yet whining.

"But you got that cloak clasp too. It's not right and you know it. If we didn't have to be quiet about it, I'd break your jaw, you whoreson!" The second voice was deeper and more melodious, but the owner was obviously furious.

Beobrand remained motionless. He could hear the two men whispering as they moved past him, but he could make out no more of what they said. When he could no longer hear them, he waited a few heartbeats more and then made off away from the camp and also in a different direction to the two men. He remembered that the fen rose into heathland a few hundred paces in the direction he guessed he was going. He also recalled the forest crowning the heather-covered hill. He decided to make for the shelter of the trees.

It took him a long time to reach the trees. It had stopped raining and the clouds began to blow apart. A cold wind from the north rustled the heather and the leaves of the oaks. Beobrand had hoped that movement would relieve the pain in his chest and clear his head, but this was not the case. His head reeled with every step and his chest felt as if someone was stabbing him between the ribs with each breath. But he did not stop. The temperature was dropping rapidly, the wind chilling his sodden clothes. If he stopped now, with no fire and no shelter, he was bound to freeze in the night. He pushed on, staggering into the darkness under the trees.

It seemed warmer amongst the boles of the oaks and ashes.

To Beobrand it sounded as if the forest was whispering to him, softly urging him to rest. His mind began to wander. He thought of Octa. He had not seen him for over three years and he would not see him again on this side of the afterlife. But his brother's face was clear in his mind. He smiled and beckoned to Beobrand.

Other faces vied for his attention. His mother. Edita. Rheda. His father. All gone now.

He trudged on into the forest. Some part of his mind drove him forward, away from the battlefield. Away from death.

He had been fleeing death for months now. Perhaps his wyrd would see death catch up with him.

Walking on, staggering from one tree trunk to the next, he was not aware of where he was travelling, only that he must move onward.

His thoughts turned to the events of the last few days. He had learnt so many things, made new friends. And lost so much. What had happened to Tondberct in the crush of the shieldwall? Had Bassus survived the battle?

Without realising what he was doing, he sat down with his back to a gnarled old oak. His vision clouded and memories he had fought to forget crashed in.

Spark-spattered smoke billowing into the night sky, carrying his father's spirit with it. The flames had caught quickly in the dry thatch of the house. The beams had groaned and moaned. The heat soon became unbearable and he had turned his back on his burning home.

He had turned away from his past and walked down to the coast, to find a ship to carry him northward, to his future.

As his injuries pulled him down into darkness, his mother's voice whispered in his mind, "You... are... not... your... father's... son..."

Later, in the stillest, darkest part of the night, a badger passed close by. It sniffed the man curled up by the moss-covered tree and then went upon its way.

No other living thing came close to the wounded warrior until dawn.

5

It had been a bad day for Coenred. He had first woken to find that he had overslept and missed the Vigils. Abbot Fearghas had made him scrub the chapel floor before Matins as a punishment. After that, the day just seemed to get worse.

At Matins he had forgotten a prayer and Abbot Fearghas had given him one of his looks. Since being orphaned two years before, Coenred had been at the monastery of Engelmynster. He tried hard to learn, but he was not the best of students. He received rather more of Abbot Fearghas' looks than he would have liked. And the looks were usually followed by strict punishments. This time was no exception, and after Matins Fearghas tottered up to him.

"You will think about the prayer you have forgotten whilst you are fetching firewood. You may return to break your fast when you have forty faggots of a good size."

Coenred bit back the answer that he wanted to blurt out. He had learnt that his quick retorts to Abbot Fearghas' reprimands were not welcomed, and only made the penance more severe.

"Yes, Father," he said meekly, but as he turned away,

he could feel the tears threatening to roll down his cheeks. It would take him ages to collect that much wood and he was ravenous.

When he left to head for the forest, his spirits sank even further. It was raining heavily and the ground was a quagmire. Soon, both Coenred and the donkey pulling the small cart were plastered with mud and panting at the climb up into the forest that overshadowed Engelmynster.

By the time they reached the edge of the wood the sky in the east was turning a watery grey. The rain had stopped, but heavy clouds filled the sky. It looked like it would rain again before he was finished cutting the firewood. He was glad that dawn had arrived though. He was loth to enter the dark forest during the night. Even now, very little light filtered through the rain-laden clouds, and still less penetrated the gloomy interior of the wood.

Coenred hesitated. People told tales of goblins and elves being seen in the woods. Abbot Fearghas had told him not to fear evil spirits, as God would watch over him and protect him. That was easy for Abbot Fearghas to say – he never ventured into the forest alone in the rain to cut firewood.

Coenred tried not to be frightened. But he could not stop imagining malicious creatures of the forest lurking just out of sight. The boles of the trees were grey in the dim light, the colour of dead flesh. Rainwater dripped from the limbs, echoing eerily. He began to recite the Pater Noster in a hushed whisper. He couldn't go back empty-handed just because he was scared. He would be beaten, not only for not bringing back the wood, but also for lack of faith.

He began to move slowly into the gloom, towards the small glade where the monks cut their firewood. After he had walked a short distance the donkey pulled up to a halt.

He tugged the harness but the animal refused to move. Its ears were flat against its head, its nostrils flared. Coenred gently patted the donkey's neck, trying to soothe it. The animal's obvious fear did nothing to reassure Coenred and he looked around nervously, trying to spot what had frightened the beast. He thought he caught a glimpse of something shining through the trees. He moved closer, not breathing. The donkey stood where he left it, quivering silently.

As Coenred edged a little closer to whatever he had seen through the trees, he became aware of a sound. He stopped moving and listened. He could barely make out a low moaning. It was possible that words were being spoken in a hushed voice, but Coenred could not be sure. He realised he was shaking uncontrollably. Surely this was the sound of an elf placing a curse on him or some evil spirit chanting to the elder gods of the forest. He was on the verge of turning to flee when the part of him that led him to imagine phantoms and elves in every shadow lost the battle with the part that couldn't bear the thought of not knowing what was lying just out of sight. His vivid imagination lost to his insatiable curiosity.

Still trembling, ready to run if his worst fears proved correct, Coenred looked out from behind the tree that was shielding him from whatever was moaning in the darkness.

At first he wasn't sure what it was that was making the sound. In the poor light he could only see a dark lump at the bottom of a tree. As he peered at it, he became aware of details. The glimmer he had seen was the leaf-shaped point of a war spear, propped against the tree trunk. The lump was the huddled form of a man, partially covered by a round shield, the boss of which was dull in the darkness. He began to make out words now in the sounds that the man was making. He didn't seem to be making any sense and Coenred thought that he must be talking in his sleep. Suddenly, the warrior screamed out, slumped to one side and lay still.

Coenred spat involuntarily in an effort to ward off evil spirits and then quickly crossed himself. He found it hard to abandon the old traditions, despite the number of times Abbot Fearghas had punished him for his pagan ways.

He waited. The man was silent, so he decided to move closer to the prostrate form. He took a few steps, half expecting the stranger to suddenly leap up and confront him. The closer he got, the less likely that appeared. The man seemed unconscious, not asleep. A few steps more convinced him that the warrior was not going to cause him harm. His breathing was shallow and feverish, his face a mess of caked dried blood and mud. His left eye was so horribly swollen that it looked as though a plover had laid an egg in his eye socket, and there was a deep gash on his temple. The shield boss, which had at first appeared rusty and tarnished, was in fact smeared with dark liquid, now dry and crusted. Whether the warrior's blood or his foe's Coenred wasn't sure.

Apart from the shield and the spear, there was little to indicate that the man was a warrior, except perhaps for his size. He was tall and broad-shouldered, but his clothes – a simple kirtle and trousers – were those of a ceorl, a commoner, not a thegn.

The donkey moved restlessly behind Coenred, startling him. He would have to make a decision about what to do. He could run back to the monastery and tell Abbot Fearghas what he had found. That would be the easiest option and he'd get away from danger quickly. But the stranger was obviously very sick. If he went back now, leaving the man in the chill damp morning, he was bound to get worse. He might well die. Brother Sebbi had been struck dead by a fever only last month and he hadn't looked half as ill. But what would happen if the man got well and then caused them harm? Coenred fretted. The stranger was a man of war and he looked strong enough to do considerable damage if he were fit.

Then Coenred recalled the tale Jesu had told of the Samaritan who had helped his enemy. It didn't matter who this man was – he was in need of help and God had seen fit to place Coenred in a position to aid him. He may have overslept and forgotten his prayers, but this was a trial he would not fail.

With new resolve, Coenred went to the fallen man and tried to lift him. He couldn't move him to start with, but after a few attempts, the man's right eye flickered open. It was a pale blue, but glazed with pain and fever.

"I can't lift you. You'll have to help," said Coenred, hoping the man would understand.

The wounded man didn't reply, but shut his eye again and let out a sigh. Coenred thought that he had lapsed back into unconsciousness, but a moment later the warrior gripped Coenred's arm.

With a lot of help, the stranger managed to get to his feet. He was in great pain and rested much of his weight on Coenred's shoulder. With difficulty Coenred guided him to the cart where the man collapsed. He had used the last of his strength and he didn't even groan when Coenred lifted his legs into the cart.

Beobrand awoke slowly.

Recently, he seemed to always be waking up feeling terrible and this was no exception.

He could feel something pressing on his face. His chest

felt tight and ached with each breath. He tried to open his eyes, but found that something prevented him. He reached up and found a damp bandage was wrapped around his face, covering both his eyes. As his fingers brushed the left side of the bandage, an acute pain flared in his eye and head. He gingerly made a move to remove the bandage but a voice from the darkness stopped him.

"Don't take off the bandage," said an anxious voice. "Alric says you'll go blind if you do."

Beobrand let his arm fall by his side, he had no desire to live life as a blind man. The voice that had spoken was young, that of a boy.

"Who are you and where am I?" Beobrand's voice croaked in his dry throat.

"Here, have some water," the boy replied and Beobrand felt a hand behind his head and a cup brush his lips. He swallowed a little of the cool water and let his head rest back on what he guessed was a straw mattress.

"Thank you," Beobrand said and then repeated, "Where am I?"

"Engelmynster. I found you in the woods, nearer to death than life. My name's Coenred."

"How long have I been asleep?"

"Three days. Your fever broke yesterday and Alric said that you would probably live, with God's will. I prayed for you every day, as Abbot Fearghas told me to do." Coenred seemed pleased with himself.

"Thank you."

"Whose side were you on? In the battle? Edwin's?"

"That much should be clear...," answered Beobrand, feeling weak and empty, the sarcasm jagged in his voice. "Is there anything I can eat?"

"Of course. Sorry," stammered Coenred. "I'll fetch you some broth."

Beobrand heard him stand up, move away from him and then pause.

"What is your name?" Coenred asked from some distance away.

"Beobrand, son of Grimgundi."

There was a pause, and then he heard Coenred leave the room.

Beobrand lay there. He was unable to look around, so he looked inside himself.

Where would he go now? Was he blind? A despair as dark as a winter night filled his soul. Why had he not died? To live as a cripple, depending on others' pity for food and shelter was worse than death. Why had Octa died leaving him alone in this northern kingdom? He thought of his father and the burning house back in Hithe. Had his actions offended the gods so, that they would leave him in a state of living death? Was that his wyrd?

He heard someone returning to the room. Coenred's voice brought him back to more mundane matters. The gnawing emptiness in his stomach first amongst them.

Coenred helped him to prop himself against the wall behind the mattress where he was lying. The pain of moving made Beobrand cry out.

"You have some broken ribs," Coenred explained, "but they are bound tightly and should heal well."

As soon as he sat still, the pain subsided. Coenred helped him to drink the warm broth he had brought.

As he fed him, a spoonful at a time, Coenred talked incessantly. Beobrand didn't mind listening. Coenred's voice was pleasant and strong and although he talked with the enthusiasm of a boy about all manner of things, he did not prattle. Beobrand could sense the intelligence behind the voice and was pleased to be able to use Coenred's descriptions of the foibles of the different monks and members of the community to keep his own dark thoughts at bay.

After he had finished the soup, Beobrand asked about the aftermath of the battle at Elmet.

"I don't know much," said Coenred. "A pedlar came through yesterday and said he'd heard that Edwin and his son had been killed. Most of his warhost too."

"Have no other Northumbrian survivors come this way?" asked Beobrand.

"No, you are the only one."

Beobrand wondered what had befallen his new friends. Bassus had seemed invincible. Yet so had Edwin, and he had not survived the battle. Tondberct was probably dead too. He had got on well with the light-hearted young warrior, but if Edwin had died could Tondberct have surpassed the trials of battle? Beobrand mourned the loss of the possible future friendship they could have had.

Everyone he had ever cared about, or who had shown him any kindness was dead. He must be cursed.

Darkness was imposed upon him by the bandage over his eyes, and darkness threatened to engulf him from within. Behind the bandage his eyes filled with tears, but they soaked into the cloth and none reached his face. He was glad that Coenred could not see him weep. He was tired of his own weakness, yet he was helpless to stop the tears.

"You should rest now," Coenred said, standing up.

The boy was right. He was exhausted. Both his body and mind had suffered terribly. He lay down carefully, trying to avoid jarring his ribs or his eye. He heard Coenred mutter something about returning later to check on him.

Beobrand lay on the lumpy mattress, images flapping at his inner eye like ravens' wings. He was sure he would not be able to sleep. Too many black fears assaulted him. However, a few moments later, his breathing became rhythmic and he fell into a sleep without dreams.

He awoke suddenly.

For a few heartbeats he was unsure what had woken him. He did not know whether it was day or night. The air he breathed in felt cold and his body was stiff from inactivity. He lay still, listening. Footsteps rushing over wooden boards. Muffled whispers, urgent and sibilant in the dark. By the gods, how he wished he could see. He was helpless. Blind and powerless against the threats in the darkness. He sat up as quickly as he could. In the distance a man shouted something angrily. A dog barked. Then there was a scream.

Beobrand needed no more signals. All was not right. His life was in danger. Moving his hand to the bandage around his head, he tentatively tweaked the cloth up to uncover his uninjured, right eye. Before he had moved the bandage more than a hair's breadth, he heard someone enter the room. He stiffened, ready to pull the bandage off. He would not be killed by an unseen assailant.

"Wait! Don't pull off the bandage! You will lose your sight for sure if you do!" the voice of Coenred spoke from the cold gloom. He spoke urgently, but in a whisper. "I will lead you. We must leave."

"What is happening?" Beobrand demanded. He felt Coenred place the blanket from his bed around his shoulders.

"Waelisc are here. If they find you, they will kill you.

Come on, there is no time." Coenred tugged frantically at Beobrand's hand and pulled him to his feet.

Beobrand felt giddy. Disorientated. The searing pain in his chest was like fire and his head throbbed. His legs buckled as he stood upright, but Coenred held him steady and after a moment he rallied. Coenred's urgency and fear were almost palpable. As if to accentuate the peril they were in, another scream rent the darkness. The dog's barks grew louder and more frenetic, and then were cut short with a yelp. Coenred pulled Beobrand, urging him to move and together they stumbled out of the room.

Beobrand knew nothing of the monastery's layout, so he had no idea where Coenred was taking him. All he could do was to concentrate on his footing and try not to jar his aching chest. Coenred had obviously decided in advance where they should hide and he moved through the night with haste. From time to time he would warn Beobrand to duck his head or that there was a step down or up, but other than that they moved in silence. Listening to the sounds of the night. There was more shouting. Then some crashing. Wood splintering. Screams.

Coenred faltered for a moment, but his resolve quickly returned and he pushed on. Beobrand felt the air grow colder on his skin. The atmosphere and acoustics changed. They had stepped outside.

"Come on," hissed Coenred and set off at a faster pace. Beobrand thought he would surely lose his balance or trip on a tree root, but for once wyrd smiled on him and he managed to keep up with Coenred without falling. After a short distance walking uphill, Coenred told Beobrand to stop and to sit down. The ground beneath them was soft and dry. There was a strong redolence of bark and sap in the air.

"We are inside a hollow oak," explained Coenred in a whisper. "If we are quiet, I hope they won't discover this place. It is hard to see from the path and the entrance is hidden completely from Engelmynster."

They made themselves as comfortable as they could and spoke no more, both fearing discovery. Sounds of screams and coarse laughter drifted up from the buildings they had left. Coenred prayed the Waelisc would not find them in their hiding place.

After a long while, the scent of smoke was borne on the wind and they feared that the monastery had been put to the torch. The smell of burning passed soon enough though and they were left wondering what fire they had noted.

So it was that they spent the rest of that chill night, huddled together, not daring to speak. Each was glad of the other's company, though they barely knew each other. Time passed and the sounds of destruction and torment from the monastery died down.

By morning, Beobrand had decided that he would risk moving the bandage from his right eye. Coenred had said he may go blind, but he had probed with his fingers through the night and it didn't hurt at all, whereas the left eye was a constant dull throb. He reasoned that if he had been able to see with the right eye when he left the battlefield, he should still be able to do so. And he certainly didn't want to face a day of uncertainty and danger as a blind man being led by the young monk.

In the dark of the bole of the huge hollow tree where they hid, Beobrand reached up and carefully pulled up the bandage where it covered his right eye. There was a brief flare of pain in his left eye as the bandage tightened against it, and then the dull ache returned. He opened his good eye.

For a hideous moment, he thought he was truly blind, just as Coenred had warned. Then he noticed a slightly lighter area in the darkness that surrounded him. It was still night, but the moonlight that filtered into the forest made the opening in the tree's trunk a grey swathe in the black wall. He let out a sigh of relief. He was unsure whether he could see perfectly, but his eye was definitely working. That knowledge lifted his spirits more than he would have thought possible.

Later, as the grey patch grew paler, Beobrand risked a whisper.

"I can see out of my right eye."

Coenred jolted fully alert. He had been dozing and the sound of speech startled him awake.

"What?" he hissed.

"I can see," repeated Beobrand. "I've taken the bandage off of my right eye."

Coenred shook his head at the foolhardiness. He could have made himself blind for life. But it would be better to have a companion who could see for himself.

"God be praised," he whispered. Just what Abbot Fearghas would have said.

They spent that day cowering in the tree. The day was cold and foggy and the two young men only had one blanket between them. Both wore only light sleeping tunics, so they squeezed as close together as they could and wrapped the blanket about them.

The sun rose slowly in the sky, casting dim light into their hiding place. There were cobwebs strewn in the upper reaches of the hollow tree. Beobrand studied his rescuer as the gloom lifted. Coenred was three or four years younger than him with mousy brown, short-cropped hair. He was slender and Beobrand noticed that where he clutched the blanket, his fingers were long and thin and stained with some dark substance. Beobrand felt weak with relief at being able to see these details. Whatever happened to his other eye, he did not need to face the future as a blind man.

There was no sound of anyone coming near to the tree, so Beobrand risked a whisper.

"What is this place? Engelmynster you called it? What sort of name is that?"

Coenred again started at the sound of Beobrand's voice. "It is a monastery. Abbot Fearghas named it after the angel he found on the floor of the building he turned into the chapel."

This made little sense to Beobrand. "What is a monastery?" he asked.

"It is where monks train. Holy men. I am studying to be a monk. I learn about the one true God and His son, Christ. I learn prayers and how to read and write."

Praying and letters sounded terribly boring. There had been a priest of the Christ in Hithe. A sour, sombre man, who always spoke of sacrifice, love and turning the other cheek. While people attended the priest's sermons by the newly-erected cross in the village, most still prayed to the old gods in private. They wore hammer amulets in honour of Thunor, gave mead and meat at feasts in offering to Woden and buried bread in the fields so that Frige would bring plenty.

"How did you come to be learning about the gods?"

"Not gods, the one true God. Abbot Fearghas says there are no other gods." Coenred smiled. "I know it is hard to understand."

Beobrand didn't think it was difficult at all. Just stupid. But he said nothing. He thought there were enough people on middle earth for all the gods to have their share.

"I came here two years ago," said Coenred. "Abbot Fearghas found us in Eoferwic." In the shadows his face took on a strained look.

"Found who?"

"Me and my sister. We were all alone. He gave us a new life." He ran a hand through his hair. "What about you? Do you have family?"

"I did," said Beobrand. "They are gone now. I'm all alone now too." He bit his lip.

"You're not alone now," said Coenred. His teeth flashed in the gloom.

Beobrand forced a smile, but deep inside he felt empty and lost.

Sometime towards midday they heard movement from the monastery. Laughter, talking and the sound of horses and waggons being readied for travel permeated the fog. When the Waelisc finally left, they moved up the hill in the direction of the hollow tree. Beobrand willed them not to detect their hiding place. Coenred closed his eyes and clasped his hands together. Beobrand was sure he was praying for his god to make them invisible to the heathens.

The group of Waelisc walked within an arm's length of the entrance to the tree trunk. They were so close that Beobrand and Coenred could smell their sweat, but none of them turned to look in their direction and after some time, the pair dared to breathe again.

They waited a while longer before venturing out of the oak. They were hungry and stiff. Beobrand found it hard to stand and needed to hold onto the trunk of the tree for support. His breath was ragged as he concentrated on staying on his feet. The pain in his chest flared up acutely and his throbbing head made him dizzy.

Once he felt more confident, Beobrand put his arm around Coenred's shoulders and allowed the young monk to lead him back towards Engelmynster. The fog had cleared, but the day was still cold and damp. The sound of their feet in the thick carpet of wet leaves seemed unnaturally loud in the still forest.

Coming to the edge of the trees, Beobrand got his first look at the monastery. It was made up of a hall, circled by several smaller dwellings. The group of buildings nestled in the bend of a small river. On both sides of the river, the forest sloped upwards. All the structures save for one were made of wood and had thatched roofs. The exception to this was the largest building, which had walls partly made of stone. The finely hewn rocks were mortared and went to about the height of a man's waist. At that point they were topped by walls of the more common wattle and daub. All this was crowned by golden thatch, one corner of which was charred and blackened.

They paused before continuing down to the monastery buildings. There was no movement down there. No sound or smoke from a fire. Neither Beobrand nor Coenred spoke. Both feared what they would find when they gathered enough courage to enter the compound. Coenred shuddered. Beobrand gripped his shoulders more tightly, both comforting and gaining comfort from his grasp.

They went first to the largest building. Near the entrance, there was what at first glance appeared to be a fur cape, crumpled in a heap where it had been dropped. When they got closer, Beobrand saw it was a small dog. It had been hacked almost in two. Coenred mumbled something under his breath. Beobrand couldn't make it out, but he thought it was the name of the animal. He cast a glimpse at Coenred. Tears had begun to roll down his smooth cheeks, leaving salty furrows in the grime. Beobrand looked away and back to the building they had now reached. The corner of the thatch had been set alight, and part of the lintel of the doorway was black and cracked. The damp weather had saved the structure, and the Waelisc had apparently lost interest when they had failed to get a blaze going easily.

Hesitantly, Beobrand and Coenred entered the building. They strained to see in the gloom. The interior was as silent as a burial mound. As their eyes grew accustomed to the dim light, they made out a shape on the altar at the end of the hall. They moved slowly forward, drawn towards the shape. Beobrand did not wish to believe what it was, yet he was already certain. He walked past the broken pottery and ripped sacks that were strewn on the ground, hardly noticing them. Beobrand did not heed the fabulously intricate design of a man's face in small tiles on the floor. His eyes were held in the inexorable grasp of the unthinkable form on the altar.

When they were close enough he saw the true horror. The pale skin of the blood-stained thighs. The teeth-shaped bruises on the breasts. The tongue, lolling from the blue-lipped mouth. And those sightless eyes. Staring, staring, in imploring silence.

He wished he had trusted his instincts and turned away. This was a sight he would never forget. It would haunt his dreams. Its gory vividness seared into his mind.

Beobrand did not know the young woman who lay like an animal carcass ready for butchering, but he shuddered to think of how she must have suffered. Coenred let out a cry on seeing the girl and fell to the ground. He buried his head in his arms and wailed. Beobrand, now without support, staggered. He stumbled to the side of the hall, and leaned against the wall.

He wanted to avert his eyes from the body of the girl, but some perverse fascination drew his gaze back. He shouldn't look, he knew, but he was powerless to stop. He felt sordid, shameful.

Coenred's sobs filled the chapel. "Tata! Tata!" he cried. Beobrand didn't know how to console him. His own recent losses seemed to have inured him to the sorrows of others. He just wanted fresh air. To be away from the milky white flesh of the slaughtered girl. Using the wall for support he made his way out of the building and left Coenred alone with the corpse and his grief.

He stepped out into the watery light of the afternoon and pulled the blanket more tightly around his shoulders. It was cold, and they would need a fire soon, and food. He looked in the direction of some of the living quarters. Did the houses contain similar gory secrets to the chapel? He wasn't strong enough to enter any dwelling yet, not alone. When Coenred had calmed himself they could go in search of clothes and food. Maybe get a fire going. But for now he would just sit and wait.

He had been sitting with his back propped against the door frame for a short while when he sensed a presence nearby. He looked up, afraid that the Waelisc had returned. Perhaps they had feigned leaving in order to lure people from hiding. The man standing over him leaned down and said in a soft, unusually accented voice, "Do not fear, my child." Beobrand had been avoiding looking in the direction of the dog and the sound of Coenred crying must have covered any noise the man made when he approached, but his sudden appearance was unnerving. The man was old, with thinning grey hair and intelligent, sad eyes. Beobrand tried to stand, but pain coursed through his chest and his vision blurred. The old man put a gentle hand on his head, bidding him to stay seated.

"Jesu be praised that you have been spared," the old man said. "Is it Coenred who weeps inside the chapel?"

Beobrand nodded, but found no words worth uttering.

"Does he weep for Tata?" the old man asked, but went on without waiting for a reply. "Her faith in the Lord was stronger than mine. She said he would deliver us from evil, but we fled. God have mercy on our souls." He drew in a ragged, deep breath and walked slowly into the gloomy chapel. Towards the sounds of Coenred's grief.

If this was how the Christ god protected his faithful from evil, allowing their enemies to rape and murder them, Beobrand preferred the old gods. They smiled on the brave and laughed at the weak. They didn't offer false hope.

Others were now moving into the clearing. Having watched the old man enter the chapel safely, thirty or forty people came out of the trees at the foot of the slope and walked sheepishly into the settlement. Beobrand estimated that there were some ten monks, wearing the same dark robes as the old man, a handful of other men, wearing the normal breeches and tunics of ceorls, and the rest of the number was made up of women and children. They all had the pale faces and nervous eyes of those who expected the worst at any moment. It would appear that they also lacked faith that their god would protect them if the Waelisc came back.

Inside the chapel, Coenred's sobs had ceased and Beobrand could make out the lowered voice of the old abbot consoling him. The other monks and men came towards the place where Beobrand was sitting. The women hung back with the children. When he was surrounded by the men, Beobrand struggled to pull himself upright. His chest was stabbed through with pain, but he was vulnerable at the feet of so many strangers and so suffered the agony in order to meet them face to face.

Once he was standing, a gruff looking man with a black beard stepped forward. "You are still weak," he said. "Come into my house, we could all do with some food."

Beobrand allowed himself to be led to one of the buildings on the edge of the clearing. The bearded man gave orders to four of the men to keep watch for the Waelisc and for the women to get fires lit and food cooking. Beobrand was staggering slowly towards the dwelling when tiredness washed over him and he almost fell. The man caught him by the arm and guided him into the dark interior of the thatched house. He righted an overturned stool and indicated that Beobrand be seated. Two young men and three of the women had gone into the building first and were in the process of putting things in order.

The Waelisc had clearly stayed in the house. There was food and rubbish strewn about the floor. Two of the women found brooms and began sweeping the detritus out of the house, while the third started laying a fire. The monks fetched firewood from outside and soon the house was in a semblance of normality.

Once the place was tidy, one of the women, a middle-aged woman with sallow cheeks and dark eyes came to Beobrand. "You must rest," she said in a surprisingly deep voice for one so thin. "I have made a bed for you by the fire." She helped Beobrand to stand and he murmured his thanks. The bed was a mattress stuffed with rushes and Beobrand needed no coaxing to make him lie down. His body had yet to recover from its wounds and the fear from the night before had taken a heavy toll on him. He eased himself down onto the mattress with the aid of the woman. His chest hurt terribly, as did his head, but he barely noticed.

"You are safe here," the woman said.

Even through the fog of approaching sleep Beobrand couldn't help but wonder what made the woman so sure of that. Perhaps faith in her god or an optimistic nature prompted her assurance of safety. Or maybe she was just saying what they both wanted to hear.

6

On waking Beobrand felt refreshed. His body still ached but he had slept through the afternoon, all through the night and long into the morning, and the rest had done him good. He lay for a while and listened to the movements of the people around him. He could hear the crackle of the fire on the hearthstone and feel its warmth against his cheek. There was the sound of someone stirring something in a bowl, and the cloying scent of malt and honey. Underneath the smell of ale being prepared, Beobrand detected the subtler aroma of baking bread. He could hear a woman's melodious voice intoning a ditty quietly, absently, under her breath. Life was going on normally, despite the tragedy of the last days. The woman had been right about their safety. The Waelisc had not returned.

He sat up. His ribs hurt, but the constant headache had subsided somewhat. The woman from the afternoon before noticed his movement and motioned for him to stay where he was. She promptly picked up a trencher containing some bread and cheese and made her way to him. She then brought him some ale. He gulped it down quickly, his parched throat welcoming the cool liquid. The brew was delicious, despite the bitter taste that indicated it was nearing three days old and would soon only be fit for the pigs. He thanked her and slowly began to eat. It was the first food he had tasted in days and his stomach started to grumble the moment he began chewing on the first piece of cheese.

When he had finished his meal, the woman collected the plate and mug and introduced herself. Her name was Wilda. When he made a move to raise himself from the bed she ordered him to lie back on the mattress and rest. Beobrand obeyed and Wilda went back to busying herself at the hearth.

Beobrand spent the rest of the day in this way. He only got up to go outside to relieve himself, but was quickly and sternly told to get back to bed by his hostess as soon as he returned. Wilda didn't talk much and Beobrand took pleasure in simply watching her work. She cleaned the trencher he had used, strained the fermented ale, removed the baked bread from the clay oven that was just outside the house, chopped carrots and cabbages for a stew. Later she sat at the loom. She did the things any woman did and watching her reminded him of his mother.

In the late afternoon, he was visited briefly by the old monk, who introduced himself as Abbot Fearghas, and the bearded man, who turned out to be Alric, the man who had bandaged his ribs and eye. They asked him where he was from and what his plans were. Beobrand had no real answer for the second question, but understood that the prospect of feeding a man who could not work was not a welcome one for the modest community. Especially after having their stores plundered by the Waelisc. They didn't dwell on the matter, but he sensed they were worried. How would they survive the winter with few supplies and without the protection of King Edwin? Beobrand assured them that he would move on as soon as he was able. This seemed to satisfy them and they made to leave shortly after, as Wilda, who was Alric's wife, told them that Beobrand needed his rest more than they needed to pester him.

Before they left Beobrand had one question to ask them.

"How is Coenred?"

Abbot Fearghas turned at the doorway. "He is well enough, considering." Then, after a pause, "Tata was his sister and his only living kin."

The words sent a pang of pain through Beobrand. He knew what it was to be orphaned and the despair of losing his siblings was still raw. His heart ached to think of the pain Coenred must be suffering.

Fearghas moved closer again to Beobrand. "It is a good thing to be able to feel the pain of others. There is much good in you, young Beobrand."

Only then did Beobrand realise there were hot tears streaming down his right cheek. The bandage over his eye soaked up the tears on the left. He wasn't good. There seemed to be no good left. The world had opened up to him and shown him what it really was – a dark, frightening place filled with unspeakable evil, fraught with dangers that a few months ago he could barely have imagined.

And now he was responsible for a young girl's death. Coenred had gone out of his way to help him. Had more than likely saved his life. And this was how he repaid such kindness. The gods had cursed him. Suddenly he was sure of it. Everyone who showed him tenderness died or suffered terrible consequences.

The image of Tata's pale, broken body flashed in his mind. He could not forget the pallor of her skin. The smears of blood. The blossom of bruises.

If Coenred had protected his sister, instead of him, she would be alive now and Beobrand would have died. Perhaps he deserved death.

"Do not blame yourself," Abbot Fearghas spoke in his gentle, lilting voice, incisively understanding what was troubling Beobrand. "The Lord gives us life, and He takes it away when He sees fit. Coenred does not hold Tata's death against you."

Beobrand could not speak. He rolled onto his side and closed his good eye, but the tears kept flowing.

The next days were spent in healing. The community of Engelmynster had suffered a terrible intrusion. One of its most beloved members had been violated and murdered. Coenred, while initially displaying his suffering more than the rest, had the resilience of youth and an ebullient nature that saw him begin to recover remarkably quickly. He began to visit Beobrand whenever he had time to spare.

They could often be found sitting on logs in the lee of Alric and Wilda's hut, talking about all manner of things. It was warm there next to the bread oven, out of the wind.

"Tell me about Cantware," said Coenred. "Is it the other side of the sea?" He gestured vaguely with his delicate hands, his fine fingers making the motion of waves.

Beobrand smiled. Coenred's hands seemed as flighty as his imagination and moved as much as his tongue. "No, it is to the south. A kingdom of this island of Albion."

"So we could walk there?"

"I suppose we could. But it would be a long trek."

"How did your family die?" Coenred asked, changing the subject abruptly.

Beobrand frowned, looking out over the buildings to the

darkness of the forest beyond. He didn't want to talk about his family, but he owed this boy his life and was responsible for the loss of his sister; he could not deny him. "The plague took my sisters and my mother."

"You said you had a brother too. What happened to him? And your father?"

Beobrand was silent for a moment, before deciding to speak. "My brother, Octa, was one of King Edwin's gesithas. He was murdered a few weeks before the battle of Elmet."

"Who killed him?" Coenred couldn't keep the excited interest from his voice.

"I don't know," said Beobrand. "But if I find out, I will kill him."

Coenred squirmed uneasily. "You could kill so easily?"

Beobrand fixed him with his one, blood-shot eye. He remembered the men he had slain in the shieldwall, recalled the fire consuming his home. "As Woden is my witness, I could and I will."

He saw that he had shocked Coenred and was sorry for causing him more distress. But he would not lie to him. Life was harsh, as he well knew, and vengeance was the warrior's way. He would not forgive as Coenred's Christ taught.

As Coenred's company helped keep his spirits out of the depths of despair, so Wilda and Alric's care helped his body recover its strength and start to mend. Every day Wilda saw to it that he was well-fed and, although she was not demonstrative, she treated him as well as either of her two sons, Leofwine and Wybert.

Each evening, the family would eat together and afterwards Alric would check Beobrand's bandages. He was pleased with the way the ribs were healing but would not let him uncover his left eye.

"The poultice needs time to do its work," he said, when Beobrand asked for how much longer he would need to have his eye covered. "The time to remove the bandage will come soon enough."

Often, after the evening meal, Leofwine would sing for them in his fine, strong voice. He knew many tales and songs, which he played on the lyre. His fingers were deft, nimbly picking out tunes in counterpoint to his voice. When he began singing it was never long before other families and some of the monks would appear in the doorway of Alric's house. They would wait expectantly to be invited in, eager to listen to the stories of magic and heroes.

Beobrand loved listening to Leofwine. He lost himself in the tales. He would close his good eye so as to better imagine the warriors and monsters the young man sang of. During those evenings, with the sound of Leofwine's resonant voice washing over him, the heat of the fire on his face and the warm, comforting presence of Coenred, Alric, Wilda and the others around him, Beobrand began to feel he belonged. It was almost as if he had a family again.

But then he would imagine himself in the battles of Leofwine's stories, wearing bright metal armour and wielding a patterned sword that glittered as it slashed through his enemies.

He had tasted battle, and as Bassus had said, some people found they revelled in it. The pain of defeat and loss had been awful. But as his wounds healed, the pain became remote, difficult to remember.

He had gloried in the battle-play. He relived the battle in his mind's eye, and he found he relished the moment when his spear had hit home, the instant his seax had sliced flesh. He wondered whether it was simply the ale and mead talking to him. But the next day, in the chill sunshine of late autumn, he watched Alric and his sons going about their chores – cutting wood, mending thatch, carrying water – and he could not see himself doing those menial tasks again.

He had been a warrior, albeit only for a few days. He had carried spear and shield for a lord and had defeated foes in battle. He could not return to the life of a farmer that he had once known.

When he was strong enough, Beobrand took the spear and shield that Coenred had found him with and went out to the edge of the clearing. There, by the river, shivering under the bite of a cold north wind, he began practising what Bassus had taught him. He pictured the huge warrior standing in front of him, as he had on the beach at Bebbanburg, urging him to push himself harder. Uncle Selwyn had never driven him so hard when teaching him with wooden blades. It had always seemed like a game. But Bassus had been adamant that he learn the ways of the spear; his life would depend on it in the shieldwall. But there had been little time to hone his skills. Now Beobrand was determined to strengthen the muscles he would need in future battles, and to improve the speed with which he could bring spear and shield to bear. He soon realised that no matter how much he wanted to train himself and build up his muscles, his wounds were nowhere close to fully-healed. His ribs began to hurt as soon as he lifted the shield and when he tried to raise it to block an imaginary foe, the pain was so acute that his vision blurred.

He refused to be deterred. He unslung the shield and practised lunging with the spear. Each thrust caused him excruciating pain, but he did not give in. He carried on in this way for some time, before he heard someone approaching from the monastery. He turned, the sweat cooling on his face in the cutting breeze that shook the trees on the far side of the river.

Coenred stood on the shingle beach. "Do you think you are strong enough to kill already?" he asked. His tone was harsh. He was clearly furious.

Beobrand was out of breath. His panting caused his chest to burn with each intake of air. "I cannot afford not to be strong. I have been weak and I do not like the feeling."

"Well, I think you'd better leave off the training for today," Coenred's voice softened. "Alric has tried to save that eye of yours, and I don't think he'll be too happy that you've made it bleed again!"

Beobrand raised his hand to the bandage on his head. It was wet and when he looked at his fingertips, they were smudged red.

Beobrand sighed. He was exhausted. Coenred was right. Losing his eye because he was angry at the world was pointless. He began to bend to pick up the shield, wincing from the pain.

"I'll get it," said Coenred. "You'll end up breaking your ribs again." There was no ire or recrimination left in his voice, and he smiled as he retrieved the shield from the stony bank.

Together, they made their way back to the buildings.

That night, after Vespers, Coenred left the chapel and came to Alric's house.

Abbot Fearghas had been lenient with him since Tata's death, allowing him to visit Beobrand frequently. He recognised that each young man's healing was aided by the company of the other. One night Coenred had even missed

Compline, having been too engrossed in a debate about the merits of Christ over the old gods. When Coenred realised his fault, he was distraught, terrified of the punishment Abbot Fearghas would mete out. But when he had gone to the old monk, head hung in shame and penitence at his transgression, Fearghas simply told him to be more careful in future and bade him go to his bed. Coenred could hardly believe he had not been chastised. He wondered how long Abbot Fearghas would remain so tolerant towards him.

He entered Alric's house quietly and sat by Beobrand for some time, quietly listening to Leofwine recounting a story of a beast that came in the night and killed warriors in their beds. Outside, it had begun to rain, and Coenred was not looking forward to returning to his dormitory. He would get drenched and muddy on the way back. And the trees around the village loomed and quivered like the unholy monsters from Leofwine's tale. If he had braved the elements simply to hear Leofwine, it would not have been worth it, but Coenred wanted to be near Beobrand. He knew his friend was getting restless but didn't want him to leave. He had no family now. But this young, strong, quiet Cantware man was the only thing that partly filled the gap left by Tata's death. Thinking of her brought the sting of tears to his eyes and he quickly blinked them away. Beobrand seemed tense. His jaw was set, and his blue eye was piercing in the smoky gloom. He had changed, as if he had made a decision.

"Why do you want to kill?" Coenred asked suddenly, in a voice that only Beobrand could hear.

Beobrand turned towards him. He didn't seem surprised at the question. Coenred and he had become close and it was hard for them to hide their feelings from each other. "I do not want to rely on the gods or my wyrd to protect me or my

own, so I must learn to fight. If I have to kill, then so be it."
He tensed, his hands balling into fists. "There are some who
deserve death. If you could kill the men that —," he hesitated,
as if not wanting to say the words. They rarely spoke of
Coenred's sister; talk of her hurt him so. But Beobrand needed
to explain how he felt and so forged ahead.

"If you could kill the ones who killed her," Beobrand
continued, still not bringing himself to say her name, "wouldn't
you do it?"

Coenred sat in silence for a long time. He thought about
his lovely sister and how she had looked after him when their
mother had been unable to work and they had been turned
out into the wilds. How she had laughed at his jokes, how
they had cooked together, how she had done whatever was
needed – unspeakable things with strangers that he had never
asked about – so that her little brother had something to fill
his belly. Later, once they had been rescued from that life and
come to Engelmynster, she had joined him in learning about
Christ. She had believed in the one God absolutely and loved
the stories of Jesu, the Christ. She would often regale Coenred
late into the night with tales from the Bible that she had heard
told by the monks. He could not stop the tears now and he let
them wash over his cheeks freely.

Finally, Coenred turned his tear-streaked face towards his
friend. "No, I wouldn't." And it was the truth. Tata would
not have wanted more death, for that is not what Christ
would have wanted.

"That is the difference between you and me, Beo. I wasn't
made for killing."

Coenred stood up quickly, and before Beobrand had a
chance to reply, he left the house, disappearing into the dark,
no longer afraid of what might lurk outside.

The driving rain that soaked Coenred to the skin on the short walk back to his sleeping quarters made him wonder if God was crying too.

After all the visitors had left, Leofwine wrapped his lyre carefully in a linen cloth and placed it in a leather-covered box. Once the instrument was safely hanging in its box from a peg above his cot, he returned to the fire and sat beside Beobrand.

"What happened with Coenred?" Leofwine asked.

Beobrand had been lost in his thoughts, almost dozing in the warm glow of the hearth. He stirred, turning his head towards Leofwine so he could see him with his uncovered eye.

"He is angry with me," he said.

"Why?"

"He thinks I am a killer."

"Aren't you?" Leofwine cracked his knuckles, loosening his fingers from the strains of playing the lyre.

Beobrand was silent for a while, staring into the flames.

"Yes, I am," he said at last. "And I will kill again to defend my loved ones. Or to avenge them."

"That is as it should be," said Leofwine. "You are a warrior, even if it has not always been so. Yours is the arm that defends the people. Every person has his place. I help feed the animals, cut wood, plough the fields and harvest the crops, but those things are not what my wyrd has woven for me. My wyrd is to tell tales, play the lyre and sing. I am a scop in here." He tapped his chest. "And here." He touched his forehead. "And you are a warrior. That much is plain."

Beobrand remembered Edwin's words back in Bebbanburg and nodded.

"But your song is yet to be written, Beobrand. A warrior's tale tells of his deeds. What he does with spear and shield, whether he serves his lord loyally. Where will your wyrd take you? What songs will be sung about you?"

"I do not know." Beobrand's eye glittered. "My deeds have been far from song-worthy. I feel lost. Alone."

"You are not alone or lost. You have friends here. Coenred is a good boy and will be a true friend, if you let him. And he is not angry with you."

"No?"

"He is worried for you. And for himself. He likes you and doesn't want to lose you."

Beobrand frowned. Leofwine's words rang true.

From the shadowy recess of the hut where Leofwine's parents slept, Alric said, "Can you two stop wittering like good-wives and go to sleep? Some of us need to be up with the dawn for the milking. And that means you, Leofwine. Perhaps you can think up a song about the kine while you are at it." Leofwine's brother, Wybert, chortled from his cot.

"You see, Beobrand. We are both misunderstood. Normal people do not understand our brilliance." His teeth shone bright in the firelight. "But we'll show them, won't we? What deeds you'll perform and what tales I'll sing!"

He stood and slapped Beobrand on the shoulder. "But first it seems, I must sleep if I am to have the strength to deal with cantankerous beasts in the early morning darkness."

A few days later Alric walked up to Beobrand where he was sitting on a log outside the house. It was an unseasonably warm day and Beobrand was sweating, his hair plastered to his forehead. He was helping Wybert prepare firewood.

Wybert used a large axe to split logs and then tossed the smaller pieces of wood to Beobrand who chopped them into kindling with a hand axe. Beobrand had tried wielding the two-handed axe himself, but quickly regretted the decision as the pain in his left side flared up. Wybert had laughed at him and Beobrand had felt his temper rising. He didn't much like Wybert, who was the antithesis of his brother. Where Leofwine was sensitive, artistic and charismatic, Wybert was surly and crude.

Alric stopped by the two young men. "Good to see you are feeling so much better, Beobrand," he said. "Come inside with me."

Beobrand wondered what Alric could want, but followed him inside, leaving Wybert looking sullenly after them. The relative darkness of the interior left Beobrand blind for a few heartbeats before his eye grew accustomed to the gloom.

"I thought it would be better not to have your injured eye looking straight at the bright sun." Alric said as he sat by the fire, bidding Beobrand to join him.

"You mean to remove the bandage now?" Beobrand felt a sudden ripple of anxiety down his spine. "Will my eye be alright?"

"I don't know. I thought you were going to lose sight in both eyes, but you can see from your right well enough. Sit, and soon we will see… or not." Alric smiled wryly, but Beobrand failed to appreciate the humour.

Alric unsheathed the sharp seax he carried on his belt and bent towards Beobrand.

"In truth," he said, "one of the reasons I had you wear this bandage so long was so that you would understand that if the worst comes to pass and you cannot see from the other eye, you are quite capable of living with only one."

Before Beobrand had a chance to contemplate this, Alric placed one hand on the bandage and gently cut it away with the knife.

"Don't try to open it yet," he warned. "I'll give it a good clean first."

He reached down and picked up a small wooden bowl filled with hot water. He dipped a cloth into the bowl and began to softly mop Beobrand's left eye socket and cheek. The skin tingled at the touch of the cloth. Even the air made it throb, it had been covered for so long.

Alric worked methodically, cleaning away the dried blood and the residue of the ragwort poultice from the gash under the eye.

"Now you can try to open it. Gently."

Beobrand tried to open his left eye, but found that the lids were sealed, the lashes still scabbed with blood. He reached up with his fingers and very carefully prised the eyelids apart. The dim light from the fireplace was enough to make him gasp. Once again he felt blinded, but now because the light was too bright. As he shut his left eye from the glare, a smile appeared on his face. He could see!

"You will have to rest it for a while before going out into the daylight," Alric said.

Beobrand opened his eye just a crack and once again light streamed in. But this time, he could make out the movement of the flames and Alric's form moving away from him. His vision was blurred, but he was confident it would get better, just as his ribs had.

"Thank you, Alric," Beobrand called out to the older man.

Alric tossed the dirty water from the bowl out of the door of the house.

"Look after my handiwork. That's all I ask!"

7

The following day saw the end of the warm spell. A bank of dark clouds rolled in from the north. Coenred shivered as the wind cut through his black robes. Once again he had been punished with the task of fetching firewood. That morning it had been because he was talking during the Vigils. Abbot Fearghas had caught his eye with a frosty glare and Coenred knew at once that his reprieve from punishments was over.

After the prayers the old monk had approached Coenred. "Do you still wish to be a monk?" he asked Coenred quietly.

Coenred was surprised at the question. Perhaps he was not going to be punished after all. "Yes, father. You know I love Christ and wish to serve him. You are my family now." As he said it, he knew this was the truth. Beobrand was his friend and they shared a bond that was unusually strong considering the short time they had known each other, but Beobrand's path would lead him away. To war and killing. Of that he was quite sure. And that was a path Coenred wanted no part of.

Fearghas looked at the boy long and hard. He would be a fine monk one day, if he would stop day dreaming.

His heart was good and there was a strength of character that was disguised by his light-hearted nature.

"Well, if you are to be a monk, you must start behaving like one," Fearghas said at last. "Forty faggots of wood before you eat. I seem to remember that the last time I asked you for firewood you came back with something different entirely." With this last comment he had raised an eyebrow sardonically, leaving Coenred to organise himself for the task he had been given.

So here he was, shivering in the bitter wind that was whipping through the trees. He needed to continuously goad the donkey with a stick to get it to pull the small cart up the incline into the forest. It was black under the trees and Coenred's mind began to wander, as it always did when entering the wood on his own. Were there elves hiding behind the boles of the beeches and oaks? Bows at the ready with sickness-bearing darts.

He shuddered and caught himself hitting the donkey harder than was necessary. He was frightened. Still, that was no reason to hurt the dumb beast. He patted its neck and it looked at him with a dolorous eye. Coenred tugged on its rope and eventually it set off without having to resort to the stick again.

The sun still hadn't risen when he reached the glade just off of the main path where he would collect the wood. The walk had warmed him up somewhat, but the darkness and the moaning of the wind through the trees did nothing to calm his fears. He set about gathering branches and twigs, not wishing to dawdle in the forest.

He had just tied some twine around the twentieth bundle of firewood and was mopping sweat from his brow when he heard a sound from the path behind him. He crouched down and stopped breathing. He listened. All his senses were trained on the small bracken-verged track that led back to the path to Engelmynster. To safety. For a moment he could hear nothing save for the wind and the creaking of the branches above his head. Then he heard the unmistakable jingle of metal on metal followed by a stealthy footfall. This was followed by what sounded like a voice, muffled and indistinct, further to his right. Someone was moving along the path. Whether people or some denizens of the forest he did not know. Neither prospect was good. If these were the Waelisc returned to finish what they had started a few weeks earlier, he had to warn the monks. If they were elves or other creatures from the spirit world, it would be best to leave them well alone.

Without realising it he had begun to shuffle slowly towards the track and the sounds. It seemed his body had decided for him. He would see who was passing the glade. Once again his curiosity had got the better of him.

The next sound he heard put a stop to all questions of the identity of the strangers in the forest. The rasp of a metal blade being drawn from a sheath split the stillness directly behind him. Before he could turn to see who had crept up on him, he felt the cold edge of iron against his throat.

A sonorous voice whispered in his ear, "Well, well, little monk. Spying on us, were you?"

Coenred's legs buckled with terror.

Beobrand had been up for only a short while when Alric ran into the house. He usually left before first light to see to the cows and to feed the pigs, but he didn't normally return so early, and certainly never at such a pace.

"A band of warriors is on the path," Alric said. He was out of breath but didn't pause for rest. He hastened to a chest at the back of the house and began rapidly pulling out items. "Arm yourself."

Beobrand did not need to be prompted a second time. He quickly retrieved his spear and shield, wincing despite himself as the linden board's weight put pressure on his ribs.

Leofwine and Wybert came bursting through the doorway after their father. Wybert was carrying the large wood axe. Leofwine went to his sleeping quarters and quickly returned with a seax. Alric had armed himself with a short throwing spear and a small shield.

"Are you not going to hide, as you did when they came before?" asked Beobrand.

"We cannot," answered Alric. "They have a hostage. They have caught Coenred in the forest."

For a heartbeat Beobrand did not comprehend what Alric had said, but then something inside his chest lurched.

How could this be happening? Beobrand felt cold inside. Were all his friends and loved ones destined to suffer and die? Could he truly be cursed? He had lost so much already and now Coenred was in the hands of some unknown enemy. Coenred, who had saved his life when he was blind and defenceless, leaving his own sister to a fate of rape and terror.

For an instant, Beobrand felt weak with the fear that Coenred was already dead. That he had been powerless to help him. Then all of his sorrow and loss coalesced inside him. The deaths of Edita, Rheda, his mother and Octa. The anguish at losing his new friends in the battle of Elmet.

A new resolve formed within him. He would not allow harm to come to Coenred. He would save him, or die in the attempt.

He felt no fear now. The part of him that knew fear and emotion would be of no use, so he hid it deep within himself. Strength and decision were what would save Coenred.

Wybert had a look of flushed excitement on his face. Leofwine looked serious and pensive. Alric started to speak, addressing the three young men. "Listen, we don't know how many—"

Beobrand pushed past the three of them and strode from the house. There was no time for chatter now. Coenred was in danger. He walked into the blustery grey daylight and immediately saw some of the men from the thorpe gathered at the edge of the clearing. Others were joining them. Beobrand sensed Alric, Leofwine and Wybert leaving their house behind him. They struggled to keep up with him when he broke into a run.

The men turned towards him when he ran up. Fear was etched in their faces in the early morning gloom.

"What do they want and how many of them are there?" Beobrand asked, cutting through the conversations of the men.

"We don't know how many there are," one slight man, with thinning hair and a grey beard said. "They say they want food."

Beobrand looked around him at the men. They were scared and looked pathetic. Not a force worth reckoning with. Beobrand closed his eyes for a moment, thinking hard. When he opened them again, Alric and his sons had arrived and all of the men were looking at Beobrand. His head ached, and his left eye squinted involuntarily in the dim light of the morning. For a moment his vision swam. Was his sight permanently damaged? But there was no time to worry about that now. The more time that elapsed, the more likely it would be that the brigands would get tired of waiting and kill Coenred.

"We must make them fear us," Beobrand addressed the men in a quiet voice. He did not wish the men on the forest path to overhear him. The villagers were silent, content for someone to take control of the difficult situation. All except Wybert.

"How do you think we can do that?" Wybert asked, sarcasm in his tone.

"We must make them think we have more armed men than we have."

The men looked baffled.

"When I give the order to fetch the rest of the men, get all the women and monks, and even children who are tall enough to pass for men and have them arm themselves with anything to hand. Hoes, brooms, hunting bows, anything. Tell the women to put on men's clothes, or to wear men's cloaks over their dresses. The men in the forest," Beobrand paused, making sure all of them were listening to him, "the men who have Coenred must believe we have too many warriors for them to fight us easily. Now, when I give the order, go, and make it quick!"

Wybert looked unimpressed with Beobrand's plan. The others looked frightened, unconvinced it would work. Beobrand turned to Alric. The old warrior had a thin smile of determination on his face. This gave Beobrand the confidence he needed. This might actually work.

He raised his voice so that it carried far into the forest. "Go fetch the rest of the fighting men. Bring all of them, and bring them quickly. We must defend our own. Now go!"

The man with the grey beard turned to go, then hesitated when the others didn't move. Beobrand was sure that their enemies were watching from the trees. Any mistake now could spell the death of Coenred. Maybe even give the warriors the courage to attack the settlement openly.

Just when he thought that his plan would fail before it had even begun, Alric shouted in a loud voice, "You heard the man! Get the rest of the warriors. Now!"

With Beobrand's order thus supported by one of their own number, the men rushed back to the houses to get the rest of the 'warriors' to swell their ranks.

Beobrand smiled his thanks at Alric, who nodded his approval in return.

Both wondered secretly whether the plan would work.

It took some time to assemble all the villagers who could pass for warriors. As time passed Beobrand's anxiety for his friend's safety increased.

Finally, as the last of the monks joined their ranks, Beobrand surveyed the group. There were some twenty 'warriors'. Some only carried long sticks or brooms, and several were obviously children, too small to pass for grown men. He quickly arranged them so that the largest and strongest men, armed with spears, axes and seaxes, were positioned in the front rank. The others were placed behind with strict orders to hold their 'weapons' high. He hoped that any watchers did not notice the quick repositioning of the gathered villagers.

He was surprised at how quickly these people had let him take command. He had never led a group before, except as a child. In Hithe he had usually been the leader and instigator of the village children's games and mischief. He tried not to think about how those childish adventures often ended with him being beaten by his father.

He turned to face this group, pushing his memories away. All but Wybert, who was in the front row, looked back with the hopeful expectation of those happy to be led. Wybert was trouble. Beobrand could not afford to have him question his authority. The illusion of an organised force would be shattered.

Beobrand thought quickly. He did not want Wybert near him, but he needed to get him to accept the situation and his authority.

Beobrand addressed them all. "I will go into the forest and parley with the men who have Coenred. Alric and Leofwine will come with me." He saw Wybert scowl, but before he could speak, he continued, "Wybert will stay here and lead you should anything befall us." Wybert frowned and opened his mouth to speak, then closed it again, looking uncertain. After a moment's pause, he nodded his assent. Beobrand let out a breath. He had no time for Wybert's petty dislike of him and was glad he'd accepted the semblance of power over his fellow villagers.

"Now, stand tall and make a good show of strength," he said quietly to the group. Then, in a louder voice, "Alric, Leofwine, come with me. We will approach the men in the forest."

With that, he turned on his heel, raised his shield with a grunt as it strained his still-tender ribs, and, not waiting to see if the others joined him, strode up the path towards the darkness of the forest.

Once they were out of earshot of the villagers, Alric whispered, "I hope you know what you're doing, boy. This is like betting your life on a single toss of the knuckle bones!"

Beobrand didn't answer. He gritted his teeth and carried on walking. He was well aware of the gamble he was taking, but he'd made up his mind to rescue Coenred or die trying. What he hadn't bargained on was leading others with him. Too late to worry about that now. He'd done what seemed right and to his amazement the villagers had accepted the leadership of a young, inexperienced warrior quickly and easily. He just hoped that their faith in him being able to protect them wasn't as misplaced as Tata's had been in the Christ god.

They were breathing hard by the time they reached the first trees of the forest. Their breath billowed in front of them briefly before being swept away by the chill wind. They stepped into the murk and slowed their pace. All their senses were heightened. After a few steps, Beobrand stopped. Alric and Leofwine flanked him, holding their weapons menacingly. They looked further into the shadows under the trees. They cast glances to either side, expecting an ambush. But they saw no one.

Beobrand stood his ground and leant on his spear, planting the haft in the earth. His pose displayed a confidence he did not feel.

"Come out and release our friend!" he shouted in a strong voice that showed no sign of nervousness.

For a few heartbeats there was no reply, and then a deep voice replied from the gloom, "Why should we give him to you? We're hungry. Give us provisions and we'll give you back your little monk. Otherwise we'll cut his throat and then take what we want!"

Beobrand's anger settled into a cold fire in his chest. The calm he'd felt in the battle of Elmet descended upon him.

He took a step towards the voice and replied, "No. You will give us the boy back now, or the warriors in the village will come to my call and we will kill you all. Do you think we are not prepared for brigands? Look at them, they await my command. We have come here without them to avoid bloodshed, but this is your last warning. Release the boy now, or die!"

There was no reply for a long time. It seemed as if the whole forest was holding its breath. The wind stopped its bluster and Beobrand could feel his pulse in the scar under his left eye. This was the moment when the bluff was tested. As time passed he feared the worst. He began to prepare for battle, seeing no other outcome from this impasse, when a different voice replied.

"Beobrand? Is that you?" The voice was younger and less self-assured.

Beobrand was startled. At first he couldn't place the owner of the voice. Then he realised it was that of Tondberct, the young warrior he had befriended in Edwin's warband.

"Tondberct? What are you doing here?" Beobrand replied, dropping his guard slightly, but still wary.

Tondberct stepped from the trees ahead onto the path and smiled. "I could ask you the same thing." He then spoke over his shoulder, "It's alright, I know him."

Five others emerged from the shade of the trees, four large men, carrying the accoutrements of war, and one smaller figure. Beobrand's heart leapt when he recognised Coenred. He seemed unharmed.

"Let the boy go back to his people. Then we can talk." Beobrand kept his voice easy now, hoping that Tondberct held enough sway in the group to allow Coenred to go free.

Tondberct turned and talked quietly with the others, then said, "Fine. Have him back. But I hope you'll give us some food and drink. We're starving!"

Beobrand was elated to see Coenred leave the group of warriors and walk quickly down the path to where he waited with Alric and Leofwine. Coenred gave them a weak smile as he passed and then broke into a run for the monastery and hamlet below.

Once Coenred was at a safe distance, Beobrand turned his attention back to Tondberct and his companions.

"I know you are hungry and cold, but the people here have little to offer and you have attacked one of their own."

"We did him no harm," replied the tallest of the warriors. He stepped forward. He wore a leather jerkin reinforced with metal plates. He carried a large shield and had a sword in a plain scabbard at his side. His bearded face was angular and handsome. He was perhaps ten years Beobrand's senior and carried himself with a warrior's natural grace. Beobrand had a glimmer of recognition. Had he met the man before?

"He sneaked up on us in the woods and we thought we could use him to get some food," the warrior continued. Beobrand recognised the voice from the earlier exchange. "We never meant him any harm. It was just a bluff. We knew it would be hard to convince people here to give us provisions. So we improvised." The man offered an engaging smile.

Beobrand was not wholly convinced, but the man appeared genuine and Tondberct travelled with him, so perhaps things were as he said.

"I will go and speak to the villagers and see what they have to offer you. Stay on the edge of the forest where we can see you and do not approach the monastery, or we'll be forced to defend ourselves and you are truly outnumbered." Beobrand looked from the group's leader to Tondberct, searching the face of the younger man for any signs of duplicity. Tondberct's open and friendly face was pinched with cold and hardship, but Beobrand saw no malice there. He nodded at Tondberct, then turned and walked back to the settlement. Alric and Leofwine fell into step beside him. As if by common agreement, they did not talk on the brief walk back.

When they reached the group of villagers posing as warriors they were greeted by a hubbub of voices. Many of them were asking Coenred questions about his ordeal. Who were the men in the forest? What had they done to him? Why had they let him go? Coenred was doing his best to answer, but there were too many people speaking at once for any intelligible conversation. As Beobrand, Alric and Leofwine approached, the faces turned to them and slowly they quietened, waiting for Beobrand to speak.

"There are five of them. They are warriors. Probably all survivors from the battle of Elmet. They want supplies. I've told them we don't have much, but I think it would be best to give them some food and encourage them to move on from here." Beobrand lowered his voice, "At the moment, they still believe you are a band of armed men, but that won't last long if you continue to prattle like washerwomen!"

He turned to Alric, "What say you?"

Alric nodded. "I think Beobrand is right. And let us not forget that his quick thinking has returned Coenred to us unharmed. Wilda, organise the women to bring together enough provisions for five men for a few days."

Wybert looked furious as the women moved to do Alric's bidding. "Who made Beobrand our leader all of a sudden? Why should we give up our food to these strangers? We have little enough left after those Waelisc stole most of our stores." Wybert spat.

Before Beobrand could reply, Alric spoke to Wybert in a firm, but sad tone. "It is decided, Wybert. Do not make a quarrel where there is none. Now go and help your mother collect the food."

Wybert's face flushed. He looked at Beobrand with loathing, and then stalked off after the women.

Coenred had been petrified while he was held by the warriors in the forest. They had not harmed him, but the threat of harm was ever present. He had been sure they would kill him. Would he meet Tata in the afterlife? Would she forgive him for leaving her to the men who had defiled her? Would she forgive his lack of faith?

He had tried to pray. To block out the voices of the men as they discussed how best to convince the villagers to give up their winter stockpiles of food. He would begin to recite the Pater Noster in his head, but the words would tangle in his mind and he would find himself picking out strands of the hushed conversations.

He shivered from the cold and the memory. They had discussed whether they should kill him and how best to do it. How long they should wait before making a show of strength by murdering him and what would have the most impact on the village. After some debate they had agreed that it would be most impressive to cut off his head and put it on the end of a spear. That way, all the villagers would be able to see.

It was at that point that Beobrand had called out. A wave of relief had washed over Coenred. He could hardly believe it as the brief exchange progressed and he was allowed to return unscathed to the monastery.

He wrapped his cloak around his shoulders against the wind and approached Beobrand.

"Well," he said, managing a smile, "looks like you've saved my life once. I think that leaves you still in my debt. By my reckoning, I've saved yours twice."

Beobrand returned the smile. "Never let it be said that the sons of Grimgundi do not honour their debts." He clapped

Coenred on the shoulder. "I am truly glad you're safe," he said earnestly. "Now you should get yourself inside by a fire. You look ready to drop with cold."

"Will you take the provisions to them?" Coenred asked. "You must be careful. They are killers, Beobrand."

"Don't fret about me. I know Tondberct and I'm sure he will offer me no harm."

Coenred thought back to the discussion of how to murder him and mutilate him. He shivered again.

"Just be careful and don't go to them alone."

He walked back to the monastery with a feeling of doom in his heart. It was not that he was fearful for Beobrand's safety; it was that he feared his friend resembled the rogue warriors waiting at the skirts of the forest.

Beobrand spent the remainder of the day in the company of the warriors by the forest. He helped carry the provisions to them and they invited him to break his fast on their new provender. They lit a fire and he fell into easy conversation, first with Tondberct, and then with the band's leader, the tall, bearded warrior, whose name was Hengist.

"Have we met before?" asked Beobrand.

Hengist gave him a long appraising look. "Aye, I travelled south from Bebbanburg. I was there in the hall when you swore allegiance to Edwin. I was one of his hearth-warriors." He lowered his eyes, looking distraught at having survived his lord.

The other men were taciturn and hardly spoke. Dreng was a wily old man, well over forty years of age, with thinning grey hair and only three teeth in his wizened mouth. He sat quietly by the fire, stirring the porridge. Beobrand could feel his hooded eyes on him all the time, like a hungry wolf watching a lamb.

The remaining two were Waelisc. They were brothers. The older of the two, Artair, was about ten years older than Beobrand. He was stocky and the shortest in the group. The younger brother was called Hafgan. He was maybe a couple of years Beobrand's senior and almost the exact opposite of Artair. He was as tall as Beobrand, but much slighter of build. The only thing that marked them out as siblings was their hair. They both had long, startlingly black hair, tied back in ponytails. They wore no armour. Each was armed with javelins and long, vicious-looking knives. They sat close together and whispered in their own tongue. Both whittled sticks with their long blades.

All of them had fought at the battle of Elmet.

"What happened? I didn't see the end of the battle," Beobrand said.

"It was chaos at the end," said Tondberct. The others sat quietly around the fire, eyes hooded as they relived those last moments of the battle in their minds. "The shieldwall broke and then it was all death. King Edwin was slain, his son too. My father died then, in that final crush." He cuffed tears away from his eyes before they could drop down his cheeks.

"Men closed in on the king to defend him, but it was useless. My father pushed me away before the end. Told me to flee. I saw that the battle was lost, so I ran." He was silent then for a moment, perhaps ashamed at having deserted his father.

"I am sorry about your father," said Beobrand.

Tondberct offered him a thin smile and a nod of thanks. "I went south for a couple of days. I didn't really know where I could go. I had no food, so in the end I decided I needed to travel north. Back to kin and friends who would help me. That is when I met Hengist and the others."

The conversation moved on to what had happened to Beobrand after the battle. He told of his injury, being found by Coenred, the attack of the Waelisc and how the people of Engelmynster had nursed him back to health.

"What are your plans?" Beobrand asked when he had finished his story.

"Hengist says that we can find a new lord to serve in Bernicia or Deira," said Tondberct excitedly. "We have heard that Osric, cousin of Edwin, has taken the kingdom of Deira as his own. And there is tell that Eanfrith has returned from exile to claim the throne of Bernicia."

Edwin's father, Aella, had united the two kingdoms of Deira and Bernicia into the one realm of Northumbria. It was certain that both of these new kings would need warriors to help them maintain their tenuous holds on their dominions. It made sense for these men of war without a liege to head north in order to seek patronage.

"Which lord will you seek out, Hengist?" Beobrand asked. He thought that Osric, as kin of Edwin, would be the honourable choice, but he knew nothing of the politics of these northern kingdoms.

"Whichever gives his gesithas the best treasure," answered Hengist. The others laughed. Beobrand joined in the laughter, but felt a sliver of doubt. He must not truly be a warrior yet, to worry about such things as kinship and honour. Those were the values his uncle had instilled in him. The traits of warriors in sagas and songs. It seemed that real warriors were not so concerned with these niceties. He would have to make an effort to be more like Hengist and the others.

"What are your plans, young Beobrand?" asked Hengist,

raising an eyebrow. "Would you join us in our quest to find a lord worthy of our might in battle?" The older warrior smiled at his own sardonic comment.

Beobrand had been enjoying the company of Tondberct and Hengist, basking in the warmth of the fire and the camaraderie that comes from having fought the same enemies. He had not considered joining them and leaving Engelmynster. Now that the option was presented, it seemed the perfect solution. He had nothing to offer Wilda, Alric and the others. He was just another mouth to feed in what would surely be a difficult winter, especially having lost much of their stores to the Waelisc.

And Leofwine was right. He was a warrior inside. He had stood in battle, and while it scared him to think of it, he wished to feel again that surge of energy and power he had experienced. If he was to be a warrior like Octa, he needed a lord. Hengist had been a gesith to a king and had a plan to find one.

Once he had a lord, he could try to discover who had killed his brother. He had sworn vengeance for Octa's murder. Yet to mete out justice, he would first need to find his brother's slayer. Only then could he confront him.

"Would you train me to fight?" Beobrand asked.

Hengist grinned. "It's all I *can* teach. Death is my mistress and she and I feed the ravens wherever we go. I'm sure she wouldn't mind spreading her legs for you too, boy. There's always someone who needs killing."

Beobrand blushed.

"I would like to come with you, if you'll have me," he said, in a smaller voice than he had intended.

Tondberct slapped him on the back and laughed. "I'm glad we came to this shit hole," he said. "It will be good to have you with us, Beo."

Hengist nodded his agreement, offering only a wry smile as answer.

Dreng's eye's narrowed and he licked his lips, pink tongue wetly smearing around his chapped lips, as if his appetite was soon to be sated. Hafgan and Artair continued whittling their sticks. Whether they had not understood, or didn't care, they showed no response to the news that Beobrand would be joining them.

A chill stroked the length of Beobrand's back. He shivered.

He hoped he had chosen wisely.

Beobrand returned to the monastery in the afternoon, leading the donkey with its small cart back from the forest where Coenred had left it. He found the young monk waiting for him in the doorway of the chapel.

"You're leaving with them, aren't you?" Coenred spoke the words like an accusation.

"It is best for everyone. They can help me find a lord. Here I am a burden."

"They would have killed me just to get what they wanted. Does that mean nothing to you?"

"It means they are men of action. They said what they needed to say. They are ruthless, but that is the way of the warrior." He thought of the warriors in tales. Of honour and loyalty. "I am a warrior now, and I stopped them from hurting you."

Coenred's eyes brimmed with tears. Beobrand didn't understand what these men were. What he might become if he travelled with them. Coenred was only young. A boy. But he had already learnt that you cannot make someone see something if they choose to be blind.

"I'll pray for your soul," Coenred said, and turned and walked inside the chapel.

Beobrand stood for a moment in the dank, grey afternoon and wondered at his friend's reaction. It hurt him that they were to part on these terms.

Once he had found a lord, he would return and visit Coenred.

8

Beobrand stared down into the mist-filled valley. He loved these moments of peace just after the sun had risen. The air was chill. He wrapped his cloak more tightly about his shoulders. The cold made his ribs ache, but the dull throb was not difficult to endure. In some ways, it was comforting, reminding him of who he now was.

He drew air deep into his lungs, wincing slightly as his recently healed wounds stretched. Behind him, the others were packing up their meagre belongings. They had been travelling steadily northward since leaving Engelmynster. Towards Bernicia and King Eanfrith he presumed, but Hengist refused to be drawn out on the subject.

"Just follow me and you'll find a ring-giving lord, young Beobrand. Don't fret," he had said the day before when Beobrand had once again asked where they were heading.

The uncertainty was unnerving. Not for the first time, he wondered whether he had made the right choice in joining these men. Could Coenred have been right about them? He had a nagging feeling of foreboding, but they had done nothing to cause alarm. Tondberct was talkative and convivial as ever. When they sat around the fire at night, Hengist was content to tell of his previous exploits in Edwin's warband. Beobrand and Tondberct would listen raptly, drinking in the tales of heroism and valour.

During one such tale, Beobrand asked, "Did you know my brother, Octa?"

Hengist's features clouded for a moment and he cast him a sidelong look. "Aye. I knew him. He was a great warrior. It is easy to see you are his kin." He paused and stared into the flames, his eyes gazing into the past. "It was a sad thing that happened to him."

Beobrand had many questions, but Hengist wrapped himself in his cloak, lay down by the fire and spoke no more.

Dreng said little, but was friendly enough. Beobrand was wary of the Waelisc brothers. Hafgan and Artair kept themselves apart from the group, but Hengist and the others trusted them.

Beobrand hoped that Hengist spoke true about finding a lord. All he wanted was to find somewhere to call home. He asked for nothing more than somewhere to sleep and simple fare on the board. Somewhere he could leave his past behind and start a new, better future. For that, he would give up anything he had. He smiled to himself, but there was no humour in it. It was the smile of a man who knew he was fooling himself. He owned nothing, save for an old spear, a shield and the clothes he wore.

Looking over the country below him, he thought how beautiful this land of Northumbria was. More mountainous than his native Cantware, and the winter was harsher than he was used to. Yet gazing out from the hilltop, seeing the mist following the course of the river, the sun rising out of the pink-tinged clouds, he knew that he wanted this to be *his* land. *His* home.

But Northumbria had become as deadly as she was beautiful. The land was lawless. Neither Osric in the southern kingdom of Deira, nor Eanfrith in the more northerly Bernicia held enough sway over the populace to bring peace. Without a king's protection the land was becoming more dangerous by the day. Bands of warriors and ruffians travelled the tracks and paths preying on the innocent. They took what they could, using whatever means necessary.

So far when they had met with such groups their weapons and number had kept them safe. They had avoided confrontation and travelled on their way.

They finished packing and set off once more, down the hill toward the misty valley below. They were all hungry. The provisions they had taken from Engelmynster had run out the day before.

Beobrand was wondering where their next meal would come from when they spotted a homestead. Just a small hut nestled in the bend of a stream. A man was chopping wood outside the dwelling, wielding a formidable looking axe. They were still distant. The sound of his axe reached them a moment after they saw his swings impact into the logs.

They walked down towards the hut. They had spent a cold night in the forest; the wood too damp for a fire. Hengist was in a foul mood. He had been sullen all morning, rubbing his temples as if his head ached. At spotting the man stripped to the waist, his temperament seemed to improve.

"What are you doing, Breca?" Hengist called out. He clearly recognised the man. "Thought you were dead."

Breca turned, wiping sweat from his brow. His eyes narrowed as he took in the men approaching him.

"What does it look like I'm doing, Hengist?" He spoke without rancour. His voice was light. A smile played at the edge of his lips. "I'm chopping firewood to pay for my keep. I waited for you after the battle. I'd heard you'd gone south…"

Hengist interrupted him. "Work like a slave, would you?" he scoffed at the young, stocky warrior. "You're a warrior, man! You should make your living fighting, not grovelling to some peasant woman." Hengist continued to stride down to the hut. Breca held the axe in both hands across his sweat-slick body. His eyes darted nervously back to Beobrand, and the four others approaching behind Hengist.

Dreng said in a quiet voice, "Hengist is in a bloody mood. Looks like he'll have him a fight now. Will settle his blood." He licked his lips and chuckled to himself, as if he had said something to rival the wit of the best bards.

"What do you want?" Breca asked, in a strong voice.

"I want you to grovel to me, like you grovelled to this old crone." Hengist waved his hand in the direction of the hut's owner, who had emerged from the smoke-filled interior to see what was happening.

Breca said, "I have no quarrel with you, Hengist. Just be on your way." Then, in an effort to calm the situation with good humour, "There'll be no grovelling today, friend." He smiled briefly, perhaps imagining that Hengist was jesting, or maybe drunk.

Hengist stared at him for a few heartbeats and then flung himself at Breca. He drew his broadsword as he sprang forward and bellowed with an insensate rage.

Breca stumbled backwards, but managed to keep his footing. He swung his axe up and was barely able to parry Hengist's wild lunge. He deflected the sword thrust upwards and then surged forwards, using the axe two-handed, like a quarterstaff, to push Hengist away.

They circled each other for a moment, then Hengist attacked again. He feinted a savage blow towards Breca's face, changing the direction of the blade at the last moment into a scything strike aimed at his midriff. Breca dodged backwards, and then darted forward, attempting to swing the axe head upwards into Hengist's groin. Hengist parried the blow easily and backed away.

He was smiling, relaxed and happy. He rolled his head to loosen his neck muscles. Breca was focused, concentration etched into his features. Both men were panting, their breath smoking in the winter air.

Dreng giggled, a sound like the cackle of a crow. The bird of death.

Beobrand watched on in shock at how rapidly the morning had descended into violence. The fight looked one-sided. Breca was skilled and had strength, but his movements were clumsy in some indefinable way. Not natural to him. Hengist carried his sword as if the blade were an extension of his hand. It was awe-inspiring and terrible to behold.

"You will grovel today, *friend*," Hengist spoke softly, the last word dripping with sarcasm.

"What are you doing, man?" said Breca, a note of desperation entering his voice. "We have stood together in the shieldwall. We were sword brothers."

Hengist attacked for the final time. He swung his sword overarm, leaving his body unprotected. Breca saw the opening and took it, sweeping his axe at Hengist's chest. With the benefit of having anticipated Breca's move perfectly, Hengist took a step backwards and hammered his blade down, hacking into Breca's left hand. He screamed, dropping the axe and grasping his smashed left hand in his right. Blood seeped between his fingers and trickled down his forearm, mingling with the sheen of sweat.

Breca gritted his teeth, his breath rapid and shallow against the pain.

"Kill me then, you bastard!" he gasped. "I always knew you were no better than a dog. You have no honour." He raised himself up to his full height.

Hengist shook his head, smiling still. "I don't want to kill you," he said, and walked past him, towards the hut, where the old woman was cowering in the doorway.

For a moment Breca looked confused. Then relieved. Believing the contest over, Beobrand and the others started to move forward.

Then, with the speed of a striking adder, Hengist spun around and dragged his sword in a slicing motion deep into the back of Breca's legs. Sinews and muscles were severed. Breca screamed again. He collapsed to the ground, his legs failing to support him.

Hengist knelt by Breca and whispered into his ear, "Now you can grovel all the time, *friend*."

They rested in the hut all the rest of that day and the following night. For a long time, Breca whimpered and cried out for help.

"He sings as badly as he fights," Hengist said, smiling, pleased at his joke. The others laughed. Beobrand's eyes met Tondberct's, but he couldn't tell what he was thinking.

After some time Breca's moaning grew tedious to Hengist and he signalled to Dreng. The old warrior got up from where he sat close to the warmth of the hearthstone and walked out into the gathering dusk. A few moments later, Breca screamed out, his words easily heard by the men in the hut.

"He'll betray you all! He has no honour!" Then his cries ceased.

Later, when Hengist went outside to relieve himself, Beobrand turned to Tondberct and whispered, "What's got into him? Why did he attack Breca? Is he touched by an evil spirit?" He could think of no explanation for Hengist's violence.

Tondberct looked uncomfortable, but before he could respond, Dreng spoke into the silence.

"If you live to see as many battles as Hengist, you will not be the same man you are today, young Beobrand. Feeding the ravens with corpses changes a man. You'd do well to remember that."

They fell silent as Hengist came back inside.

The old lady was terribly afraid. She cooked for them and treated them with deference. Hengist smiled benevolently at her, but still made sure that one of them was on guard at all times in the night. None of them wanted to have his throat slit during his sleep.

Sleep was a long time coming to Beobrand that night. When he closed his eyes he saw Breca cut down again. Hengist's speed and skill was somehow obscene, but questions whispered in his mind. Could Hengist teach him? Could he learn to wield a sword with such prowess? He had thought his uncle had been a skilled swordsman, but he was nothing when compared to Hengist.

Then he remembered Breca's final words and his sobbing cries for pity.

Deep inside he knew he should have heeded Coenred's warning about these men. But what could he do now? He had chosen this path. He only hoped he could follow it without becoming lost.

They pressed on north, leaving the old woman behind. She was relieved to be rid of them but they had taken much of her food. How she would survive the winter she did not know.

Breca's stiff body lay outside where it had been left. Wolves or foxes had worried the carcass in the night, but it was mostly whole. Walking away, Beobrand cast a glance back at the hut and saw the woman straddling the corpse. He glimpsed the glint of a sharp seax in her hand. He turned away, appalled.

Over the next few weeks winter set in. With the trees covered in frost, brooks turning to ice and snow falling from leaden skies, the band of warriors fell into a routine. They would forage for food, hunting when possible, and travelling little. Once they had set up a camp, much of their energy was taken up with collecting firewood. The cold seeped into their very bones. At night they would huddle around their small campfire for warmth. Their hands and faces became chapped and cut by the cold. They were desperate for anything that would provide protection from the winter chill. The skins of any game they caught were quickly made into rough hats and mittens.

Hafgan and Artair were fine huntsmen. They would often leave the group for a day or more, always returning with meat. After their first hunting trip they had returned, each weighed down with a side of venison. They had smoked much of the meat in thin strips and it lasted them for several days. But despite the brothers' skills, they often went hungry over those winter months. On those days when they had no food, they would be irritable and lethargic. Their stomachs silently screaming with the agonising pangs of emptiness.

Then Beobrand would remember warm days hunting

boar with Octa and his friends. The forests around Hithe were rich with game. They would leave small offerings on the edge of the trees for the forest spirits and head into the cool darkness. There they would look for the paths used by the great boars of the forest. Splitting up, one group would drive the boar towards the other, who would wait, spears ready.

They brought down many a bristling, tusked beast. The animals would burst forth from the undergrowth into the area they had prepared and the boys would pounce, spear points glinting dully in the gloom. Squeals, grunts, shouts and the sounds of breaking branches would follow, and then stillness and the panting of the hunters. Laughter at their success and having survived in the face of the forest beasts.

The meat from an animal you have killed yourself tastes sweeter than any other. Boar meat, skin crisp and flesh succulent and dripping had always been a favourite of Beobrand's. Thinking of it in the bleakest of winter days set his stomach growling and made him yearn for his brother, and his friends.

It seemed to Beobrand that they had been avoiding settlements as they travelled. Ever since the incident with Breca, Hengist had seemed keen to camp in the forest, despite the cold. On a few occasions they had seen smoke, but each time Hengist had rejected the idea of seeking the warmth of shelter they could expect from a village. Perhaps the fight with Breca had unnerved Hengist too, but that seemed unlikely.

One late afternoon, as the pale sun dipped towards the trees on the horizon, they came upon a village. Not the usual kind of place they saw of a few huts and animal pens, but several stout buildings, with white walls, surrounding a sizable hall. The last of the sun gave the thatch of the hall's roof an inviting warm glow. Smoke billowed through the chimney hole into the still winter air, where it hung, wreathing the building in a hazy crown. The sound of laughter and chatter reached Beobrand's ears and he half imagined the smell of cooking meat.

They all turned to Hengist, enquiring silently whether they could seek refuge at the hall for the night. They were freezing and wet. It had been raining all of the previous night and that morning, only abating a short while before they had stumbled upon the welcome sight of the hall that beckoned to them with its invitation of warmth.

Hengist shrugged. "I'm cold too. A fire and a roof over our heads would be good." They all smiled, their spirits lifting as they picked up their pace on the road towards the hall. Faces peered at them from doorways as they passed by the houses. A man looked up from where he was fixing a fence and nodded a taciturn welcome. A few children ran up behind them and dogged their steps until Dreng turned around and growled at them playfully. The children ran away screaming.

Before they reached the hall at the settlement's heart, four men approached them. Each carried a spear and shield. The oldest of the four, a dour-looking man of perhaps thirty years, with flecks of grey in his beard, held up his hand and said, "What business have you in this shire of our Lord Ecgric?"

Hengist said in a voice as smooth as burnished silver, "We are travellers. We are weary, cold and wet and seek your lord's hospitality. One night at his table and under his roof and we will be on our way."

The man glanced at their weapons, clearly assessing how much of a threat they posed. "Travellers, you say? Where do you travel so laden with weapons?"

Hengist smiled. "The roads are dangerous for travellers, but we are warriors, as you can see. We mean you no harm. We travel north in search of patronage. We seek to offer our service to the new lord of Bernicia, King Eanfrith."

"Then perhaps the gods smile on you this day. One of Eanfrith's men is here. Wait here while I speak to my lord."

The man turned and left the other three guards to look over Hengist, Beobrand and the others. He walked to the hall and disappeared inside. The guards shifted their feet nervously, frequently looking over their shoulders at where their leader had gone.

Beobrand watched Hengist as they waited, trying to gauge his mood. He looked relaxed enough, but there was a tension in him that could not be totally hidden. Beobrand hoped for all their sakes that nothing would ignite his pent up anger. Breca had been alone, but here, in a lord's hall, they would all be in danger if a fight broke out.

The lead guard returned. "You may enter the hall, but you must leave all weapons outside with me."

Beobrand watched as Hengist bridled. He always wore his sword and even slept with it wrapped inside his cloak. He was never parted from it. But they all knew that to enter a lord's hall, weapons were left at the door, so they handed over their spears and seaxes, only being allowed to keep their small eating knives. Hengist unbuckled his belt and handed it with great ceremony to the door ward. "Do not draw her blade. If it is freed, it must taste blood," said Hengist. The guard's eyes widened, but he nodded solemnly as if such assertions were common.

Satisfied that they were bereft of weapons, the door ward stood aside and ushered them into the hall. It was not a large hall, nor was it as sumptuously decorated as the royal hall of Bebbanburg, but in comparison with sleeping wrapped in a cloak by a guttering fire in the forest, it was luxurious indeed. A fire burnt brightly in the centre of the floor, casting moving shadows into every corner. Above the hearth hung an iron cauldron, from which emanated the rich scent of a meaty stew. Beobrand's stomach rumbled. Around the edge of the hall, tallow candles burnt, adding extra light and making the room warmer and more inviting.

Boards were laid out along the length of the hall and several men were already seated at the benches. At the head of the room stood the high table, where there sat on a gift-stool, a large, heavy-jowled man with grey hair. To his right sat a slim man, with hawk-like features. He was dressed in fine clothes and a gold chain glittered at his neck.

The large man heaved his bulk out of his seat and stood, wobbling on his feet slightly, as if he had already drunk too much mead.

"Welcome travellers," he said, his voice loud over the din of conversation. "Is that you, Hengist? I thought you surely killed at Elmet."

Hengist took a step forward. "Well met, Ecgric, son of Eacgric. I survive to tell the tale of the fall of Edwin, son of Aella. But many men fell to my sword before the end, when my liege was struck down by the Waelisc scum."

Some of the men in the hall banged cups, knives or fists on the boards in approbation of Hengist's words.

Lord Ecgric peered at Hengist for a long time, as if he was struggling to make him out in the dim light and the haze of smoke from the fire. After some time, he raised his hands for silence.

"You must join us at the high table, Hengist. I would know how it is that you survived when so many fell. I myself sent four men to join the fyrd and none returned. Tale of the slaughter has reached us. There are many widows this winter in Bernicia and Deira."

A hush fell on the room. Beobrand glanced at Hengist and saw that his lips were pressed tightly together. A vein throbbed at his temple.

"Do you accuse me of being craven, lord? I am not armed, but I cannot let a slur on my name go unchallenged."

The mood in the hall changed. A stillness and tension such as descends before a thunderstorm fell upon the throng.

Ecgric held up his hands to placate Hengist. "Brave Hengist, I would not dream of questioning your mettle or your courage, not even in my own hall. I merely wish to hear of your exploits and how you escaped from that carnage with your life. I meant no harm." His words were spoken in calm earnest, but the twinkle in his eye belied his innocent tone. Beobrand wondered whether this lord knew how dangerous Hengist could be. But then again, they were surrounded by the lord's gesithas and Hengist was unarmed.

Ecgric said, "Come, join us at the table."

Hengist took a step forward and the tension began to ease out of the gathering. But before the volume of chatter could reach the level it had been when they had arrived, the hawk-faced man at Lord Ecgric's side said, "How is it, Hengist, that I saw you at the table of Cadwallon and Penda after the battle of Elmet?"

Silence slammed down on the room. All eyes turned to Hengist. Beobrand stood closest to him and could feel the waves of ire washing off him. He was ready to explode into violence at any moment. Beobrand took a step away from him involuntarily.

Hengist fixed the man with a stony glare. "What did you

say?" His voice was clipped, each word forced out through clenched teeth. The muscles in his jaw bulged.

The man next to Ecgric seemed oblivious of Hengist's anger. "I asked how it was that you were dining with your enemies while your king lay dead, his body not yet cold?" he said.

A whisper ran through the hall as men muttered their disbelief. Whether at the substance or the audacity of the accusation Beobrand could not tell.

Hengist swallowed. His hand trembled where it groped unwittingly for the hilt of the sword that no longer hung from his belt.

"Who are you?" Hengist asked. "I would know the name of a man before I kill him."

"I am Galan, son of Galen. I saw you when I bore a message to Cadwallon, king of Gwynedd from my master and lord, Eanfrith, son of Æthelfrith, rightful heir to Bernicia." He smiled. "But why do you threaten to kill me rather than answer my question? I have a reason for my presence in Cadwallon's camp. Do you? It seems my questioning upsets you. Could it be that I have uncovered a dirty secret?" He raised his eyebrows and a faint smile played at the edge of his mouth.

Beobrand sensed in the instant before he moved, that Hengist would attack Galan. Hengist surged forwards with a roar and lunged towards the high table. All along the hall, men leapt to their feet.

Hengist brushed off the hands that tried to seize him and reached for the board that was between him and the object of his wrath. Grasping the board's edge he heaved it over. Trenchers, plates, food, knives and drinking horns were cast to the ground with a clatter that was lost amongst the clamour of Ecgric's gesithas as they sprang to their lord's defence and that of their lord's guest.

Hengist tried to kick his way through the debris. Galan took a step back, but seemed calm in the face of Hengist's onslaught.

Before Hengist was able to push his way through the barricade of the fallen board and its contents, several of Ecgric's men grabbed him roughly. He struggled and screamed, like a wounded animal.

"I will kill you," he shouted.

A moment later, Beobrand felt a cold blade at his throat and a strong arm around his chest. A voice spoke in his ear, "Do not move, or I'll bleed you like a pig at Blodmonath." Beobrand did not struggle. The ferocity and suddenness of Hengist's violence stunned him. What was Galan talking about? Could it be true that Hengist had been a guest at Cadwallon's board after the battle of Elmet? It seemed impossible.

"Stop this! You are a guest in my hall!" Ecgric's bellowing voice rang over the throng, silencing them all. He was shaking with fury, all semblance of affability gone.

"This man dishonours me!" screamed Hengist, flecks of spittle flying from his mouth.

"No," said Ecgric, "it is you who brings dishonour to my hall and to yourself. You and your companions are no longer welcome here. You will leave my hall and my lands. As a mark of the respect Edwin had for you, I will allow you to leave unharmed and with your weapons. But if I see you again in my lands, I will not be so lenient a second time. Now, get him out of my sight."

He turned his back on Hengist and spoke quietly to Galan, who laughed. Thralls moved out of the shadows and started setting the boards and fetching fresh food and mead.

The man holding Beobrand turned him towards the door of the hall and pushed him towards it, still holding the knife at his throat.

Outside dark had descended. Hengist, Beobrand and the others were all pushed out of the hall porch and into the cold darkness. The leader of the door wards picked up their weapons and threw them into the mud at their feet. He could see Hengist contemplating attacking.

"I wouldn't if I were you," he said. "Pick up your things and be gone. Unless you think you are quicker than an arrow." He nodded to his left, where two men were standing in the shadows of the hall with hunting bows. Each had an arrow on the string and the bow pulled taut, ready to loose. At such close range they could not miss, and an arrow, though not often a weapon of war, would kill or maim a man, as soon as killing a hare.

For a long moment nobody moved. Beobrand looked at their adversaries and decided he would charge at one of the bowman if they started to fight. Perhaps he could put off his aim and close the gap close enough to tackle him with his hands. More of Ecgric's gesithas stepped out of the hall, stacking the odds further.

In the end, it was Dreng who moved first. He stepped forward, not taking his eyes from the door ward, and reached down to retrieve his own gear and Hengist's sword. He handed the sword to Hengist and Beobrand heard him whisper, "We should leave. It is not worth it. Wyrd placed Galan there, it cannot be helped now."

Hengist was tight-lipped and quivering with pent up anger, but he offered Dreng a small nod and took his sword.

"Pick up your things, men. We are leaving."

Beobrand and the others cautiously collected their belongings, wary of treachery from the door wards and warriors congregated at the entrance to the hall. But the men proved honourable for they allowed them to leave Ecgric's lands safely. When they had walked some distance from the hall and were swallowed by the night, Beobrand heard sharp laughter behind them, then the doors to the hall slamming.

They walked on in silence into the gloom. Nobody talked, but Beobrand's mind was full of questions. He wondered at Galan's insistence that he had seen Hengist dining with Cadwallon. What had he to gain from lying? Was Hengist's reaction proof that it was true, or merely a seemingly typical violent response to his honour being slighted?

After some time, Tondberct broke the silence, his breath misting in the cold night. "Oh well, I didn't really like the smell of that stew, and a warm fire would just make us soft."

Nobody laughed.

Beobrand focused on the shape of Hengist's set shoulders and trudged along in his wake. He would get no answers to his questions tonight.

As the days grew shorter, and the weather ever harsher, the small band set up a semi-permanent camp beside a stream.

The site was protected from the wind by a steep, wooded bank. There was an overhang of earth and tree roots that provided them with shelter from the elements. To this natural barrier, they added some wattle fences and built up a makeshift roof of branches and leaves. On the coldest and wettest days, their constructions did little to protect them. They would miserably hunch under their meagre shelter and wait for more clement times. But on clear days, when the wind did not rush along the stream bed and rattle the bones of the denuded trees, the camp was as comfortable as any hall.

A few days after the encounter at Ecgric's hall, when it had become clear that they had settled into this new camp, with no intention of travelling on, Beobrand broached the subject of the incident with Hengist. The day was cold, but dry and they were sitting by the fire as night approached. It had been a pleasant day of activity, preparing firewood and constructing the fences for the shelter. Now they all sat, tired but content in the warmth of the crackling flames. It was easy to almost forget how Hengist's anger and violence had erupted like fire from dry tinder.

"Hengist?" Beobrand said, stretching his legs out to loosen the muscles and also to warm his feet closer to the flames.

"Aye?"

"Why did you get so angry with Galan? Surely it was a mistake and you were not with Cadwallon."

Everyone turned to look at Beobrand. Artair stopped whittling the piece of wood he held. Dreng licked his lips nervously. Tondberct fidgeted, as if preparing to flee. Beobrand was suddenly afraid.

Hengist stared at him for a long moment and then said, "Do you think to question me, Beobrand, son of Grimgundi? Do you also believe me dishonourable? Treacherous?" Hengist's eyes bore into him, unwavering and unflinching.

Beobrand looked away. He searched the faces of the others. All averted their gaze; none would stand at his side in this. He was all alone. He felt small and weak then. As he had so many times when his father had taken his fists to him.

"No, I just…"

"Just what?" asked Hengist. "Think carefully before you speak again, young Beobrand." The air was heavy with unspoken threats.

As so many times before when facing his father, all Beobrand wanted was to make the situation go away. "I'm sorry, Hengist. I meant no harm."

The tension ebbed from the camp and Hengist leaned forward and threw another log onto the fire in a shower of sparks.

Beobrand was ashamed at his own weakness. The taste of it was in his throat as he stood and walked away from the others and he hated it.

It was while they were at the camp that Hengist began to train Beobrand in the art of combat. Beobrand was horrified at Hengist's sudden explosive violence, but was equally eager to learn to fight like him. If he could fight well, surely he would not feel so impotent.

Hengist seemed to enjoy training the young warrior, and it was clear to the others lounging by the fire, that Beobrand was a natural. He picked up stances and moves quickly and began to look at ease with a shield on his left arm and a spear in his right hand. His injuries still hurt, but he was able to push the pain out of his mind. He continued practising until his body ran with sweat and his muscles steamed in the cold air. By the end of each day, he collapsed by the fire and fell asleep listening to the others telling stories of battles, drinking and women they had known.

For much of the time Hengist commanded Beobrand to run through patterns of lunges, parries, crouches and defensive blocks. Sometimes he would call on one of the other warriors to spar with Beobrand. At first, he was outclassed by all of the others, receiving many knocks, scrapes and bruises to add to the injuries he'd sustained in Elmet. But by the end of the second day's training, he bested Tondberct.

Tondberct was overconfident. He had seen the experienced Dreng beat Beobrand resoundingly in a few heartbeats.

He readied himself in a defensive stance, shield high, spear held higher. Beobrand suddenly bellowed and thrust his own spear into Tondberct's shield, pulling it down, as Bassus had shown him. Tondberct, caught off guard, had tried to retreat, but this only resulted in his shield being pulled further from his body, leaving him more exposed. He panicked and decided to go on the offensive, aiming a vicious spear thrust at Beobrand's face.

Beobrand caught the spear shaft on the rim of his shield, lifting it harmlessly over his head. At the same moment, he let go of his own spear and drew in a smooth motion the bone-handled knife that Immin had given him. He rolled inside Tondberct's reach, almost embracing him, his knife's keen edge against his friend's throat.

There was a moment while Beobrand and Tondberct stood close together, unmoving. Then Hengist started laughing. Dreng and the two Waelisc brothers joined in. It was an audacious and risky move. If he had mistimed it, he would have been left with a small knife against the much longer spear. But he had executed the manoeuvre with precision and grace. If it had been a real fight, Tondberct would have been dead.

"That is what I like to see," said Hengist. "I teach you moves for two whole days. Then you go and do something like that. Nobody can teach you that. You have a warrior's instincts and you're not scared of anything, are you?"

Beobrand felt scared of a lot of things. Particularly Hengist. But while he was fighting, he did not think of his fear. For those moments there was only him and his adversaries, and the inescapable desire to overcome them at any cost.

Beobrand's gaze met Tondberct's and there was something there he hadn't expected. He wasn't smiling ruefully at having been beaten by his friend, and he wasn't angry at having lost so easily, either of which reactions Beobrand would have understood.

The look he saw on Tondberct's face was fear.

With each passing day Beobrand got stronger, faster and much more deadly. Tondberct would no longer spar with him, after having lost seven or eight times in a row. They still joked together and were seemingly friendly, but there was a tinge of resentment in Tondberct over Beobrand's rise to prominence in the group. This, coupled with Tondberct being threatened by Beobrand's skill, meant that their conversations were often stilted.

Artair posed little problem for Beobrand after a few days. The stocky Waelisc was strong and skilled, but lacked Beobrand's speed and instinctive feeling of how to beat an opponent. He was too predictable. His brother Hafgan, was a different matter. He was tall, like Beobrand, and as fast as a cat. He wasn't as experienced or skilled as his older brother, but he made up for this by being much less predictable and extremely quick. After a fortnight of practice, Hafgan was still able to beat Beobrand on almost every other encounter.

When Beobrand asked Hengist if he could face him, the older warrior laughed. "You wouldn't prove more than a mouthful for me if you can't best the others."

But Dreng proved impossible for Beobrand to vanquish for several weeks.

The old man had so much experience, was so accomplished in the art of parrying with both shield and his long-bladed langseax, that Beobrand would wear himself out trying to find a gap in Dreng's defences. In the end, Dreng would effortlessly flick out the tip of his langseax and touch Beobrand wherever he chose. Sometimes he would draw blood. He always pretended it had been an accident and apologised to the younger man. But there was a glimmer in his eye, and he would lick his lips with his fleshy tongue and smile for a time afterwards.

The balance shifted when Hengist told Beobrand he had learnt the basics with the spear and he should now pick up a blade to train with.

"A sword is a true warrior's weapon," said Hengist, fingering the fur-lined hilt of his broadsword. "If you can't get a sword, a langseax is the next best thing. Here, you can use mine." He tossed him his long-bladed langseax. Longer than a dagger or knife, it was a more formidable version of the seax, the single-edged knife that gave their people the name the Waelisc used to describe them: Seaxon.

The instant Beobrand held the blade, it felt right. It wasn't the sword he had always dreamt of, but its balance was good and all of those days he'd spent with Selwyn gave him a seemingly instant prowess.

He began training with renewed vigour and the others realised that where he had been a natural with the spear, with a long-bladed weapon, he would soon be unstoppable against all but the most highly accomplished opponent. He had an affinity for the langseax that the others had not seen before in any warrior, except in Hengist, who was the best swordsman any of them had witnessed.

"You have used a blade before," Hengist said, intrigued. "Who taught you?"

Beobrand swung the langseax through the air in a flourish, flashing a grin at Hengist. "My uncle, Selwyn. He was a great warrior and trained Octa and I to use a sword."

Hengist rubbed his beard, watching Beobrand's stances. "Well, he taught you well," he said.

After only a couple of days with the langseax, Beobrand was able to vanquish Hafgan three times out of four. And a few days after that, he beat Dreng for the first time.

The older warrior made the mistake of letting his guard down in an attempt to draw Beobrand in, but he had underestimated the young Cantware warrior. Beobrand made a feint towards the exposed area, as Dreng expected. Then, at the moment Dreng committed himself to hit Beobrand's extended right arm, Beobrand spun fully around, landing a brutal blow to Dreng's rump with the flat of his langseax's blade.

Dreng fell sprawling to the ground while the others burst into peals of laughter. Dreng pulled himself up and rubbed his backside and smiled sheepishly, but the look he flashed at Beobrand was dark and murderous.

"That was a risk to turn your back on an enemy, boy," Dreng rasped. "I wouldn't do that again if I were you."

The laughter died down and Beobrand thought that Dreng's comment was more a veiled threat than a tip on his fighting technique. He swallowed hard and vowed not to let Dreng out of his sight.

9

After Geola, the longest night of winter, Hengist started to withdraw into himself. He talked less and was no longer interested in training Beobrand. The others were wary around him. Only Dreng seemed at ease in his company. After Hengist had one of his increasingly frequent outbursts, screaming at Artair for burning the tiny squirrel he'd been roasting over the fire, Dreng smiled and said, "Getting bloody again, he is. We should move on tomorrow."

The next morning it was bitterly cold. The trees creaked and cracked around them, settling themselves for the harsh weather to come. Dreng silently started to pack up the camp and the others joined him, rolling up their blankets and squeezing their few provisions into bags. Hengist sat some way off, cloak wrapped about him, his back to them.

They set off, following the stream southward, which surprised Beobrand. Perhaps Hengist had changed his mind over their destination. He wondered if this change of direction had anything to do with the chance encounter with Galan.

They had not been travelling long when they smelt woodsmoke. They stopped, each sniffing the breeze, listening intently for any sound that would indicate where the smoke was coming from. After a few moments, they heard a horse whinny off to their right, someway in the distance.

They stealthily unslung their weapons and placed their bags on the frozen earth underneath a huge beech tree. With no words spoken amongst them, they silently moved forward, like wolves on the scent of a newly-birthed lamb. Beobrand was not sure what they planned to do, but he felt his blood rise at the anticipation of action. He'd trained these last few months, now perhaps he could put what he'd learnt to good use. He carried his spear and shield, and still had Hengist's langseax hanging from a loop of leather on his belt.

Hengist's face was a picture of concentration. His eyes sparkled, his mouth was slightly open and his breath plumed around his face as he signalled to them all to move forwards. They crept towards the sound of the horse, using the boles of the trees for cover, spreading out into a skirmish line. They had only taken a few steps when the still of the forest was rent by a shrill scream. This was followed by the sounds of battle: metal against metal and shouts of anger and pain.

Beobrand, Hengist and the others paused for a heartbeat and then made their way forward more quickly.

They came to a clearing. A large oak had fallen in some past storm and its roots now stuck out in an earthy, tangled web. Where the tree had fallen it had cleared a sizable piece of ground, taking a few smaller trees with it. With the shelter provided by its upturned roots, it was a perfect campsite, and there was a small campfire built there.

Two horses were tied to the fallen oak and there were eight people in the clearing. Six of them were engaged in combat and two more were prostrate on the ground. It appeared that two of the people, a young woman armed with a short spear and a man wielding a broad-bladed seax were defending the camp. It looked like their four assailants, men armed with seaxes and spears, had ambushed them. The two figures on the ground seemed also to be from the camp, probably killed quickly as the four brigands attacked with the element of surprise.

Beobrand didn't pause to think. The cold of battle descended upon him. His instant reaction was to help those who were outnumbered. He didn't question this, he simply took a step into the clearing and threw his spear overarm with such force that it took one man in the chest and lifted him from his feet. The spear's metal tip disappeared between the man's ribs, and he was dead before he had hit the frigid forest loam.

Beobrand did not stop to watch the flight of his spear. He was sure that enemy was dealt with. He turned his attention to the next man, drawing his borrowed langseax and rushing out of the trees to meet him. He let out a bellowing cry and chopped into the second man's collarbone with a vicious downward blow. Blood fountained out of a severed artery, splattering Beobrand's face and hands, as the man fell sideways.

The two defenders of the campsite fell back, providing this crazed warrior from the woods with space. Beobrand's savage onslaught had given the remaining two attackers pause. A moment ago, they had outnumbered their foe two to one. Suddenly their advantage had disappeared in a frenzy of violence that had come as quickly as it was unexpected.

Before they could make up their minds to attack or retreat, Hafgan stepped from the trees and flung a javelin at the man furthest from Beobrand. The javelin struck the man in the hip, spinning him round. He stumbled and then fell onto his hands and knees.

The last man looked at his fallen comrades and then back to the warrior who had burst from the forest. Beobrand looked like an apparition from the underworld. Blue eyes burning from a mask of blood, his langseax dripping and steaming with gore.

The man turned to flee. Dreng walked out of the cover of the trees to block his path. The man made a desultory effort to raise his seax to fight the old warrior. Dreng swatted the blade away, stepped inside his reach and buried his blade deep into the man's entrails. He held him upright for a moment, the man's face as close to his as a lover's, then plunged his blade several more times into the man's stomach, before finally letting him slump forward onto the earth.

For a moment the glade was still. Then the injured man tried to scrabble away on all fours. Beobrand made a move towards him but Hengist called out, "Wait, don't kill him!"

Hengist strode quickly to the injured man. He'd realised he could not escape and had rolled over onto his back so as not to have his attackers behind him. He was now frantically trying to free a knife from the scabbard on his belt. He got the blade out just as Hengist arrived. Hengist stamped on the man's wrist, pinning the knife to the ground. He then fell onto the man's chest, immobilising him.

A broad grin shone from his bearded face. He looked truly happy. "Thanks for leaving one of them alive, Beobrand," he said. "You're much too efficient with your killing. Where's the fun in that?"

The man underneath Hengist, a young man with ratlike features, started to babble. Hengist looked down at him for a moment contemplatively while the man's pleading whines grew in volume. And then, apparently not wishing to hear any more, he began to rain blows into the man's face.

Hengist put a lot of his weight behind the blows. It wasn't long before the young man was silent, his face a battered, bruised and bloody mess.

"He looks like you now, Beobrand," laughed Hengist "I'll save him for later." He got up and turned to look at the survivors of the camp. "What have we got here?"

The woman and man stood side by side. Their backs were as close as possible to the roots of the fallen tree.

The man was middle-aged and heavyset. He wore clothes of fine quality, a bear fur cloak over a woollen tunic. He had greying long hair and a fine moustache. He held his broad seax at his side. Wary, but not threatening.

The woman was younger, only a little older than Beobrand. Despite the fear and shock that contorted her features, she was beautiful. She sported a blue thick wool cloak over a cream mantle and brown tunic. Her head was covered by a cap and her blonde hair fell in a single long plait down her back.

Her gaze flitted around the clearing, looking at each man in turn as they stepped from the cover of the forest. Her eyes settled on Beobrand last and there they lingered. He stood panting, his breath billowing with each ragged breath, sweat beading his blood-drenched face despite the cold. He was as suddenly spent of energy as he had been consumed with the cold lust for battle. He looked down absently at his hands and was surprised to see them shaking.

"My name is Cynric," said the man in the bearskin cloak. His voice was shaking as much as Beobrand's hands. "This is my daughter, Cathryn." He placed a protective hand on her arm. "Thank you... for rescuing us," he tried to maintain his composure, but his voice caught in his throat. "Now, we must attend to our fallen."

Cynric fell to his knees next to the two bodies of his companions. He touched them, seeking signs of life. When he found none, with increasing urgency he shook the bodies. Cathryn knelt beside him, tears streaming down her face and darkening her mantle. She put her arm around her father. He shuddered convulsively and began to sob.

They clung to each other for some time, lost in a grief that Beobrand understood all too well.

Later, after the dead had been tended to and were lying covered by their cloaks, they all sat around the fire and Cynric told their story. They were travelling from Pocel's Hall, about two days travel to the south, and heading for Gefrin, in Bernicia. They had family there and had heard that Eanfrith's court was Christian. Pocel's Hall had been sacked by Cadwallon's forces. Cynric and his three children had fled with as much as they could carry. They had been travelling more slowly than they'd have liked, having only managed to take two horses with them.

Both of his sons had been struck down as the ambush began. They'd had no chance to resist.

Hengist appeared uninterested in the personal woes of Cynric and his family. "How many were in Cadwallon's warband?" he asked. "Which way were they headed?"

Cynric looked bemused, but answered as best he could. "I don't really know. It seemed to me that the Waelisc were fleeing westward. I imagine Osric of Deira had taken to the field and was in pursuit of them."

Throughout all of the conversations, Cathryn sat silently at her father's side. Her eyes shone from her tear-streaked face. Beobrand was in a kind of stupor. All energy had fled and he sat morosely listening to Cynric's words, not really taking in what was said. He frequently looked at Cathryn, and he often found her looking back at him.

Hengist was alert and interested in the news of troop movements and the shifting of power within the northern kingdoms. The recent fighting seemed to have settled him temporarily, but there was an undercurrent of tension in him. From time to time, his gaze flickered over to the unconscious brigand who still lay where he had left him.

Dreng, Tondberct, Hafgan and Artair were all content to sit and stare at Cathryn. They were all openly admiring of her looks and her shapely figure. Whenever she got up from the fireside, their eyes tracked her movements. If it made her uncomfortable, she did not show it. Cynric was not oblivious to the attention his daughter was attracting, but didn't know how to stop it. Six heavily armed killers sat by his fire. They'd rescued them from certain death, or worse in Cathryn's case. Letting them ogle his daughter was not such a bad price to pay for their protection.

As the sun fell in the sky, the forest rapidly became dark. Hengist agreed with Cynric that they would all travel together to Gefrin. Perhaps Hengist and his companion warriors could find favour with King Eanfrith there. Beobrand was surprised to hear this. He was sure they had set off south that day and he could not imagine how they would be received after Hengist's confrontation with Galan, one of Eanfrith's men. But it was good to hear Hengist openly speak of their destination.

They readied the camp for the night. Stocking up on firewood, agreeing the watches, and preparing a sparse meal from their supplies and what little game they had left from Hafgan and Artair's most recent hunt.

Beobrand roused himself and went down to the stream to wash off the dried blood that covered his face and hands.

The bitterly cold water snapped him out of the languor he'd fallen into after the fight at the camp. The blood was congealed and dried, difficult to remove. His skin soon ached from his frenzied rubbing and the freezing water.

It took longer to scrub away the blood and stench of death than it had to kill the men in the clearing. Beobrand splashed more icy water on his face. It was hard to believe the ease with which he had taken the lives of the men.

He had not been away from the camp for long, when he heard a gurgling scream pierce the still night air. It came from the clearing of the fallen oak. He jumped up and ran back to the camp. He stumbled over roots and fallen branches in the gathering gloom.

The flickering light from the fire lit a nightmare scene. Hengist and Dreng were straddled over the form of the injured brigand. He was now conscious and Hengist and Dreng were working on his body with their knives. The flames lighting from below made their faces distorted, monstrous. As Beobrand watched in dismay, Hengist slit the man's left eye with the tip of his blade. Liquid oozed down his already blood-slick cheek. Dreng sawed at the side of the man's head, then held up his severed ear in triumph, a look of rapturous glee on his face. The man was screaming, but the sounds he made were muffled and guttural. Beobrand saw then that the man's tongue had been cut out.

He turned away in disgust, and looked straight into the eyes of Cathryn. She was lying on her back on the frozen earth. The milky skin of her thighs, where her dress had been pulled up, was a stark contrast with the dark of the forest floor. Hafgan was holding her wrists, pinning her arms to the ground with his weight. Artair was on top of her. His bare buttocks, white in the darkness, moved up and down as he thrust himself into her with a furious passion. Tondberct was standing by, watching with rapt enjoyment on his face.

Grey-haired Cynric lay sprawled and inert near the fire.

Cathryn's eyes pleaded with Beobrand. Tears streaked her face, glistening in the firelight. The brigand's tortured cries filled Beobrand's ears. Artair reached out and ripped Cathryn's mantle aside, exposing a breast. He squeezed it viciously, pinching the nipple hard between thumb and forefinger. Cathryn let out a cry and closed her eyes tight against the pain, blocking out the night.

Beobrand felt himself becoming aroused. He'd only been with a girl once before, back in Hithe. But Udela had been no beauty like Cathryn, and he hadn't really known what he was doing. That encounter had ended quickly and had become an exciting but embarrassing secret memory, to be dwelt on in the deep of night. Is this what it was to be a warrior? To hear the screams of your enemies in your ears while taking beautiful women with impunity. His arousal grew more intense, his gaze roaming over Cathryn's flesh.

Artair's pace quickened. He leaned forward and gave Cathryn's breast a savage bite. She moaned, clenching her eyes even tighter in an attempt to shut out what was happening.

Beobrand's memory filled with the image of Tata's lifeless body on the altar in the small chapel. The teeth marks on her breast, her eyes staring, unseeing, as if in accusation. Coenred's terrible grief. Had he really changed so much in a matter of weeks that murder and rape now meant nothing to him? His mother's dying words came to him then: "You... are... not... your... father's... son..." He shook his head, trying to focus. No, his father had used his strength to beat those weaker than him, never to protect them. He had thrived on violence against the helpless.

Beobrand could not allow this to carry on. He would never be able to face Coenred again if he stood by and did nothing. He wasn't sure he'd be able to live with himself. Edwin had seen something in him. A determination, a strength that he predicted would make him a great warrior. If he was to be a great warrior, worthy of his brother's memory and Edwin's praise, he must act now.

He was not his father's son.

Without pausing to consider the consequences, he stepped quickly into the firelight. Artair was reaching his climax, arching his back, his face a rictus of pain and pleasure. Beobrand stooped to pick up a log from the pile of firewood and swung it into Artair's head. Artair collapsed immediately, falling to the side of Cathryn. Whether unconscious or dead, Beobrand did not know nor care. He spun towards Hafgan, who let go of Cathryn's wrists and leapt to his feet. He moved away from Beobrand and drew his hunting knife. Beobrand had left his langseax by the fire, so he drew his small knife and stepped forward to meet Hafgan.

Before they could close in combat Beobrand felt a crashing blow to the back of his head. His ears rang and his vision blurred. He fell to his knees. He struggled to regain his feet. Hafgan sprang forward and kicked him full in the face. He landed on his back, legs folded awkwardly beneath him.

Cathryn's eyes met his. His sight began to cloud and he knew he had failed her.

10

B eobrand was surprised to awaken the next morning.
He ached all over, head throbbing from the blow he'd received. His left eye was again swollen shut. His ribs felt broken once more, or at least badly bruised. His legs were numb from having lain on them in an unnatural position for a long period of the night.

He got slowly onto all fours. Then, after catching his breath and working the blood back into his limbs, he got to his feet. There was a thick frost on the ground. Mist hung under the trees.

A few paces from the smouldering embers of the fire he found Cathryn.

She was dead. Her mutilated corpse unrecognisable save for her long braided hair and clothes.

His head spun. His stomach twisted convulsively. He fell forwards, onto his hands and knees, and vomited.

He stared groggily at the outpouring of evil, purged from his body in a steaming puddle. Would that the memories of the night could be expelled so easily.

*

For the first few days following Cathryn's murder, Beobrand wished they had killed him that night. He could not understand why he yet lived.

He was a mass of bruises. His head pained him if he moved too quickly, and breathing deeply caused him to wince.

Slowly, his body recovered. But worse than his physical wounds were those of his soul. He had been unable to stop them. Perhaps confronting them had inflamed their savagery enough to kill Cathryn. Had he caused her death by intervening?

He could not bring himself to talk with any of his companions, but Tondberct was persistent. He sat close to Beobrand in the evenings and chattered inanely. He was desperate for Beobrand's attention. As though he thought if he could get Beobrand to consent to talk with him, he would somehow be exonerated from the atrocities of that night.

Eventually, Beobrand relented. "Why did they not kill me?" he asked, keeping his voice low so only Tondberct could hear.

"It was Hengist," answered Tondberct, pleased that Beobrand was talking to him at last. "He calmed Hafgan down. Told him it was the battle lust. Said you wanted your part of the spoils. That you were impatient for your turn. Hafgan stopped arguing once he got on top..." His voice trailed off. Beobrand's bruised face had taken on a thunderous aspect.

"And Artair?" asked Beobrand, his words clipped.

"He cared little about it. Said it was normal. You are young. Jealous."

"And the others?"

Tondberct looked blank.

"Did they each have a turn?"

Tondberct nodded.

"And you?"

Tondberct was unable to meet his gaze. That was answer enough.

"Who killed her?" Beobrand whispered.

"Dreng and Hengist." Tondberct was keen to shift the focus to someone else. Beobrand's piercing eyes were like ice. "They woke her up, so they could... enjoy her."

Beobrand could listen no more. He stood abruptly, making Tondberct flinch.

He spat and stalked from the camp. Impotent rage burning inside him with a savage heat.

Beobrand was wretched with self-doubt. Could he have saved Cathryn if he'd acted sooner? He recalled the feeling of arousal at seeing her naked flesh and shuddered in revulsion. How was it possible that he'd been aroused at the sight of her being raped? He tried not to think of his own lust for Cathryn, but his mind, like a tongue probing a rotten tooth, always turned back to the moment when he had stood and watched. And enjoyed it.

He dreamt of Cathryn's eyes, pleading with him, asking for him to save her. In his dreams he would leap into the fray and attack her rapists, killing them all with savage fury. But then he would wake up and know the truth. He had watched for a time before acting and thus had failed to protect her.

She became the focus of his every waking thought. Unlike the men who had killed Octa or Tata, he knew exactly who Cathryn's assailants had been. All of his rage at the loss of his brother and the self-loathing he felt at having failed to protect Cathryn seethed within him. It formed into a crystal-hard resolve. By all the gods, he would avenge her, or die trying.

However, there were five men responsible for her death, and he was but one. Despite his prowess and natural ability with a blade, Beobrand knew that he was no match for the group all together. He would have to bide his time, and until such time as he was able to mete out justice, he would have to act as one of them.

He had become withdrawn after that night in the forest. Now he forced himself to settle back into the life of the group. After the conversation with Tondberct, he slowly rejoined the group. He sat closer by the campfire and resumed conversing with them. Their words often stung. His own words tasted like bile in his throat. But he let none of his anguish show on his face.

Following Cathryn's death they had travelled someway further north, into the hills of Bernicia. But they were now headed south again.

Hengist was leading them on a circuitous route and Beobrand was unsure where their final goal was. It clearly wasn't Eanfrith's hall at Gefrin. Beobrand became increasingly certain that the encounter with Galan at Ecgric's hall had disrupted Hengist's plans. He thought of Breca's words warning of Hengist's treachery, then he pictured the scene of torture and murder in the clearing and it was not hard to believe that Hengist had been involved in some betrayal of his king, as Galan had implied. Why else would he have been with Cadwallon and Penda? Perhaps he'd intended to seek patronage from Eanfrith in the beginning, but Galan recognising him made that impossible now.

Whether he had in mind to find a different lord, Beobrand didn't know. Hengist's nature craved blood and violence and there were few lords who would allow their thegns to mistreat their ceorls so badly. If any of them asked Hengist where they were heading, he would give a noncommittal shrug, saying they'd know when they got there.

As they moved further south, from the hills of Bernicia back into the forest they'd left behind in Deira, Beobrand began to get an uneasy feeling. By his reckoning they were heading back towards the campsite at the fallen oak. Hengist and Dreng rode the horses they'd taken. Beobrand and the others trailed someway behind them on foot.

For the first time since Beobrand had joined the band at the beginning of the winter, Hengist seemed to have a clear destination in mind. They travelled hard, leaving little energy for talk, but Tondberct tried to start a conversation with Beobrand.

"Where do you think we're going?" he asked.

"I don't know, but I hope there will be some good food and a bed there!" answered Beobrand, quickening his pace in an effort to dissuade Tondberct from further chatting.

Tondberct frowned after him, but Beobrand didn't care. He wanted to get where they were going as soon as possible so that he could find out whether his fears were correct. He had noticed Hengist smiling to himself as he rode and Beobrand couldn't shake the feeling that they were getting ever closer to something evil. They passed the fallen oak without stopping.

Hengist waited for Beobrand to catch up and said, "You remember this place, Beobrand? You were the only one who didn't have fun that night." He laughed and Dreng chortled.

Beobrand gritted his teeth. He swallowed the angry words he wanted to shout at Hengist. The time would come for more than words.

They travelled on through the forest, the late winter sun not managing to warm the undergrowth. As night began to fall, Hengist ordered them to set up camp and they fell into their now well-practised routines. In a short time they had a fire lit, water collected from the stream they were following, and a thin stew beginning to simmer.

They talked into the night, but Beobrand kept himself apart from the others. Dreng watched him from the other side of the fire with humour in his eyes. It was as if the old warrior knew some funny anecdote about Beobrand, or that they shared a private joke. The old man's leer only made him more uncomfortable. More on edge.

Beobrand chose to take the first watch that night. After rousing Artair to relieve him, he fell into a fitful sleep, rolled up in his cloak near the fire.

He dreamt of Cathryn. She was lying on the ground on warm, lush grass. Bathed in the golden glow of a summer's afternoon. She wore a flimsy, white robe that clung to her breasts and thighs. He could make out the shape of her nipples pushing the fabric taut as she reached towards him, beckoning him to join her. Her lips parted in a half smile, her mouth inviting him to kiss her.

As he bent to embrace her, his lips seeking hers, he saw a splash of red blossom under her robe. Blood gushed from some hidden wound, drenching her dress, leaving it plastered to her body. He looked back at her face and saw that it was no longer beautiful and inviting. Great strips of skin had been flayed from her cheeks. Her nose had been carved crudely off, leaving a gaping hole, which bubbled with fresh blood. Blood flowed down her face and into her mouth, which was moving erratically. Gurgling sounds came.

She was laughing.

He awoke with a start, choking back the scream building in his throat.

The others were already up and about, moving around the

campsite. Hafgan was prodding the fire with a long stick, adding tinder to get it burning again. Dreng was sitting with his back to a tree trunk. He was staring at Beobrand, his gimlet eyes lidded. As Beobrand caught his eye, Dreng licked his lips and smiled. Beobrand's shudder was only partly caused by the cold.

Shortly after they'd broken their fast with a few scraps of dried venison and some hazelnuts, it began to rain. At first, the rain was light enough that little of it filtered through the branches of the trees to the men below. But soon it was falling steadily, filling the forest with noise and soaking the travellers.

They struck camp and moved off, continuing southward with Hengist in the lead. They trudged along behind Hengist and Dreng, walking to the edge of the trail of hoof prints in an attempt to avoid the worst of the cloying mud. Very soon their cloaks were sodden, doing nothing to protect them from the chill or the wet. Beobrand was dejected. A dull ache throbbed in his chest, yet he was accustomed to it and paid it no heed. But his dream had unnerved him. He walked with his head bowed as if under a heavy weight.

It was sometime around midday when Beobrand and the others caught up with Hengist and Dreng, who had stopped at the edge of a clearing. Looking through the grey sheets of rain Beobrand recognised the small group of buildings huddled below them. They had returned to Engelmynster. They had returned to Coenred, Alric, Wilda and the others who had given him succour in his time of need. He had protected them from these men once before when he didn't know how dangerous they were. Now he knew their true nature and, seeing the smile that twisted Dreng's toothless mouth, and the glint in Hengist's eye, he understood why he had been brought back here.

They wanted to complete their unfinished business.

11

The winter had passed slowly for Coenred. He couldn't quite believe that Beobrand had left with the men who had threatened to kill him. He had fallen in with them so naturally, it made Coenred wonder if he was wrong about the young man from Cantware. Coenred had always made up his mind about people quickly, and once he'd decided to be someone's friend, he was unswervingly loyal. He had been sure that Beobrand was a good person and even after his sudden departure, Coenred still liked to think that he wasn't the same as the other warriors.

The month of Blodmonath, with the slaughter of the cattle, made way into Geola. The monastery began to prepare for the feast of Modraniht, the mothers' night, when they celebrated the birth of the Lord Jesu. As the preparations progressed, Abbot Fearghas talked increasingly about the story of the birth of the Christ. Doubt began to gnaw at Coenred. Why had Beobrand decided to join the warriors despite his protestations about their intentions? What was it that drove him? He had said he sought vengeance for his brother's death, but from whom? He had as much idea of who had killed his brother as Coenred did of who had murdered Tata. And what good would revenge do? Neither Octa nor Tata were going to come back from the afterlife. For a moment, Coenred thought bitterly that if Beobrand found his brother's killer, he might be able to exact the weregild from his slayer's kindred. Octa had been a thegn after all. But nobody would pay the blood price for a young orphan girl. He had immediately felt ashamed. He didn't want money or goods for his sister's life. Nothing could replace her and the thought of revenge just saddened him.

The winter had been harsh, and travellers had been few after Beobrand left. But the villagers and monks remembered what had happened to Coenred and how Beobrand had organised them. So Alric had taken on the task of setting up regular patrols at night. Nobody ever left the encampment alone. On a few occasions, other remnants of Edwin's scattered army had arrived seeking food. Or mischief. Each time, Alric and the organised villagers sent them on their way. Coenred reflected how the Christian ideals of charity to others seemed to wane in direct proportion to how little food was left in the stores for the rest of the winter.

They all agreed that if another large warband descended on the village, they would flee again into the forest. Some of the villagers began to question the wisdom of the location of the monastery. It was on a well-used route through the forest, but was isolated and not easy to defend. Fearghas spoke eloquently in defence of the site. He said it was especially holy. The old ones who had built the first buildings there had been blessed. As proof he had pointed to the picture that was on the floor of the small chapel. It had been there when he had first come to the place and was surrounded by low stone walls. He and the monks had built up those walls with wooden lath, covered them in daub, then roofed them with thatch.

The floor was made of small coloured stones or tiles. It was of immense beauty. The swirling patterns around the edge framed the face of a bearded man, who Fearghas said was an angel. He had travelled to this place on his way from Hii, the island in the north-west, to Eoferwic. He hoped to start a Christian church there, converting the heathens to the one true faith, as Columba had done for tribes far north of the Wall. As a young man he had known the great Columba. He was the most inspiring of men and Fearghas had always secretly longed to have as much impact on people as the great man had. Perhaps he had not converted kings like Columba had, but he could not help feeling pleased with his achievements. He knew it was the sin of pride, but he told himself that he was doing God's will, setting aside all earthly pleasures.

On his journey he had rested here for the night and when he had awoken the next morning, a shaft of light had illuminated the angel on the floor. It had been a sign from God Himself and Fearghas had not doubted that he should begin his mission there. Soon, others had joined him. Within a few years, the monastery housed several monks, took on young novices and catered to the spiritual needs of the dozens of villagers who inhabited the clearing.

Abbot Fearghas was happy that he'd not reached Eoferwic as he'd originally planned. He had since travelled to the capital of Deira and he did not like the crowded streets, the noisy traders, with their constant shouting or the smell. He enjoyed the quieter life of contemplation and teaching that he had created at Engelmynster. One of his greatest joys was seeing the boys he taught gain enough knowledge of the scriptures and the teachings of the Christ to leave the monastery.

To make their way into the world to carry the good word to others.

Coenred was still young, but he was quick-witted, thoughtful and sensitive, if a little headstrong and impulsive. Fearghas thought it would not be long before he would be ready to leave the confines of the monastery. It was clear to Fearghas that the boy yearned for greater challenges than learning lines from the hagiographies every morning and reciting prayers with the other monks. Coenred had shown an aptitude at reading and writing, and his Latin was passable. Perhaps he would be a scribe, thought Fearghas. If he didn't run off and do something stupid.

The old monk thought of the grief that had consumed Coenred only a few months before. The resilience of youth never ceased to amaze him. Coenred still had dark moments. He had matured since his sister's death and his capture at the hands of the warriors in the forest, but his irrepressible character was not much changed. Fearghas had prayed for him and Jesu had answered his prayers.

Coenred had applied himself to his studies with a new enthusiasm over the winter. The short days had often not been long enough for the young novice, who always wanted more information. Frequently, at the end of the day, Coenred would ask Fearghas to explain to him one of the finer points of the scriptures. Or he would ask Fearghas to repeat the life story of the saint of the day. Fearghas welcomed the quest for knowledge and understanding. Coenred clearly had a yearning for answers to the imponderable questions of his existence.

But Fearghas was getting old. He was sometimes so tired that these constant requests for more teaching left him short-tempered. Or even more short-tempered than usual. He smiled ruefully. He was well aware of how the young novices, and most of the older monks for that matter, thought of him. Old, irascible, hard to please and quick to anger. All of this was true, but he loved his brethren unconditionally and always sought to bring out the best in them.

Abbot Fearghas was feeling particularly annoyed at that moment. The weather was horrendous. A constant, cold rain fell in waves from a featureless, iron-grey sky. Little light filtered into the room where he sat with Coenred and four other novices. The damp and cold made his back ache.

"No, no, no," Fearghas snapped. "For the hundredth time, you must add the iron salt after the encaustum is thickened. Otherwise the colour will not hold fast."

He took the powder away from Coenred, spilling a little of the expensive ingredient onto the rough workbench where they were working.

"Now look what you've made me do. We have little enough of this stuff as it is."

One of the other four novices, a pimply boy called Dalston, sniggered, attracting one of Abbot Fearghas' infamous looks.

The old monk turned his attention back to Coenred. "Well, what do you have to say for yourself?"

But Coenred did not answer, he had turned and was looking beyond Fearghas, where someone was framed in the doorway.

Coenred's face was pallid. His mouth had dropped open. The other novices' gazes followed Coenred's. Fearghas turned slowly to see who had intruded into his class on ink mixing.

The moment he realised they were at Engelmynster, Beobrand knew he was in trouble. He was sure that Hengist meant to harm those who had harboured him.

That was something he would not allow. His mind raced. What could he do to stop them? He had been waiting for the right moment to seek vengeance for Cathryn but the time for waiting had passed. Now was the time to act.

Yet there was only one of him, and five of them. He rubbed his left side, remembering all too well what had happened the last time he had attempted to fight them without any plan or advantage.

Hengist turned in his saddle with a sardonic grin. "Time for some fun," he said. Dreng licked rain water off his lips and chuckled deep in the back of his throat.

"Don't take too long joining us," Hengist said. He spurred his horse forward into a canter, shouting over his shoulder, "I'm sure you won't want to miss this, Beobrand."

A heartbeat later, Dreng's steed also surged forward. Mud thrown up by the horses' hooves splattered Beobrand and the others. Both riders moved off quickly and were soon almost hidden from sight by the torrential rain.

Beobrand didn't like the situation. Hengist and Dreng would reach the village long before he could. He broke into a clumsy run, slipping and sliding through the quagmire left by the horses. He ran down the slope as fast as he could, sensing the others chasing behind him. Now he had two enemies in front and three behind.

He ran awkwardly, his shield slapping against his back. He had a head start on Tondberct, Hafgan and Artair and while he ran he scanned the buildings before him for something that could tip the odds in his favour. The place looked empty. The storm was too violent to allow any hearth smoke to be seen and the weather was evidently keeping people inside. He watched as Hengist and Dreng turned towards the small group of buildings that made up the monastery.

Coenred would probably be there. Beobrand was certain now that the main objective of Hengist bringing them back here was to kill Coenred. Hengist knew that Beobrand and the young monk were friends. Beobrand was sure that making him witness Coenred's death would appeal to Hengist. Beobrand had stood against him and denied him the pleasure of the kill the last time they were here. Then, the night of Cathryn's death, Beobrand had confronted them again. Hengist had been toying with him ever since, leading him back here for the perfect punishment for his defiance.

Hengist and Dreng reined their horses to a halt outside the monastery and dismounted. Seeing this, Beobrand began to make his way towards them, desperate to prevent them from fulfilling their brutal goal. But what would he achieve when he got there? Hengist and Dreng together would be more than a match for him and the others were on his heels, calling after him. Surely Hengist would want to have him present before hurting Coenred, that must be the whole reason for bringing him here. Inflicting pain gave them pleasure. To be able to inflict pain on Coenred and cause Beobrand anguish as a result, was the ultimate prize.

Beobrand gambled this was the case.

Please, Woden, father of the gods, let me be right.

He changed direction all of a sudden, his mud-clogged feet skidding. He lost his balance and started to fall, only righting himself by pushing off the ground with his hand. He cast a glance behind him and saw his three pursuers stop, momentarily unsure of which direction to go. He offered up thanks to Woden and pressed on with renewed speed.

He shouted as he ran. "Arm yourselves! Enemies are amongst you! To arms, to arms!" The thunder of the rain partially drowned out the sound of his voice, but his words must have reached the houses. He saw a few faces peer out from doorways, but he kept going, screaming at the top of his voice all the while.

His breath ragged, he saw his destination approaching. The thatched cottage had been home to him for weeks back in the autumn. He was about to rush inside when the stocky figure of Wybert stepped out, blocking his path.

"Come back have you? What do you want?" Wybert sneered.

Beobrand stole a quick look over his shoulder. Hafgan was almost upon him, with the other two following only a few paces behind. There was no time to be wasted. This was not the time for talk.

He stepped in close to Wybert, putting all of his weight and considerable strength behind a straight punch to his jaw. Wybert's head snapped back and he fell backwards into the hut.

Beobrand leapt in after him, jumping over his supine form. The hut's single room was smoky and dark. Before his eyes could adjust, the light from the guttering fire glinted off of a spearhead that was hurtling towards his chest. With instinctive lightning reactions, Beobrand spun to one side and the spear narrowly missed his body, instead snagging his sodden cloak.

"Wait! It is I, Beobrand," he said before Leofwine could make a second lunge. "You are under attack, but not from me. There are others right behind me."

As if in response to his words Tondberct's voice, breathless from exertion, called through the doorway. "Beobrand, come outside. We don't want to hurt you."

Beobrand's eyes were becoming accustomed to the gloom inside the hut and he was able to make out Alric, armed with an axe, standing beside Wilda, who was clutching a large knife. "Beobrand?" she asked, "Is that you?"

Alric stepped forward. "What have you done, boy?" He moved towards Wybert. "You'd better pray he's alright."

"He should be fine," answered Beobrand. "I'm sorry. There was no time to talk."

"I can hear you talking in there!" came Tondberct's voice. "Come on out and we can all talk together."

Alric helped Wybert up and moved him with Leofwine's help to the back of the hut, where they laid him on a low pallet. Wilda moved to his side, fussing over him. He moaned groggily.

Alric and Leofwine turned back to Beobrand. Alric hissed, "What is happening? Who are the people outside?"

"There's no time to explain," said Beobrand. "You have to trust me. There are five armed men in the village. Three here and two more at the monastery. I think they mean to kill Coenred. Perhaps others too."

Alric's face hardened. "We'll see about that." He reached up to one of the roof beams and brought down a horn that had been hanging there. He moved towards the doorway, placed the horn to his lips and blew five short blasts. The sound was loud in the confines of the hut, but much of the sound was directed out of the open doorway. Alric paused, took a deep breath, then repeated the five blasts on the horn.

"That should bring us some reinforcements," he said, with a cold smile. "We've not been idle since you left, Beobrand. Now you'll see."

Wybert sat up, despite his mother's protestations. "You bastard," he rasped, looking at Beobrand with utter hatred. He made as if to stand up, but Wilda firmly pushed him back.

"We need to fight our enemies, Wybert," said Alric, looking at Beobrand appraisingly. "Not our friends."

Reaching his hand to his chin and wincing at the touch of

his probing fingers, Wybert answered, "Friends don't punch you in the face."

"Enough!" said Alric, drawing a conclusion to the conversation. "If you are strong enough, Wybert, pick up your weapon and prepare to stand strong in defence of Engelmynster, your friends and your kindred."

Wybert got up shakily. He gave Beobrand a sour look, but said no more.

For a moment, nobody spoke and the only sounds were the constant drone of the rain falling on the thatch and the crackle of the fire on the hearthstone. Then a horn sounded somewhere not too far away. Three long blasts. A reply to Alric's call to arms.

Alric raised his horn to his lips again and blew.

Hefting his axe, he turned to Beobrand, Leofwine and Wybert. "Let's show these ruffians what happens when you attack Christ's children."

With that Alric strode out of the hut into the driving rain. Beobrand didn't think he counted as one of Christ's children. Nonetheless, he drew his langseax, unslung his shield from his back, lifted it on his left arm, tensing slightly at the jolt to his still-tender ribs, and followed Alric outside. Leofwine and Wybert trailed out after them.

In front of the hut stood Tondberct, Hafgan and Artair. All three brandished their weapons, but didn't have the confidence they'd displayed only moments before when attempting to draw Beobrand out from shelter. Beobrand was now flanked by three armed men, making them outnumbered. The horn sounded again, this time closer. More allies were coming. The three of them stood close together, gaining strength from their proximity to each other. Their eyes were frightened.

They could see the reinforcements approaching now. Five more men, armed with knives, cudgels and spears, were walking determinedly towards them through the mud and rain.

The new group of villagers was getting close. Soon Tondberct and the two Waelisc brothers would be surrounded. They would have to fight. It was a fight they knew they could not win.

Some silent communication passed between them, and, as one, they turned and fled towards the forest.

The new group of villagers let out a cheer and ran forward, meaning to give chase. Alric held up his hands to stop them. "Wait, there are two more," he said. "At the monastery. We think they mean to kill Coenred. There's no time to waste."

Without waiting for a response, Alric broke into a lumbering run towards the monastery buildings at the other end of the village clearing. Beobrand ran at his side. Leofwine, Wybert and the others needed no further encouragement.

"Well, well, well, what have we here?" Hengist sneered from the doorway. He moved into the room, allowing Dreng to enter behind him. The small chamber was already crowded with the five novices, Abbot Fearghas and the workbench. The overbearing presence of the two large warriors made it cramped. The novices moved as far from the two intruders as they could, cowering against the far wall.

Fearghas stepped forwards, placing himself in between the warriors and the boys. "This is a place of worship and reflection. These boys are studying the works of God. Do you seek food or shelter from the rain? I'm sure we can find something to give you. Perhaps you could dry your wet clothes by a fire in the village."

Fearghas knew the men had not come for food or shelter, he could see the malice in their eyes. They reeked of wet wool, sweat and woodsmoke. A lust of violence radiated from them like one more stench. Perhaps they were possessed by evil spirits. He did not know how, but he must protect the boys in his care from these men. Please Lord, protect these innocents from these men of war, he prayed silently.

Hengist laughed. "We can take the food we need. We want to complete what we started back in the autumn." His eyes roved across the novices and settled on Coenred. "As I recall, we were going to cut off your head and display it on a spear. Before your friend interrupted us."

Coenred felt sick. He had tried not to think about his brief time in the woods with these men. He'd thought he'd never see them again. That they would become a bad memory. Yet here they were, the large bearded leader and the evil-looking, toothless old one and there was nobody but Abbot Fearghas to protect him. Fleetingly, he thought that he should pray. Christ would protect him. Then he looked straight into Hengist's eyes. He saw the madness and cruelty there and all thought of prayer left his mind, like smoke borne away on a breeze.

Hengist made to take a step towards Coenred and the novices. Fearghas stood his ground. "You cannot have him or anyone else. In the name of the Father, the Son and the Holy Ghost, be gone from here!" Abbot Fearghas' voice was surprisingly strong for one so frail.

Hengist paused. He didn't know what magic this old man was capable of by invoking the names of his new gods. He had seen people wither away after being cursed. His own mother used to weave her spells with words of power. Who knew what powers this new Christ god had, especially inside his sacred buildings? He shuddered. The old priest must be silenced and they should get outside, where the wind and rain could wash away his incantations.

Without warning Hengist struck Fearghas across the face with the back of his left hand. His knuckles connected solidly with the old man's nose, crunching the cartilage. His eyes glazed over, rolling back into his head. Blood was already flowing from his nose, as he sank to the floor, dazed. Any other man who had stood against him as the old priest had would already be dead. But something in his demeanour made Hengist decide not to use his weapon. Perhaps striking him down with the words of his spell still on his lips in this enclosed space would bring down the wrath of the Christ god. Hengist feared no man, but he had a healthy respect for gods, both new and old.

Dreng had drawn his seax and pounced on Fearghas' senseless form.

"Leave him!" shouted Hengist, the extent of his own fear surprising him. "We've come for the boy." He pointed at Coenred, who felt his legs grow weak. He moved as far as he could from the two warriors, pressing his back against the rough wall.

Dreng moved grudgingly away from Fearghas. He pushed past the workbench to get to Coenred. The boys moved aside, allowing the old warrior to get to his new prey. When he reached the last boy before Coenred, the young monk did not move. It was Dalston and he was paralysed by fear. Dreng grabbed the young novice by the hair, using it to pull him out of the way. Dalston let out a whimper and his bladder released. The sharp tang of warm piss filled the air, as shivers began to rack the boy's body.

Ignoring the weeping youth, Dreng seized Coenred by the ear. Twisting it savagely, he pulled Coenred towards

Hengist and the doorway. Coenred didn't resist. He tried to keep pace with the old warrior to alleviate the pain in his ear. He managed a quick look back at the frightened faces of the novices in the room before he was dragged out into the pelting rain. There would be no help from that quarter.

The cold rain and wind buffeted Coenred's face. Dreng let go of his ear and gave him a hard shove in between his shoulder blades. Coenred sprawled in the mud. He pushed himself up onto his knees, but before he could stand or contemplate running away, Hengist kicked him in the stomach with such force that he was lifted off the ground. He landed on his back, unable to breathe. He lay in the mud looking up at the dark clouds roiling overhead. He struggled to draw a breath. Panic engulfed him. So he really was going to die. His vision blurred, darkening at the edges.

After what seemed like a long time, when he thought he was about to pass out, Coenred finally managed a shuddering intake of air. As the air filled his lungs, his senses flooded back and with them an intense pain in his midriff where Hengist's boot had connected.

From the village came the sudden sound of five notes on a horn. They were muffled by distance and the storm, but clearly audible. Coenred recognised the signal Alric had made to warn of attack. About time. Perhaps he wasn't going to die after all. Would Christ see fit to spare him again?

He turned his head and saw Hengist and Dreng standing over him, rain streaming down their faces. They were not looking at him.

"By Tiw's cock, what is that? And where are Beobrand and the others? I thought they were right behind us," said Hengist, peering into the driving rain in the direction of the sound of the horn.

The mention of Beobrand made Coenred start. So he was still alive and with these men. What part did he have in this? Surely he couldn't want to kill him.

Just then another horn sounded. Longer notes this time, a different pitch.

Despite the pain in his stomach and the waves of nausea that were now making his mouth fill with saliva, Coenred saw an opportunity to escape while the warriors' attention was diverted. He hadn't prayed for help, so it was unlikely God would save him.

He had better help himself.

The first horn sounded again. The warriors were distracted. Coenred scrabbled up from the ground away from Hengist and Dreng. But they were standing and Coenred was starting from lying flat on his back in the mud. After only a few strides he was pulled back by a strong hand gripping his robe. He was brought to a halt and he felt the cold iron of a blade pressed painfully into his throat.

"Where do you think you're going, eh?" Hengist held him tightly. The blade at his neck kept him still. "We've got plans for you."

"Looks like we've got company," said Dreng. He went to the horses and retrieved both of their shields from where they had been tied to the saddles. Dreng held his shield in his left hand and then grabbed Coenred by the throat while Hengist readied his own shield.

Running through the rain towards them came Beobrand and eight other men. All armed, but none wearing armour. Only Beobrand carried a shield. His face was dark with fury. Hengist grinned.

Dreng spoke quietly beside him. "It is good that Beobrand's angry. The boy is good with a blade, but he's no match for you."

Hengist snorted. "Beobrand won't be a problem. But where are Tondberct and those two damn Waelisc inbreds?"

Dreng scanned the village for sign of their friends. "Two against nine are not good odds."

"No, but not impossible odds. Not against these peasants," said Hengist.

Beobrand and his companions stopped a few paces away from them.

"Come to see us kill your little friend, Beobrand?" said Hengist. "Did you believe I wouldn't come back for him? He's been dead these last months. He just hasn't known it."

Beobrand stopped a few paces from Hengist. He looked Coenred in the eye and saw the fear there. It struck him that Coenred didn't respond in any way to him. He is not sure if I am here to help him or to help them kill him. The thought saddened him.

"If you kill Coenred, you will both die. There are nine of us." He waved his arm in the direction he had come. "Tondberct, Hafgan and Artair have fled."

Dreng looked around furtively. He licked his lips. The rain stopped falling abruptly, throwing a blanket of eerie silence over the village.

Hengist smiled. "We will kill the boy if you try to attack. We can take him with us. Ride away from here. You'll never catch us."

Beobrand saw the truth in Hengist's words. A shiver ran down his spine. It was not brought on by the cold wind on his rain-soaked clothes. He had to stop them from leaving with Coenred.

"You came here for a death. Let him go and face me instead."

Hengist's eyes narrowed. "Why would I want to do that?"

"To prove you can best me. I have beaten all the others, but you have never fought me. I wonder if you are craven."

"As soon as I release him, they will set upon us. You think I'm a fool?"

"You have my word that if you beat me in single combat, they will let you leave in peace." Beobrand turned to Alric. "Swear an oath on whatever you hold sacred that your people will let this man go if he beats me."

Alric appeared troubled. He looked Beobrand in the eye for a long time. Beobrand gave a slight nod.

"Aye. I swear on the bones of our Lord Jesu Christ that you will be given free passage should you beat Beobrand in combat. But first you must let the boy go."

Hengist hesitated. Dreng shuffled his feet in the mud. Coenred looked from Beobrand to Hengist.

Beobrand broke the silence. "A coward it is then. Too scared to face me? Unbelievable. The great Hengist is scared of the boy he trained."

"Let him go." Hengist waved at Dreng, but his eyes never left Beobrand's. There was murder and death in that stare. Madness too. Fear suddenly gripped Beobrand. He'd seen what Hengist was capable of. He was no match for the older warrior. His stomach tightened.

Dreng pushed Coenred away. Hengist sheathed his knife and drew his sword slowly from its plain scabbard.

All eyes were on the blade as Hengist pulled it out with great ceremony. He held it aloft for a moment, and then pointed it at Beobrand. The shimmering patterns from the forging of the blade made it look like the skin of a serpent. Or the rippling waves of the ocean. It was a thing of beauty and great value. It was a noble blade.

"Where did you get that sword, Hengist? Why do you never

unsheathe it?" asked Beobrand, readying himself for the attack that would come all too soon. He sensed the men behind him back away, giving them space to fight. A glimmer of emotion passed over Hengist's face, sowing a seed of a thought in Beobrand's mind. "Did you steal it?" he asked. Hengist's eyes widened. Then, almost as an afterthought, Beobrand said, "Like the coward you are." To the onlookers, he seemed calm, in control. Inside he churned with pent up emotion. And fear.

Hengist's jaw clenched.

"I am no coward, Beobrand. It was I who saved Edwin. This sword is named Hrunting and it was my wyrd for it to be mine. I didn't steal it. I brought the justice of the gods on them both!" Beobrand didn't understand Hengist's words, but he had clearly struck on something to rile his foe. He needed any advantage he could get, so he pressed on.

"Your words make no sense, Hengist. Are you spirit-touched? You talk of justice. What do you know of justice?"

"I know that betrayal should be paid for with death. That is why I killed Elda," spittle flew from Hengist's mouth. He was working himself up into a rage. "And why I killed Octa!"

Without warning Hengist charged.

Despite being prepared for the attack, Beobrand was startled. He threw up his shield to ward off Hengist's long-reaching lunge but he did not feel the impact of metal on the leather-bound wood. Hengist skipped to the side, lithe and agile, sure-footed even on the muddy ground. As he moved, he flicked out the tip of his sword behind Beobrand's shield and opened up a cut on his arm. Beobrand staggered backwards. Off balance. Feeling clumsy. His arm stung. The warmth of blood trickled inside his sleeve.

His mind was in turmoil. Had Hengist really killed Octa and Elda or was he trying to make him lose concentration?

Beobrand could not allow that to happen. He pushed the thoughts from his head. He was going to need his full focus and everything he had learnt if he was to have any chance of surviving this fight. He regained his footing and resumed the fighting stance Hengist had taught him.

Hengist laughed. "Come on then, Beobrand. Show us what you've learnt."

They circled each other. Beobrand tense, keeping his guard up, Hengist relaxed and loose, his shield held at his side, his sword dancing in intricate patterns. The watchers were silent. Coenred held his breath.

Hengist attacked again. He led with his shield, crashing boss against boss. He followed through with a cut to Beobrand's feet, but this time Beobrand anticipated the move and leapt backwards.

They circled again. Each looking intently for signals that would give away the other's next move.

Beobrand was biding his time. He hoped more than anything for Hengist to make a mistake. He kept his shield up and continued to mirror Hengist's movements. His shield arm was tiring. The pain from the cut was getting worse. He would have to attack soon.

As fast as a cat, Hengist attacked once more. They clashed shields again, Hengist using his forward momentum and strength to lever Beobrand's to the side and down. He sent a probing cut with his sword over the shield's rim, aimed at Beobrand's face. Beobrand twisted his body and was able to parry the strike with his langseax. Though how, he was not sure. He had barely seen Hengist's attack. Sparks flashed briefly in the dim light as the two blades collided.

They parted. Beobrand went on the offensive almost instantly in an attempt to catch Hengist by surprise. He wielded his langseax with all his strength and skill, landing a flurry of blows upon Hengist's shield. Hengist effortlessly deflected all of Beobrand's attacks. He laughed again. "Is that the best you can do?"

Beobrand could feel his strength sapping. The cut on his arm must be deeper than he had originally thought. Soon he wouldn't be able to lift his shield at all. He could see no way of breaking down Hengist's defence. Beobrand had been walking all day, then he had run and now he was losing blood. Hengist was hardly out of breath.

Every time they moved Beobrand could feel his feet shifting and sliding, making him clumsy, slow to react. Hengist seemed unaffected by the poor condition of the ground.

They exchanged more blows, ending up shield to shield. For a moment they were staring at each other. Hengist's eyes were full of malice, a gleeful violence. Then he gave a shove, lifted his sword up and under Beobrand's shield, cutting into his side, beneath his ribs.

Beobrand let out a cry and jumped back. Hengist did not press home his advantage; content to watch his young adversary suffer some more before delivering the killer blow.

The pain in Beobrand's side was excruciating. He wanted to probe it with his fingers to find how bad it was, but he could not risk letting his guard down for a moment. The warmth of his blood soaked into his woollen jerkin. He scanned the faces of the people watching the fight. It looked as if everyone in the village had arrived while he had been fighting Hengist. Now they would all be able to witness his death. At least they now so vastly outnumbered Hengist and Dreng that there was no chance of the two escaping.

"Octa died a coward's death," said Hengist. "Alone in the dark. No sword in his hand."

If Hengist hoped to unnerve Beobrand, his words had the opposite effect.

"You mean you murdered him in the dark when he was not prepared to fight you," Beobrand panted. "There is no dishonour for my brother. But you are craven. The worst kind of man."

The pale face of Coenred caught his eye. The young monk was staring at him earnestly, worry etched on his features. But something else too. Could it be pride?

Beobrand said, "It is not dark here and I am armed and ready, Hengist. Come to me and let us finish this."

Hengist let out a roar and took three bounding steps towards Beobrand, lunging forwards with his sword point, hoping to strike inside Beobrand's guard.

Beobrand was slow to react. His near exhaustion, coupled with his loss of blood, made him sluggish. He moved to meet Hengist's charge, but he was too late. Hengist's sword was aimed at his right shoulder and there was no way he would be able to lift his shield in time. He attempted a desperate leap to one side, but his left foot slipped in the slick mud. He fell, sprawling into the mire.

His timing could not have been more perfect if he had made the move intentionally. Hengist's sword slid safely over him. Instead of running him through the shoulder, it pierced thin air. Hengist's speed carried him forward, unable to slow himself down or adjust his attack. His feet crashed into Beobrand's thighs. He lost his balance and he toppled over on top of Beobrand.

Beobrand instinctively raised his langseax to ward off Hengist's falling form. His blade sliced into Hengist's unprotected face. The sharp blade opened up a cut from Hengist's chin to his left eyebrow. He dropped the sword, let out a shriek and rolled away from Beobrand, clutching his face with both hands.

Beobrand staggered to his feet, not quite sure what had happened. The onlooking crowd let out a ragged gasp. Dreng moved to Hengist's side. Helped him to his feet. Blood was streaming from the gash in his face. Hengist clamped his right hand to it. His left still clutching his shield. His right eye stared balefully at Beobrand.

"What have you done, you bastard? By Tiw, I'll eat your heart!"

Beobrand stood his ground, swaying slightly, his legs weak. Alric and some of the villagers took a few steps forwards.

Dreng pulled Hengist towards the horses. He helped Hengist onto his horse, then mounted his own. "Come, brother," he whispered, "You cannot win this fight today."

"This hasn't finished!" screamed Hengist. "I will have my revenge on you, Beobrand. I swear it on all the gods." He had dropped his hands to the horse's reins, his face a bloody ruin. "I'll kill you and take back Hrunting. Your life and the sword are both mine." He turned his steed, kicked his heels to its flanks and galloped away northward.

Dreng followed him, his horse flinging up gobbets of mud in its wake.

A stillness fell on those watching. They stared after the two horsemen until they had been swallowed up by the gloom of the forest road.

Beobrand could not quite believe what had just transpired. He silently thanked Woden, father of the gods. For surely the gods had guided his hand and caused him to slip at exactly the right moment. To think it had been blind luck was too frightening. He began to tremble. He could feel the strength ebbing from his limbs. Perhaps he could go and lie down in the dry of Alric and Wilda's hut, when a strangely familiar voice penetrated his foggy senses.

"Well, Edwin said you'd be a mighty warrior!" roared the voice.

Beobrand spun round, dizziness blurring his vision. Striding towards him was the hulking figure of Bassus, King Edwin's champion and Octa's best friend. He was resplendent in his war gear and leading a chestnut horse. There were several other riders dismounting behind him.

The huge warrior tossed the reins of his horse to Coenred, who was standing looking dumbstruck. Bassus stooped and picked up the beautiful, patterned-bladed sword from the ground where it lay and walked to Beobrand, smiling broadly.

Beobrand was confused. "What? How are you here?" he blurted out.

"Well, there I was thinking you might actually be pleased to see me. I have to say I am pleased to see you. I was sure you were with Octa, drinking in the hall of the gods." He gave Beobrand an appraising look. Beobrand's face was gaunt from a winter of sleeping rough and foraging off the land. He had a scar under his left eye. His left arm and side were stained crimson from his injuries. He was soaking wet and covered from head to foot in cloying mud.

"From the look of you, you haven't got far to go to join your brother."

With his cloak, Bassus wiped Beobrand's blood from the sword's blade, admiring the workmanship. "Well, I never thought to see this sword again. It seems it has chosen to be reunited with the kin of its previous owner." Beobrand looked at Bassus, confused by his presence.

He proffered the sword to Beobrand, hilt first. "Hrunting

was gifted to your brother by King Edwin. It seems it was not lost in the sea after all."

Beobrand took the sword. "Hengist murdered Octa. I must avenge him…" His voice trailed off.

Bassus placed a hand on his shoulder, steadying him. "We can talk of this later."

Beobrand was in no state to have a conversation. He was wavering on the verge of consciousness. Bassus turned to the assembled crowd. "My companions and I are travelling north. We mean no harm. We seek refuge here for the night. We will pay well for food and shelter." The tension eased from the villagers. "But first, let's get young Beobrand here somewhere warm and dry and his wounds tended to."

Alric stepped forward. "He can come to my family's home. Come, Beobrand." He placed his hand on Beobrand's arm.

The glazed look left Beobrand's eyes and he turned to Coenred. "Well, I make us even now. That's twice I've saved you. I told you a son of Grimgundi always repays his debts."

Bassus stretched his feet out to the fire. He had ridden all day and for many days prior to that, and riding always made his feet cold. The weather since leaving Cantware had been foul. Wind and rain most days, and freezing nights. Still, it was better than travelling by ship, which is what Queen Ethelburga had wanted. He hated sailing more than he hated riding. It was not natural for men to get into fragile wooden boats and travel over vast expanses of endless ocean. Every year, when ships were lost at sea, or wrecked on the rocky coastline of Northumbria, Bassus couldn't help but feel that the sailors had got what they deserved. You could fall off a horse and get back up with a bruise or a broken bone.

Fall out of a ship and you were never coming back to dry land. Ethelburga had said that by sea he would get the message he was carrying to King Eanfrith of Bernicia sooner than if he travelled by road. Bassus had replied that if he drowned, Eanfrith would never get the message, so he would ride.

In the end, Ethelburga had relented and not ordered Bassus to do her bidding exactly. Since the death of her husband, she was less certain of her position and was unsure whether her husband's men would follow her as they had followed him. After Edwin's defeat at Elmet, a handful of his most trusted thegns had survived. Led by Bassus, the small group had escaped the field of battle, ridden hard north to Bebbanburg, where Ethelburga, the princess Eanflæd and the little atheling Wuscfrea waited. From there they had sailed south to the lands of Ethelburga's brother, King Eadbald, in Cantware.

Bassus remembered those dark days clearly. The defeat at the hands of Penda and Cadwallon had been absolute and terrible. First Osfrid, Edwin's heir had fallen. Edwin, dismayed and blinded by his loss, had struck out to avenge his son. He had charged forward on his own, causing the shieldwall to split and falter.

Bassus blamed himself. He should have reacted more quickly to the danger. He should have sensed the tide of battle shifting and acted accordingly. Instead, his king had been struck down and it was all Bassus could do to pull him away from the thick of the fighting before they were completely overrun. In those last moments, Edwin saw clearly what he had done and what the outcome of the battle would be. He had gripped Bassus' wrist and made him swear on all the gods, both old and new, that he would follow Queen Ethelburga in his stead. Bassus would have gladly laid down his life for his lord, so he was powerless to refuse the request. But now, in the rare moments when he allowed himself to think on the past, he felt a deep-seated shame that he had not died on that battlefield.

Despite being back in her homeland in the south, Ethelburga still feared for the safety of her children. There was no clear ruler over the northern kingdoms. The exiled heir to Bernicia, Eanfrith, had returned. Osric, Edwin's cousin, had sat himself on the throne of Deira. Cadwallon continued to vie for control of the two kingdoms, emboldened by his victory over Edwin, who had ruled both.

With the first green shoots of spring, a trader from Eoferwic had arrived in Cantware recounting tales of Osric being killed and his forces routed by Cadwallon during a siege.

It was this unsettled situation that had led Ethelburga to send a message north. It was possible that Eanfrith would seek to unite the two kingdoms as Edwin had done. If he was successful, he would surely wish to dispatch with as many potential usurpers of his throne as possible. So Ethelburga had decided to send a message of peace and Christian love to Eanfrith. He was reputed to worship Christ, albeit following the Hibernian traditions taught in the Pictish lands where he had been exiled, and not the teachings as laid out by Bishop Paulinus and Pope Honorius in faraway Rome. Nevertheless, she wished him prosperity and victory over his enemies in the name of the Lord. She also let it be known that her children were no threat to him. Despite this, Ethelburga decided to remove Wuscfrea, her one remaining son, along with Yffi, her stepson Osfrid's son, from the courts of the noble houses of Albion. At the same time as Bassus had been sent north with the message to Eanfrith, the boys had been sent south to be fostered in the court of her cousin, Dagobert, in Frankia. She prayed they would be safe there, far from the machinations of the different royal lines of Albion.

Bassus sighed as the warmth of the fire began to seep into his bones. His toes tingled as the blood returned. With a conscious effort, he brought his focus back to the present. He had decided long ago that dwelling on the past was for fools. You could not go back and change your actions, so why go over and over your mistakes in your memory? Because he was a fool. A sentimental fool, who was getting old. He smiled at the thought. It was true that he was not young anymore, though he still had several useful years left in him, he hoped.

He looked over at the sleeping form of Beobrand. Now there was youth. Beobrand had endured terrible hardship, both of body and mind, and yet he shrugged off his ills as a duck's feathers shed water. Well, perhaps not that easily. His wounds had been cleaned and bound and it would take several days until he was fighting fit again, but the colour had returned to his face after a small meal of pottage and some mead. Now he slept soundly. The sleep of a child. But he was a child no longer. The last vestiges of childish roundness had left his cheeks. His body and face had taken on a hard edge that was lacking when last Bassus had seen him.

Bassus still found it hard to believe the boy's story as it had been told to him that afternoon. How he had survived against all the odds, escaping the battlefield at night. Then being nursed to health here in this village, narrowly avoiding marauding Waelisc from Cadwallon's force. And finally joining up with some survivors of Edwin's warband and travelling the wilds throughout the winter. Beobrand had told him little of what had happened during the long winter months, but he had clearly learnt how to fight. When Bassus and his companions had arrived, the fight between Beobrand and Hengist was almost over. Beobrand had been injured and was struggling, yet he still carried himself well, blocking, parrying and attacking like a seasoned veteran. Bassus knew Hengist too. He was a warrior to be reckoned with, savage, skilled and ruthless, with a nasty penchant for wanton violence. So Bassus was surprised at the outcome of the fight. The moment he'd recognised Beobrand, he'd decided to step in to stop Hengist from killing Octa's younger brother. Just at the moment he'd taken a step forward and was preparing to shout out a command to both warriors to put up their weapons, Beobrand had slipped and ended the fight with the terrible blow to Hengist's face.

Beobrand wasn't just a natural warrior, mused Bassus. He had the commodity that warriors prized more highly than any other: luck.

Bassus turned his attention to the young monk who sat next to Beobrand like a faithful hound. He had been introduced as Coenred and there was clearly a strong bond of friendship between him and Beobrand. It was he who had found Beobrand and nursed his wounds after the battle of Elmet. It seemed that Hengist had threatened to kill the boy, which is what prompted Beobrand to fight him. Just like his brother. Brave to the point of careless, and a more loyal friend you would not find.

As he watched, Coenred's head sank slowly forward. His chin ended up rested on his chest and he fell ever so slowly sideways, until his head rested on Beobrand's legs. Bassus smiled. He really did look like his dog now.

Alric, who was sitting quietly next to Bassus, broke the silence. "I'm surprised Coenred stayed awake as long as he did," he said quietly. "It's been a terribly long day, and he took a real beating from those bastards."

Bassus grunted. He didn't feel like speaking. He was happy to sit here watching over Beobrand and the monk.

From outside came the sound of distant laughter. Bassus' companions had been put up in different homes in the village, and they seemed to be enjoying themselves. The storm had blown itself out. The night was still, allowing the noise to travel far.

Alric didn't press him into conversation. Instead he refilled Bassus' drinking horn with ale. Bassus nodded his thanks, taking a deep draught. It was good. Fresh and light.

Both men raised their drinks in silent toast.

PART TWO
THE TEMPERING

12

Sunniva was late.

She was supposed to have the fire burning and the forge ready before her father came out to start work. He said he worked harder than her all day, so it was only fair that she get up before him to prepare things. She wasn't sure she'd call it fair. She helped lift the glowing hot billets of iron out of the fire and onto the anvil for him to hammer in a shower of white sparks, and she worked the bellows until her back and arms ached, but she didn't argue with her father. Strang was a man most men feared and with whom few would pick a quarrel. His shoulders and arms looked capable of bending the metal he worked without the use of fire, anvil or hammer. He was quick to anger, and while he rarely raised his hand to Sunniva, she had learnt to avoid conflict.

Strang's sullen moods were worse than his rages. Sunniva's mother, with her quick smile and easy manner had always been able to snap him out of his depressions. But ever since her death the winter before, Strang spent most of his days gloomily focused on his work. Not having the forge set for him in the morning was not a good start to the day.

Sunniva rushed to blow air into the charcoal with the bellows. She could hear her father moving inside the house. He would be pulling his leather apron down from its hook by the door. Readying his tools. Sunniva pumped the bellows harder. She was pleased to see the satisfying glow from deep within the mound of charcoal. A wave of heat washed over her with each heave of the bellows. The forge would be ready after all. Stray wisps of her long blonde hair, that had escaped her plait, were plastered with sweat to her forehead.

Strang stepped out into the dim daylight and gazed at his daughter for a moment before she realised he was there. She was half-turned away from him. The heat from the forge made the air flicker above it. She brushed a strand of hair away from her face, and then gave the bellows a last few pushes. She was so beautiful it made his heart ache. It was as if her mother stood before him, as she had looked when he first met her. Etheswitha was more than Strang could ever have hoped for. She was graceful, quick-witted and devoted to him and Sunniva. But she had not been strong. She had been ill for much of their time together. She had borne him four children. Two had been stillborn and one, a boy, had only lived for a few days before succumbing to a terrible cough. Sometimes, in the still of the night, he thought about those tiny babies that had died before they even had names. If it hadn't been for Sunniva, he would have thought that the gods had cursed him. But then he would see his beautiful daughter and his heart would swell.

Sunniva looked up and saw Strang standing watching her work the bellows. "The forge is ready, father," she said, smiling brightly.

He returned the smile as best he could and began work on

the dozens of spear heads that the new king, Eanfrith, had commissioned.

Around them, the rest of the town was awakening. Voices could be heard, dogs barked, somewhere a cockerel crowed.

The winter had been quiet in the town of Gefrin. After Edwin had fallen in battle, Queen Ethelburga and her children had left Bernicia and many people fled with them. The lands became dangerous, with wandering groups of lordless warriors preying on travellers. Marauding Waelisc, from Cadwallon's forces, also roamed the land. There had not been as much work as normal. But then Eanfrith, the exiled heir, had returned from the north with his retinue of retainers and the settlement began to feel alive once more.

Sunniva had watched the king closely when he came to speak to her father about making new spear heads for his warband. She was unsettled by how handsome he was. He was broad-shouldered, tall and strikingly attractive, despite being many years her senior. He flashed her a sparkling smile as he swept into the forge, flicking his fine crimson cloak over his shoulder. She'd blushed at the knowing look in his eye. He appraised her in the same way that many of the warriors did, but with one important difference: the warriors around Gefrin kept their distance, fearing Strang's wrath should they approach Sunniva. Eanfrith had the confidence that if he wanted to act on an impulse, he could. He was the king, after all. When his green eyes had met Sunniva's, she could see the mischief lurking under the surface. She had been suddenly aware that she had benefited from her father's protection all these years without paying it any heed. She didn't like the feeling of confronting a man who was not afraid of her father.

Eanfrith had quickly lost interest in his dealings with Strang. He had begun by inspecting a few pieces of Strang's work before coming to an agreement on price. But when Strang had begun to explain some of the finer points of the forging process, Eanfrith's concentration had waned and he had said he had other business to attend to. Sunniva had taken offence, later saying to her father that it was not right that a smith of his experience should be treated in that way.

The smith had been much more pragmatic. "He is the king. He can treat me any way he pleases."

The commission would keep the two of them occupied for weeks and would provide enough for them to live comfortably for several months, so Strang was as happy as he could be. Keeping busy and providing for his daughter were the only things that concerned him since Etheswitha had left him. Producing all of these spear heads for Eanfrith's gesithas fulfilled both of those criteria. Perhaps he'd even have enough money to buy a slave. Sunniva could not be expected to work the forge with him forever. She was already old enough to be married and the gods only knew why no man had proposed to her already.

The day was warm with only a few feathers of cloud scudding high in the azure sky. Despite the shade over the forge, which helped protect the fire from the elements and made it easier on sunny days to gauge when the glow of the metal was right for working, it was sweltering work. By midday father and daughter were drenched in sweat and eager for a rest.

Sunniva went into the house and brought out a loaf, some cheese and a pot of ale. They took off their leather aprons and sat in the shade of the oak tree that grew beside the path. They ate their meal in companionable silence. The township bustled around them. A drover walked a small group of oxen past them on the way to the tannery. The acrid smell of the piss used to cure the leather wafted to them from time to time on the light breeze.

A group of mounted men approached from the south. At the head of the column was a giant of a man. He was armoured, had a shield and metal helm hanging from his saddle. A sword strapped to a baldric was slung over his shoulder. The rest of the men were similarly accoutred, though none with finer armour, steed or weapons.

The huge warrior was familiar, but for a moment Sunniva could not place him. She knew all of the warriors in Gefrin by sight. Many had arrived early in the new year with Eanfrith. These men were riding from the south, not from the northern kingdom where the heirs of Bernicia had been exiled. She looked up at the figure silhouetted against the bright sky and was at last able to put a name to the warrior. Bassus. King Edwin's hearth-ward. His most trusted thegn.

Strang recognised him at the same instant. Father and daughter both tensed. Bassus pulled on his reins and drew up in front of them. Now that they had placed Bassus, many of the other riders' faces quickly came back to them. All had been Edwin's men. Edwin had seized the throne of Bernicia from Eanfrith's father and caused his sons' exile for years. The arrival of several armed men who had previously served Edwin could quickly spark violence.

Sensing their nervousness, Bassus smiled. Strang stood, defensively moving in front of his daughter. "Do not fear, good smith Strang," said Bassus, who had also recognised the smith and recalled his name, "we have no quarrel here with you or anyone in Gefrin. We carry a message for King Eanfrith. He is residing at the great hall?"

"That he is, lord." Strang said.

Bassus thanked him and Strang stepped back from the path. The riders moved off towards the largest building in Gefrin. They passed quickly. From where they stood, Sunniva and Strang could now make out a couple of people straggling behind. Curious, they waited to see who these travellers were rather than returning to their work at the forge.

After some time they were able to pick out details. One was large with blond hair. He carried himself with the confidence of a warrior, had a spear in his hand and a sword hanging at his side. On his back were a circular shield and a pack. The other was a bright-faced young man, who walked with a light step. Over his shoulder he had a strangely-shaped, leather-encased box.

As they got close, Sunniva studied the warrior more closely. From afar she had thought him older. Now she could see that despite the hard edges and scars on his face he was probably not much older than her. Under the grime of long days of travel, piercing blue eyes shone with a cold intensity.

With a start, Sunniva realised she was staring and the warrior's eyes had met hers, returning her gaze. At the same instant, both looked away, but not before Strang had noticed the silent exchange. This boy warrior would be trouble.

Strang stepped forward once more, unconsciously placing himself between his daughter and these newcomers. "Do you travel with Bassus?" the smith asked.

"Yes," answered the blue-eyed warrior, somewhat tersely.

"But not as quickly. Our legs are not as long as their horses'," interjected the other young man, smiling.

Strang pointed up the path to the great hall that dominated the village. "They've gone up there to see the king."

"Thank you," said the blond warrior, and then, looking at Sunniva, "My name is Beobrand."

Sunniva felt her cheeks redden. There was a pause, and when it became apparent that Beobrand was not going to introduce his companion, the young man carrying the unusual box took a step forward and said in a fine, clear, musical voice, "I am Leofwine."

The smith glowered at them for a few moments. He did not want to have anything to do with Bassus or these strangers. They would only bring discord, he was sure. And the young warrior standing in front of him, staring unashamedly at his daughter, would be the most problematic of all. He toyed with the idea of not returning the introduction, but thought better of it. However young they were, one of these men was heavily armed. They were also friends with Bassus and his band. It would be very unwise to antagonise them with rudeness.

He forced a smile. "I'm Strang and this is my daughter, Sunniva. Well met, but now we must be getting back to work."

With that, he ushered Sunniva back to the forge. He gave the travellers a curt nod.

Sunniva pumped the bellows to get the forge hot enough to start working again. She waited until her father had turned away from her to pick up an iron billet and then she cast a furtive glance at the young warrior, Beobrand, as he made his way up the hill towards the king's hall. As if he sensed her gaze, he looked round. Their eyes met again for the briefest of moments. Sunniva looked back at the forge and pushed on the bellows with all her strength, trying to convince herself that the heat from the fire was what was making her face burn.

The sight of Sunniva, the girl at the forge, was enough to make Beobrand forget the pain of his blistered feet from the days of walking. She was the most beautiful girl he had seen since... his mind brought back to him the face of Cathryn. He felt a chill down his spine as he realised how similar Sunniva was to the ill-fated girl. They could easily have passed for sisters. He couldn't help staring at her. It was as if the gods had brought Cathryn back as a reminder to him of his failure to protect her. Sunniva had seemed equally interested in him, which made Beobrand all the more unnerved. Sunniva's likeness to Cathryn, coupled with her intense focus on him, added to his feelings of unease.

During the brief conversation with Strang, Beobrand struggled not to see Cathryn's blood-drenched face, staring up at him from the cold earth. Beobrand had not told anybody of the death of Cathryn. He held the secret tight inside. Ashamed to talk of it, but also unable to let it go. Frequently, his mind picked at the hidden memory as his fingers picked at the scabs that itched over the wounds he'd received in the fight with Hengist. In contrast to the bitter days of death and pain in the forest, it was now warm and the sun shone bright in the sky. And Sunniva was vibrant and alive, and looking at him with a warm interest that both excited and scared him. By the goddess Frige, the girl was magnificent.

Beobrand stole a glance over his shoulder to catch one more look at her as they walked away. To his embarrassment, he found himself staring straight into her eyes. He quickly turned back, but not before noting the shape of her body under her mantle as she stretched to pull on her leather apron. Beobrand walked forward, resolutely staring at the ground ahead. His cheeks were warm and they reddened further when Leofwine began to hum a love song under his breath. It seemed the connection between Sunniva and Beobrand had not been missed by his companion. He could expect jokes for several days to come. He tried to frown, but a smile threatened to form on his mouth. In an effort to divert the attention away from him, he pointed at the great hall that loomed over the other buildings in the township of Gefrin.

"Bassus said it was impressive," he said.

"But he didn't mention smith Strang or his equally impressive daughter," replied Leofwine, smiling broadly.

Beobrand tried to ignore him and focused on the great hall.

It was lofty, as well as long. Higher than any building he'd seen, its roof was made of wooden shingles. The gables were adorned with carvings of animals and swirling decorations, painted in vibrant shades of red, green, yellow and blue. At the apex of the roof, at the top of the south-facing gable, the roof was garlanded with what appeared to be two wooden horns. It was a truly magnificent building and was clearly designed to instil awe.

The main door into the hall stood open. There were two men standing either side of it. Both were armed with spears and eyed the two young men with interest.

Beobrand and Leofwine approached with some trepidation. Each had come to Gefrin for his own ends and was now unsure how to proceed.

Leofwine had decided to seek his fortune as a bard. He was talented and played the lyre with great skill. These traits, in addition to his innate charisma and easy-going nature, made him sure to succeed in Beobrand's opinion.

Beobrand sought a lord to serve. Someone worthy of the majestic sword that had become his. At night he would draw out the blade and gaze at it in the firelight. He was entranced by the patterns on the blade. It shimmered like the skin of an iridescent serpent.

A lordly gift to his brother for his bravery should now serve a good lord again. Wyrd had brought Hrunting back into the hands of its rightful heir. Beobrand would make sure it was put to good use.

"How could such a blade have failed Octa?" Beobrand had asked Bassus one night, as they sat by the campfire.

"I do not know," Bassus had replied. "But I would guess that Hengist surprised him with Elda, and killed them both."

"Hengist is like an animal."

Bassus had looked at Beobrand for a long time, his eyes reflecting the red of the flames. "No. Animals do not kill for pleasure. Hengist loves killing and death."

Thoughts of Hengist roiled in his mind, often bubbling to the surface the way scum floats atop a cauldron of broth. How he wished he had seized the moment in Engelmynster and slain his brother's murderer. The night after the fight, he had sworn his oath anew on Hrunting and before all the gods that he would avenge his brother's murder. At Octa's grave he had not known his killer's identity, now he had an object for his revenge.

Perhaps Hengist had succumbed later from his wounds. It was possible. Probable even. Yet somehow Beobrand doubted he would die that easily.

After the fight with Hengist, Beobrand had been unsure of what to do. He was quietly proud of his victory over the older warrior. Despite the element of chance involved, he knew he had held his own better than most warriors would have done and it was no mean feat. Alric, Bassus and the others had all praised his bravery. Leofwine had told the story of the battle between Beobrand and Hengist the following night at a meal attended by most of the inhabitants of Engelmynster. The way Leofwine recounted the fight, Beobrand battled against a giant of a man with the strength of ten bears, the cunning of a fox and the prowess of Tiw, god of war, in battle. Beobrand, stiff from the exertion and injuries he'd suffered, had smiled at the story, embarrassed at the embellishments. He had been surprised that even the people who had witnessed the fight began to believe some of the more outlandish elements of

Leofwine's telling. By the time he had turned in that night most of the village would have sworn he had disarmed Hengist with a single blow of his langseax before picking up the fine sword that had once belonged to his own brother and delivering the winning blow to Hengist's face with a flourish.

Falling asleep that night, the noise of the merriment washing over him, he had mused on the power there was in Leofwine's words. His story had already grown in the telling and he wondered whether the truth would be remembered at all once it had been told a few more times.

Following the celebration, he had begun to feel better. His wounds were clean and healing well. The weather had broken. Clear skies brought warmth to the land and, it seemed to Beobrand, to that part inside of him that was still chilled from the winter and the events he had witnessed.

Bassus had come to him that morning shortly after he had woken.

"What do you plan to do now?" Bassus asked.

"I don't know." Beobrand thought of the sudden rush of excitement that overtook him in battle. Of the total focus and control. And of the feeling of power he had felt at taking lives. At beating armed men who sought to kill him or harm others. It was a much better feeling than that of impotence he had felt at the death of Edita, Rheda, his mother, Octa... Cathryn. "I'm not sure why, but I want to fight," he said.

"I know why – you're good at it. Come north with me. You could join Eanfrith's warband. He'll need good men. Or, if you prefer, you can come back with me to Cantware."

Beobrand had gingerly touched his wounded side, wincing. He could not return to Cantware and the memories he had fled from. "I can't travel yet. My wounds will open."

Bassus had given him a long look. "We can wait for you to

heal. We've made good time from Cantware," he lied, "and the men could use a few days of rest before continuing." Bassus felt he owed it to his friend, Octa, to protect his younger brother. But more than that, he liked the boy and would welcome his company.

And so they had lingered in Engelmynster for several more days until Beobrand was fit enough for the long walk north into Bernicia.

When they finally left, Leofwine had joined them. "If we stay longer here, we'll end up with half the village joining us," joked Bassus, as they said their farewells to the inhabitants of Engelmynster.

Coenred took the parting hard. He loved Beobrand like an older brother and looked upon him with the awe of a younger sibling. He clung to Beobrand as the horsemen rode from the village.

"You will come back again, won't you?" he had sobbed.

"I will return, if the gods will it." Beobrand could not bring himself to give false promises.

Coenred had nodded and turned away. He did not know what the Christ or any of the old gods willed for Beobrand.

Alric and Wilda had looked upon Leofwine's leaving with a mixture of pride and fear. They each hugged him briefly. Then, while he said goodbye to Wybert, Alric had approached Beobrand.

"You look after my boy," the older man had said, gripping Beobrand's arm and looking searchingly into his eyes. "God go with you."

The journey north to Gefrin had taken another week, the pace slowed by the walkers. A couple of the men had commented that Ethelburga wouldn't be pleased with the delay, but Bassus had shrugged and said with a tinge of menace in his voice that she would never know, unless someone told her. The comments had stopped after that.

They took turns riding, allowing the injured Beobrand to ride for longer stretches than the others in the first days, until the sour looks he was receiving from some of the men made him do more than his fair share of walking. Bassus noticed that despite starting out annoyed at Beobrand and Leofwine for slowing them down and making them walk for part of the journey, the men began to warm to them. Each of them was likable in his own way, and it wasn't long before they were both accepted into the group.

The terrain had gone from forest to rolling hills of scrubby grassland. They travelled past the great Wall. Beobrand had seen it before when travelling with Edwin's host to Elmet and had questioned Bassus about it. "It cuts the land from east to west," Bassus said. Beobrand thought there could be no way such a huge thing could exist, but it disappeared into the distance in each direction and Bassus seemed serious.

"Who could have built such a wall?" Leofwine had asked as they made their way through a gap in the Wall, amazed at the scale of the stone edifice.

"The same people who made that angel floor back at Engelmynster, I'd imagine," Bassus had answered. "Some say they were giants, but they were just men from a land far to the south. They built the road we're walking on too, I'd wager."

"I wonder what happened to them," Leofwine had pondered.

That night sitting by the campfire, Leofwine told a tale of giants building mountains and fighting each other, throwing rocks across the sea from one island to another. The tale made the men laugh, but Beobrand awoke in the night, shivering, when thunder rolled in the distance, convinced that the giants who had made the Wall were returning.

The weather had been mild on the journey, but the people of the land were still afraid after the harsh winter of roving bands of brigands and Cadwallon's forces marauding with impunity. Often, when they approached houses, they found them empty, the occupants having fled. Once they found a cow lowing pitifully. Its udders were painfully full of milk, so Beobrand, who had worked the land in Cantware since he was a tiny boy, milked it into a wooden pot they found in the abandoned house. The cow quietened and the men all had a drink of fresh warm milk. As they left the cow and house behind, Bassus placed a clipped half of a small golden coin inside the empty pot.

This pattern was repeated whenever they stopped at a dwelling for food. Whether they took something from an empty house, or were fed by bolder inhabitants of some of the villages on their way, Bassus always paid for their provisions, either in coin, or in some form of labour. At one homestead, the men helped chop firewood, at another, they carried water up from the nearby stream. The lord of one hall had accepted Leofwine's singing as payment for food and lodging for the night. Leofwine had told again the story of Beobrand's victory over Hengist. Beobrand was embarrassed and proud in equal measure as all eyes had turned to him.

How different it was to travel in this way, thought Beobrand. Paying your way instead of taking what you desired by force. People still feared them. They were armed warriors, after all. But the look in their eyes held something else too: respect.

As they stood now in front of the great hall of Gefrin, it was not respect, but amused disdain they saw in the eyes of the warriors flanking the door.

"What do you want?" enquired the shorter of the two. He was heavyset and had a round, almost soft face, but the silver rings on his arms denoted him as a warrior of some renown. "You with those others, from Cantware?"

"We are travelling with them, yes," answered Beobrand. "We also wish to have an audience with the king."

"Oh, you do, do you?" sneered the thickset man. "Well, we'll see about that. What's it worth, boy?"

Beobrand was nonplussed. He felt his face redden. The man was treating them with contempt, as if they were nothing more than children. Beobrand dropped his hand to the hilt of his sword and the two guards stiffened.

Before anyone could make a move, a tall man approached them from the other side of the great hall. "There you are, boys! What took you so long? You didn't stop to sample the local lasses already, did you?" It was Gram, one of the men who had travelled from Cantware with Bassus. He was about ten years older than Beobrand, almost as tall as Bassus, but leaner. He flashed his quick smile at the two guards, assessing the situation instantly.

"Don't kill these two, lads. They're not ripe yet!"

The shorter guard laughed. The other one smiled in return to Gram's amused grin. All the tension vanished.

"Why don't you boys come and help me brush down the horses and get them stabled? Bassus is inside talking to the king and the likes of us will have to wait until we're invited in." He put his arm around Beobrand's shoulders and led him away around the side of the hall towards the other buildings there. Leofwine followed.

When they were out of earshot of the guards, Gram whispered, "You need to be careful of your quick temper. When I first saw you, you were doing your best to anger King Edwin in his hall at Bebbanburg. The next time I saw you, you were knee-deep in mud and slugging it out with none other than Hengist, one of the scariest sons of a whore I've ever seen fight. And now you've been on your own for no time and you are almost coming to blows with the door wards of King Eanfrith's great hall! I've seen you with a blade, and you have some skills, but you won't live long if you carry on like this."

"He's right, Beobrand," said Leofwine, as they reached the horses. "The man was clearly a buffoon, but he didn't get those arm rings by playing a tafl game."

Beobrand knew they were both right. It worried him how easily he was ready to fight somebody. He had no qualms with fighting when it was necessary, but he would be stupid to get himself injured or killed over a petty offence.

His hands were shaking as he reached out to take the brush Gram proffered to him. Leofwine pretended not to notice. He shrugged off his pack and began helping with the other horses.

Beobrand felt his nerves settle as he rubbed the horse's flank, the rhythm and rasp of the motion calming both him and the mount.

He took deep breaths, the scent of the horse and leather enveloping him. He walked around the horse to brush the other side. From this vantage point he could look down the road and make out the roof of the forge, nestling beside the large tree where they had spoken to Strang and his daughter, Sunniva. Beobrand thought of how her hair had glowed in the sunlight.

Leofwine cast a sidelong look at his friend. It was obvious where Beobrand's gaze was directed. Leofwine smiled in the knowledge that he had been right to joke about him falling for the blacksmith's daughter.

This time though, he chose to keep his thoughts to himself.

13

The great hall was almost as noisy in the early morning as it had been the night before.

Beobrand winced as one of the women cleaning the hall broke into song. Her voice was not pleasing to the ear and several groans came from different parts of the hall where others had slept following the feasting.

"Well, if you don't like my singing, be off with you," shrieked the woman, in a voice that would easily have cut through the clamour on a battlefield. There were more groans, followed by movement, as men shook themselves awake and staggered to get away from the cacophonous crone. She laughed at their discomfiture.

"You should have thought about this morning last night." She continued to mutter to herself about men and their lack of thought for the consequences of their actions. From time to time she let out another screeching line of song in counterpoint to her murmuring. All the while she swept, cleaned, moved furniture and told the younger women what to do.

"By all the angels in heaven, what unearthly creature from the underworld is abroad in this hall?" Leofwine sat up, all bleary eyes and dishevelled hair. His voice was hoarse from the strenuous singing he'd done to entertain all those present at the feast. The singing had paid off. Eanfrith had seen that Leofwine had talent and had asked him if he would join his retinue as the royal scop. The king was conscious that he had returned from exile after many years and that he needed all the help he could get to bolster his position. Having a singer and storyteller at one's disposal was a great opportunity. Eanfrith of Bernicia's exploits would be told around the hearths in the great hall and in the other royal villas as the king and his retinue travelled throughout the kingdom. All his subjects would hear of his prowess in battle and others would pick up the tales, retelling them in all corners of Bernicia and beyond.

Leofwine was overjoyed. They had only arrived in Gefrin the previous day and he had already found patronage from the king himself. His happiness had led him to a heightened amount of exuberance, which only made the king more pleased in his choice of bard. Leofwine had celebrated with abandon, but now, as the old slave woman cleaning the hall indicated, he was regretting his excesses.

He got up shakily and made his way outside.

Beobrand smiled to himself at the sight of Leofwine stumbling from the hall. He was pleased for his friend's success, but he was not jubilant about his own prospects in the court of this new king of Bernicia. He had naively expected Eanfrith to simply accept him into his warband, as if carrying a sword at his side was proof enough of his abilities. He thought how ridiculous it was that only a few months before he had been a farm boy and now he imagined it was his right to enter the service of a king as a warrior. Bassus had done his best to give Eanfrith a good impression of Beobrand, but as he recounted his exploits, it had become apparent that

Beobrand had fought on Edwin's side in the battle of Elmet. Eanfrith's face had darkened and his interest in Beobrand had waned. He wanted warriors he could trust to be loyal to him.

Later, as the mead flowed, Leofwine recounted the heavily-embellished tale of Beobrand's defeat of Hengist and many turned to look at the young Cantware man with new respect. Beobrand had surveyed the room and noticed the king looking at him through the fug of the great hall. Eanfrith had met his eyes and seemed to smile slightly. He had raised his drinking cup in a silent toast to Beobrand. Beobrand wasn't sure if it had been sincere or in jest, but he had raised his drinking horn in reply and then drained its contents. When he had looked back at the king, Eanfrith was deep in conversation with the silver-haired thegn sitting at his left.

He stretched and walked stiffly from the great hall. He mulled over all of the events of the previous night and was unsure what he should do next. He had not drunk as much as many, but his head was still muzzy. He decided to walk down to the river that ran near the township. The air would clear his head and at the river he could get a drink and splash some water on his face to wash away the sleep that still clung to him like cobwebs.

It was going to be another bright and warm day, but it was still early and there was a slight bite in the air. The peak of the huge hill on the west of Gefrin caught the morning sun. The hill to the east was in shadow. The river was enshrined in a gossamer cloak of mist. As he walked he realised he would pass in front of the forge. His heart quickened at the thought of seeing Sunniva again.

He picked up his pace, hoping for a glimpse of her working with her father. He toyed with the possibility that she might be out walking on the path too, away from her father's cloying protectiveness. They could meet and talk freely. Talk of what? He knew nothing of the girl, and she was probably uninterested in him.

As he drew close to the forge he heard the ringing sound of metal on metal. When the shaded work area of the forge was in sight, he could make out the imposing figure of Strang, bent over the anvil beating red-hot metal with a heavy hammer. As he watched, the smith picked up the metal he was working on, inspected it closely for a moment, and then plunged it into the charcoal embers of the fiercely hot forge fire. There was no sign of Sunniva.

Strang looked up and caught Beobrand's eye.

Beobrand quickly turned away, focusing his attention back to the path and the river ahead.

When Beobrand arrived at the river, the mist that had veiled it from afar was already beginning to burn off as the sun rose in the sky. Thin wisps clung to the shaded areas, where trees overhung the water. He walked down to the water's edge, feet crunching on the smooth pebbles and looked around. Gefrin was awake and there were several people in sight, going about their everyday business.

In the distance, cattle were lowing in the large fenced off area where all the livestock of the town was kept. A cart, pulled by an ox, was being driven by a short, swarthy man towards the river crossing. The ox was labouring under the weight as the path went slightly uphill before it dropped down toward the ford, and the man beat the beast mercilessly on the back with a long, supple stick of birch.

In the other direction, back towards the great hall, the smoke from many cooking fires hazed the air, casting a pall in the sky over the town. A boy chased a group of geese down the road towards the river, waving his arms and whooping. The geese protested noisily, honking and flapping their wings as they waddled to keep ahead of the boy.

Beobrand turned and walked along the river bank, away from the path, upstream to where the water would be clean of any of the waste from the people and animals of Gefrin. There were trees and bushes along the banks, which meant that from time to time he had to move away from the water's edge, but they would provide some cover from any prying townsfolk. Beobrand wasn't overly concerned if someone saw him bathing, but he would prefer some privacy if possible.

After some time, he found a gap between two trees which provided some shelter and also a gentle slope down to the water. He pulled off his kirtle and hung it over a low branch. He had no weapons to worry about, having left his sword and spear back at the great hall. He had handed them to the king's door wards the previous evening before the feast. He was not one of Eanfrith's trusted companions and was therefore not permitted to carry arms inside the hall. Bassus, Gram and the others had also relinquished their weapons, accepting that the hospitality of their host would only stretch so far.

He knelt by the water and scooped up a double-handful, splashing it onto his face. It was icy and it made him gasp. He repeated the process, enjoying the tingling sensation that the water left on his skin. He sat back and checked his most recent wounds. They were healing well, but his side was still tight, and the scar was a vivid red. It remained tender to the touch.

As he looked up again, just about to reach into the water for a drink, he noticed something floating in the water. It was a leather bucket and it circled slowly in the current as it drifted towards his position. He could see that he would not be able to reach the bucket from the bank, so he quickly pulled off his shoes and stepped into the water. He waded out towards the deeper, colder water at the middle of the river. The water came up to his thighs in a couple of steps. From here, he was easily able to reach out and snag the bucket as it reached him.

He waded back to the shallows and hauled himself up onto the bank. Whose bucket could it be? It might have floated from another village altogether. That was when he heard the girl's voice, raised in anger.

"By Thunor's balls!"

The expletive came from upstream, but didn't sound very far away. Beobrand leapt up, suddenly wishing he had thought to retrieve his weapons before leaving the safety of the hall. For a moment he thought of the cold, dark forest clearing where another girl's screams had split the night's silence. Then, without pausing for more thought, he ran in the direction of the noise.

He leapt over a fallen branch, and skidded to a halt when he saw the source of the commotion.

Sunniva had her back to him, but he recognised the curve of her neck and the spun-gold brilliance of her hair. She was leaning over the river, looking downstream. He supposed she was trying to see where her bucket had gone. She continued to shout curses that would make hardened warriors blush.

Beobrand watched her for a moment, enjoying the scene and learning some new insults.

When she paused for breath, he cleared his throat. "Looking for this?" He held out the bucket.

She spun around, instantly on the defensive. He smiled at her, trying to put her at ease. "I've never heard anyone swear like you before. And I've been in battle and sailed aboard a ship."

"Well, I dropped the bucket," she said, as if that was explanation enough. Her cheeks were coloured, whether from the exertion of shouting abuse at the errant receptacle, or from being overheard by him, Beobrand could not tell.

"I rescued it for you," he said, proffering the bucket to her again.

She stepped closer and took it from him. "Thank you," she said, then, looking down at his dripping trousers, "You're soaked. Did you jump into the river to get it?"

He smiled sheepishly. "It seemed like the right thing to do." He was suddenly acutely aware that his chest was bare. "I'd better go back and get my clothes and shoes," he said, awkwardly.

"Wait," she said. "Let me fill both the buckets and I'll come with you. I have to take the water back to my father. He'll be wondering where I have got to anyway."

She stooped, picked up both the bucket Beobrand had retrieved from the water and another one that had been resting at her feet, and dipped them into the river. When they were full, she stood, balancing the load with one bucket in each hand.

"Let me help you," Beobrand said. She didn't protest as he took one bucket from her. Their fingers brushed and he felt his stomach flutter. He could sense her gazing intently at his muscled torso as he walked in front of her to where he'd left his clothes.

He sat to pull on his shoes and flinched slightly as he stretched to pull on his tunic.

"Those scars look new," she remarked. "And painful. How did you get them?"

"You'll have to ask my friend, Leofwine, to tell you the story. It sounds much more exciting when he tells it."

She laughed.

They walked back to the forge slowly. Each wanting the moment to last as long as possible.

"Where are you from? You speak strangely," she said.

"You're the second girl to say that to me in Bernicia," he answered.

"Oh?" She raised an eyebrow archly.

"Yes. She had golden hair too."

"And who was this golden-haired beauty?"

"I never said she was beautiful." His cheeks grew hot as he teased her.

"Wasn't she?"

"Yes, she was. And a princess."

Sunniva let out a small gasp. "You jest with me."

"No, it is true. She was Edwin's daughter, Eanflæd."

"But she is only a child!"

"I know, but she is beautiful." He paused for effect. "But not as beautiful as you."

Now it was her turn to blush.

Beobrand smiled. He had never been good talking with girls, but talking with Sunniva seemed natural to him. It was hard to believe they had only met the day before. He had not felt happy for a long time, but the encounter with Sunniva lifted his spirits. He didn't want the moment to end, but he could sense her getting restless as they got close to her home.

"I've already taken much longer to fetch the water than I should have. I need to get back," she said. "Shall we meet again by the river? Tomorrow at the same time, or a bit earlier?" She sounded breathless, as if shocked by the audacity of her own words.

Beobrand's step faltered. A few drops of water splashed from the bucket he was carrying. He turned to look at her, trying to see whether she was making fun of him in some way. She looked in earnest, her cheeks flushed and her eyes bright. He swallowed hard. "I'll be there," he said.

"Make sure my father doesn't see you going down there. Go round behind the forge."

"Sunniva! What are you doing dawdling there with that good-for-nothing foreigner?" Strang had stepped out from the forge and was holding his hands on his hips, glaring at the two of them.

Sunniva turned, lowering her eyes and walked back to where her father waited. "He's not good for nothing, father, he stopped me losing one of the buckets…" she mumbled.

Strang looked exasperated. "Well get it back then, child!"

She turned and quickly retrieved the other bucket from Beobrand. "Goodbye," she said, followed by a whispered "See you tomorrow." While her back was still turned to her father.

"Come on, girl," Strang shooed her into the forge, giving Beobrand one last long, piercing stare before returning to his work.

Beobrand could feel the distrust washing off of Strang like the waves of heat from his forge, but it did not bother him. His headache had gone and he felt wide awake. Exhilarated.

He looked up at the sky and smiled. It was going to be another gloriously warm day and he no longer cared whether Eanfrith would offer him a place in his warband.

Beobrand had just talked to the most beautiful girl in Bernicia and she wanted to see him again.

★

"The man's an idiot!" Bassus roared. "And a rude idiot at that."

Gram and Beobrand both looked around furtively to see if anyone had overheard.

Gram said, "Hush yourself. You're as foolhardy as young Beobrand here. You know as well as any man that you cannot speak about a king that way. Unless you don't want to be returning home, that is."

"He's not worthy to be called king. I've a good mind to knock some sense into him, the little runt." The veins on Bassus' temples bulged. "He called her Edwin's whore! By Christ's bones and all the old gods, if I'd had my sword, Bernicia would be looking for a new heir now!"

It was afternoon and they were walking in the livestock enclosure on the southern edge of town. There were sheep, cattle and some geese in the enclosure, but none of the watching ceorls or thralls were near enough to make out Bassus' words. At least Gram hoped not, or they would have to leave Gefrin in a hurry.

Until a few moments before, Gram and Beobrand had been sitting in the afternoon sun outside the great hall while Bassus had been inside giving Eanfrith the message from Ethelburga. They had been relaxed and drowsy in the heat of the sun, enjoying the peace when they had heard a crash from inside the hall. The guards posted on the main entrance had made to enter the building, but before they could, Bassus had burst forth in a terrible rage and barged them both out of the way, oblivious to any danger posed by their weapons.

Beobrand and Gram had leapt up and followed Bassus, managing to steer him to this relatively isolated area of the town.

"But what exactly happened?" asked Beobrand.

Bassus continued to pace, his face red. "I gave him the gift.

He laughed in my face. Said he'd hoped for something more useful than a psalter. Asked what good a book was going to do him when Cadwallon was banging on the door of the great hall." Bassus' breathing was finally slowing and he seemed to be in control of his emotions once more.

"Well, he has a point," ventured Gram.

Bassus shot him a withering glance. "I don't care if he's right, he had no reason to insult her. When I gave him her message, he said he cared not for Edwin's whore's whelps!" He walked on, brooding. "I lost my temper then."

Gram and Beobrand shared a look, unsure what to say.

Bassus stopped abruptly and said to Gram, "Round up the men. We'll not be staying another night in this place."

"But…" Gram stammered, trying to find the words that would convince Bassus to allow them to stay at least another night. He'd spent the previous night with a comely slave girl who had performed some rather memorable feats with him and he'd been looking forward to seeing what further delights she had to offer. He didn't bother to continue protesting, however. Bassus was not going to change his mind, that much was certain. He'd known the man for years and he was as stubborn as the animal that gave him his name.

Bassus calmed down quickly. He'd purged himself of the anger and made a decision, now he moved on. To continue raging over Eanfrith's insulting behaviour was a waste of energy and would get him nowhere. This ability to push his emotions to one side and remain calm, coupled with his passionate rages, made him a formidable opponent in battle. Calculating, yet ferocious.

"Gram," Bassus said, "get the men together. Find our weapons and buy us some provisions. I want to be ready to leave well before nightfall."

Gram looked crestfallen, but resigned to obeying Bassus' orders. As he trudged away, Bassus called after him. "Don't worry, there are plenty of other dirty slave girls south of here!"

Bassus turned to Beobrand. "Sorry, boy. I think my temper has left you in a tight spot. Eanfrith wasn't all that keen on you, and now I can't use any influence on him to make him take you in. Your best bet would be to come with me, back to Cantware. What do you say?"

Beobrand thought of his homeland. The low rolling hills, the dense forests of ash and beech, the white cliffs of the coast. He thought of the old friends he'd left behind, his boyhood friends, Alwin and Scrydan, with whom he'd played on the long summer evenings after his chores were done. He fingered the whale tooth pendant that hung around his neck and thought of Hrothgar and the other sailors who had treated him with such kindness. Part of him cried out to return to Cantware, to what he had once known, to what seemed safe. But his thoughts turned to the billowing furnace of his home as the flames lifted his father's spirit up to the gods. He swallowed hard. He could not return to Hithe. There were too many ghosts and too many questions would be asked of him.

He thought of all that held him in Northumbria. Hengist was still here somewhere and he meant to find him, and kill him. Hengist had killed Octa and Beobrand would use his brother's sword to exact vengeance. He also had friends here. Leofwine was in Gefrin and then, of course, there was Sunniva. He knew it was madness to say he would stay for her, and he would not dream of voicing it out loud, but deep down, he knew it was the truth. Since that morning's chance meeting by the river, she absorbed his every waking thought. He could not stand the thought of going away and not seeing her again. He hoped beyond reason she felt the same way.

"Thank you for the offer," Beobrand said. "In many ways I wish I could go with you, but I feel must stay here. After all, I have to finish what I started with Hengist. Octa must be avenged."

Bassus nodded grimly. "You take care, Beobrand. Hengist is like a serpent, cunning and fast."

"A serpent can be crushed under a boot," replied Beobrand.

By the time the men from Cantware were ready to leave, the sun was dipping low on the horizon, silhouetting the horsemen against the cloudless sky. Bassus and Gram were the last to mount. Gram secured a final bag of provisions to his saddle, then pulled himself up onto his horse in a well-practised motion. Bassus approached Beobrand, who was standing with Leofwine, watching the preparations.

Eanfrith had not deigned to speak with Bassus or any of the Cantware contingent since the afternoon's outburst, but neither had he impeded them in any way. They had been allowed to procure provisions and to retrieve their weapons without hindrance. Not one of Eanfrith's entourage of thegns was there to wish their guests farewell. But Bassus seemed to care nothing for the petty snub of a man he believed unworthy of holding the title of king.

"May your wyrd favour you in your quest for revenge, Beobrand," Bassus said, as he grasped the younger man's wrist in the warrior grip. "I hope our paths cross again one day." Bassus' voice was gruff, but Beobrand knew the older man was sad to be leaving him behind.

"Thank you, Bassus," replied Beobrand, clapping the huge warrior on the shoulder with his left hand and squeezing his wrist firmly with his right. "You've been a true friend.

To me and Octa before me." He wanted to say more. How he'd never forget his kindness. How he would almost certainly be dead without Bassus' help. But, unable to find the words, he merely said, "Have a safe journey."

Bassus nodded. "Leofwine, tell tales of Beobrand's exploits that will travel all the way to Cantware so that I can hear about his progress." He winked, and Leofwine smiled in return.

"I'll sing songs to rival those told of the great Beowulf," the bard replied. "May the Lord watch over you and guide your steps on your travels, and may the wind always be at your back."

Bassus mounted his large chestnut mare, heaving up his bulk with a grunt. He shifted his weight to make himself comfortable, then turned his steed to the south, dug in his heels and made out of Gefrin at a trot. Gram waved at Beobrand and Leofwine and then he and the other warriors followed behind Bassus.

A thin cloud of dust hung in the still, late afternoon air, the sun picking out larger motes like sparks rising in the smoke of a fire. Beobrand watched as the horsemen rode out of the town. Some of the townsfolk had stopped what they were doing to watch the men ride by and with a jolt Beobrand recognised the gold hair of Sunniva, glowing like molten metal. She had run out of the forge and was standing beside the path intently watching the warriors leave. Her father walked slowly from the forge and placed his hand around her shoulders.

When the men had passed, Sunniva turned, scanning her surroundings. When she looked in Beobrand's direction, he raised his hand and smiled a wide grin. She had been looking for him amongst the men headed for Cantware. She was quite some distance away, but she must have spotted him, as she raised her own hand. No sooner had she done this than Strang spun her round and pushed her back towards the forge.

Any doubts he'd had about staying in Bernicia were washed away with that single glance and a wave from Sunniva.

Leofwine witnessed all of this. He'd learnt not to make fun of Beobrand and his interest in this girl from the forge, but he couldn't help chuckling to himself.

Beobrand didn't notice. He felt a strange mixture of emotions. He could still see Bassus, Gram and the others riding in the distance, but seeing Sunniva and having her acknowledge him so openly, made his heart flutter in his chest and left him light-headed. He stood there for a long moment, watching until the horsemen were lost in the haze of distance, unaware that he was smiling all the while.

Beobrand had found it hard to sleep.

He had decided he could not return to the great hall after the scenes between Bassus and the king, so he had asked the hostler, a kindly-looking man, whether he could sleep in the stable. The man, a thrall, felt pity for the young warrior so far from his homeland, so had allowed Beobrand to curl up in his cloak in a corner. But it wasn't the hard floor or the stomping and snorting of the horses that kept him awake, it was the anticipation of seeing Sunniva again in the morning. He had relived the moments when he had seen her the day before. In his memory he watched her waving at him when she saw he hadn't left with the other Cantware men. He felt again the fluttering sensation of excitement in his chest. He wasn't sure what he would say to her, but he could think of nothing else but Strang's daughter.

A long way into the darkest part of the night, he had fallen into a fitful sleep. His dreams did not permit him any rest. In them he had been standing at the water's edge talking to Sunniva. She had turned and her face was awash with blood, her hair sopping with gore. He had felt a terrible pain in his side, which had made him cry out. When he'd looked down he had seen that Sunniva had stabbed him with his own bone-handled knife.

He had awoken, stifling a scream. The hostler's snores resonated around the dark room. Outside, the birds sang to the day that was soon to arrive. Beobrand made his way out of the stable, careful not to disturb the slave's slumber.

The fresh, cold air of the pre-dawn darkness revitalised him and the dream's terror faded quickly. He shivered, his breath misting before him. On the horizon, the sun tinged the sky pink. It would be light soon. He could make his way to the river now, unseen before the town roused itself.

He walked down to the river, the growing glow from the dawn making the buildings and trees loom large and strange around him. By the time he arrived at the river there were a few people beginning to go about their business. It would be another fine day and there was much work to be done for those who worked the land or tended the livestock.

Beobrand retraced his footsteps from the day before and found the small secluded space on the riverbank, hidden from the town by trees. He sat with his back to a tree and waited, listening to the burble of the water as it flowed over the smooth pebbles of the river bed.

Some time passed and the steady sound of the water helped soothe his mind, drawing him down into the sleep that had eluded him during the night.

He awoke to the touch of a hand on his arm. Disorientated

and frightened, he slapped the hand away and sprang to his feet, ready to fight. The sun had risen in the sky, casting deep shadows beside the trees and making the water of the river shine lambently.

Sunniva let out a small gasp, lost her balance and fell backwards, sitting down hard onto the dewy ground.

Beobrand's head cleared quickly. "I'm sorry," he stammered, his cheeks flushing crimson. "Are you alright?" He held out his hand to help her up.

"I'm fine," she said, dusting herself down. "I shouldn't have startled you."

"I wasn't startled," he said, embarrassed, "just asleep."

She raised an eyebrow and they both smiled. Both knowing he'd lied.

"I wasn't sure you'd come," Sunniva said. Then, in a rush, "I thought you'd left with the others yesterday. That I'd not see you again." She looked embarrassed as soon as the words left her mouth.

"Bassus asked me to leave with him," Beobrand replied in a quiet voice.

"Why didn't you?"

"I told him I needed to stay to avenge my brother."

Her face sank. She bit her bottom lip.

"And that is true," Beobrand continued. "But I didn't tell him the other reasons." He looked into her eyes. They were limpid, nervous tears brimming there.

"And what were those reasons?"

"I would not be welcome back in my homeland."

"Oh," disappointment coloured her voice with a hint of sarcasm. "Why is that?"

"I... I cannot say. I will tell you one day, but now, I just cannot." He had not spoken to anyone of his actions in Hithe.

This was as close as he could go to the truth. He did not wish to frighten her away.

She looked at him seriously for a moment and then said, "You mentioned more than one reason. What are the others?"

"Only one other reason," he said.

"And that is?" Sunniva asked.

He hadn't known how to tell her how he felt. It was all so sudden. A girl as beautiful as her must have had plenty of men tell her all sorts of clever things. But she had confirmed what he had suspected: that she'd been scared he was leaving Gefrin bound for Cantware. He dared to believe for a moment that she reciprocated his feelings towards her.

Beobrand swallowed. His throat was dry. "You," he said simply.

Sunniva's face lit up and she grinned. Beobrand felt warm, as if basking in her glow.

After that, their conversation took on the easy playfulness of the day before. They sat close together, not quite touching, but close enough so that the other's physical presence was a constant distraction.

After some time their talk turned to her family.

"Mother died last winter. I still forget sometimes and expect her to be weaving at the loom, or cooking when I go home." She was silent for a moment, looking into the ripples of the river. "It is just father and me now. What of your family?"

"They are all dead. A year ago I had two younger sisters, parents and an older brother. The pestilence came and a murderer killed my brother and now I am alone." Sunniva reached out and placed her hand over his. Her touch made him breathless.

"What do you plan to do?" she asked.

"I don't know. I have sworn to avenge Octa's murder, and I know who killed him. But first I need to gain a place in a lord's gesithas. It is my hope that Leofwine will speak favourably of me with Eanfrith. Perhaps the king will allow me to join his warband."

At the mention of King Eanfrith, Sunniva remembered her father's work on the spear heads. She had been gone a long time and she needed to get back. He would already be suspicious. He was not stupid and he had seen the way she'd waved to Beobrand.

She jumped up. Beobrand felt a stab of loss as her hand left his. "I have to get back home," she said. "I've been gone far too long. My father will be furious."

Beobrand didn't protest. He knew she was right. "When can I see you again?" he asked.

"I'm not sure. I don't think my father will allow me to come down to the river for water again tomorrow. Not now that I've been late back twice." She stooped to the river and filled the two buckets she had brought with her. "Don't walk back with me today. If he sees you, he'll only be angrier."

"Can you get away tonight?" Beobrand asked.

Sunniva bit her lip, calculating. "Maybe. He often falls asleep soon after sundown. I could sneak out then."

"Very well then. I'll wait here for you after dusk. Try and get away. If you can't, I'll visit you tomorrow at the forge."

"Oh no, father would be so angry."

"Well, you'd better make sure you get out tonight then," Beobrand grinned.

Despite her nervousness at the prospect of her father's anger when she was late back and the possibility of being caught in the evening, Sunniva found herself smiling too. She leant in quickly to Beobrand and kissed him on the cheek.

"I'll bring a blanket. It will be cold down here at night," she whispered huskily, her breath warm against his ear.

Without waiting for a response, she turned and walked away as quickly as she could while balancing the weight of the two buckets.

Beobrand watched her leave. The sway of her hips and the ghost of her kiss on his cheek made him ache for her.

14

"Well don't just stand there. Tell me where he is," thundered Eanfrith. It was important to keep up a show of strength in front of his men.

The messenger bowed his head, unsure what to say.

"Cadwallon, you fool! Where is he and is he on the move?"

The man was awestruck at talking to a king. He swallowed deeply. He had not been offered a drink before having to talk to Eanfrith. He opened his mouth to speak, but his voice cracked in his throat. He swallowed again and finally managed to utter the message he'd been sent to deliver.

"My lord, and your humble servant, Bebeodan, would inform you that Cadwallon, may God cast his soul into hell, has camped south of the great Wall and is amassing his troops there. When I left my lord's hall, two days hence, they were not moving. It is hard to know when they will. But it was clear they were readying for war again."

A murmur ran through the men assembled in the great hall. They all knew that war was almost a certainty, but to have it confirmed, brought the truth of it closer to reality.

A grizzled, grey-bearded warrior who stood close to the

king said, "Cadwallon can be upon us in a matter of days. We should fall back to Bebbanburg. It is impregnable."

"I shall not retreat from this upstart," answered Eanfrith. Scand had once been a warrior of renown, but Eanfrith found him to be cautious almost to the point of cowardice. "Bernicia will not be cowed by a rabble of Waelisc. I do not fear Cadwallon."

There was another ripple of murmured comments, but nobody wanted to point out the obvious to the king. Cadwallon, with Penda's aid, had already defeated Edwin, who had called himself Bretwalda, king of all Albion. After that the Waelisc king of Gwynedd had gone on to kill Osric, heir to the throne of Deira.

Scand set his shoulders. "We will of course stand with you against Cadwallon, but we should not throw away any chance of advantage we may have. Gefrin is exposed. This place is not built to defend, it is built for leisure, and for making speeches in that ludicrous stepped contraption." Scand spoke with obvious disdain of the tiered, wooden auditorium that stood at the centre of the royal township. Apparently, Paulinus, Edwin's priest, had preached to masses of people there. Scand thought it an extravagant waste of good timber which would have been better spent creating defences. "If we stay here, we are vulnerable. We should join your brother at Bebbanburg."

"Nonsense," replied Eanfrith, an edge of anger entering his tone at having his authority challenged in front of his men. The thought of having to spend time with his righteous brother, cramped atop the crag of Bebbanburg was more than he could bear. He had told Oswald to hold the rocky fortress to keep him away. His brother had his uses, but he was not enjoyable company. Besides, Eanfrith preferred the open land about Gefrin to the rocky outcrop of the cliff-top stronghold.

"To retreat would be to appear craven in the eyes of our enemies and the people of Bernicia. Gefrin is the most majestic of halls and should be my base. I must be seen to be strong."

Scand clenched his jaw, but nodded, resigned to losing the argument. He glanced to the shadowy edges of the hall, where Eanfrith's queen, Finola, sat with their son, Talorcan. She was almost childlike in size, tiny and fragile. Her finely-brushed tresses of flame-red hair fell down her back, a shimmering sheen in the moving light from the fire. Finola looked back at Scand, but her face was expressionless, resigned. Talorcan's eyes twinkled with interest, but he knew to keep quiet in the presence of his father.

"You are right, my lord," said Scand. "But think of your queen and the atheling. We should at least be prepared to defend ourselves if the moment arises. Would you send some men out to keep watch on Cadwallon and to bring us news when he moves northward?"

Eanfrith waved his hand magnanimously. He cared nothing for Finola; he had married her to build an alliance with the people of her Pictish tribe, and he found her boring and unappealing. At least she had given him a son. But Scand doted on her as a father and his gesithas seemed to enjoy her presence in the hall. Talorcan frequently angered him by speaking out of turn, but he saw much of himself in the boy and could not help feeling proud as he grew into a hand-some child.

"Very well, send out some riders. And you," Eanfrith turned back to the cowering messenger, "have done well and have our thanks. After you have eaten and rested, you must take my men south with you and show them where Cadwallon is camped."

The messenger bowed nervously before leaving.

Eanfrith returned to the game of tafl he had been playing with some of his thegns. Conversations started in the hall as the news was discussed.

Scand watched as the messenger left the hall and then looked at the king. Eanfrith was laughing at the predicament of his opponent. His pieces were surrounded by the king's and he looked set to lose all of the stake he had bet in the next turn of the game.

Scand frowned. He loved Eanfrith. In many ways he was a good king. He had served him for many years. Stood by him in exile and fought in the shieldwall at his side. He was brave in battle, and was a good strategist and planner. This translated into making him a formidable tafl opponent. He always seemed two moves ahead.

Scand hoped that Eanfrith knew what his next moves were in the deadly game he was playing with Cadwallon. Staying at Gefrin made no sense to Scand and the Waelisc king was not someone to be taken lightly. But Eanfrith was as stubborn as he was skilled at tafl. His mind would not be changed.

Eanfrith made his final move, winning the game. The beaten thegn angrily swept the pieces off of the board onto the rush-strewn floor. The watching men jeered and laughed as the man handed over an arm ring to his king.

Scand smiled too, despite himself, before remembering his misgivings. He prayed they would win the real game as easily. They all stood to lose a lot more than scyllings or silver arm rings if they lost.

The messenger's news of Cadwallon amassing troops in the south and King Eanfrith's response rapidly spread through the small township's populace. By noon everyone in Gefrin knew that the Waelisc warlord was once again threatening their land. Edwin, a great leader of men, had faced Cadwallon in open battle and been defeated. Many were the voices that whispered about the wisdom of this new king's decision to remain at Gefrin. The place had already lost many of its inhabitants in the last few months, as they'd drifted away to seek a safer place to live. Those who had stayed were hardy and not easily frightened, but most took the precaution of ensuring they had their important belongings packed and ready to carry with them should they need to leave suddenly. That night some would sneak into the darkness to bury items of worth that they could not easily carry.

Beobrand heard the news at midday. He met with Leofwine to share food.

"Cadwallon prepares to invade," said Leofwine, his face flushed with excitement.

"Why so happy? Death and sorrow will come when Cadwallon marches."

"And glory too," retorted Leofwine. "I will have tales to tell and songs to sing."

The bard's high spirits were infectious and Beobrand smiled despite himself. "I have seen nothing to suggest the men prepare for battle."

"Well, that is the thing. They aren't. Eanfrith said he is not frightened of Cadwallon and he will not retreat, or march south. Old Scand was furious."

"The greybeard?" asked Beobrand. He had seen him sitting at the high table and walking with the king and queen.

"Aye. In the end, they sent some men south to watch the Waelisc."

"Hardly the stuff of legends for your songs then."

"Not yet, but battle will come and I will have my stories and songs. It is wonderful, Beobrand." Leofwine realised what he had said and continued quickly. "That sounded wrong to my own ears. I mean it is wonderful to have a good king who allows me to spend my days musing over tunes and rhymes and then to perform them every night. That is the stuff of legends! I never thought I would be able to do this." He waved his hands animatedly.

"It gladdens me to see you content. I give you joy, Leofwine."

"A few days ago I was working with my father in Engelmynster and now I am attended by slaves and fed delicacies I had not even heard of before, let alone tasted."

Beobrand laughed aloud at his friend's happiness.

"Wyrd is a strange thing, Beobrand," the scop continued. "I followed you here with no idea what would come of it, and now look at me. Singing to a king and pampered like an atheling." He clapped his hands. "I will write a song about it.

"The good news for you is that Eanfrith will need all the warriors he can find. I'll make sure I mention some of your exploits tonight."

"Some warrior I am, I haven't even got my sword back," complained Beobrand, but with little vehemence. As far as he knew, Hrunting still rested in the storeroom where he had relinquished it on first entering the king's great hall. He would retrieve it when he needed it, but it seemed as safe a place as any for the time being. He was more concerned with how much longer it would be until nightfall and he could meet Sunniva again.

"You should seek an audience with the king tomorrow. Ask to have your sword returned to you so that you can use it in the service of Eanfrith and Bernicia. Hopefully, I'll have convinced him of your worth with my stories and songs by then." Leofwine smiled broadly and Beobrand nodded, absentmindedly.

"I'll do that."

Leofwine clapped him on the shoulder and rose. "Well, I had better get started on a song about you for tonight," he said, smiling broadly.

Left to himself, Beobrand decided to scout around the environs of Gefrin in an effort to keep himself busy and to make time pass more quickly. He walked past the fenced off enclosure where the cattle were safely housed. He noticed for the first time the mound at one side of the enclosure. He had seen such barrows before and paused, wondering who was buried there.

He headed towards the great hall and decided to investigate the strange structure that was in the middle of the royal buildings. Leofwine said it was especially designed for speeches and preaching and hoped that Eanfrith would allow him to perform there to all the occupants of Gefrin.

It was triangular, narrow at the end where Beobrand presumed the speaker would stand on a small raised dais and broadening out to seat an ever increasing number of witnesses. Each row of benches was wider than the next as you moved away from the dais and also each bench was raised up higher than the one before. This would allow those seated to all see over the heads of the people in front. It was ingenious and Beobrand wondered at the person who had come up with the idea. Leofwine seemed to think it was the brainchild of the Christian priest who had served Edwin. It was said he had come from a land far to the south, close to where the Christ was born and lived.

Beobrand was not interested in the Christ or his priests, but he was moved by the cleverness of the design of the structure.

With the news of Cadwallon's movements still fresh in his mind, as he walked through the township he looked at the whole of Gefrin from the point of view of battle and how it could be defended. The royal buildings were surrounded by the smaller houses of craftsmen and bondsmen. The whole township nestled contentedly on a flat piece of lush grassland, overlooked on three sides by towering hills. To the south, the land dropped away gently to trees and the river.

He was not knowledgeable in the ways of warfare, but he could see that this place was not made for defending. It seemed designed for leisure and as a focal point for people from all around to come and petition the king. And to pay tribute, of course.

"Hey, you!" a harsh voice called out. He looked over and saw three men lounging by the side of the path. He recognised two of them as the door wards of the great hall. The men he had almost fought on his arrival in Gefrin.

"You look all lost now your friends have gone," the short, stocky one said. His name was Acennan. Beobrand had learnt this during the first night in the hall. He was loud and outspoken, but seemed popular. "Poor little boy." He feigned crying like a baby. His companions laughed.

Beobrand ignored them and walked on, but Acennan stepped into his path, blocking it. The other two also stood.

"Don't be so rude. Aren't you the mighty Beobrand, who defeats men twice his size with a single blow of his majestic sword?" He looked around him in exaggerated movements as if searching for something. "But wait a moment. Where is your wonderful sword? Oh, that's right, you had to give it up to enter the hall. Pity. It is a fine weapon."

Beobrand could feel his face grow hot. His hands clenched into fists at his side. But he remembered Gram and Leofwine's words. He must control his anger. He should not let this fool bait him.

"I think you would not be so brave were I to have my sword in my hand, Acennan. I have heard tell you too are a mighty warrior. It would do you good to remember that, and act as such. You demean yourself." He took a step to the side and made to walk past. The short warrior moved again to block his path. His companions had stopped laughing now. The encounter took on a hard edge. Acennan placed his hand on Beobrand's chest.

"Watch your tongue, boy," he hissed.

"No, watch your own," retorted Beobrand, his voice full of ice. He looked down pointedly at Acennan's hand, then stared him directly in the eyes. He had to lower his gaze to do so. "Do not start something you do not mean to finish, Acennan. The next time you touch me in anger, I will make you regret it."

The two stared at each other for a long time. Acennan could see no give in those frosty blue eyes. Eventually he removed his hand and let the younger man pass. But he could not resist having the last word. "You'd better watch yourself, boy. You don't have any friends here. Nobody to go crying to." The men with him guffawed and slapped him on the back in an attempt to take the sting out of the meeting but they all knew that Acennan had lost face.

Beobrand walked out of the town and made his way north and east, to higher ground. Gradually, his heart slowed and the anger that Acennan had provoked in him subsided.

It was a beautiful day and he refused to have his mood soured by a bully.

He passed a shepherd with a small flock of scrawny looking sheep. He nodded to the boy, who just stared back at him, eyes wide and unblinking.

The day was warm and Beobrand walked until he had worked up a sweat. He sat in the shade of an aspen, wishing he had had the foresight to bring some water with him. It was peaceful under the tree. Bees droned over the heather and a soft zephyr rustled the leaves above him.

When Beobrand opened his eyes he was at first unsure where he was. He could make no sense of the light. The shadows were long on the ground and the sky was red in the west. He had not meant to sleep, and now it was almost dark. He leapt up. He was supposed to meet Sunniva by the river far to the south.

He started running. He knew there was no way he could get there before sundown, but she would not be able to leave her house until Strang was asleep. Beobrand consoled himself that he would probably get there before her, or soon after, if she was able to get away as soon as it was dark. His breath quickened with the pace and he grimaced at the ache from his scars. But he thanked the gods that, having walked mainly uphill on the way northward, he now had the benefit of a downhill trip back to Gefrin.

He slowed his pace as the sun set and darkness made it hard to find his footing. He had covered much of the distance while it was still light and now felt less concerned that he would miss Sunniva, or leave her waiting for him alone by the river.

In the night air, he could smell the cooking fires from Gefrin before he was able to see the houses. A full moon began to rise, casting a silver glow over the buildings in the distance.

With the added light, and his goal in sight, he quickened his pace once more, deciding to head straight down the main track through the town towards the river, rather than attempting to conceal his destination. There would be few people out at night so it was unlikely he would be seen.

Drawing close to the great hall, the smells of roasting meat were strong and the hubbub of the people inside filtered through the wood and daub of the building. Beobrand smiled as he caught the timbre of Leofwine's fine voice, rising over the noise of the feasters. Perhaps he was singing about him.

He pressed on. He passed the forge and it was silent and still, the house beside it dark. It looked as if the inhabitants were sleeping. Beobrand hoped that one was, and that the other had crept out to meet him.

He was almost at the meeting place now. The river was ahead of him, reflecting the pale rays of moonlight.

He slowed to a walk and thought he heard something. He stopped, listening. Wondering if perhaps Sunniva was on the road and had seen him. For a moment there was no sound beyond the distant murmur of the merry-makers in the great hall. An owl hooted somewhere in the night. Beobrand was about to move on when he heard it again. The crunch of a footfall on the small stones of the path.

The hairs on the back of his neck bristled and a shiver ran down his spine. He turned his head in an effort to make out where the sound came from. There it was again. Off to his left. There was someone lurking behind the hawthorn that grew alongside the path.

Beobrand walked stealthily around the bush, hands held in front of him, ready for action. He regretted not retrieving his sword.

It was difficult to make out anything in the blackness of

the moon shadow behind the hawthorn. There was a figure there, standing facing the bush. Then the tangy smell of piss reached him and he realised it was a man relieving himself.

Embarrassed, he started to turn away and leave him in peace, but before he could, the man turned to him and said in a slurred voice, "What are you looking at, boy?"

It was Acennan's voice, distorted by drink, but recognisable. Beobrand sighed. This was not going to end well.

"Where are you going? Scared, are you?"

Beobrand moved back towards the road where there was better light. He could barely see here in the shadows and if he was going to have to fight, he wanted to be able to make out as much as possible of his enemy's moves.

"I am not scared of you, Acennan." he said. "I do not want to fight you. You're drunk."

Beobrand stepped into the relative brightness of the path. The moonlight made his features appear like stone. Chiselled and lifeless. His eyes black pits.

"Drunk, am I?" roared Acennan, staggering onto the path. The light of the moon glinted off his arm rings.

"Yes," Beobrand answered, his voice level, "it would not be a fair fight. Killing you would be too easy."

Acennan's round face, distorted by the shadows, cracked into a grin.

"Kill me? You're not even armed," he said in a slurred voice.

He reached down to his side and drew the sword that hung there. The moonlight played on its surface, giving it an ethereal quality, as if the blade was made of mist. Beobrand knew that blade. It was Hrunting.

Beobrand went cold. He had hoped he could get away without a fight.

"Don't be a fool, Acennan. Someone will get killed."

"That's the idea!" Acennan replied and took a massive swing at Beobrand's neck.

Beobrand stepped back, avoiding the blade by a finger's breadth. Acennan was drunk and slow, but he knew how to wield a sword and Beobrand knew all too well how deadly that blade was.

That sword was his by right. It had injured him once, but it would not taste his blood again. The cold fury of battle descended on him. All his senses were heightened. He could smell the mead on Acennan's breath.

Acennan lunged at his chest, hoping to embed the tip of the blade between his ribs. Beobrand saw the move coming and spun away to the side, light on his feet. Acennan followed through, using his own momentum to change the direction of the blade. He turned on the balls of his feet, again swinging at neck height in an effort to decapitate Beobrand.

Remembering his fight with Hengist and how his slip had saved him, Beobrand dropped to one knee. The sword passed harmlessly over his head and Acennan lost his balance. Stumbling, the force of his attack carried him on until he was facing away from Beobrand, who surged up and pushed him hard on the back with both hands.

Acennan took several running steps to stop himself from falling, giving Beobrand a chance to assess the situation. There was no way he could continue to avoid the sword. In the end one of the blows would connect and the fight would be over.

"That is my sword. Passed down to me from my brother, Octa son of Grimgundi, thegn of King Edwin. You have no right to touch it. You are a craven and a thief."

Acennan sneered. "Craven, am I? Better than dead!"

He leapt forward slicing the sword down in an overhead arc with enough force to split Beobrand in two.

Beobrand, with the acute focus of battle, sidestepped the attack easily. The sword flashed past his face. He waited for just the right moment, when Acennan was committed and losing his balance again, then he reached out and grabbed his wrist with both hands. He pulled, adding to Acennan's forward motion. At the same time he twisted his body and raised his knee. It connected with Acennan's groin with terrible force.

Acennan let out a guttural grunt.

Still holding Acennan's wrist with both hands, Beobrand brought the arm down sharply, again using his knee as a weapon. This time Acennan's elbow was the target. Beobrand was not positioned ideally. He was too close to Acennan, who was trying to double himself up to ease the pain to his groin, so the knee only dealt a glancing blow to Acennan's elbow. Nevertheless, it had the desired effect and the sword fell from his grasp.

Beobrand ignored the sword now. He knew he had bested his opponent, but something inside him was driving him on. Acennan stood, bent over, nursing his arm and panting. There was no fight left in him.

Beobrand took a step back and swung a vicious uppercut that caught Acennan soundly on his nose. Cartilage cracked, blood burst from his nostrils and he fell onto his back. He was dazed, but as Beobrand stepped closer again he curled himself into a ball.

Beobrand couldn't stop now. This man had threatened his life, with his own sword, by Woden! And he had baited him repeatedly. He had told Acennan he would regret it if he picked a fight with him. Now he would see that was no idle threat.

He let himself fall onto Acennan's chest, leading with his

knees. Acennan vainly tried to ward him off by raising his hands to his face, but Beobrand simply punched through the piteous defences. He pummelled Acennan. His lips spilt against his teeth. Cuts opened on his brows. His face was soon slick with blood. Black in the moonlight.

After some time, strong hands pulled him back. He turned quickly, jumping up and away from the grasp. Strang the smith stood there. A solid, sombre, yet somehow calming presence. "Enough boy, you'll kill him, if you haven't already," he said.

Sunniva stepped past her father and touched Beobrand gingerly on the arm. They must both have approached in the darkness, unnoticed by the combatants. Behind them, light spilt from the doors of the great hall illuminating more people gathered there.

Beobrand picked up his sword from the path and began to shake.

15

The great hall was crowded. All of Eanfrith's thegns, companions and counsellors had come to see what would happen to the upstart from Cantware who had so savagely beaten Acennan, a trusted warrior in Scand's gesithas. There were a good number of craftsmen and merchants from Gefrin present, and more slaves than had a real reason to be there. Everyone in the throng hoped to see something memorable.

Many of Eanfrith's warband knew Acennan well and saw his defeat as an affront to one of the king's oldest and most trusted thegns and thus, by association, to the king himself. Something that could undermine his authority and threaten their own superiority over the ceorls. If a young man could stand up to one of their own and win, especially when unarmed, what would stop others from doing the same?

In equal measure many of the villagers disliked the way Eanfrith's thegns lorded it over them. Taking without payment. Preying on their daughters. And so far they had seen no benefit from them being there. Their enemies gathered in the south and the land was still lawless. From the rumours, the young warrior had had no option but to fight Acennan, and surely if a warrior who served one of the king's comitatus, his closest companions, starts a fight, he should be prepared to finish it, or accept his defeat bravely.

The doors opened and Beobrand walked in, escorted by two armed guards. He had once again had to relinquish his sword, but at least he had not been bound. That was something.

All eyes turned to stare at him, as he strode towards the end of the hall where the king sat.

It was a damp day. Clouds had rolled in overnight and now a constant drizzle fell from a low sky. The grey, watery light filtered through the doors and windows of the hall, providing little more illumination than the moonlight of the night before. Rain worked its way through some loose shingles of the roof, and dripped here and there into the hall. People shifted to avoid the drops, causing the tightly-packed onlookers to jostle for drier positions.

Beobrand surveyed the king and the amassed group of thegns. With a start he recognised the hawk-faced thegn, Galan, who he had encountered in Ecgric's hall. Galan was standing close to the king, just behind Queen Finola. Their eyes met and he saw recognition there.

Beobrand squared his shoulders. He was defiant. He'd done nothing wrong. He'd only defended himself and retrieved what was rightfully his, but he was not so naive as to believe that he would get away with beating one of the royal warband without consequences.

Eanfrith stood. The crowd hushed.

"Speak your name for all to hear," Eanfrith said.

"I am Beobrand, son of Grimgundi, your majesty." Beobrand's voice had the hard edge of defiance, but he was mindful to address Eanfrith with the politeness due to his station.

"Is it true that last night you attacked Acennan, a warrior loyal to my trusted companion, Scand, son of Scaend?"

"It is not true, your majesty." A murmur ran through the gathered watchers. Beobrand raised his voice to be heard over the noise. "I did not attack Acennan. He attacked me. I merely defended myself."

"Yet you are unharmed, and he is unable to rise from his bed. He has been beaten about the face in a terribly savage way. It appears you attacked him when he did not expect an attack, thus gaining the advantage of a coward who attacks from the shadows."

Beobrand's anger rose. He struggled to keep it in check. He'd spoken to Leofwine briefly that morning, and the scop's advice had been to not lose his temper. "If you get angry, it will become a fight between the king and you, and that is a fight you cannot win." Beobrand knew this was sound advice and he swallowed hard, biting back the words that threatened to burst forth in a torrent of ire and outrage.

"That is not the truth of it, sire. He attacked me. I was unarmed, whereas he carried a sword. And not any sword, but my own sword, which I had left in this very hall at the behest of your guards. I know nobody here will speak up for me. I am a stranger here, but I am no coward."

A ripple of conversation ran through the hall. Then, at the back, a huge figure pushed his way through the crowd. Beobrand turned to see Strang stepping forward.

"I will speak for Beobrand," said the smith in a loud voice. He had not wanted to come here and confront the king on behalf of this boy. But Sunniva had been weeping since the night before. When she heard that he was to be taken before Eanfrith she had begged her father to intercede for him. He disliked the idea of his daughter with a warrior, but he realised sometime in the darkest part of the night that if he stood against her, he would lose her. He had seen the way she had led the young man back to their home, soothing him with her voice. How she had brought him drink and sat with him in the dark, talking quietly until he had stopped trembling. She cared for the boy and if he was hurt, she would suffer terribly, so he had agreed to speak for him. Besides, he told himself, he hated injustice and was only going to speak the truth.

"I witnessed what happened and he speaks true. Acennan attacked him with his sword. Beobrand disarmed him and then beat him fairly. Let any man who says otherwise accuse me of lying."

Again the murmur of conversation ran through the hall.

Eanfrith turned to consult with Scand. They spoke quietly for a moment, and then beckoned to a thin, birdlike man to join them in their deliberations. The man took several sheets of calf-skin vellum from a table and approached the king. He spread the sheets on a table and pointed at certain points in the closely-scribed scratched out writings.

The conversation in the hall got noisier, the onlookers restless to know the outcome of the discussion.

Beobrand could not tell from their faces whether the judgement would fall in his favour or not. He caught Leofwine's eye. Leofwine offered him a small, bleak smile, and he nodded in return.

Turning slightly, he looked to Strang, hoping to acknowledge his help, but the smith stood resolutely looking forward and refused to meet his gaze.

The crowd quietened down as Eanfrith stepped forward and raised his hand.

"I have consulted with the Dooms as laid out for the king-dom of Bernicia and find you guilty of mutilating the nose of a warrior of the king. For this you must pay the weregild of twelve scyllings."

The audience erupted. Friends of Acennan were pleased with this result. Those who disliked this new king's warriors were disgusted. The young man had done nothing more than defend himself and reclaim what was rightfully his. This had been corroborated by Strang, who they knew as an honourable member of the community and one who would not lie about such things.

Beobrand's heart sank. He had no livestock or coin, and the only thing he had of real worth was Hrunting, which he could not bear the thought of losing.

Eanfrith lifted his hand again until the hall was silent.

"Furthermore, we find Acennan, warrior of Bernicia, guilty of using a weapon where there was strife, but no evil had been done. For this, he must pay a reparation of six scyllings." He raised his hand to quell any interruptions. "For the use of the sword owned by Beobrand son of Grimgundi, Acennan must pay a further six scyllings, thus paying twelve scyllings in total."

The noise from the watching crowd reached a new height. This time, Eanfrith did not seek to quieten them. He let them chatter excitedly about the clever decision he had reached. By fining them both the same amount, their penalties negated each other. He smiled at Fugol, his scribe, clearly pleased that the complicated situation could be diffused while still upholding the law.

Eanfrith looked around the room, as if weighing up options and then, mind apparently made up, he turned to one of his men and said, "Bring Beobrand's sword to me."

Silence fell over the hall. The king was going to speak again. He held the sheathed sword in his two hands, outstretched before him.

"Beobrand, son of Grimgundi, approach and take what is rightfully yours."

The guards either side of Beobrand stiffened, and the thegns around the king shifted, dropping hands to hilts of blades, readying themselves for action. This young warrior from Cantware was dangerous and they did not like the thought of him being armed with a good sword so close to their liege.

Others watching, were moved by the bravery inherent in the gesture. Beobrand himself was moved by the king's trust in him. He was reminded of a time only a few months ago, but it seemed a lifetime away, when he had approached another king of Northumbria in front of dozens of onlookers. His stomach squirmed, but he forced himself to move forward.

Everyone was silent as he stepped towards the king. He reached out and took the sword from Eanfrith's hands. He took a deep breath, sweat running down his cheek, despite the cool in the hall. He sensed the men beside him tensing as he held the hilt of the sword. He knew he had to act now.

With a flourish, he drew the blade from the scabbard and then proffered it hilt-first towards Eanfrith. There were gasps in the hall behind him and Beobrand heard the guards springing forward, fearing he meant to attack their lord. Beobrand ignored them all, focused his gaze on Eanfrith's wide eyes and dropped to one knee.

Hands clutched at his shoulders, trying to pull him away. The room was in an uproar. To draw a blade in the presence of the king was amongst the worst of crimes, punishable by death. Beobrand continued to stare into the king's eyes and raised his voice to say, "I offer you my sword, King Eanfrith, son of Æthelfrith, lord of Bernicia." Beobrand remembered the oath he had spoken to another lord, in a different hall. He continued, recalling the words he had used. "I will to you be true and faithful. I will love what you love and shun what you shun and never displease you through deed or word." It was close enough to the warrior's oath. Some of the thegns nodded in appreciation.

Beobrand paused. The room was silent once more. The throng hung on his every word. Eanfrith stared at him, quite taken aback that this young stranger would take the moment that he, the king had created, and use it to his own ends.

"Will you accept me, lord?" asked Beobrand, his voice small now.

The silence stretched out for what seemed a long time to Beobrand.

"You ask much of me, Beobrand, son of Grimgundi. You come here accused and now seek my patronage."

The king paused. There was total silence in the hall now. The sound of rain dropping into a puddle on the floor could be heard over the collectively held breaths.

"I cannot accept you as my man. That is too much honour for one such as you." Gasps from the onlookers. Beobrand's shoulders slumped. He had terribly misjudged his moment.

The king continued. "But as you submit yourself to my will, Beobrand, son of Grimgundi, I will accept you as one of my gesithas, if you swear your oath to Scand, the thegn whose man you wronged. What say you? Will you swear your oath to him?"

Beobrand felt a rush of relief. He turned to the grey-haired Scand. He looked severe and distant, but there was a glint in his eye, as if he was secretly amused by what he saw before him.

"I will swear the oath to Scand, my lord king. Willingly."

Scand stepped forward. "Then stand and sheathe your blade. You are now one of my men." The crowd, released from silence, broke out into cheers. This young warrior was brave indeed.

Beobrand slid his sword into its scabbard. Scand stepped close. "Do not make me regret this day, young Beobrand," he said quietly, so that no one else could hear. Then he turned and left the hall behind Eanfrith.

Against all the odds, Beobrand had a lord again.

16

The next weeks were a time Beobrand always remembered fondly. Scand was a good lord. There was food in the great hall, and mead. He was accepted by the other warriors in Scand's retinue and by those in the king's warband. He had been worried that after the beating he'd given Acennan he would have enemies within the group, but apart from the usual ribald humour of any group of men, no real enmity was apparent. Acennan recovered and acknowledged Beobrand with a nod when their paths crossed, but both of them were reticent to talk after the fight. The rest of the warriors displayed a reluctant admiration for him.

The people of Gefrin were anything but reluctant to show their appreciation of how he had stood up to one of the warriors in the king's service and then managed to get accepted into the coveted position of warrior companion of a thegn in the king's inner circle. Everyone in Gefrin knew his name and talked to him whenever he walked through the town. Although he was from Cantware, his connection to Edwin through Bassus and his brother Octa made many of the townsfolk consider him somehow one of their own.

Beobrand was embarrassed by the attention, but flattered too. On a few occasions people would talk about the king derisively in front of Beobrand, questioning why Eanfrith did not send out more patrols or prepare the town for attack. When this happened, Beobrand was quick to remind them to whom he had sworn allegiance, but he also made sure to mention the concerns to Scand later. The old man valued the newcomer's honesty and his ability to hear from the people of Bernicia what was really happening.

He spent much of each day engaged with the other warriors in arms practice. He was perhaps not the best swordsman of them all, but he was certainly better than most, despite many of them having a decade or even two decades more experience. His skill raised a few eyebrows and comments. He was naturally gifted with the sword and they all remembered what he had done to Acennan with his bare hands. Beobrand enjoyed the chance to test himself against new opponents and to hone the skills he had picked up from Uncle Selwyn and later Hengist. It was also good to feel his muscles strengthen and the aches from his various wounds subside. A roof over his head, wholesome food and regular training healed him better than any poultice or potion could have. The colour returned to his cheeks and Leofwine noted that the haunted look in his eyes was increasingly less frequent.

During this time he often sat in the shade of the afternoon talking to Leofwine. The storyteller was a wonderful listener and Beobrand found it easy to open up to him. As the conversations moved onto painful subjects, such as the death of his brother, Beobrand would sometimes come to an abrupt halt, like a man walking in a marsh who realises he's strayed from the path. At these times, it was as if a spell had been broken and the thread of the conversation could not be picked up again. In their conversations Beobrand touched on many difficult subjects, but never spoke of the events of the forest in the winter. He didn't even mention Cathryn's existence. He was scared to say her name. Wyrd had brought him out of the darkness and cold and he was frightened that it could plunge him back in without warning. Above all, he was ashamed when he thought of her. Of how he'd let her die. To think that Hengist was present at both her death and Octa's kindled a fire deep within him that he stoked with his shame.

For Beobrand, chief amongst the good things of his life in Gefrin was Sunniva. He had long since abandoned any attempt at secrecy when visiting her. They could be seen together in the town or the environs whenever she could get away from her work at the forge. Strang had put up some resistance at first. He still did not approve of the young Cantware warrior, but he knew that to fight against the obvious attraction his daughter felt for him would get him nowhere. She was as stubborn as her mother. So, he had begrudgingly accepted that Beobrand could court her. However, Strang made sure she was as busy as possible so that she had less time to spend with him.

But even when he made her work longer than he had ever done before, she still had the energy to meet Beobrand afterwards. The days were long, with dusk coming late, so the couple would stroll arm in arm, the light of the setting sun turning Sunniva's hair to liquid fire. They were happy and revelled in each other's company.

"You're sure it was him?" Hengist leant forward, eager and expectant. A wolf scenting a spring lamb.

Dreng settled himself by the small fire. "Aye. There is no doubt. He is swiving the daughter of the smith." He moistened his lips with his tongue. "She's a tasty morsel. You'd like her."

Hafgan and Artair didn't look up from where they sat. They both whittled sticks with avid attention.

Tondberct tensed. He straightened his back and focused on the flames of the campfire. He feigned disinterest, but was clearly listening intently.

Hengist grinned, instantly regretting it as the wound on his face split once again. He lifted a cloth to his cheek and dabbed at the seeping liquid that oozed from the cut. The cloth was already stained and damp from constant use. He could hardly believe Octa's brother had done this to him. Training Beobrand had amused him at first. He had seen the killer in the young man. Having Beobrand join their band and look up to him as his leader was the ultimate revenge on that bastard Octa. There was a dark side to Beobrand that Hengist recognised. He had hoped to coax it out into the open.

The weapons practice had provided them with entertainment over those interminable winter days. He'd never expected the young Cantware man to be able to best him.

By Tiw, it was not fair!

Time and again Hengist had run over the fight in his mind. He was certain it was mere chance that had caused Beobrand's victory.

He should have won. He had been toying with him. A cat tormenting a mouse. And then that muddy slip and the savage cut. His face was ruined. Nobody would look at him with anything but fear now. Or loathing. No woman would have him willingly ever again. When last it rained he had looked into a puddle and seen the face of a monster staring back at him.

Hengist spat into the fire. The bitter taste of rage stung his throat. His wyrd was to topple kings. He was destined for greatness. He would fulfil his mother's prophecy. But first he would destroy Beobrand. He hawked up phlegm and spat again, grimacing at the sting of his stretched scar.

A curse on both sons of Grimgundi. They had caused him such anguish. Taken so much from him.

But soon now, Hrunting would return to him and he would bathe it in Beobrand's blood before the end.

"He did not see you?" he asked.

"No," replied Dreng. "Gefrin is crowded with warriors and artisans. They prepare for war. I was careful. When I saw him with the girl, I followed them for a time, then returned here. Beobrand didn't see me."

"Good. You have done well." Hengist absently pressed the filthy rag to his face. "The smith's daughter you say? Perhaps we should pay her a visit."

Hengist stared into the fire, dreams of death and vengeance burning in his eyes. He did not see Dreng shudder at the look on his leader's shattered face.

Scand scratched at his beard. The sweat made it itch and he wondered absently whether a tick had got in there and burrowed into his chin. Perhaps he'd shave. That was the best way to get rid of the lice and in this warm weather it would be a blessing to be clean-faced.

The sun was low in the sky. A group of warriors had just finished a gruelling series of practice bouts and were slumped on the ground, resting in the shade of the great hall. All except Beobrand. Scand watched as the young Cantware man rose from the group, splashed some water from the trough on his face and made his way downhill towards the lodgings of the township of Gefrin. Towards the forge. Some of the men shouted jokes after him about who he was going to meet, but he merely waved over his shoulder and continued on his way. Too tired to get angry, or perhaps he was just settling in to the warband and the ways of the men.

He liked Beobrand, and admired his audacity in handling the audience with Eanfrith. And it had done Acennan no harm to have someone stand up to him. Beobrand seemed honest enough and eager to fit in. Scand considered himself a good judge of men, and Beobrand struck him as a man of honour. There was a dark side to him, but who could say they had no secrets? Scand had a feeling that God was smiling on them when he sent Beobrand to Gefrin.

He cast his eyes beyond the town and surveyed the horizon. He didn't expect to see anything out of the ordinary. There were scouts posted around Gefrin and he had men watching Cadwallon's troops, so a surprise attack was unlikely. Nevertheless, the old warrior found himself scouring the land to the south with increasing frequency.

Battle was coming. As sure as smoke rose from fire. He could almost smell it. When it would come, and in what form, he did not know. But come it would.

Rumours were rife. Information flowed into Gefrin with the new warriors who gathered under Eanfrith's banner. Cadwallon continued to build up his numbers in the south, but he still showed no inclination to attack Eanfrith. The land was dangerous with wandering groups of warriors. Landless and lordless after the rout at the battle of Elmet, many now chose to come to Gefrin, where they were welcomed by Scand. They needed all the fighters they could get, so he asked few questions. But he kept the new arrivals away from the king and the great hall. Instead they were camped within the animal enclosure on the edge of the town. It was all too possible that one of these new warriors could be sent by an enemy of Bernicia to kill the king. He might not be able to talk sense into Eanfrith and have him pull back to the fortress of Bebbanburg, but he could make sure that the king would not fall to a stealthy dagger in the night.

The swelling numbers of men boded well for Bernicia, but they could not stay in Gefrin for much longer. They were low on provisions and would need to move in order to be able to collect food from farms and other royal villas. Perhaps that would be a way to convince Eanfrith to move to Bebbanburg, thought Scand. He'd talk to Fugol about the numbers so that he could tackle the king armed with knowledge. If they didn't attack as a large force soon, the host would need to be broken up. They would simply not be able to feed them.

Eanfrith planned to summon all the ealdormen of Bernicia to Gefrin to swear the oath of allegiance to him. Those lands with no ealdormen would be granted to his most trusted thegns. The warriors who had come seeking a lord would be spread amongst the ealdormen of the kingdom.

The plans were good, as far as they went, but Scand knew they were premature. The time to talk of dividing up the land had not yet come. First would come the time of killing and death. Land could not be settled until it had been paid for with the blood of men.

And Scand was sure the day the land would exact its tribute was fast approaching.

"What are you gawping at, young man?" asked Sunniva. She was bending down to spread her oldest cloak onto the warm grass. When she turned to look at Beobrand, he'd been watching her with his mouth wide open. "If you don't close your mouth, you'll catch a fly!"

Embarrassed, he shut his mouth quickly. He was often embarrassed when he was with Sunniva. She was so effortlessly beautiful and quick-witted that she made him feel stupid and clumsy. He knew she didn't mean to, and she showed no sign of thinking badly of him, but he couldn't help but feel he was not worthy of her.

She sat and patted the cloak next to her. "Well, what were you staring at?" she asked, smiling archly.

Beobrand sat. "I was just looking at you," he mumbled.

"Oh. And did you like what you could see?" She was enjoying herself now.

"Yes, of course."

"As good as the shepherdess I saw you looking at on the way here?"

Beobrand didn't know what she was talking about. It was true that they'd passed a flock of sheep on their way to this meadow, but he hadn't noticed the shepherdess. Then he saw the gleam in Sunniva's eye and realised she was teasing him.

"Well, you're not bad, but that shepherdess was like a goddess." He tried and failed to keep a straight face and they both burst out laughing.

Sunniva felt wonderful. This young man was all she'd ever hoped for in a husband. He was strong and brave, but there was a tenderness and thoughtfulness there too.

She leant forward, placing her hand on his thigh and kissed him lightly on the lips. He shivered and returned her kiss gently. She knew the power she had over him, and she loved that he never attempted to force himself on her. He always responded to her, but she could tell he was holding himself in check, not allowing his passion to run wild. This only excited her more.

Over the last few weeks they had seen a lot of each other and their encounters had become increasingly physical and passionate. Sunniva had decided that this would be the day that she would give herself to him.

Strang had told her three days before that he would be travelling to collect charcoal and had asked her to accompany him. She had waited until the night before and then feigned the arrival of her monthly bleeding. She knew her father would not remember when her last blood had come and when she said she had stomach cramps and wished to stay in the house, he did not argue. Her mother would have quickly seen through the ruse.

After her father had left Gefrin, she had gone down to a secluded spot by the river and bathed. Then she had changed into her favourite dress. It was blue, with white embroidered edges. She and her mother had sewn it together.

She had packed a basket with food, some cheese, a piece of ham and bread, folded her old cloak on top of the provisions, and gone in search of Beobrand.

She had found him training with some other warriors. He was stripped to the waist, his muscular torso glistening with a sheen of sweat. He was wielding his fine sword effortlessly, thrusting, parrying, lunging. The blade flickered in the bright sun, flashing silver like a fish darting in the shallows of the river. She had watched as Beobrand drove his opponent backwards, his footwork lithe and precise. He was in total control, despite his adversary being several years his senior. In the end, the warrior tripped and fell onto his back on the dusty ground. Beobrand stepped over him, holding the point of his sword at the man's throat.

All the onlookers were silent. There was a cold fire burning in Beobrand's blue eyes. The man on the ground lay motionless, staring fixedly into those eyes. For a moment he looked in fear for his life, but then Beobrand looked up, saw Sunniva, and smiled in welcome. He switched his sword to his left hand and held out his right to help his opponent up.

Relieved, the man grasped the offered hand and Beobrand pulled him to his feet. "Be glad your girl arrived when she did. Another moment and I would have humiliated you!" the older man said loudly with a grin. The watching warriors laughed. Beobrand clapped him on the back and made his way over to Sunniva. The tension had gone, but the men were all wise enough not to jest further about Sunniva. Many of them looked sidelong at the couple. The girl was a beauty, and not a few of the men were jealous of Beobrand's luck.

Beobrand had pulled his kirtle on and Sunniva had asked if he cared to join her for some food. He was never going to refuse so she'd led him away to the north of Gefrin. They'd walked for some time until they had reached the meadow. It was one of her favourite places, and she loved to come here and doze on warm days. It was close enough to Gefrin to be reached on foot, but far enough away to grant them some privacy.

The small swathe of meadow was roughly square in shape. It was on a slope and overlooked by a stand of rowan and pine trees on three sides, which meant it was secluded.

Sunniva's hand was warm on Beobrand's leg. He felt himself growing aroused and he returned her kiss with mounting passion, his tongue probing her mouth. Breathless, he pulled away. He had caught himself thinking of Cathryn. He remembered his arousal in that dark forest clearing. He shuddered. Self-loathing cooling his desire.

"What is it, Beobrand?" Sunniva asked, unsure what she had done wrong.

"Nothing. I'm sorry."

"Don't you want me?"

He watched entranced as she unfastened the brooches that attached her peplos, her over-dress, to her under-dress. She removed her belt and then shrugged out of the blue and white peplos, leaving just her cream-coloured linen undergarment. It clung to her form, accentuating the swell of her breasts. She reached up and unlaced the string that held the neck of the garment closed.

Beobrand swallowed. "Of course I want you. It's just that…"

"What?" Her voice took on an edge of pique. Was he going to reject her now, after all her plans?

"I don't want to hurt you. You are so perfect."

"You won't hurt me," she smiled, mollified.

"I… I am not a good person," he stammered.

"You're good enough for me," she laughed and kissed him again. "Let's not talk any more. There are much better ways for us to spend the afternoon." She took hold of his hand and pulled it to her chest, sliding aside the cloth so that his fingers touched her warm, bare flesh. His palm brushed her nipple and she let out a small gasp of pleasure.

She grasped his kirtle with both hands and tugged it over his head. For a moment she gazed in admiration at his muscular torso, taking in the scars she had seen before, tracing them with her fingertips. He shivered again, but it was warm in the meadow. She moved in close and kissed his chest, his neck, his mouth.

He stroked her breast again, feeling her nipple harden. He kissed her deeply.

After some time, they paused, both breathing heavily, as

if they'd been running. Beobrand's manhood throbbed. He was desperate for her to touch him there. He fumbled with his clothes. She helped and they managed to pull his britches down. She reached out and gripped him in her slender hand. Her fingers were callused from working in the forge, but her touch was tender. Now it was his turn to gasp.

Sunniva kissed him again, then, hitching her undergarment up, she lay back onto the soft grass and pulled him down on top of her.

He could feel the pressure building. She used her hand to guide him to her moist opening and as he felt the touch of her, he entered her, cautiously, not wishing to hurt her.

She moaned and pressed her fingers into his back.

All thoughts of shame and guilt fled from Beobrand's mind. Then, for quite some time, he could think no more.

The sun was barely peeping over the treetops and dew still bejewelled the grass when Strang set out for charcoal. He was getting through more of the valuable resource than he was accustomed to. The forge had been in use constantly with all the warriors now in Gefrin. Not only did he have the order for weapons from Eanfrith, but each of the newcomers seemed to need something mending, or had a request for a new item to be forged. Of course, there was only so much he could do with nobody but Sunniva to help him, but the money that was coming in would soon be enough to get a slave. Perhaps he could find one with useful experience, but it was unlikely. What did the Waelisc know of making good steel? No, he'd be lucky to get a strong healthy one with enough brains to be able to pick up some of the rudimentary skills needed for metalwork.

One thing was for sure, Sunniva would soon be gone. She had fallen for the Cantware boy and he thought it would only be a matter of days or weeks before he plucked up courage enough to ask for her hand. Strang had disliked him from the moment he'd seen him walking up the hill towards Gefrin. He knew he'd bring trouble. Still, Sunniva could do worse, though he wouldn't admit as much to her. Beobrand was brave and honest, and he doted on her.

Strang tapped the ox on the rump with the stick he carried for the job. It picked up its pace, easily pulling the unladen cart along the path towards the forest. Both beast and man knew the path well. They had made the trip dozens of times before. They would be walking for most of the morning, then they would stop at the clearing where the charcoalers built their huge fire mounds. There they would eat and Strang would tell them all the news from Gefrin before they loaded the cart with charcoal and he headed back to the forge. It would be a long, dirty, hot day, but Strang was pleased to get away from the forge. Walking the oft-travelled path allowed his mind to wander.

He thought of Etheswitha. What would she have thought of Beobrand? But he knew the answer already. She'd have liked him. He could almost hear his wife saying to him, "You don't like him because he is too much like you!" He smiled at the thought. He supposed it was true. Neither he nor Beobrand talked much, they were both serious and faced their problems with strength and pragmatism, rather than cunning and guile.

He walked on, enjoying the peace of the open country. He saw nobody on the path and made good time. The ground was firm and dry after weeks of warm weather and sooner than he'd expected he was entering the shadow of the forest. He would be at the charcoal burners' clearing soon. He could already pick up the scent of the wood fires on the light breeze. It would be good to sit for a while and chat with the men. Strang had brought them a small barrel of mead, and his mouth filled with saliva at the thought of slaking his thirst on the sweet drink.

It was cool in the shade of the trees. Pleasant after the hot sun that had beat down from the clear sky. The sweat cooled on his brow. The pungent smell of woodsmoke was stronger now. As they drew near to their destination, the cart's right wheel slipped off the path into a hollow. The cart listed abruptly to the side and Strang was pleased it hadn't been piled high with charcoal; he'd have lost much of the load. He hadn't been paying attention, relying on the ox to follow the path. He'd been lulled into a thoughtful reverie by the silence and shade of the woodland track.

Silence.

Strang was suddenly aware of the hush that was on the forest. On a warm spring day there should have been many sounds surrounding them. The song of birds. The rustle of the movement of animals in the trees. The quiet buzzing of insects flitting in the undergrowth. But there was no sound. They were close enough to the clearing that he should have been able to hear the charcoal men talking.

A feeling of unease settled on Strang like a cloying mist.

The ox had stopped as the cart tipped to the right and Strang now made his way back round to the wheel. He used his bodyweight and strength to push the cart upright, at the same time clicking his tongue and giving the ox the order for walking forward. He had to push for some time and raise his voice before the ox did as instructed. Eventually, the cart was lifted from the ditch and was once more on the path. The small keg of mead had fallen over and Strang righted it. He also picked up his large axe that had been resting in the back of the cart.

Tentatively now, unsure of what to expect, but unsettled by

the stillness, he urged the ox forward once more. He pulled it to a halt just before they reached the clearing. He could see the fires were burning. There were three large, earth-covered mounds in the clearing, each seeping smoke, making the space between the trees hazy in the midday sun. He could see no people. Strang knew that the fires needed constant attention to make sure that the burning wood was not consumed in its entirety, so the absence of the charcoal men was not only unusual, it was unheard of.

He gripped his axe with both hands and stepped into the clearing.

"Hail!" he called. Hopefully the men were off in the trees for some reason and would now come back to meet him. He felt foolish to be so nervous.

Then he saw the feet. Protruding from behind the closest mound. He took a small step forward to get a better look. His knuckles were white on the axe handle.

The hair on his neck bristled. The feet belonged to one of the charcoal men. An elderly man who Strang had known for years. His body was contorted in an unnatural position. His death had been violent. Blood covered his soot-smeared clothing. The red wetness of it almost shone in the hazy light. Fresh blood.

Movement behind him made Strang spin around, letting out a small, involuntary gasp of surprise.

Several men made their way out from where they had been hidden behind the mounds or in the trees. They were a rough looking bunch and all were armed. Some even wore pieces of armour and carried shields. The man closest to Strang held a seax which was smeared in recently-spilled blood. He was old, and when he licked his lips, Strang saw he had only a few rotten-looking teeth in his smiling maw.

A voice from behind him made him spin around again.

"Well, welcome to our little feast. Thank you for bringing along something to drink. It's been thirsty work."

From between two of the charcoal mounds stepped a tall warrior. He walked with the relaxed confidence of one assured in his power. He was clad in leather and metal, his hair was dark and unkempt. He exuded strength and malevolence in equal measure.

Strang stared at the man's face. If he needed any further proof of what had happened and what was soon to pass, that face took any doubt from his mind. It was hard, with dark shadows veiling the eyes. And it was horribly disfigured. A raw, red, seeping scar ran from the man's left eyebrow all the way down to his lightly-bearded chin. When he smiled, the scar seemed to smile too, pulling his face into a distorted mask. The other side of his face was undamaged, and he would probably once have been handsome. But he was now repulsive. His was a ghoulish face, like some monster stepping from the darkness of a mead hall tale into the light of day.

Strang shivered. Then raised his axe.

He was painfully aware of the men encroaching on him from behind, but unwilling to turn his back on the monstrous warrior before him.

He drew himself up to his full height.

Ready to fight.

He smiled, a small private smile at his optimism. But Etheswitha had always said he was a terrible liar. He certainly couldn't fool himself.

He was not just ready to fight.

He was ready to fight. And to die.

*

Beobrand and Sunniva made their way back to Gefrin as the sun was setting. The great hall stood out on the horizon, bathed in golden light, details of each plank picked out in harsh relief. Clouds were gathering in the east, far out over the unseen sea. A breeze was picking up and a slight chill was in the air.

They did not feel cold. They walked close together, touching frequently with a new-found intimacy.

An elderly woman who was feeding slops to a pig saw them and smiled. She remembered when she had been young and in love.

The couple walked on, oblivious of the looks of the villagers and the warriors lounging near the great hall. They were intent on their own company.

The forge was quiet and dark when they arrived. The cart was not there and they couldn't see Strang on the road. Sunniva had expected him to be home before her. She had been preparing her excuses for when he questioned where she had been.

Finding the house empty broke the spell that had settled over them since their love-making in the afternoon sun. Sunniva was suddenly worried. It was unlike her father to be late.

"Don't worry," said Beobrand, stroking her arm. "Perhaps the cart has broken a wheel, or the ox has turned lame. He'll probably be here soon."

Beobrand could see she was getting anxious and a tiny worm of unease worked its way into his mind. "Come on, let's go inside and light a fire. It's getting cold. I'll wait with you until he arrives."

"He'll be furious if he comes in to find you here."

"I'll worry about that when he arrives. I'm not leaving you alone."

She lit a fire on the hearth and prepared food. They waited. A long time later, when neither of them thought he would return that night, but hoped he was sheltering until morning, it started to rain.

Sunniva began to cry quietly. She didn't mean to, but the thought of her father out in the darkness and the rain, injured or worse, was too much.

"Hush, my love." Beobrand caressed her hair. It felt good to provide comfort to her. She rested her head in his lap and closed her eyes.

"Do you think he's dead?" she asked.

"Shhhh. Do not think such things. I will go and find him tomorrow."

She didn't speak any further and after a time, her breathing became rhythmic.

He watched her in the dim light of the embers and thought of wyrd. His life had changed irrevocably in the last months, but the turns and twists in the paths he'd trodden had brought him to this beautiful creature. He closed his eyes, listening to the rain and wind buffeting the small house, and thought of the afternoon they had spent together. She had unleashed a passion in him that he had not known. They had made love with ferocious tenderness and had later lain together in the warmth of the sun, the sweat drying on their skin. They had dozed in each other's embrace, truly content.

Alone here with her now, in the warm glow of the dying fire, he was still content. But he was not sure what the morning would bring. He hoped Strang would be found in good health.

If not, he feared their happiness would be short-lived.

17

The rain lashed down with a vehemence that would have seemed impossible the day before. It was hard to believe that the skies had been clear and the weather warm for weeks before this stormy downpour. Beobrand made an effort to pull his cloak around his shoulders to offer some protection from the elements, but he needed his other hand for the reins of the horse he was riding, so his attempts did not get him far. He tried to bring back the memory of the previous afternoon with Sunniva. Something warm and happy to think about, rather than the cold and wet trail he was on, but any happiness seemed as far away as the sun.

He rode at the head of a group of eight riders. To his left was Scand, who had insisted on joining them on the search for the smith. The old thegn's face was a stern mask of determination, his eyes squinting against the wind and rain dripping from his grey beard. Beobrand had gone to him in the morning when Strang had failed to arrive back at the forge. Sunniva had been distraught with worry, but he had promised her he'd find her father. Scand had cursed the news that the smith was missing. It had been foolish for the craftsman to travel alone, but he was angry at himself for not thinking to have the man watched and guarded. They had no other smith in Gefrin. Scand had quickly gathered a small band of men together, led by Acennan, Beobrand's old foe, who had acknowledged him with a nod. While they had armed themselves, Scand had ordered bondsmen to prepare provisions for the men for a couple of days riding and to saddle eight horses.

"Do you know where he was going?" he'd asked Beobrand.

"Yes. Sunniva says follow the path that leads to the forest and then continue into the trees for a short way to the charcoal men's clearing. Half a day's walk."

So they had set out into the rain, not riding hard, instead preserving the horses in case they needed to push them later. They made good time and were soon walking the horses into the forest. The rain still fell hard, but the noise of the storm was softened by the trees. The wind had abated somewhat but the rustling of the leaves and the sounds of the horses and men moving along the path prevented them hearing anything from a distance.

The men did not talk as they approached the clearing. They were subdued. A foreboding had fallen over them. The smell of smoke from the fires reached them first, then, as they stepped into the clearing, a different smell. Strangely familiar, yet out of place. The smell of cooked meat.

They found Strang on one of the charcoal fire mounds.

The mound had been partly broken, letting the embers inside spill out. Strang's body had been thrown onto the burning charcoal. The wood still smoked, hissing where the rain hit it. Steam and smoke swirled around the smith's body. His head and shoulders lay in the fire. His hair had burnt away. The face was blackened and charred, lips pulled back from the teeth in a grisly smile.

Some of the men crossed themselves. Others spat and touched the iron of their weapons. A few did both.

There was evil here that must be warded off.

None of them wanted to touch Strang.

Beobrand stared for a long time at what was left of Sunniva's father. With his death, his hopes of happiness fled. The gods must be laughing at him.

Scand and the others searched the rest of the clearing. They found three charcoal men dead. All of them had been stabbed or cut, but not burnt. The men carried the bodies into the centre of the clearing and laid them out next to each other.

"I'll need some help to move Strang," Beobrand said eventually. He no more wanted to touch the smith than the others did, but the man could have become his kin one day. Besides he would not be able to face Sunniva if he did not remove him from the fire.

To his surprise, Acennan stepped forward. Their eyes met, they exchanged a slight nod of understanding and together lifted the huge body. The body was warm and pliant in Beobrand's hands. He suppressed a shudder of disgust.

They laid it down next to the others.

They found a fifth body on the edge of the clearing, just within the tree line. This one had been struck a terrible blow to the head. The top of the skull was caved in. Bone, blood and brain matter was splattered over the face and the long black hair. They stretched him out with the other corpses.

"Do you think it was Cadwallon's men?" one of the men asked.

Scand shook his head. "No, at least not in numbers. From the signs there was only a handful of men here. But whoever did this must pay. These men were men of Bernicia. Strang was a freeman and his death cannot be left unpunished. You men, help me get the bodies onto the horses. We'll walk back to Gefrin." He signalled to two of the men who lifted one of the bodies and began to secure it to a horse.

"Acennan, take Beobrand and the others and hunt these man-slayers down. Their tracks are fresh and they seem to have taken the smith's cart, so they should be easy to follow. We will see to it that these five men are laid to rest in the proper way."

"Four of them," said Beobrand quietly.

"What?"

"Four of them should be treated with respect." He was looking intently at the fifth body, with the massive injury to the head.

"What are you saying?" asked Scand.

"This fifth one is Waelisc and helped to kill these men."

"How do you know?"

"I recognise him." Beobrand's voice had taken on a hard edge. "His name was Artair. He travelled with the man who killed my brother. When we find them, their leader, one called Hengist, is mine."

They could not ride as hard as they wanted. The path through the trees was winding and difficult to navigate on horseback. After a short while, they decided to dismount and lead the horses through the trees. This also meant that they could better survey the ground for sign of their quarries' passing. The ground was soft now, but the men they hunted appeared to have left the charcoal burners' glade before the rains, so they had left little in the way of tracks on the path.

Fortunately, they had taken the ox and cart, so there were,

from time to time, indications that they had travelled that way. With the cart, there was nowhere else for them to go but the path, at least until they left the woodland.

The men did not talk. Their faces were grim. They all knew that this journey would end in bloodshed. The task was clear. They would have no qualms exacting justice on the men who had killed those they were sworn to protect, but the unknown size of the group preyed on their minds. Beobrand told them what he knew of the group from when he had travelled with them, but they did not know if their numbers had changed since then, and none of them were expert trackers.

The men looked sidelong at him.

Beobrand felt their eyes on him. Knew what they were thinking. What sort of man travelled with the likes of these murderers? Had he no honour? Could his oath be trusted? He set his jaw and pressed on. There was nothing he could do to make them trust him apart from showing them with actions where his duty now lay. He cursed his stupidity at having fallen in with Hengist and the others. Wryd. It was pointless to question it. Bassus had told him never to dwell on the past, but to think of the future. He did that now. He planned his revenge. There were so many that cried out for vengeance. Octa, Cathryn and her father, Strang and the countless others Hengist had killed. Beobrand gripped the reins tightly enough to hurt his hands and picked up his pace.

They were soon out of the woods. They mounted again and continued along the path that stretched into the distance through nettles and grasses. The rain had stopped, though clouds still brooded in the sky and the wind was cold and blustery. The tracks of the cart were clearer now. The path was not frequently used and was quite overgrown, so the wheels of the cart had crushed foliage as it had passed. There was dung from the ox too, and then from a horse, so at least one of them was mounted. They spent a short while scanning the ground trying to work out how many men there were and the number of horses. They couldn't agree, but all thought that there was only one, or perhaps two horses. If the band was the same size as Beobrand mentioned, with one of their number dead, there were four left.

The five pursuers kicked their horses' flanks and cantered forward. The men they hunted had a day's head start on them, but they were not all mounted and the cart would slow them down.

In the early afternoon, they found the men's campsite. They had huddled under the lee of a steep hill. The remains of their small fire were still warm to the touch, despite the heavy rain. It was easy now to see where the men had lain. Near the fire were four areas of flattened grass.

Beobrand, Acennan and the other three warriors paused there briefly. They ate sparingly of the provisions they had taken from Gefrin. They had also taken the food originally given to the three who had returned to the great hall with the bodies. They did not know how long the hunt would take, but all were anxious to bring the men to justice and get back to Gefrin. War was in the air, and this seeming random act of violence unnerved them. They did not want to be cut off from the warband when battle commenced. It was their duty to stand with their lord. The shieldwall was where their names would be made and silver arm bands won.

The wind picked up again, blowing directly into their faces as they mounted and rode once more into the west. Into higher ground. Towards the wilds where the people were as untamed as the lands they dwelt in.

They drew their damp cloaks around them, and rode on.

Scand and the others arrived at Gefrin late in the afternoon, leading the horses with their grisly burdens. They trudged between the dwellings, the hooves of the mounts squelching in the mud of the path. A bondsman, guarding livestock at the enclosure on the edge of the township, saw them and asked who the men over the backs of the horses were. When they told him, he ran off with the bad news, ahead of them. Bearing bad tidings was evidently a rare excitement for the man.

By the time the men had led their horses to the great hall, they were followed by a small procession of townsfolk. The wives of the charcoal men joined the throng with their children. Their faces were almost as ashen as their dead husbands'. They hoped beyond reason that the news they had heard was not true. That the corpses on the horses were not their men, but when the thegns dismounted and cut them down, lowering the bodies with reverence to the wet ground, they saw what they already knew. Their men were gone. Without them, they would not be able to feed their children. They cast their eyes down when the king stepped from the hall. Everyone there knew the women would likely have to place their heads in Eanfrith's hands if they were to survive. They would cease to be free then. By throwing themselves on their lord's mercy they would become thralls.

But first they would tend to the dead. The womenfolk of the town gathered around the bodies and started giving men orders to pick them up and take them to their abodes, where they would be cleaned and prepared for burial in the old tradition.

Sunniva came dashing up the hill, her golden hair bright against the grey sky. When she saw her father on the ground, she let out a wail of grief and fell to her knees. She was still young and had seen less death than the older women, who had buried husbands, fathers, brothers, sons. She would learn, they thought. They crowded around her, raised her up from the ground and took charge of the preparations for her father. Etheswitha had been their friend and they all loved Sunniva. She was kith to them.

As they drew her away, leaving the menfolk to talk of the events, she suddenly turned. "Where is Beobrand? Is he...?" She could not bring herself to finish.

Scand spoke loud enough for all to hear. The king needed to know what had happened, and the people may as well know too. He was tired and had no inclination to have to repeat the telling.

"Beobrand is unhurt, or was when we left him. He travels with Acennan and the others in search of the men who committed these murders most foul. We found these men in the charcoal clearing, where they had been slain. This fifth man was one of their attackers. Beobrand knew him and told us of the men he travelled with. They are men who believe themselves outside the law. Five of my gesithas, mounted on fine steeds and with sharp blades and strong war harness are hunting these outlaws. They will find them and they will be brought to justice." He turned to the king and bowed his head. "I trust I have done what you would have ordered."

Eanfrith was shocked at how old Scand looked. Remove the battle-dress and weapons and he would be one of the longbeards who sat sucking their gums by the fireside.

The king drew himself up to his full height and spoke clear and true. "You have done well, most trusted Scand. We must protect our people and bring to justice any who raise their hand against us. Now come into the hall and share a cup with me. It has been a hard day for you and you need rest."

Scand scowled. Eanfrith's comment belittled him, making him appear weak and tired in front of his men. He didn't protest though. Eanfrith was his king, and the truth was that he was exhausted. He began to make his way into the hall, already anticipating sitting on the mead bench and resting his weary legs in the smoky warmth inside, when there came the thrumming of galloping hooves behind him.

They turned to see a single rider approaching. He rode a large black stallion, a fine horse, with braided mane. The rider was unknown to them. He had hair as black as his horse. His cloak was white and it billowed behind him. At his side he had a sheathed sword and at his neck shone a golden torc.

Scand's fatigue vanished and he quickly stood in front of Eanfrith. The other warriors formed a protective line in front of their king. Weapons were drawn. It was only one rider, but he bore down on them like a black devil. The corpses on the ground reminded the men what happened to those who do not prepare for battle.

The crowd of people parted and let the rider through. At the last possible moment, he pulled hard on the reins, bringing his steed to a skidding halt. Gobbets of mud spattered the bodies.

Scand stepped forward. "Who are you and what brings you here? You come at a time of sadness, as you can see."

The man remained mounted, his horse turning skittishly, unnerved at the smell of blood. "My name is Gwalchmei ap Gwyar and I bear a message for Eanfrith, son of Æthelfrith, king and ruler of Bernicia and all its peoples."

Those watching were hushed. This man was one of the Waelisc, the proud foreigners from the west who had long battled against the Angelfolc. He was brave indeed to ride alone to the very doors of the great hall of Gefrin.

Eanfrith spoke in a clear voice. "I am Eanfrith, son of Æthelfrith, son of Aethelric, and I rule this land by the right of the old gods and the new. Who sends me a message, Gwalchmei ap Gwyar?"

"The message I bring you is from Cadwallon ap Cadfan, king of Gwynedd and ruler of the kingdom your people know as Deira. My lord would meet with you to discuss terms of peace."

18

Cresting a hill the riders saw an overturned cart in the valley below. The path was steep and treacherous, made up of loose stones. They rode cautiously down towards the cart. Drawing close they could see large gashes in the scree of the path, where the cart had slipped and finally come to rest on its side. One of the cart's wheels had come off and was lying some way from the path.

The ox that had pulled the stolen cart had clearly outlived its usefulness. Its carcass lay in the long grass beside the broken vehicle. It had been quickly butchered. Choice cuts had been removed, but most of the meat was still on it. No time had been wasted.

"I'd say they know they are being followed," said Acennan, swatting at the flies that buzzed up around his face, disturbed from where they feasted on the bloody wounds of the beast.

"Or they know someone will be following them soon and they want to make up as much ground as they are able before they are hunted," replied Beobrand.

Acennan did not disagree. "Whichever the reason, they are

travelling fast. Now, without the cart they can make better time in these hills. We might lose them."

"There is still some light in the sky. Let's press on till dark. And we should not light a fire this night. It will be cold, but we do not want them to see us coming."

They swung back into the saddle and carried on.

Shortly after finding the cart, they came across some buildings nestling in the crook of a stream. There were four small, thatched cottages. A thin line of smoke rose from three of the buildings. The sun was low in the sky. It shone in their faces briefly as it dipped below the clouds. Then it was lost behind the horizon. The valley they were riding into was shadowy and dark. There was no movement from the buildings.

Warily, they rode into the settlement. There were small wattle enclosures for animals, but they were empty and the whole place was eerily silent. One of the enclosures stood open, its gate swinging in the breeze. Part of the gate was stained dark. Beobrand dismounted and touched the gate. Blood. There was more on the ground underneath it.

"Hail!" Acennan shouted, shattering the silence. The men waited for a long while. There was no response. "Hail!" he shouted again. Nothing.

They all dismounted and tied their horses to the gate. The smell of the blood made the horses nervous. They stamped their hooves and lay their ears flat on their long heads.

Acennan spoke quietly now, so as not to be overheard should there be people listening from the huts. "We will go to each house in turn. Beobrand and I will open the doors. The rest of you watch the other buildings in case anyone comes out to attack us."

They went first to the hut where there was no smoke.

Beobrand drew his sword and hefted his shield. The others all brandished their own weapons. Dusk was falling and none of them wished to be in an exposed position once it was full dark. Acennan looked Beobrand in the eye. They both nodded and Acennan swung the door to the hut wide. Beobrand leapt forward, holding his shield before him, wary for a blow being struck from the dark interior of the house. No attack came. They peered inside and saw a simple hut arranged in the way of such dwellings. There was a hearth in the middle of the single room. A table, stools, a chest. Some herbs and dry fish hung from the rafters.

The hut was still and cold. Empty.

Beobrand had the feeling that they were being watched. The back of his neck prickled.

They moved on to the next house and went through the same process. Again the house was empty and there was nothing out of the ordinary about it. In this building, the embers of a small fire still glowed on the hearthstone.

The next house was just as empty as the first two. Again, the fire was still hot, the embers winking dimly like the eyes of a wolf in the darkness.

It was almost full dark now and the men moved nervously onto the last building. The feeling of being watched had increased as they'd moved through the buildings and Beobrand was convinced that something evil would leap from the fourth door. The others felt it too. They were all tense. Muscles taut and aching from remaining at the ready for too long.

Acennan swung the last door open. The bearded face of Hengist burst out from the gloom towards Beobrand. He took an involuntary step backwards. Raised Hrunting before him.

Hengist did not leap out of the hut. Beobrand let out a ragged sigh of relief. His eyes had played mischief with him. It was just a dark cloth hanging behind the door, probably to lessen draughts. It had billowed out with the door as it had been opened.

Feeling foolish, he swung his sword and cut down the cloth. Behind it they found another empty room.

The settlement was deserted.

"My guess is that they are hiding with their livestock," said Acennan. "Perhaps they saw us coming." Mounted and armed strangers would frighten most people. "Or perhaps they hid from the men we hunt. We can rest here. There is shelter and a fire. We would not be able to follow the tracks in the night, and we do not know this land well."

The men were pleased to rest. They added kindling to the fire in the largest house and set up watches for the night.

Acennan said, "Remember, these are houses of men of Bernicia. Treat them well. Rest while you can. We leave before first light."

Beobrand offered to take the first watch. He was on edge. Thoughts and images tumbled through his mind as he stood by the tethered horses. He saw Strang's face in the dark. Charred. White teeth bared in a rictus. Cathryn's beautiful face, eyes pleading. Hengist as he had last seen him, face opened to the bone, blood gushing in a sheet over his chin. Octa waving as he left Cantware, smiling. Hair streaming in the wind. Tiny Edita, wrapped in linen, being lowered into the ground. Rheda, trying to smile, even as she died. His mother, gripping his hands as she spoke her final, haunting words to him. His father, hands reaching out imploringly as the flames licked at the straw mattress.

It was a cool, dry night. The wind was shredding the

clouds. He looked up, wondering where the dead went. Could they see him? Were they looking down from Woden's hall? Or perhaps they gazed upon him from the heaven the worshippers of the Christ talked of. He shivered. The moon and stars stared down implacably.

He tried to summon up the face of Sunniva. Radiant, hair glowing in bright spring sunlight. But he couldn't see her. His mind was only able to bring up images of death and sadness.

Somewhere, a long way off, a wolf howled.

"This is madness!" Scand could hardly believe that Eanfrith was seriously considering accepting the invitation to meet Cadwallon. "It is a trap. He offers sweet words like honey, and you, like the bear in the forest, fail to see the bees ready to sting."

There was a murmur from the men in the hall. Scand and Eanfrith were seated at the end of the long table, while the king's retainers sat at the other end, leaving them enough space to speak without being overheard. As long as they spoke in hushed tones. But both of their voices had been raised for some time now. Scand was tired and outraged. He was also genuinely frightened for his lord's life should he go to Cadwallon.

The king slapped the table with his palm. "Enough! You forget yourself. I am your king."

Even those thegns who had been feigning disinterest in the conversation turned their heads and stared.

Scand knew he had overstepped his position. "I apologise, my lord. You are right. But I only speak in this way for I see great peril in what you are planning. You are my lord and protector of the people, but I also have sworn an oath to you and your father before you to protect the rightful king of

Bernicia." Scand felt helpless. Eanfrith would not be swayed in this. He could see it in the set of his jaw. "I would not be doing my duty if I did not speak out against your decision in this matter."

Again, there was a rumble of assent from the gathered thegns. They too were worried. Dispirited at the uncertainty of the future. They had known war was coming. Now their enemy spoke of peace and their king seemed to accept the words without a second thought.

The messenger, Gwalchmei, had delivered his message and then departed as quickly as he had arrived. Cadwallon called on Eanfrith, accompanied by twelve of his most trusted thegns, to be his guest in the camp of the Waelisc three day's hence. There they would feast and talk of how they should rule their neighbouring kingdoms peacefully.

Scand had started to dismiss Gwalchmei, believing only a complete fool would consider the offer, when Eanfrith had raised his hand for silence. To Scand's dismay he had replied to the haughty Waelisc in a courteous voice, telling him to return the next day for his answer. The messenger had galloped off. God alone knew where he was planning to camp, or if he travelled with more warriors. Scand had doubled the guard that night, fearing a surprise attack.

Now Eanfrith stood and bid Scand to follow him to the back of the hall, where curtains partitioned off his sleeping quarters.

Unable to contain himself, Scand continued to rail against the king, but now in a tense and forced whisper. "Again, lord, I am sorry for my outburst, but you must see this is a trap."

He could see that Eanfrith was angry, furious at being dishonoured in front of his most trusted followers, his comitatus. Yet he saw him rein in his ire before he spoke.

"Do not fret, old friend," said Eanfrith, his voice calm. Quiet and soothing. "Cadwallon will do me no harm."

He spoke with an assurance that was unsettling. Something in his voice made Scand give pause. A tiny sliver of dread needled him. "How can you be so sure, lord king?"

Eanfrith smiled. "He is in debt to me."

"What do you mean?"

"I gave him aid."

"What aid?"

"Wealth, to buy weapons and armour. Information about Edwin's court." Eanfrith's smile broadened.

"And what did you get in return?" Scand's voice was flat.

"Bernicia, of course. My birthright!" He was pleased with himself at having kept these things secret for so long. Almost as pleased as he was at having collaborated with the Waelisc king in order to secure the throne of Bernicia once more. The look of pure shock on Scand's face made him laugh aloud, unable to suppress his glee.

Eanfrith couldn't stop talking now that the secret was out. He continued in a hurried rush. "Don't you see? That is why I was not concerned at our apparent lack of protection here at Gefrin. I prefer the hall here and there is no reason to flee to Bebbanburg. We don't need its cliffs and walls. We are not under threat here. I have taken Bernicia without losing a man in battle. The tale-tellers will talk of this for generations. I will have Leofwine begin work on a song as soon as I return from the visit to Cadwallon."

Scand was speechless.

"What did you think? That I had lost my senses?"

Scand stared at the king. He was like a young boy who had played a trick on his elders.

Eanfrith laughed again. "No, my friend. I am no fool."

Scand said nothing.

He dared say nothing. For he had a terrible feeling that his king was wrong.

There was fog in the early morning. Thick and blinding. Shapes loomed out of the gloom like shadowed memories of bad dreams. Beobrand and the others saddled their horses, closed the door of the house they had used and left the lonely steading. They had seen nobody during the night, but one of the men had spotted what he thought was the glimmer of a fire someway off to the west, on higher ground. Whether it was the owners of the buildings, the men they pursued, or some other dweller of these lands, they could not tell.

They rode on into the west. More slowly due to the fog. They were unsure of their quarries' path, stopping whenever there was a fork in the track to look for a sign and discuss which way to go. They felt lost in this land of shades and mist. At sundown they had thought they were almost upon their prey, now they were less sure.

They rode on in silence, listening keenly for any sound beyond their horses' hooves or the creak and jangle of their battle gear and harness. They heard nothing and rode on blindly, increasingly anxious and irritable.

They were pleased when the sun rose high in the sky and dispelled the fog. They had been climbing steadily all morning, moving along valleys, but now they decided to get a better look at what lay ahead. They kicked their horses up a goat path until they rode atop the ridge of a large hill. The land opened up before them. They reined in their mounts and surveyed the land.

They did not talk for some time, soaking in the rays of the

sun. It breathed new life into them and their spirits lifted. The horses dipped their heads to crop at the long, sturdy grass that survived on this windswept peak.

Below them was a desolate landscape of moors. Grass, heather and gorse. Small brooks trickled from higher ground. Mist still clung to dips in the land.

Acennan broke the silence suddenly. "Over there!" he pointed. They peered into the distance, and saw three figures trudging over the moorland. They were too far off to see details, but they were convinced they had found the men they hunted. Beobrand believed it also. He thought he could make out who the three were, but he said nothing. He did not want to remind the others that he had once travelled with these men.

He was not the only one to note that there was no horse with them.

"Perhaps their horseman has ridden back to outflank us," Acennan said. "Be on your guard for an ambush."

Beobrand thought of Octa. Had Hengist ambushed him? Hengist had surely been the rider in the group they were following, he would have allowed no other to ride before him. He shuddered at the thought of Hengist attacking them unannounced. He hoped none of the others had seen the shiver.

"We should get off of this ridge," he said. "They will see us against the sky and we may still have the element of surprise."

Taking a last moment to fix the men's position with regard to the scant landmarks available, they spurred their horses down the hill at a canter. Their enemies were within their grasp now. They would catch them before the end of the day and mete out justice.

Beobrand looked around at the horizon one last time for any sign of Hengist, but he saw none. He kicked his horse after the others, a feeling of disquiet wrapped around him like a wet cloak.

"Woden's teeth!" screamed the man, as his horse tripped and stumbled. He was thrown over its head and fell heavily. Rider and mount both rolled down the slope. The steed narrowly missed crushing the thegn, but did give him a nasty kick as it careened past. It was a glancing blow to the foot, but the man still let out another cry. Glancing blow or not, it hurt to be kicked by a horse.

Acennan, Beobrand and the other two riders who were still in their saddles were unable to contain their mirth. They were feeling cheered by the sighting of their quarries and the sunshine. Seeing their companion tossed onto the ground and then kicked by his own horse struck them as one of the funniest things they could recall. The object of their humour was not laughing. He stood shakily and scowled at the others where they had reined in to watch. The look on his face set them off again.

He rubbed his foot and hobbled over to where his horse stood. It was shaking and skittish. It took him a while to calm it with soothing words. In that time, it became clear to all of them that the horse was hurt. The mood changed at once. This was no laughing matter now. A lame horse would mean their pace would slow. They might not catch up with the three figures they'd seen from the top of the bluff.

They dismounted and crowded round. They enquired after the horse's leg, asked if the man was well. He was not easily mollified. The horse was lame, as they'd expected. It had a pronounced limp and would not bear the weight of a rider.

"We must not waste time here," Acennan said. "We will

lead the horse and you can share one of the other mounts. We'll take turns so as not to tire them too much."

They quickly agreed who the horseless rider should share with first and they set off again, more slowly now, into the west.

They passed a small clump of bushes, surrounded by a circle of stones. Each stone was nearly the height of a man. The bushes fluttered with tatters of cloth and trinkets that had been hung from the branches. Left there by people who sought divine intervention from whichever god was revered in this place. As they drew close to the shrine, a cloud moved over the sun. At the same moment, they saw that one of the stones was decorated with a ghastly token. A human skull peered sightlessly at them, grinning teeth crooked and yellow.

This was a bad omen. Perhaps the men they pursued had prayed here, or offered sacrifice.

They hurried past. The sun returned from behind the clouds.

They pressed on, but all of the men now felt anxious. Acennan touched the boar that was carved into his fine war-helm. He caught Beobrand's eye. Beobrand saw fear there. They outnumbered their prey, were men of strength and honour and carried strong battle weapons, yet the omens had sapped their resolve. They rode on, despondent now. Where they had been convinced of victory and success, now they only expected failure and defeat. The change in them was as striking as it was fast in coming.

Beobrand could feel his own will waver. Perhaps we should turn back, whispered a small voice in his head.

But this was not the voice of a warrior. Of one of the comitatus, of the mighty thegn, Scand, right-hand man of the king. This was the voice of a coward. He refused to listen to it.

"Come, men," he said in a strong voice, startling them out of their gloomy reverie. "Are we womenfolk who would cower at the shadow of a cloud over the sun? Should we fear the portent of a horse falling on a steep path? No, we are warriors of Scand and we ride to bring our lord king's justice to outlaws. We should not be afraid of omens. It is our enemies who should be frightened, for we will bring vengeance to them! We will smite them with our lord's wrath for what they have done."

The men laughed. The young man spoke well. The spell of the standing stones was broken and their mood lifted somewhat.

Acennan watched Beobrand's back as he rode on.

Maybe he had been too quick to judge. The boy might do.

19

In Gefrin, they feasted long into the night. The king was in fine spirits and this rubbed off on his thegns. All except Scand. He sat gloomily in the corner and did not join in the merriment. The men glanced at him, and one of them, Galan, as jubilant as the king, called out to him, offering him mead and meat, but Scand was not interested. Perhaps he was ailing with something, they thought. Or maybe the king had rebuked him when he had pulled him away from the group. Whatever cloud hung over Scand, the others forgot about him as the drink flowed and the hall became raucous with boasting talk and tales.

Leofwine seized onto the mood and sang with a fine loud voice. Then, later, as the night drew in and the only light in the hall came from the embers of the hearth fire, he told the story of a troll that crept into a hall on just such a night. He told the story well, and the up-lit faces of the men were rapt. They were slack-jawed in expectation as he described the beast dripping with grime from the mere where he lived and how he ravaged the people of the hall with terrible strength. To fight the beast, the lord of the hall called upon a great warrior from across the sea. Leofwine called this warrior, Eanfrith, which gained a huge cheer from his audience and a broad smile from the king, who banged the table with his eating knife in appreciation.

In the way of stories, the hero defeated the fell beast and the warrior, Eanfrith, was rewarded handsomely for his bravery. Leofwine had told this story before with a differently-named hero, but in the full version the hero got old and died. Judging his audience well, he decided against completing the tale, preferring to leave the hero wealthy, famous and lauded by all.

As the applause and cheering abated, Eanfrith, his cheeks shining in the hearth-light, pulled a gold ring from his finger and tossed it towards Leofwine. It was a poor throw and the light was dim, so Leofwine dropped it. He reached down quickly and scooped it up, holding it high for all to see. His cheeks burnt.

"Gold for a golden voice!" slurred Eanfrith. "His skill at catching does not match that of his singing!" It was a poor jest, but the throng laughed loud and long.

Elsewhere in Gefrin there are women preparing their dead for burial, thought Leofwine, yet here we are feasting. He did not know what else he could do, but the thought sat heavy on him. He gripped the golden ring in his fist and hoped that Beobrand's woman was not alone with her dead father that night.

A light rain fell during the night, drizzling over Beobrand and the others where they lay wrapped in blankets. Beobrand slept fitfully and rose before he was roused to take his turn on guard. He stood and stretched, his lower back and thighs stiff from the riding. They had ridden hard all the previous day, but they had not come upon the men they sought. Nor had they seen any other people. The land was desolate and lonely. As night fell, they had made camp and collapsed with tiredness.

A wind was blowing out of the north and the rain clouds were scudding south, breaking up as they went. Beobrand could make out the still figure of Acennan silhouetted against the deep, silken purple of the night sky. The stocky warrior was standing, leaning his head against the shaft of his spear. Beobrand wondered if he was asleep on his feet, but Acennan proved he was alert by speaking up as Beobrand approached.

"I could see their fire again. Before the rain. I don't believe they know they are being followed. They make no attempt to conceal themselves."

"We should leave before first light. With any luck we will catch them by surprise."

"Yes. We should put an end to this tomorrow. We are far from our lord's hall. It feels wrong. War is brewing and we should be with our lord."

The use of the term "our lord" was not missed on Beobrand. It was a good feeling to be included by Acennan in Scand's comitatus. He was unlikely to get anything closer to an apology or open acceptance.

"Why don't you sleep for a while?" said Beobrand. "I will awaken you before dawn."

"Very well. Don't fall asleep or I'll have to give you a beating." Beobrand could not see his face in the darkness, but he could hear the smile in his voice.

Eanfrith's mood was still ebullient in the morning. Despite the amount of mead and ale he had consumed, the king seemed as fresh as a child who had slept the whole night after a drink of warm milk. He ordered his steward to prepare horses and provisions for a journey for him and twelve of his most trusted thegns.

Thralls and bondsmen ran hither and thither filling sacks with hams, cheeses and all manner of other food. Skins were filled with water. Two slave girls brushed and wrapped the king's best clothes for him to wear when attending the king of Gwynedd.

By the time Gwalchmei rode once more into Gefrin, Eanfrith and his thegns were ready to leave.

As the black-garbed rider approached, Eanfrith turned to Scand. "I leave you in charge, old friend."

Scand could not bring himself to smile, instead he bowed his head. "I will keep Gefrin safe in your absence. I will watch over Finola and Talorcan and see that no ill befalls them." The queen had not come out to bid her husband farewell, but young Talorcan stood by Scand's side, watching proceedings with a keen eye. Scand placed his hand on the boy's shoulder protectively.

Eanfrith gave his son a brief smile and a nod. "Do as Scand says, Talorcan."

"Yes, father," he replied, but he did not look at Eanfrith.

Eanfrith turned his attention back to Scand. "You have nothing to fear here. Find yourself a nice girl. You should enjoy yourself."

Eanfrith's attempt at levity fell flat. He faced the approaching Waelisc rider.

Gwalchmei halted and said, "What decision have you taken, Eanfrith King?"

Eanfrith smiled. "I will ride to your camp and meet your lord." He mounted his horse, a fine grey stallion held ready by the hawk-nosed Galan. Eanfrith swung into the saddle lithely. He was not a young man, but he had always been a good rider. The men who would ride with him mounted too. They were caparisoned in their finest trappings of war. Polished helms, silver-hilted swords, freshly painted shields. They were a formidable band of warriors, hale and strong.

Eanfrith turned to the men who were staying behind. "You are to follow Scand as if he speaks with my voice until I return. I will come back soon and I will bring good news of peace. Watch to the south, for our returning. Lead on, Gwalchmei ap Gwyar."

They rode out of Gefrin, leaving a pall of dust hanging in the air. The day was clear and dry and the sun was warm, but as he watched the thirteen men riding after the black rider on the black horse, Scand felt a chill run down his back.

"Are you sure you want to burn him, child?" the elderly woman asked Sunniva. It was the old way, but most of the people of Gefrin now embraced the Christ priests' teachings and buried their dead.

"I am sure. It is what he would have wanted. He lived with fire and would want to be sent on with fire."

She was determined in this and had been awake since the first light of dawn collecting firewood. She had refused any help, piling it high into a pyre behind their house.

Now, four men helped to carry her father out to the mound of wood. They laid him down with reverence on the branches. The tightly-wrapped cadaver shifted and for a moment they thought the pyre would collapse. But after a moment, it settled. They moved away to a safe distance.

Sunniva walked slowly back to the forge where she had

stoked the fire that morning, like so many other mornings. She scooped some of the charcoal into a pot. It was fitting that fire from Strang's forge should start the flames that would consume his earthly remains.

She walked back around the house to her father's waiting form. Men and women were gathered around to witness the smith's final passing.

Sunniva stooped at the base of the dry wood, spilling some of the coals at different points. The kindling had been cunningly placed and flames quickly licked up the wood. She was good with fires. It was one of the things her father had taught her.

She stood close to the flames, the early morning breeze fanning them.

The heat grew too much for her. The onlookers were suddenly afraid that she meant to throw herself onto Strang's bone fire.

Her tears were hot on her face. Her hair was whipped about by the wind rushing in to breathe life into the fire. Her father's body was dark, blackened and blurred by the conflagration.

Wisps of her hair singed and shrivelled. Her eyes stung from the heat.

At last she staggered back. The women caught her. Their hands held her. Supported her. She sobbed, but there was no sound over the roar of the fire that sent her father's body on to the afterlife.

The fire burnt for a long time.

The others slowly moved away. There were more dead to see to.

And life went on.

All around Gefrin people saw to their business. People

mourned their loved ones. Newly-widowed mothers fretted about how they would feed their children. Livestock was taken to pasture. Warriors practised the art of killing.

But all the while the smoke from the smith's funeral pyre painted a dark smudge on the sky.

Sunniva, daughter of Strang, watched over it all that long day. She watched until the embers collapsed in on themselves.

Never again would she hear her father working the metal at the forge, bending the strongest of elements to his will. Nor would she again sit with him and share food in companionable silence.

She was alone.

Her thoughts turned to Beobrand. She prayed over her father's ashes, where his spirit could take the message to the gods. She prayed that her lover would find her father's murderers. She asked that the gods would guide him. That he would find them, and kill them.

And then, the blood price exacted from her father's slayers, she prayed Beobrand would come back to her.

Beobrand shook them all awake when the birds were announcing the imminence of the dawn. They ate sparingly of their provisions, drank a few gulps of water and did not light a fire. The lame horse was no better, but no worse.

They mounted up and moved off into the pre-dawn gloom. They had loosened their blades in their scabbards, donned helmets and sharpened spears. They all hoped that today would bring an end to the hunt. They rode quietly towards where Acennan had spotted the fire in the darkness.

The sun rose on a clear day. All of the clouds had blown away during the night. The riders' shadows streamed in front of them, pointing the way westward. Further into the unknown.

As the light picked out the details of the terrain, their quarries' camp could be seen clearly. It was closer than they had expected, on the lower slope of a large, tree-topped hill. Acennan, who rode at the front of the group, pointed and signalled for the men to prepare themselves. They drew their weapons and spread out. They rode up the hill in silence and were barely a spear's throw away when one of the camp's inhabitants saw them and raised the alarm.

The figures jumped up and readied themselves for combat quickly.

Acennan said, "Give them no time to prepare. Forward!"

The riders heel-kicked their steeds forward, quickly closing the gap.

The three figures in the camp drew together, forming a tiny shieldwall. Beobrand recognised each of them. Hafgan, the tall, lithe Waelisc was on the right, Dreng, the old, blood-thirsty warrior stood on the left and Tondberct, the young Bernician warrior whom Beobrand had considered a friend, stood in the middle. The three locked shields and stood against the horsemen who lumbered up the hill.

There was no sign of Hengist or a horse in the camp.

The incline took the speed out of the charge and before they could join in battle, Hafgan let fly with one of his javelins. Beobrand watched its flight. It wobbled as it left Hafgan's hand, but the throw was true. It arced into the bright sky, a dark sliver of death streaking on duck-shell blue, before falling quickly to lance into the neck of the horse carrying two riders. The horse whinnied and shied off to one side. The javelin had not penetrated deeply and was shaken free. The men managed to slow the horse and dismount, but they would have to climb the rest of the way on foot. The horse galloped away down and eastward, towards the lame horse that had been left at the bottom of the slope.

Beobrand kicked his horse on, urging it to go faster. Acennan and another rider rode on either side of him.

When they got close to the puny shieldwall, the others pulled their mounts to a halt and quickly dismounted. It was not the way of the Angelfolc to fight from horseback. Shield to shield was the warrior way.

But Beobrand drove his horse on, raking its flanks savagely with his heels. He felt the cold, clarity of battle descend on him. If they faced them with their own shieldwall, the outcome would be uncertain. They were attacking uphill, they did not drastically outnumber their foe and they had sustained the first injury to their ranks with Hafgan's javelin. Their only advantage was the bulk of the horses they rode. There was no time to think clearly about what he was doing. He'd made the decision almost before the idea had formed in his mind.

Acennan slid from his horse and pulled his shield onto his arm, ready to stand shoulder to shoulder with his companions. He saw Beobrand riding on and saw he had no intention of stopping. He shook his head in disbelief.

"Onwards!" he shouted, and ran up the slope as fast as he could.

At the last moment Beobrand saw recognition in the faces of the three men who stood defiantly before him. Recognition and the realisation that he did not plan to stop. Fear too. This was the man who had faced Hengist and survived. They had seen Beobrand kill savagely with the ease of a ceorl scything hay.

Hafgan was the fastest to react. At the instant before impact he lifted another javelin from the ground and plunged it into the unprotected chest of Beobrand's mount. The animal screamed. Dark blood splashed. The javelin snapped and whipped across Tondberct's face, stunning him. The horse's momentum carried it on, even as its lifeblood pumped from the wound in its chest. It crashed into Tondberct and Dreng's shields, sending them both reeling backwards.

Prepared for the collision, Beobrand leapt from the saddle, launching himself at Dreng and clear of the flailing horse. He mistimed the jump and landed hard, sprawling to the dew-wet ground. The fall winded him, but he pushed himself up. He was exposed and vulnerable while prone. He drew Hrunting.

Dreng was also climbing to his feet. Tondberct did not move. Hafgan pulled his long knife and turned, squinting into the rising sun, to face the men running up the hill towards them.

The horse thrashed on the ground, unable to rise now. Its whinnying cries were pitiful to hear.

Acennan and the other three warriors soon reached the camp. They stood, shield to shield, metal-garbed and menacing. They were some way behind Beobrand, but he did not want to lose the moment of advantage he had gained.

He took a step towards Dreng and spoke in a strong, clear voice. "Put down your weapons or be killed!"

Tondberct groaned. Hafgan and Dreng looked uncertain. Behind them, the horse's harsh breaths were growing weaker. Its hooves now silent.

"Now!" thundered Beobrand. He took a step to close the gap with Dreng.

The old warrior licked his lips, his eyes darting this way and that, searching for an escape. In the faces of the five warriors before him, he saw none. Certain death awaited him if he chose to fight. He dropped his langseax.

A moment later, Hafgan dropped his knife.

Acennan let out a long breath.

"Lie down on the earth. Face down," said Beobrand. His voice as cold and sharp as the blade in his hand.

Dreng, resigned to his defeat now, complied.

Hafgan still stood. He stared at Beobrand defiantly. "Why should I lie before you? You are no better than I." His accent was strong, but the words were clear and easy to understand.

Beobrand walked slowly towards the Waelisc, stopping in front of him, close enough to smell his breath. "You will lie as I have commanded it. We are gesithas of Scand, thegn of Eanfrith, king of Bernicia. This is his land. By your hand innocent men have died." All of his impotent rage at Cathryn's death rose up within him. "Women too," he said more quietly, so only Hafgan could hear. Their eyes met. Beobrand let his anger consume him. Without warning, he hammered his forehead into Hafgan's face. The blow carried months of pent up aggression and shame and Hafgan's head was flung back with the force of it. His nose broke and blood spurted. He fell to the ground in a daze.

"I said, lie down," said Beobrand. He spat on Hafgan's unmoving form and turned away. "Tie their hands."

Acennan raised an eyebrow at Beobrand assuming the mantle of command so effortlessly, but now was not the time to confront him. He stared at the tall, pony-tailed man on the ground. Acennan's hand involuntarily touched his own scarred nose, crooked since the fight with Beobrand.

He said, "I'll say this for you, Beobrand. You know how to get your way." He smiled wryly.

"Come on," he said to the others, "tie their hands. Then we can decide what to do with them."

★

"We cannot take them back with us. We will be slow enough as it is." Acennan looked at Beobrand as he spoke. He was not happy with losing another horse, but he had to admit that the young Cantware warrior's action had saved them a fight. Shieldwall to shieldwall, there was no telling how that fight would have gone. The three men they'd captured certainly looked able to acquit themselves in combat. It had been a foolhardy thing to do, but the gods smiled on the brave.

One of the men said, "We need talk no more on this. We saw what they did to the smith and the charcoal men. The old one wears Strang's cloak brooch. They are all doomed by their actions."

Their three captives lay on the ground some way from the fire that they themselves had built. Acennan and the others had added fuel to the embers and were now preparing a warming meal of roast horse meat. Acennan had made Beobrand butcher it. It seemed fitting, as he had caused its death. It had been a fine mount. Scand would not be pleased at its loss. But the cooking meat smelt so good that Acennan's anger had already dissipated.

The lame mare and the javelin-injured horse had been brought up the hill, a little way from the campsite. There they had been tethered, along with the two other horses, to stakes in the ground. They were nervous from the fight. The smell and sight of the fallen horse made them skittish. But the men had been pleased to see that the javelin wound was superficial; the bleeding had already stopped.

Beobrand was silent for a long while after the confrontation with his erstwhile companions. His hands started to shake and he felt dazed. He concentrated on butchering his horse, hiding his trembling hands from the others. He left them to discuss the fate of their captives. Once his hands were still again, he spoke up.

"These men are guilty of all you saw in the charcoal men's clearing. But there are other acts for which they should be given justice." He paused, aware that all the men were listening to him. "I have been a witness to man-slayings of the worst kind. And the forcing of women."

A man laughed, ready to make a ribald comment, but one look from Beobrand saw the words dry up in his mouth.

"It is no matter of jest to see a young woman violated and then murdered." He stared at each man in turn, daring them to make light of his words. None accepted the challenge. "I know you have seen battle. In that there is honour. But these men, and the man who rode with them, enjoy killing and torturing those who cannot defend themselves."

"You rode with them," a man said. "Aren't you as guilty as them?"

Beobrand lowered his eyes. "I was weak. But I did try to stop them. I fought their leader."

"We have heard the tale told by Leofwine in King Eanfrith's hall," Acennan said. "Let no man here doubt Beobrand's honour. Any that does, will have to answer to me. I say Beobrand should decide what we do with them, as he knows their crimes better than us. What say you, Beobrand?"

Beobrand stared at the three tied men. Helpless now, just as Cathryn had been. Dreng lay with his eyes closed, reconciled to his fate. Hafgan glared at him, his face caked with dried blood. His swollen, puffy eyes defiant and full of hate. Lastly, he looked at Tondberct. Easy-going and quick to jest. He had thought him a friend. Yet Tondberct had done nothing to stop Hengist and the others from their savagery. He had stood by and would have watched as Hengist killed Coenred. He had turned against Beobrand completely in Engelmynster.

"Did Hengist ride with you?" he asked.

Tondberct was suddenly hopeful. If he told Beobrand what he wanted to hear perhaps he'd let him go. "He did. He left us two days ago."

"Why did he leave you?"

Tondberct's eyes flicked to Dreng. "We quarrelled. He wanted to go south, we wanted to travel west. He rode away. You know what his moods are like. He's been worse since… since you fought him."

"Where did he plan to go?"

"I don't know. He said he might join Cadwallon or Penda. He made no sense. He babbled a lot about your sword. Said it should have been his."

"Why don't you shut your mouth, you snivelling runt?" spat Dreng. "I am tired of listening to you prattle like a woman."

Beobrand ignored Dreng. He stared into Tondberct's eyes. They were pleading with him. He remembered that cold night in the forest when he had stared into other pleading eyes. Anger filled him.

Sensing that his doom was about to be pronounced, Tondberct said in a whining voice, "Come on, Beo. We had some good times, didn't we? You could release us. We'd never come back to Bernicia. You'd never see us again. We'd disappear. I swear it!"

"Your oath is like chaff on the wind. Your words are hollow." Beobrand's voice was as hard and chill as the ground underneath Cathryn's mutilated corpse.

"But I never killed anyone," Tondberct continued, starting to snivel. "That was the others." He sounded pathetic, like a child blaming an older sibling for some small misdemeanour.

It was probably true though. Tondberct was never comfortable with the violence in the way that Hengist, Dreng and the others were. Beobrand had also stood by and witnessed terrible acts. His shame threatened to engulf him as it came flooding back.

"You chose your path a long time ago, Tondberct. You could have left. You could have fought."

"But they would have killed me!" Tondberct was weeping now. Dreng and Hafgan turned away from him, ashamed. Dreng spat and then licked his lips.

"They might have. But it would have been an honourable death. A man's death. A warrior's death."

Beobrand didn't want to hear Tondberct's crying anymore. It grated on his soul. He wanted rid of all these men who had been present in that forest clearing. Who had witnessed his shame.

"Hang them all," he said and turned away.

Tondberct's cries rose to a new pitch.

Eanfrith had a warm feeling inside. The ride south to Cadwallon's camp only took a couple of days and the weather was kind. His men were understandably tense, feeling they were riding into the jaws of the wolf, but Eanfrith assured them they would come to no harm. He did not wish to tell them about his secret pact with Cadwallon. Most warriors were simple when it came to the ways of kings and diplomacy. They were governed by a simple code of oaths and honour and would not comprehend that a king could not always be so simplistic in his dealings. He had done what was needed to get back the kingdom that had been his father's and he was proud of that.

As they rode south, Eanfrith enjoyed surveying the land that was now his. It was vast and beautiful. Rugged and fertile. When they passed farms or settlements he made sure that the people knew who he was and that he was riding south to secure peace for the whole of Bernicia. The people were scared. They had suffered much in the winter and expected the worst when they saw riders approaching with a warlike aspect. On more than one occasion they found houses empty, their inhabitants having fled at the sight of the armed men. Those people they did see stared blankly back at the king. He had armed men with him and therefore he should be respected, but one king was to them the same as any other. If he could bring peace to the land, then the gods be praised. But the rumours from the south were that the Waelisc were amassing a warhost to ride north into Bernicia. This man with a handful of warriors was unlikely to stop war from coming.

The further south they rode, the more nervous the locals and other travellers were. When they were less than a day's ride from the Waelisc camp, they began to come across buildings that had been razed to the ground. Eanfrith was displeased. "These are my people," he said to Gwalchmei, "why have their homes been destroyed?"

The Waelisc replied, "You must not forget, Eanfrith King, that we have been at war with Edwin for a long time before now. We did what we had to do. I'm sure you understand."

The explanation made sense to Eanfrith. He understood that nothing was simple.

"I understand," he said, airily. But as they passed an increasing number of burnt out buildings, his men became more uneasy.

When they arrived at the camp they were shocked at its size. There were tents and makeshift shelters covering a huge area to the south of the massive Wall that crossed the land from east to west. The Wall made up the northern perimeter of the camp. They could see men standing on the Wall as they approached. Behind them, the camp was shrouded in a thin fog of smoke from dozens of campfires.

As they rode up to the broken gateway through the Wall, a group of riders made its way out to them and hailed Gwalchmei in their musical tongue. They spoke briefly.

Eanfrith understood their tongue well, having lived for many years amongst his wife's people in Dál Riata, but the men spoke in hushed tones and he was only able to make out his own name and that of the king he was to visit.

Gwalchmei then said, "King Cadwallon will see you directly. He is expecting you and is anxious to meet you."

They followed Gwalchmei and the new riders through the camp. Picking their way between the different shelters and fires, the Bernicians could feel all the eyes of the Waelisc warhost on them. The enmity was palpable. One man spat at Eanfrith. Others laughed and made insulting gestures. Eanfrith shrugged all of this off as the crude ignorance of the lowly Waelisc warriors. They were little more than savages. You could expect no better from them. He ignored them and rode on after Gwalchmei.

Their destination soon became clear. A wooden hall situated on a small rise in the middle of the encampment. It was a large hall and must have belonged to the local ealdorman or thegn.

At the riders' approach, a murder of crows rose in a raucous flutter from where they had been feeding. Flapping away, they left their meal exposed. They had been feasting on three bodies that dangled from roughly made gibbets. The corpses' faces were black and bloated. Their eyeless sockets stared blindly at Eanfrith and the others as they passed.

Eanfrith shuddered. "Who were those men? Why were they hanged?" he asked Gwalchmei.

Gwalchmei shrugged. "Every large group of warriors like this will always have some who choose not to obey the laws of their lord. They must be punished as an example to the rest."

They reined in their mounts at the entrance to the hall. Servants saw to the horses and helped them carry their baggage.

Gwalchmei led the way to the doors of the hall, where he turned and addressed Eanfrith and his retainers. "King Cadwallon does not allow armed men to approach him." There was consternation amongst Eanfrith's men, but Gwalchmei continued quickly. "However, as a gesture of the peace and friendship that we hope will live between our kingdoms, you may keep your weapons. There is nothing for you to fear here, and we should fear nothing from you."

The warriors, somewhat mollified, but still uneasy at being surrounded by Waelisc, followed their lord into the dark interior of the hall.

Inside, it was much like any other hall. Benches ran down either side and boards had been laid out with food and drink. A welcoming fire blazed on the hearthstone. At the head of the hall was an ornately carved wooden seat, upon which sat a slim man. He was dressed in fine robes and had a golden torc about his neck. Many rings adorned his fingers and arms. Gwalchmei strode to him and whispered something in his ear. The man nodded and stood, spreading his arms expansively.

"Welcome, Eanfrith, son of Æthelfrith, son of Aethelric, lord of Bernicia. I am in your debt and have long wished to meet you. Come drink from my cup."

He poured mead into a shallow bowl and proffered it to Eanfrith. Eanfrith stepped forward, aware of the gravity of the moment and accepted the bowl and drank deeply.

"Thank you, Cadwallon ap Cadfan, king of Gwynedd and ruler of the land of Deira. It brings me joy to meet you at last." He handed the bowl back to Cadwallon who drained the last of the mead.

The two men smiled at each other and turned to the warriors gathered in the hall.

"Let us feast!" said Cadwallon and offered Eanfrith a large chair at his right-hand side. It was not as grand as the one Cadwallon sat upon, thought Eanfrith, but no matter. The Waelisc king was clearly friendly and Eanfrith was overjoyed at the reception. He had not dared admit it even to himself, but he had been secretly worried about this encounter. He felt the tension wash away as the drink warmed him. He put his worries aside and allowed himself to relax.

The Waelisc king lavished food and drink upon his guests. They were served heron, plover, pork, hare and venison. Never had any there eaten more or better fare. The bowls and drinking horns were kept full to the brim with ale and mead and after some time Eanfrith and his men were laughing uproariously. All concerns had left them and they slapped each other on the back and told tales of bravery to their host and his retinue. Many of the Waelisc did not understand much of what was said to them, but they smiled in response to the loud Seaxon men.

When Cadwallon stood and raised both of his hands for silence it took some time for the men at the benches to quieten down. Eventually a hush fell on the room and Eanfrith and all of his men looked to the Waelisc king. He brushed his long hair back from his face and smiled at Eanfrith.

"I hope you have enjoyed the feast. It seemed the least I could do." Eanfrith and his gesithas hammered the boards with their knives and drinking horns. Some cheered to

Cadwallon's health. When they settled down, he continued, "I thank you again for your aid against Edwin, my enemy and yours. I think I could like you, Eanfrith," he paused, "if you were not one of the accursed Seaxon who blight our land." Eanfrith's smiled wavered. Had he heard correctly?

"I told Gwalchmei you would not be so foolish as to come to my camp with only a handful of men. But he had heard tell of your pride and I have to say, I am pleased that you have come. It will make taking Bernicia that much easier with you dead."

A chill washed over Eanfrith, as if a cloud had passed in front of the sun. Those of his men whose drink-addled heads could understand what Cadwallon had said were leaping to their feet. Drawing swords and seaxes. Preparing to fight.

Eanfrith remained seated. He looked upon the hall with a strange detachment. Many armed Waelisc had entered the hall while their king spoke and now Eanfrith saw the first of his men cut down as he was rousing himself from the bench where he sat. Blood misted in the smoky air. Benches were overturned. Iron rang against iron. The hall was a tumult of raised voices, screams and the clatter of weapon-play.

He saw Galan, wide-eyed and incredulous, turn to him, as if he expected his king to somehow stop this nightmare. Galan opened his mouth, but before he could utter a word, a blade was dragged across his throat. He blinked in surprise, still staring at Eanfrith in dismay, even as his blood spouted onto the board before him. And so this is how their bloodless conquest of Bernicia would end. All their scheming had been for nought.

Eanfrith watched as one by one his men were slain. All the while he sat quite still. He was numb. He could not understand how this had happened. How could he have failed his people so absolutely?

Desolation and regrets swept through him. He would never see Talorcan become a man. He had not been a good father to the boy. Or a good husband to his wife. He was surprised that in this moment, so close to his end, he should think of Finola. He had loved her in his own way, but never as she deserved.

With the killing of Eanfrith's last man, a hush fell upon the hall.

He turned to look at Cadwallon. "How...?" he couldn't speak. "Why...?"

"Because, Eanfrith King," Cadwallon replied, his voice dripping scorn, "you are a fool."

Eanfrith felt a looming presence behind him. He turned, saw the raven-haired man, Gwalchmei, stepping towards him, sword glittering in the firelight.

And Eanfrith knew that Cadwallon was right.

PART THREE
THE QUENCHING

20

They hanged them from an old yew tree.

Hafgan put up a fight at the end. They needed to beat him to get the noose around his neck. They hoisted him off the ground still kicking and screaming abuse at them in his own tongue. His shouts became gurgling, strangled gasps. He struggled for a long time. Eventually, only his feet still moved. The last twitching as his spirit journeyed beyond middle earth.

They lowered Hafgan's corpse to the ground and removed the noose. They only had one rope.

Dreng accepted the rope with a quiet dignity that the men respected.

He licked his lips and calmly asked, "Will one of you pull on my legs? It will make my passing easier."

Acennan glanced at Beobrand, then nodded and stepped forward. "I will help you on your way, old man," he said.

The others pulled Dreng off of his feet and secured the rope. Acennan gripped his kicking legs around the ankles and pulled down hard. The kicking stopped abruptly.

The sight of his two companions being hanged drove Tondberct mad with fear.

"I didn't kill anyone! Don't kill me, by all the gods, I am not a murderer!" he screamed.

He cried and blubbered. Spittle ran from his chin, like the droolings of a toothless old man.

Quickly, they placed the noose they had removed from Dreng around his throat. It was now fraying slightly and carried signs of its previous victims: hair, skin and dark blood stains where it had rubbed their necks raw. On seeing this Tondberct's body was racked by sobbing. His ravings unnerved them. They regretted not hanging him first.

One of them threw the end of the rope over a branch. Not wishing to listen to him anymore, they pulled on the rope with savage force. Tondberct was lifted off the ground at such speed that his neck broke with an audible crack.

They all let out a breath then, enjoying the sudden silence.

The wind rustled the leaves of the yew. Tondberct's body swung, the rope creaking like the sound of oars in the tholes of a longship.

When they were sure he was dead, they lowered his corpse down and laid it next to the others.

Beobrand watched each man's end with a heavy heart. The solace he sought from avenging Cathryn and Strang did not come. Tondberct's pleading did not move him. There could be no mercy. Death was the only just payment for their crimes.

So why did he still feel ashamed? How could he be rid of this deep-seated anguish?

Of those present in that winter clearing, now only two remained. Hengist and Beobrand himself. He placed his hand on Hrunting's hilt and once more swore a silent oath to all the gods that he would see Hengist dead. Only then, with the death of his kin-slayer, would he know peace.

Riding away, their mood was sombre.

They could not push the horses hard on the return journey. They led the lame horse and the five men rode on the remaining three steeds. They stopped regularly and rested the mounts, redistributing the riders.

The weather was good, but they made slow progress. Each man carried enough horse meat to last the journey home. The rest of the carcass, along with the three corpses, had been left behind for the wolves and crows.

By unspoken consent they travelled wide of the skull-topped shrine. None of them wanted to be close to that place again.

On the afternoon of the second day they came back to the steading where they had slept on their outward journey. Now they approached from the empty lands to the west, with the sun at their backs. They could see smoke drifting up from the buildings and as they got closer they saw a man moving in the space between the dwellings. He spotted them at last and ran inside. By the time they arrived at the collection of houses, there were six men in their path. Each was armed. There were a couple of spears, an axe and three seaxes, but they did not have the bearing of fighting men. They were nervous and the younger men fidgeted. Two were little more than boys.

Acennan told Beobrand and the others to wait and he spurred his horse forward. He halted in front of the men.

"I am Acennan, son of Bron, hearth-warrior of Scand, trusted thegn of Eanfrith, king of this land of Bernicia. We mean you no harm."

It took him some time to convince them of what he said, but in the end the leader of the group, a man called Cedd, gruffly offered them lodging for the night. With better grace, Cedd's wife ushered them into her house and passed around a large wooden cup of mead. They all drank, solemnly sharing the drink, accepting the ritual welcome.

They ate well that night. The womenfolk cooked plain food and were grateful for some of the meat the warriors carried, adding it to the stew.

Cedd told them how Hengist and his companions had killed their best pig. They had not stopped at the farmstead for long. When Cedd's folk had seen Acennan and his men coming from the east, they had gathered up their livestock and fled to a secret place.

He was pleased to hear of the hanging, and asked for details of the fight. When they heard the tale they were all overjoyed to be eating the very horse that had been instrumental in their assailants' capture.

They all rested well that night, but Acennan made them keep watch. "You can never trust these ceorls in the middle of nowhere. They'd as likely butcher us in our sleep and eat us in place of the best pig they lost!"

Scand was exhausted. He rubbed his eyes and looked at the setting sun. Still no word from Eanfrith or Acennan and the men who had ridden into the west. He was concerned about both. He was more convinced than ever that war was coming.

That morning he had witnessed a terrible omen. The hall doors had been open to let in light and air. A magpie had landed in the doorway, silhouetted against the bright daylight. It had stood there for a moment, then it cocked its head as if listening to something, perhaps the voices of the dead. The fell bird had then flown into the hall. It had flapped along the length of the chamber and landed on the high back of the king's seat. Scand had hardly believed his own eyes. He looked around to see the reaction of others, but unusually the hall was empty apart from him and the bird.

It had stared at him with its beady eye, head moving with small jerky motions. He was certain that the bird brought him a message. It was a harbinger of terrible portent. Eventually, having made sure that the old warrior had seen and understood, the bird flapped to the ground, seized a scrap of meat in its beak and flew back out into the light.

Scand had been shaken, but he did not mention the omen to anyone. Instead, he had made his face stern and unreadable then walked back out to where the warriors were training. They looked to him for guidance and he would not fail them or his king.

Ever since Eanfrith had left with his retainers, following that black rider, Gwalchmei, Scand had worked incessantly on preparing the warriors and the people of Gefrin for battle. Eanfrith had placed him in charge and he did not mean to waste a moment. All around him men were slumped on the ground, panting and drenched in sweat. He had made them run in whatever armour they possessed and then form two shieldwalls. It was then a contest to see which group of men could shove the other back past a mark on the ground using brute force. For the winners Scand had promised mead and ale, for the losers only water that night. By the end of the day of exercises, the winning group was too tired to cheer.

For the rest of the townsfolk he had set the task of gathering their belongings together in small enough packs and bags to be carried. He relied on the women to organise themselves. The young woman, Sunniva, seemed to have been strengthened by the death of her father. The way that steel is tempered by fire in the forge. No sooner had her father been laid in the ground than she had begun to go from house to house with Fugol ensuring that people were choosing the most important items for a hasty retreat from Gefrin should the time arise. Beobrand had chosen well there. Or more accurately he had been lucky that she had chosen him. A brief smile played on his lips before his habitual frown returned.

Finola had risen to the task of organising the royal household. She was soft-spoken and small, but she knew what she wanted and was the daughter of a king. The thralls and bondsmen quickly learnt to do her bidding without comment.

When he looked into the flames of the fire in the great hall at night, he saw the faces of men who had fallen in shieldwalls far away and long ago. Men he had called friends who had been taken from this world in the way of wyrd. He remembered his first glimpse of the island of Hii, white sand glittering like a jewel in the dark sea. He remembered individuals who had died over that sea in Hibernia, where Eanfrith and his brothers had fought for their Dál Riatan protectors. Their faces were clear to him, but not their names. He had seen too many good men die. And too many women. His own wife, Morna, had left him many years before. How he had loved her, his Pictish beauty. She had died bearing their first child, a son, while he was in Hibernia. The baby had not lasted a week and both were long in the ground when he had returned. He had never married again. No other woman could compare with Morna. His only female company now was Finola. The delicate, thoughtful young woman reminded him in many ways of Morna. She spoke in the same lilting tones and he would sometimes sit with her, talking by the fireside late into the night, wondering what could have been. But his affection for her was that of a father to his child.

He felt protective of Finola and her son, Talorcan. Both were ignored by Eanfrith, and it saddened Scand to see it.

He had sacrificed so much and travelled so far with Eanfrith through all the years of exile waiting for this moment to come, when they could return to the land that was rightfully theirs. He hoped that Eanfrith was right in his assessment of the situation with Cadwallon, but Scand had seldom heard a good word about the honour of the Waelisc king and he feared the worst: that Eanfrith's pride and eagerness for a crown had clouded his mind.

The responsibility for the queen and atheling and the people of Gefrin sat heavily on Scand, but he would not rest until he knew he had done all in his power to ensure their safety. He had several men patrolling the area surrounding Gefrin both day and night, and he had ordered beacons built at regular intervals to be lit if enemies were spotted. He worked the men harder than any of them liked until they all collapsed in exhaustion at the end of every day. Too tired for riddles and song, and all too pleased to let sleep engulf them in her dark embrace.

They left Cedd's folk shortly after dawn, eager to get back to Gefrin. They made good progress. The day was dry and bright. Soon they would be back with their lord and loved ones. Their spirits were high.

They rested the horses frequently and took a long break from the midday sun in the shadow of the trees where the charcoal pits were. When they passed through the clearing all was silent and still. The fires were cold, the clearing deserted.

The men did not speak, but each of them recalled the sights they had seen there a few days before. They were tired from the long days in the saddle, but they sat up straight on their steeds. They had delivered justice to the men who had brought death to the charcoalers and Gefrin's smith. They had done their duty and were now anxious to return.

When they were still some way from Gefrin, two horsemen approached them. They had been posted by Scand to watch the road. They exchanged news. Beobrand, Acennan and the others were shocked to hear of Eanfrith's decision to ride south to meet with Cadwallon. All of them were worried that he had not yet returned.

They rode on, but worry now gnawed at them.

It was dark by the time they crossed the river that flowed to the south of Gefrin. They could see the great hall on the horizon. A black shape that blotted out the stars of the clear night. The settlement was silent, the sound of their horses' hooves travelling far.

They talked briefly to the door wards of the hall who told them that Scand and the men were sleeping. They should rest and then they could tell their tale to Scand in the morning. Acennan and the other men made their way quietly into the hall. Some of the sleeping men stirred and they settled them with soft words.

Acennan turned towards Beobrand, who had stayed in the doorway of the hall. "Are you not going to sleep?" he whispered. Then, realisation dawned and his teeth flashed bright in the starlight. "Or perhaps you have other ideas?"

Beobrand could feel his cheeks colour, but he knew none could see him blush. "I'll go and check on Sunniva," he said awkwardly.

Acennan chuckled quietly. "See you in the morning," he said and moved into the hall.

The door wards closed the doors and sent for bondsmen

to tend to the horses. Beobrand walked back down towards the forge past the silent houses that loomed in the night.

He had not seen Sunniva since Strang's death and he was unsure how she would react to his return. But he could not imagine waiting another heartbeat without seeing her. He had missed her terribly. Only now, with the prospect of seeing her moments away, did he comprehend the extent of his longing to be reunited with her. There was nobody else now.

His heart fluttered in his chest as he swung open the door of the house by the forge. It was dark inside, but he could sense that the hut was not empty.

There was a rustle of cloth and then Sunniva's voice, frightened, tremulous, blurred by sleep. "Who is there?"

Warm relief flooded through Beobrand at the sound. He stepped over the threshold and said, "Do not fear, Sunniva. It is I, Beobrand. I am come home."

And even though he had never lived in this small building, had been in Bernicia for less than a year and in Gefrin for only a couple of months, he knew that it was true.

Sunniva watched Beobrand as he slept.

She could hear the usual sounds of the settlement outside. Someone was whistling. The distant strikes of a hammer on wood. A group of people hurried past talking excitedly, their words muffled by the wattle and daub walls.

The normal sounds of Gefrin would be replaced soon. She was sure of it. War was coming and then all would be chaos and fear. But she looked upon her man's sleeping features and clung to this moment of peace. Since he had left to seek her father, Sunniva's life had spun out of control. Her father's death threatened to consume her with grief the way hidden rocks in a riverbed can cause swirling currents to drag floating objects under. She could feel the darkness ready to smother her, so she had not allowed herself to rest.

She had collected Strang's ashes in an earthenware urn. She had buried the urn with the seax she had made for her father when she was fourteen. He had always cherished it, despite it not holding its edge. She had also interred his hammer. She hoped he would be able to forge metal in the afterlife. It was his passion. She had laid her father to rest next to her mother's remains. He had missed her so, it was right that they were together again.

As soon as the burial was finished, she had set about helping to prepare Gefrin for battle.

She had not allowed herself to think about her father or mother. When she took a moment's rest her mind turned to Beobrand. Would he return? Would he abandon her too?

When he had stumbled into her house, waking her, she thought he was part of her dreams. A shade come to torment her sleep.

But then he had spoken. Touched her hair. Held her in his arms and she had grown weak with relief.

She had fed him and he had told her briefly of what had happened. The hunt into the west. Capturing the men. The hangings.

She had sat close to him, her body warming his. In the darkness her hand had found his. He'd trembled at her touch. She'd felt a rush of desire then and kissed him. Their passion mounted rapidly and she had pushed him onto her bed. Frantically pulling his kirtle and trousers off she had straddled him, gasping as he entered her. They had made love desperately. Like two wayfarers lost in a maelstrom they had clung together, scared to let go.

Spent, they had fallen asleep in each other's arms. She had awoken first and was now content to watch the rise and fall of his chest. To listen to his breathing through half-opened mouth. Safe in the knowledge that he was alive and she was not alone.

She watched motes of dust float in the shaft of bright sunlight that pierced the gloom of the house through a crack in the door. The light fell on Beobrand's face. He stirred, mumbling something in his sleep.

She could hear the shouts of the warriors drifting down from where they were training by the great hall. Beobrand had slept late, exhausted from his journey, but he would want to join the men soon. She did not want him to leave her side again, but she knew this was the man that her wyrd had chosen for her. A brave man. A man of war. And she could no more change his nature than she could tame a wild bear.

He opened his eyes and smiled to see her gazing at him.

"That is the best sight I have seen these past many days," he said.

She returned his smile. Traced the scar on his face with her fingers. "I was so scared you wouldn't come back."

"Only death could keep me away from you."

She looked away, tears prickling her eyes.

"I'm sorry," he said. Death had taken away so much from them both. For a long time she said nothing.

"Did they have a hard passing? The men who killed my father?"

He thought of the yew tree and the creaking rope. "It wasn't easy. They will hurt nobody now."

"Like they hurt you?"

"My wounds have healed."

"I don't mean where you were cut. You carry some other pain with you."

He sat up. Reached out and brushed her hair away from her forehead.

"The one they… *we* travelled with, Hengist. He killed my brother." His voice turned hard and cold. She shivered. "I will have revenge for what he has done."

"Will it take away your pain? If you kill him?"

He stood abruptly.

"I don't know, woman! Once I have killed him, I'll tell you."

He pulled on his trousers and kirtle. Picked up his sword. Prepared to leave. Scand would need him.

She did not reply, but dropped her gaze to the ground. Bit her lip.

He sighed. "Forgive me. I am tired."

"Do not be angry with me," she said. He pulled her into an embrace and held her tightly. Her hair stroked his face. He breathed in her scent. She whispered in his ear. "I asked because you have killed and I have not. Death is a thief to me. Only taking. But you bend it to your will, taking back what others have stolen. I hope killing your enemies brings solace. If not, how can we hope to end this pain?"

Scand was pleased that Acennan and the men had returned with no losses apart from a horse. They had meted out justice to all but one of the perpetrators and this was to be celebrated. He gathered the townsfolk together and recounted what had befallen those who had slain their menfolk. The people were still anxious that their king had left them, but the news of justice gave them a grim sense of satisfaction.

There was still no sign of Eanfrith and Scand caught himself looking south ever more frequently as time went by.

He pushed the men in their training. The addition of Acennan, Beobrand and the others to their ranks lifted their spirits.

Scand was pleasantly surprised to see Acennan and Beobrand talking to each other from time to time. Even smiling and joking during some of the exercises he put them through. Friendships forged in conflict were the strongest. He glanced once more to the south, but all of that day there was no sign of their king.

That evening, despite all of the men being shattered from practising weapon-play, they wanted to hear the tale of the hunt into the west and how the malefactors had been brought to justice.

Leofwine had sat with Beobrand and Acennan during the midday meal and questioned them on every detail. Now, the firelight illuminating his face with a ruddy glow, he told the tale with the verve of an epic saga. Beobrand and Acennan became as giants fighting dragons. He spoke with the voice of the horse that had so bravely sacrificed itself to break the defence of the men they had hunted. Then the tree from which the men were hanged spoke of its sadness at being sullied by the evil of men who were not worthy to be suspended from its great branches.

Beobrand and Acennan looked at each other and grinned. Leofwine's gift at spinning a story was awe-inspiring. All of those who listened felt themselves uplifted. When the tale-teller finished, the men cheered loudly, banging their fists on the boards before them. They were proud of their men and proud of Leofwine.

Scand smiled. It was a wonderful thing to see the power of words over men. Yet he knew that words could only carry them so far. In the end it would be strength and steel that would defend this hall.

As he fell asleep that night, he remembered the magpie on the throne. He pulled his blanket around him, trying to push the memory away. But the image of the black eye of the bird would not leave him and dark dreams of death and fear disturbed his sleep.

In the darkest, quietest marches of the night, when the embers had died down and the only sounds in the hall were the snores of its sleeping residents, the creak of the cooling timbers and the distant shriek of a vixen, Scand was awoken by a sudden tumult.

Other men were rousing themselves. Fumbling for weapons and shields where they were stacked against the walls. There were shouts from outside the hall, the drumming of hooves on packed soil. Scand thought for a moment of the tale Leofwine had told of the rending creature from the mere that stalked the night.

They heard the door wards hail someone who approached. There was a muffled reply and then the doors were swung open.

All the men in the hall were standing now. The room bristled with hastily-drawn swords. A figure stood in the doorway, a shade against the starlight. Cold night air wafted in. The embers glowed more brightly.

"Who disturbs our rest?" asked Scand. He raised his voice, but his throat was dry from sleep and it came out as a croak. Like a magpie's harsh voice.

The man in the doorway took a step into the hall and the dim glimmer of the fire showed them his face. He was one of the men who had been posted to watch the south road. "I bring dire news. Cadwallon marches north with a mighty host. They are almost upon us. The beacons have been lit. We must ready ourselves for war."

There was a moment's silence and then the hall erupted in a cacophony of voices. Men shouted questions. Others screamed for silence.

Scand once more raised his voice. In battle he was able to make himself heard over the screams of dying men and the din of death blows being dealt. Now his voice cracked.

Nobody else heard him, but to Scand, the sound of his own voice echoed in his head like the cackle of a tiding of magpies.

21

"We will make our stand at the river." Scand's battle voice had returned to him and all the men gathered in Gefrin could hear his words. Gone was the uncertainty. Put aside was the fear for his lord. He had a clear objective now and he would act to see it done. Or he would die trying.

There was no time left to worry or think about Eanfrith's fate. The warhost had been seen marching northward and from the account of the man who had seen the Waelisc, they far outnumbered the Bernicians. The river was the best place Scand could think of to defend. The trees would provide a funnelling effect and the water was a natural barrier that would slow their attackers down.

All the fighting men were there. Some, the men who had lived in exile with Eanfrith, were well known to Scand. They were stout of heart and hale. He could trust their resolve. Many of the others he was less sure of. There were younger men in the group and fewer wore armour than he would have liked. Many of the men simply wore a tunic and trousers. He had seen to it in the last few weeks that all had a shield and a spear. That was something. They would have to pray that the days of training would prove enough.

He surveyed the men's faces. Most were grim and dour. Some of the younger lads looked eager, excited, almost happy. Those were the ones who had never stood in the shieldwall before. They would die first, or live to tell the tale and never smile at the prospect of battle again.

Beyond the men, the women and children, along with the longbeards, were trailing out of Gefrin and heading east. They had a couple of carts and all of Gefrin's livestock was being herded along with them. Finola's red hair caught the light of the sun. She walked at the head of the column, with Talorcan at her side. Scand's heart tightened. He loved the queen and the young atheling and hoped he would see them again in this world. It was a straggling group and he prayed they would not meet with any of Cadwallon's warbands. He contemplated sending some of the young men with them, but thought better of it. They would be of no use against a concerted attack, but here he could use their numbers.

Beobrand followed Scand's gaze. He could see Sunniva at the front of the group, just behind Finola. Her golden hair glowed in the brilliant sunlight. She turned at that moment, as if she had felt him looking, and waved.

He could remember her words as she had clung to him desperately that morning. "Don't you dare die, Beobrand son of Grimgundi. Fight with honour, but come back to me. You're all I have now." He had not replied. He had kissed her long and hard and then left to join the warriors in their preparations. He had no intention of dying, but he didn't want to tempt wyrd by saying as much. He touched the iron hilt of Hrunting for luck, then checked that the hammer amulet was safely around his neck. He waved back, forcing a smile.

"We will go to the river and there we will form our shield-wall," Scand said. "We will meet Cadwallon in battle and hold him there. We must be as iron. We will not break. We will stop these Waelisc in their tracks and make them pay dearly for marching into our land."

He did not need to tell the men that their loved ones needed time to reach sanctuary at Bebbanburg. Many thought that Bebbanburg was where they should have been all along. It was impregnable and would be a perfect base. But their king had insisted on staying at Gefrin. He hoped it would not be their undoing.

At the river they waited. Waited and sweated. The day was hot and they were glad to have the cool water of the river to hand. At least they would not be thirsty. They dipped helmets into the water and slaked their thirst as the sun rose to its zenith.

The men congregated into groups of friends and discussed tactics. Some regaled others with stories of past battles, but the boasting sounded hollow. In the same way small dogs will bark when they are scared.

Beobrand sat beside Leofwine. The tale-teller carried a shield and spear; a seax hung from his belt. He was uncharacteristically quiet and subdued. Beobrand liked Leofwine, but he wished Bassus was with him now. The giant warrior's presence would have done much to calm him. He seemed invincible. Beobrand wondered if he would ever see him again.

He found himself looking over at Acennan. A few weeks ago he would not have believed it, but now he was pleased to see him and would welcome him at his side when the weapon-play began. Acennan caught his glance and smiled briefly.

His thoughts drifted to the other time he had been in battle. He had not known what to expect then. He had been full of the tales told in mead halls. He had imagined battle as a glorious thing. Nothing had prepared him for the chaotic gyre of screams, blood, shit and piss of the shieldwall.

Some of the younger warriors tried to engage him in conversation. They asked him what the shieldwall would be like. How many men had stood with Cadwallon at Elmet? Did he think they could stand against the Waelisc king?

Beobrand didn't answer and soon the questions ceased. What could he say? That Cadwallon's men had numbered like the stars? That he could see no way that they could survive against the vastly larger Waelisc host?

He already skirted on the edge of despair. He did not want to dent the men's courage with his own fears. Courage was all they had. That and the knowledge that their actions would give their families time to reach safety.

He could still hear Sunniva's words. She was all he had too. He looked up at the sun and conjured up her face and radiant hair in his mind.

He sat in silence and prayed to Woden it would not be the last time he saw her.

As the sun started to fall into the west the men got restless. Could it be that the Waelisc had travelled some other way? Maybe their families would get cut off from Bebbanburg.

Scand told them to hold firm. They would need to fight soon and they could not afford to split up now. "The Waelisc have heard what a fearsome band of warriors awaits them and they are frightened," he said. The men laughed.

Inside, he cursed silently at the time that had been wasted. Where was Cadwallon? They could have found a better place for this battle, or they could have gone with the womenfolk.

Just as he was beginning to think that the men may be right in their fears, the mounted men he had sent south to watch the warhost galloped into view.

Their horses splashed through the ford, droplets glistening like jewels in the air.

They dismounted and their horses were led to where the few others were tethered. "They will be upon us very soon. We have ridden ahead of them for some time."

All of the men stood up. Urgency and fear were upon them again.

"How many?" asked Scand.

The man paused. He took a cup of water that was offered and took a large gulp. He swilled it around his mouth and then spat, washing away the dust of the road. He lowered his voice so that some of the men could not hear his words. "Four, maybe five times our number, my lord."

Scand looked closely at the path ahead of them. They could see the dust from the host as a pall on the southern horizon. A low-lying dun-coloured cloud.

The trees and bushes to the side of the path would squeeze the enemy force down the slope to the ford where the Bernician shieldwall was formed. The ford was as good a place to defend as any they would be likely to find. The river was too deep and wide for a long way east and west to be easily crossed. Nevertheless, they would have to make sure they kept a watch for the Waelisc trying to cross and outflank them.

Scand turned to the men, raising his voice to carry to all of them. "They are coming now. We have chosen the place of their destruction. The river will run red with their blood. There may be more of them, but you are each worth ten Waelisc!" They cheered. "Now stand strong and remember all you have practised. Keep the shieldwall strong and do not break. Their womenfolk will weep over their corpses tonight. For you are men of Bernicia and you will make them pay the blood price for attacking our land."

The men formed the line. Linden shields were hefted. Swords and seaxes were loosened in scabbards and sheaths. Helms were placed onto sweaty heads. Men kissed talismans for luck. Beobrand felt a hollow queasiness in the pit of his stomach. Somewhere down the line to his right a young man doubled over and vomited into the river. Some of the men laughed, but more than one looked as if he might do the same.

Beobrand looked around him and saw that Acennan stood to his right. He was pleased. The stocky man was a fighter and he could think of nobody else in Gefrin he would rather have at his side. He noticed that Leofwine had been separated from him and was now three or four men away to his left.

They waited and watched as the Waelisc force slowly came into view over a shallow rise. It was as the man had said. The host was several hundred strong. Beobrand thought that at Elmet there had been more men, but it was hard to tell. One thing was certain: the Waelisc outnumbered the defenders.

At the head of the host was carried a standard. Beobrand had seen it before. At Elmet. It had been topped with a human skull then, but now it also had a head, which still bore flesh and hair, but it was too far away to make out the features of the severed head. Several straggling human scalps dangled from the crossbeam.

Scand peered at the standard. It was still some distance away. The dust in the air made it hard to be sure, but the head looked familiar to him.

He let out a gasp. He had known the face well in life and its features had suddenly become clear to him. His worst fears were confirmed. His lord Eanfrith was dead! He should have been there at his ending. It was his duty to fall with him.

One of the other thegns recognised the head and let out a cry. "We have failed our lord. He is killed by his enemy and we were not there to protect him."

A ripple of disquiet ran through the men of the shieldwall. Scand knew that this battle could be lost before it began if the men lost morale. He stepped forward and addressed them, turning his back on the enemy amassing on the other side of the river.

"Do you see the head of our lord king? These Waelisc pigs have slain him with treachery. But they have made a grave mistake. They have come to us showing their vile deeds openly. Their crime is there for us all to see. And they have brought back our lord! Eanfrith watches us from Woden's hall. Will you disappoint him? Will you let him see us fail here? No! We will make them pay the weregild for a king with their blood. With their lives." He could sense the moment of doubt had passed. The men were once again ready for battle.

"Will you make them regret killing Eanfrith King?"

"Yes!" came the answer from the shieldwall. As they raised their voices, so they raised their spirits.

"Will you make them pay?" he screamed.

"Yes!" they replied in a raucous roar of inchoate anger.

"Make your king proud!"

They cheered and jeered at the Waelisc.

Scand stepped back into the centre of the line, lifted his shield and drew his sword. Yes, we will make them pay for what they have done.

The men saw a strong, grey-bearded thegn, resplendent in metal-knit shirt and polished, boar-emblem helm. But his weapons were heavy and his helm weighed down on his head.

He closed his eyes for a moment. A wave of tiredness and grief washed over him.

He felt old.

The first Waelisc to arrive stopped someway short of the river. The others were forced to spread out behind them.

Cadwallon rode at the head of the host. He sat astride a fine dappled gelding. Gwalchmei rode at his right hand on his enormous black stallion. They reined in to survey their enemy and the black horse took a bite at Cadwallon's mount. The king's steed skipped to the side to avoid the other horse's teeth. It was not the first time this had happened on the short journey up from the Wall and Cadwallon was annoyed.

"Apologies, lord king," said Gwalchmei. He tugged at his reins to let his horse know who was truly in control.

Cadwallon wondered whether Gwalchmei's horse's obvious dislike reflected its owner's true attitude towards him. The young warrior always seemed so self-assured of his position. He had always been faithful and useful, it was true, but there was no need to act as if it was an accepted fact. His smugness prickled Cadwallon. He would soon have to tug on Gwalchmei's reins. It was time he understood the reality of his situation. He would be nothing without his king.

They had stopped just beyond a spear throw's distance from the river. Before them they saw the force that Eanfrith's loyal retainers had managed to organise. There were little more than a hundred of them. They stood two-men deep in a shieldwall that bristled with spears. The afternoon light sparkled on the water and the polished helms and spear points of the Seaxons.

"They have chosen their position well," said Gwalchmei. "We will not gain full advantage of our numbers."

Cadwallon shrugged. He could see it was true. The path to the ford was heavily overgrown on either side, with large trees along the banks of the river forming a natural barrier.

"No matter. Form the men up into ranks. We will use the weight of our numbers to push them back and crush them."

Gwalchmei turned his horse and started shouting orders at the men.

Cadwallon remained where he was, looking over the water at the defenders of Gefrin.

He watched as an old warrior wearing fine battle gear stepped in front of the ranks of warriors. The greybeard turned his back towards him and shouted words of encouragement to the men in the shieldwall. It was difficult to make out the words over the noise of his own warhost behind him, but Cadwallon caught some words. He smiled. It seemed they had seen the latest addition to his standard. They shouted and cheered, but he knew the damage had been done. They had seen their lord defeated. Their resolve would soon buckle like a poorly forged sword.

He would defeat this last resistance before nightfall. He was feeling confident. He had conquered Deira and killed three Seaxon kings in under a year. Men had flocked to his banner. Even some Seaxons, hungry for spoils of war and to be on the winning side. He could accept some of their kind to make up the front ranks of the shieldwall. They were strong and savage, but he was pleased that the size of his host now meant he no longer needed that damned brute Penda of Mercia to help him.

Bernicia would be his alone.

*

Acennan passed Beobrand a leather flask of water. They had been standing now for a long time and they were all drenched in sweat. The Waelisc formed up into a strong shieldwall of several men deep. Beobrand took a swig of the warm water. It tasted sharp and tangy. He spat and handed the flask back to Acennan.

"Looks like the waiting is over," he said.

"Thank the gods for that," answered Acennan. "Perhaps we can kill these whoresons and go home before dark. I'm tired."

A few men chuckled.

Beobrand turned to Leofwine to his left. "Heed me when the battle starts, Leofwine. I'm expecting a song about it later."

Another ripple of laughter, but the mood was tenser than ever now. Leofwine smiled a thin smile, but could not tear his gaze away from the enemy host as they started to make their way towards the river.

"Hold your ground, men," shouted Scand. "Make your fathers and your lord king proud."

There was a tremor in the shieldwall as men hefted their shields and weapons, readying themselves for combat.

The Waelisc walked slowly down to the water's edge. There they paused. Several threw javelins and other projectiles. Most clattered harmlessly off of raised shields. One stone hit Beobrand on the shoulder, making him wince. The boy who had vomited earlier mistimed lifting his shield and a short throwing spear struck him in the hip. He screamed and fell back. He was replaced in the shieldwall and pulled to the back of the line, whimpering.

Cadwallon's men stepped into the shallow water of the ford. The water lapped around their ankles.

Those who had something to throw now returned the Waelisc attack. Spears and stones flew across the river. A few spears landed in the ranks behind the shieldwall and men cried out in pain. But the warriors did not falter and they were now so close that Beobrand could make out individual faces and details.

Both sides let out screams of defiance. The noise was deafening, terrifying.

Fear gripped Beobrand then. He shivered, the sweat on the back of his neck suddenly chill. He stared at the man moving towards him. The man he would meet in battle in moments. The man he must kill. Bile rose in his throat and he thought he might disgrace himself.

"Hold!" shouted Scand, his voice carrying over the battle-cheers of friend and foe alike.

Before Beobrand loomed a hulking figure. Iron-knit shirt, white, leather-clad shield, with gleaming boss. Blood-shot brown eyes and wild hair. The Waelisc line took a step forward and the shieldwalls met with a clash.

Beobrand used his weight to push forward, then pulled back momentarily. Acennan pushed his spear into the gap. The man with the blood-shot eyes wavered, tried to defend the blow from Acennan. Beobrand did not hesitate and pushed his own spear overarm into the man's throat. The man's gurgling scream went unheard over the cacophony of death. He fell into the shallow water of the ford and was trampled by his companions as they stepped into the breach.

Beobrand let his spear fall with the man and quickly drew Hrunting. His fear had fled like a coward flees combat. He welcomed the cold anger of battle lust like a long-lost friend. Gone was the time for fear or thought. He had become an instrument of death once more. He grinned at Acennan.

He swatted away an ineffectual swipe over his shield, then thrust his sword under the shieldwall and felt it connect. He jabbed it harder and it opened up flesh and sinews, till brought to a halt against bone. He twisted the blade and pulled it back. The face of the young man before him went deathly white. The sword had opened a terrible wound in his groin. Dark blood spurted and the boy collapsed.

All along the line the Bernicians were faring well. The Waelisc had poor footing at the edge of the river and were attacking up the slight rise out of the ford. The Bernicians were defending their homes and their loved ones. They could not give any ground.

Acennan and Beobrand quickly fell into a pattern of teamwork. Singly they were each formidable foes, but together, they were unstoppable. Blood misted the air before them.

Beobrand swung his sword in a downward chopping motion into the unprotected head of a man with straggly grey hair. Acennan shoved his shield forward, hacking downwards with his sword into the shins of their enemies. The river was clogged with bodies. Sweat, blood and splashed river water covered every man with a slumgullion of gore.

The Waelisc fell back from the onslaught leaving a space around the two. Beobrand stepped forward into the gap, meaning to drive towards the grisly standard and Cadwallon, who fought at the centre of the line. Acennan pulled him back.

"We must not break the shieldwall! It would be our undoing."

Beobrand remembered Elmet and how he had been cut off from his companions. He nodded and stepped back into his place. Acennan smiled, showing his teeth. They were stained with blood. His lip was bleeding but he was oblivious.

Beobrand looked left and right, trying to assess the passage of the battle, but it was impossible to tell which way things were going. All along the line men were killing and dying, but the gods alone knew if either side was winning.

Many had already fallen on both sides, but the Waelisc seemed to be taking the worst of the battle. Some men were able to stagger back behind their lines, others lay where they fell and were either pulled out of the way or trampled. All was chaos. Chaos and death.

He caught a glimpse of Scand's polished helm and white beard. He was laying about him with a fine blade that flashed silver in the sun. The Waelisc were scared to approach him. Closer he saw Leofwine and his heart rejoiced at seeing him still hale. The young scop was standing tall. He was pushing his shield against the Waelisc shieldwall, jabbing over the rim with his spear.

As Beobrand looked, he saw Leofwine's spear point find its target. It raked down his enemy's unprotected arm. Blood flowered, but the man did not fall back.

"Beobrand!" Acennan's shout alerted Beobrand to the danger that faced them. He turned back to the river. In front of them, the men had regained their courage. The Waelisc shieldwall had reformed and the warriors charged forwards. Beobrand and Acennan braced themselves. Beside them their companions did the same. The shields once again smashed together with jarring force.

Beobrand sensed more than felt a seax coming under his shield rim. He slid his shield down as hard as he could and caught the wrist that wielded the seax with the rim of the linden board. The knife fell to the ground to be stamped into the mud.

Taking advantage of the opening presented by the lowered shield, a black-haired man with striking green eyes swung a huge axe at Beobrand's face. Beobrand barely managed to lift his shield in time and the strength of the blow splintered the linden. The axeman swung again and again. His attack was so ferocious and his strength so prodigious that Beobrand found himself being battered backwards. After a few blows his shield was a tatter of splinters and leather strips, with merely the boss remaining intact. He was breathless. He could not carry on like this. He took a step back and forced himself to be calm.

The man stepped forward and once more lifted his axe over his head. Beobrand parried the downward cut with his shield boss and saw that losing most of his shield would provide his salvation. He could see his adversary's movements clearly, and his attacks had become all too predictable.

The axeman took another swing. Beobrand changed his footing and sprang forward. His sword slid through the links of the man's battle-net and deep into his belly. His green eyes were wide with surprise. A heartbeat before he had been so sure that after the battle men would sing of how he, Cadman, had slain the blond devil with his mighty axe. Now he could feel the strength leaving him as his lifeblood poured into the mud. The axe swung down and then fell from Cadman's fingers. It bounced off Beobrand's back and grazed against his calf, drawing blood. Their eyes met for a heartbeat before Beobrand punched him full in the face with his shield boss. Teeth smashed and the light went out of the green eyes as Cadman fell on the muddy beach of the ford.

Beobrand had been forced back but now returned to Acennan's side.

"I thought you would be joining your ancestors then," Acennan said, smiling his bloody grin.

"I have other plans," laughed Beobrand.

Again the area in front of them opened up, giving them a moment to catch their breath. Both lines were tiring now. Their arms were aching, leaden.

Surveying the battle, they could see that the fighting was most fierce around Scand. Cadwallon's banner was there and his closest retainers were trying to break the shieldwall by killing the Bernician leader. Scand and his gesithas were putting up a defence worthy of legend. A pile of dead and dying lay before them.

Beobrand searched for Leofwine and saw that he was still in the line, shield and spear in hand. He had a cut to his head, and blood soaked his long, flaxen hair. As Beobrand watched he saw with dismay that a new enemy stepped up to face Leofwine. He recognised him instantly. His face had once been handsome, but now it was a mask of terrible ugliness. The puckered, raw scar from eye to chin had been inflicted by Beobrand himself. He gripped the hilt of his brother's sword, anxious to be able to finish what he had started.

"Hengist!" he screamed. But Hengist did not hear him. He strode towards Leofwine, who looked like a hare that had been fixed in the gaze of an eagle.

Beobrand could not stand by and watch. He must protect his friend. Vengeance was within his grasp. Hrunting was already slick with the gore of his enemies, now it would drink the blood of his brother's slayer.

He started to move towards his enemy, but Acennan held him back.

"I must help Leofwine. Let me go!"

But Acennan shook him. "If you go, the shieldwall will part and we all will die! Look, they attack again!"

*

The battle raged on till the men on both sides were exhausted. Time and again the Waelisc threatened to break the Bernician shieldwall, but each time Scand's men rallied. Still, in the end they would have been overwhelmed despite their bravery and the toll they took on their enemies. It was as inevitable as night following day. More than half their number had fallen. Of those left standing, few were uninjured and all were so tired they could hardly think.

They would have been defeated but for wyrd.

For it must have been wyrd that made Scand's fine sword blade shatter.

Scand stood in the front of his line and fought with courage. He defeated all who stood against him. He seemed invincible, despite his age. The Bernicians took heart at their leader's war prowess. Their enemies' resolve began to falter. This battle should have been over quickly. Yet the Bernicians stood fast. The sight of their white-beard lord slaying foes like a young man filled them with pride. They would make him proud. They would make their dead king, who looked on from atop the Waelisc banner, proud too. They would not back down.

But they would be defeated.

They were only men, and men can only do so much. They fought on. For honour and to make the Waelisc pay dearly for this land. But as the sun dropped in the sky and the shadows lengthened, they did not fight to win.

Then, weary and half blinded by sweat and blood, Scand stepped forward to meet the next in a long line of men to kill. The young Waelisc staggered over the heap of dead, half sliding towards the grim warrior. He swung his short sword at the helmeted head, but Scand parried the blow with his own blade. It was notched and pitted from many battles, but it chose that moment to break. Shards flew out, flashing red and gold in the afternoon sunlight. For a moment, neither Scand nor his enemy could understand what had happened. Scand lost his balance, falling forward to one knee, as if in obeisance to the young man. The Waelisc regained his wits quickly and made a desperate lunge at the old warrior's chest. Scand's byrnie turned the blade and before the man could strike again, one of Scand's retainers leapt forward with his shield to protect his lord. Scand's closest companions rushed to their lord's aid and the man was quickly killed.

They pulled Scand to his feet and handed him another blade. They prepared for the next attack. They looked left and right. The shieldwall was ragged. Gaps had appeared. They would be overrun soon.

But wyrd had played its part and they would not die that day. The Waelisc were retreating. Their king had been wounded and they huddled close to him, backing away through the corpse-clogged stream. For when Scand's sword was broken, one of the iron shards had flown as true as if thrown by dexterous hand and embedded itself into Cadwallon's cheek. It was close to his eye and caused him great pain.

The Bernicians could scarcely believe what they were witnessing. Each had made his peace, sure that soon he would breathe no more on this earth. Now, with the last rays of the sun dappling the blood-pink water in front of them, they began to hope again.

They removed helmets and ran gore-sticky fingers through sweat-drenched hair. They were thirsty, but would not drink of the water befouled by so many dead.

Beobrand watched the Waelisc retreat. Could it be that he would live to see Sunniva again?

All around him men were staggering back towards Gefrin.

Moving away from the charnel stench of the river. Some men sat down, shock and fatigue making them slack-jawed and slow. Acennan slapped Beobrand on the back. "Well, they won't forget this day soon," he said, smiling. His face was a mask of blood and mud splatter.

Beobrand couldn't smile. He could feel his hands starting to tremble, his legs were weak. He just wanted to sit down and catch his breath. Then he could talk.

Acennan shook him by the shoulders. "Hey! No time to rest now. We are going to need to move. We cannot stay here."

Scand seemed to have the same thought. He was clearly exhausted, but he pulled himself up to his full height, stood before them and raised his voice. His throat croaked from the constant shouting, but his words still carried.

"Men of Bernicia, you have fought with courage and honour today. You should be proud. You stood like rocks against the sea. Unmovable. Ours was the victory today. Eanfrith King looked on and he saw heroes. Men worthy to sit at his mead bench.

"We have lost many, but the battle of Gefrin's ford will be remembered in song for generations. Where few stood against many and did not break."

The mention of song brought Beobrand out of his lethargy. Where was Leofwine? What had befallen Hengist? Had it truly been him he had seen in the Waelisc shieldwall? He looked for Leofwine amongst the men listening to Scand, but he could not see the bard's handsome face.

"Our loved ones will be halfway to safety by now, but we cannot rest," the old lord continued. "Dark is almost upon us. We must follow them through the night. We have bought them the time they needed, but now we must join them."

The men roused themselves and prepared to leave. The

bodies were rich pickings for weapons, armour and jewellery and many men became rich in those few moments after the battle. Acennan collected things of value from the men they had slain, but Beobrand looked for only one thing. It didn't take him long to find it.

Leofwine lay sprawled face down. His long golden hair was brown with drying blood and filth. He was unmoving. Beobrand's stomach tightened. He fell to his knees next to Leofwine and turned him over.

The young tale-teller groaned. He was alive! But his skin was white. The splashes of dirt and blood stood out starkly on his pallid face. Looking down, Beobrand saw a gaping wound in Leofwine's stomach. He knew then that his friend would die.

Leofwine's eyes flickered open. "Did we win?"

Beobrand swallowed. Was this victory?

"I think so," he answered, his voice cracking. "They retreated when Cadwallon was injured."

"I recognised him," Leofwine said.

"Who?"

"The man who has killed me. It was Hengist. You stood before him in Engelmynster. But I am no warrior, Beobrand." He smiled a wan smile. "That much is clear."

"I will kill him," Beobrand said. "He has taken too much from me."

Leofwine stared at Beobrand for a long time before speaking again. "I think you will. It will make a great tale." He started to laugh, but it turned into a cough. A trickle of blood bubbled from his lips. He closed his eyes briefly against the pain. When he opened them again, they were unfocused, as if he was looking at something distant. "But I fear someone else will have to do the telling," he said. He closed his eyes again and soon Beobrand understood that Leofwine's spirit had departed.

Never again would men sit enthralled by the melodious voice of Leofwine, son of Alric. Beobrand stroked his long hair and his mind turned to Octa. So many dead. Why did he still live? He felt tears burning his eyes, but they did not fall. He had seen too much of death in this past year. His tears had dried up in him, like a stream can run dry in the heat of summer.

Victory should not be like this. He felt empty. All about him was death and dying.

He wanted to lie down next to Leofwine and weep for his friend. Or perhaps simply to sleep. But Acennan found him and drew him to his feet.

As if in a dream Beobrand carried the burdens Acennan handed to him. In a daze he traipsed along with the others leaving the battlefield to the ravens.

They could not carry their dead and hope to escape from the Waelisc warhost if they were pursued. So their companions were left were they had fallen and this weighed heavily on them all. Those who had survived the day could not rejoice. The cost had been too high.

Their shadows streamed long before them as they walked into the east.

Soon the sun fell below the horizon. The air grew cooler and darkness wrapped the land like a shroud.

That night was interminable. They were all so tired that walking a dozen steps would have seemed impossible and yet they trudged on through the night. They knew that if they were caught in the open by the Waelisc they would have no

337

chance of surviving another battle. Many of the Waelisc had not stood in the shieldwall, so would be fresh. Their only chance was to get to the safety of Bebbanburg. And so they walked on.

There were not enough horses for them all to ride. Those mounts they had, carried the wounded.

Once all the light had gone from the western sky, they could clearly see the beacons that still burnt as a warning of attack.

The question went unspoken, but thought by many: Why had Oswald not ridden to his brother's aid from Bebbanburg at the sign of the beacons? None knew the answer.

The warriors were too exhausted and disheartened at the loss of their king and hall-fellows to talk much. They lowered their heads, hoisted their weapons and shields on their backs and forced their feet to move them forwards towards the east. Towards the coast. Towards Bebbanburg.

Beobrand followed the man in front of him and tried not to think. But he could find no peace. The image of Leofwine's pale face was etched into his mind's eye. Leofwine joined the ranks of all the others killed by Hengist. Beobrand was filled with sorrow, but his sadness fuelled his anger the way a breeze fans the flames of a fire. And as he walked the flames of his anger forged his desire for vengeance into the strongest steel deep within him. He would meet Hengist again and when he did he would destroy him.

It was when they stopped to rest that they saw the fires in the west.

A huge conflagration illuminated the clouds as if the gods themselves had lit torches or dragons were sweeping down and razing all before them with their fiery breath. The men gazed at the distant flames for some time before Acennan broke the silence.

"And so the mighty hall of Gefrin is destroyed."

They knew that he was right. The Waelisc must have moved up from the river to the buildings of Gefrin and put them to the torch. As they watched, more fires sprouted like yellow and red flowers in the black night.

No more was said. But it took no cajoling to get the men back to their feet. They had nothing to return to now. Behind them lay death and fire. Their only hope lay ahead.

The wounded were checked and those who had died were left at the resting place, so that others could ride.

And thus their numbers dwindled.

But the burning of their lord's hall rekindled the spark of their spirits. It was a final insult and could not be ignored. The Waelisc would have to pay.

They walked on, straining to see the first light in the east that would presage the dawning of a new day.

22

The first fingers of sunlight caressed the billowing clouds in the eastern sky with red. Below the clouds, silhouetted black against the dawn, rose Bebbanburg. It stood on a high, rocky crag that soared up from the low land around it. On the east it was protected by steep cliffs and the sea. Its palisades had never been broken. It had been the centre of Bernician power for generations. It was impregnable.

The men did not cheer at the sight of their goal as the sun rose. Instead, there was an air of dejected resignation about the company. For before them, blocking their way to the cliff-bound fortress, stood a line of Waelisc warriors. It was not the whole of the surviving host they had faced, but it was a sizable number. Perhaps twice that of their own warband. The Waelisc had ridden through the night and cut them off within sight of their destination. It was a bitter draught to swallow. The men, already on the verge of collapse, could find no more vestiges of energy within themselves to stand against this new foe.

The Waelisc had only just arrived. They had galloped in from the north, having circled them. Now they dismounted, tethered their horses and began to form into a shieldwall. They meant to finish what they had started the day before.

Scand cursed the gods silently. Whether Cadwallon had died from his wounds and the Waelisc sought revenge, or he had ordered them to pursue Eanfrith's men, he did not know. The outcome would be the same. His men were too tired to win a battle. The men before them would be tired too, but riding did not sap a man's strength in the same way as walking and many of the Waelisc may not have even fought in the battle at the ford.

Scand surveyed his men. They were wounded and broken. Some had sat down as soon as the Waelisc had been sighted, content just to have a moment's respite from the march. Scand knew despair at that moment. They would die now. It was like a bad joke of the gods to have had them walk all night only to be killed now, so close to sanctuary.

Beobrand looked at the grey-haired lord. Scand's face was grim. His shoulders slumped in defeat. He had the aspect of a man who had lost hope.

In the long, painful march through the darkness, Beobrand had pictured how he would exact his revenge on Hengist. He had become convinced that it was what wyrd had planned for him. The threads of their lives were inextricably entwined, but the next time they met, he would cut Hengist's thread. Then he would be free from the shame and heartache he felt at not having been able to protect those he loved.

He had not travelled all this way to be cut down now by these Waelisc who blocked their path. Sunniva must be inside Bebbanburg and, by Woden, he would see her this day. He looked around him. None of the men looked able to fight.

Acennan was as done in as the next man, but Beobrand

clapped him on the shoulder. "Stand up straight," he said. "Get ready."

What for? thought Acennan, bemused at the sudden change in Beobrand.

Beobrand put down the items he had been carrying. He had hardly noticed them when Acennan had handed them to him the previous sunset. But having accepted them, it seemed important to him not to let them go. So he had clutched them through the night, not stopping to think about them. When they had rested he had gripped them tightly, refusing to give them up. Now, in the daylight he was almost surprised to see a shirt of metal rings and a couple of seaxes clatter to the dew-damp grass.

He stretched his arms, massaging the cramps from them and took a few steps towards the Waelisc. He then turned to face the Bernicians. He could feel the Waelisc eyes boring into his back. He felt exposed and nervous, but he ignored the feeling and addressed the men who had marched from Gefrin.

"Hear me!" he bellowed. "Hear me, men of Bernicia. You are tired. We are all tired. But we have already beaten these Waelisc curs once. Shall we lose hope now, in the shadow of the fortress of Bebbanburg? Your families are there. We gave them the time they needed to reach safety. Do you want them to see you dishonoured now? Defeated by these whoresons?"

All the faces were turned towards him now. Scand raised himself up to his full height and joined Beobrand. He gave the young man a nod and said in a hoarse whisper, "You speak well, Beobrand. I had forgotten myself." He grasped Beobrand's shoulder "Thank you for reminding me who I am. Who we all are."

Scand faced the men and said in a strong voice, "Beobrand

speaks true. We are men of Bernicia. We are the victors of the battle of the ford of Gefrin. We will stand again shoulder to shoulder, shield to shield, and we will exact more vengeance for the death of our lord king, Eanfrith."

The mood amongst the men had shifted, like the breeze that changes direction and blows out a torch. Or breathes life into dying embers. A few men heaved themselves to their feet, ready to do their duty once more.

"Stand, my shield brothers. Stand and show these Waelisc that they should fear us. Stand and fight for Bernicia."

Beobrand picked up the words and repeated them. "For Bernicia!" he shouted. "For Bernicia!"

Acennan joined in, then a few more, and soon all the men were chanting. The noise gave them heart and the last men sitting raised themselves up.

Shields were hefted. The men crowded together into a tight wedge. The warband bristled with spear points.

Pride swelled in Scand's chest. Moments before, the men had been defeated and now they were a formidable force once more. Hope began to return to him. Perhaps they could win through after all.

Before them, the line of Waelisc stood watching.

Scand could make out the black-clad Gwalchmei leading the troop. Treacherous bastard. He spat. He would put that fine head of his on display from the walls of Bebbanburg before the day was through.

"Nicely done," Acennan said to Beobrand with a wry smile. "I think you've talked us into dying with honour."

"I have no intention of dying today. I thought that much was clear." Beobrand reached down and picked up the fine iron-knit shirt he had been carrying all night. "Help me on with this," he said.

Acennan helped him get the byrnie over his head. He then showed him how to cinch it with his belt, to take some of the weight off of his shoulders.

"It is a fine war harness. Here, see if this fits." He handed him a helmet that he had been carrying. Beobrand recognised it as having been worn by one of Scand's closest retinue. It was iron with bronze boars above the cheek guards. They would protect the wearer of the helm. Beobrand chose not to dwell on what had happened to the helmet's previous owner.

"I cannot take this. It was Beorn's."

"Nonsense, he won't be needing it now."

He placed it on his head. It was a snug fit, and the metal shirt weighed heavily on his shoulders.

"I've seen you fight like a warrior from a saga, now you look the part too." Acennan slapped him on the back and handed him a shield.

Scand's battle voice carried over the talking men. "Stand firm, men. The Waelisc approach."

Acennan and Beobrand raised their shields with the rest of the men. They stood at the centre of the shieldwall. The Waelisc were advancing at a walk. Beobrand scanned their line, looking for Hengist. He could not see him.

All along the Bernician line men began to shout abuse, hammering spear staves and sword hilts into shields. The noise rose to a tumultuous roar.

Someone started the chant again. "For Bernicia! For Bernicia!" With surprise, Beobrand realised it was his voice. Others joined him. The rhythm of the words and the beating crash of iron against linden sounded like a threnody.

The sun rose from behind the rocky outcrop of Bebbanburg. The Bernicians squinted into the light.

Javelins and hand axes flew from the Waelisc shieldwall,

arcing across the sky towards them. The projectiles were almost invisible against the harsh sunlight. Men raised their shields instinctively. Someone screamed in pain to Beobrand's right.

And the Waelisc advanced.

Sunniva's feet ached. The sole of her left foot hurt whenever she put weight on it. They had walked fast all through the day and well into the night and a blister had formed where her shoe rubbed. The pain and aches of her body from the long walk to Bebbanburg were as nothing when compared to the anguish she felt. She had slept fitfully on the floor of the great hall with the rest of the people of Gefrin. They had been welcomed and the gates of the fortress were thrown open, but no amount of pleading from any of them, not even Queen Finola, could convince Oswald, the lord of Bebbanburg, to go to the aid of Scand. He had been sure that they had been killed. Leaving the safety of the walled fort would bring no good.

The women had cried and wailed that their men should not be abandoned. But the lord would not be swayed.

When the burning of the buildings of Gefrin had lit up the western horizon, they all assumed the worst: Scand had been defeated and the Waelisc were destroying all in their path.

Sunniva had made her way up onto the palisade to see the blaze for herself. She had stared disconsolately into the night. The fires in the distance burnt away her chances at any semblance of happiness. Orphaned, her home destroyed, her lover killed, she wondered why her life had been cursed. Only days ago she had been happily in love. Her father had been warming to Beobrand grudgingly, and she had been blissfully content. Since then her life had been a litany of sadness. Her father's murder. Burying him next to her mother. Beobrand going away, leaving her alone with her grief. Then, on his return, the attack of the Waelisc and the destruction of her home. Now, seeing the flames, she had known that her happiness was a thing of the past. Beobrand was dead along with her parents and she was alone.

She had awoken early. Unable to rest. The floor was hard and unyielding, her mind full of darkness and despair. It was barely dawn, the courtyard between the buildings was still in shadow from the wooden walls that surrounded Bebbanburg. Above them, clouds were tinged with the pink of sunrise. She stepped gingerly into the coolness of the morning, wincing absently at the stinging in her foot.

All around her was activity. Men ran from buildings. They carried shields and spears. A stocky warrior in a padded jerkin and wearing a visored helm almost ran into her. She sidestepped lithely and wondered what was happening. Had the Waelisc marched on Bebbanburg? It was clear that the men were readying for battle. She could think of no other explanation.

She traced her way back to the ladder she had climbed the night before. She made her way up onto the palisade platform and peered over the edge.

The land to the west was in the shadow of the fortress crag for hundreds of paces. Beyond that, on the horizon, there was a dark pall of smoke where Gefrin still burnt. She looked closer, beyond the shadows but still quite near to Bebbanburg.

A group of horses stood there, and beyond them warriors. Arrayed in a shieldwall. She squinted, trying to make sense of what she saw. The warriors had their backs to Bebbanburg. They seemed to be moving away from her. But why?

Then she saw the small group of men standing resolute against the shieldwall and the whole scene fell into place in her mind. Her heart leapt in her chest. It could only mean one thing: there were survivors from Gefrin. They were too far away for her to make out individuals, but hope surged within her.

Beobrand might still be alive.

Beobrand readied himself to fight. His body ached from the previous day's battle and the gruelling pace of the night march, but he braced himself, trying to summon up some of the certainty he had shown to the others.

The enemy approached. He had a sudden urge to piss. Too late now.

Light glinted from the spear points of the Waelisc shieldwall. The faces of the men advancing on them were in shadow, featureless against the brightness of the early morning sun.

They were very near now.

"For Bernicia!" he chanted, his voice joining the screams and shouts from both sides.

His new helm's cheek guards reduced his vision, forcing him to look straight ahead. He fixed his eyes on the man directly in front of him. With a start, he saw that his wyrd had served him well. It had brought his enemy, the slayer of his kith and kin, to him.

Hengist stood directly before him. Moments ago he had been just one more of the faceless warriors in the enemy ranks. Now Beobrand could make out every detail of his foe. His black hair was slicked back under a small helm with a nose guard, but there was no mistaking his gait, his size or the horribly scarred face. Beobrand's tiredness and fear evaporated as quickly as water splashed onto red-hot metal. He had been dreaming of this moment. He had faced Hengist before and narrowly escaped with his life. Then he had not been prepared. He had stood in kirtle and trousers armed with a seax.

But now he was armed with his brother's sword. Now he was decked in battle-dress and war-helm.

Now he was not an untested boy. He had stood in the shieldwall at the ford of Gefrin and the dead had been heaped before him.

Now he would have his revenge.

Hengist stepped closer. He saw a large warrior facing him, face partially covered by a metal helm. His piercing blue eyes bore into him. Those eyes were familiar to him.

At last, Beobrand saw recognition in Hengist's face.

There was barely a spear's length between them now. Hengist's hideously lopsided face cracked into a grin. His teeth flashed white against the red of his scar.

"Time to repay you for my face, boy!" he screamed. "Now you die!"

He leapt forward and the rest of the shieldwall came with him. The line trembled as shields clashed. Both sides heaved and pushed, straining to hold their position.

Over the rim of his shield, Beobrand could see Hengist's maniacal eyes. He struggled to stand his ground.

"I'm going to enjoy killing you. I should have done for you months ago," Hengist hissed.

"I will kill you like the dog you are," returned Beobrand. "Like I killed Dreng, Hafgan and Tondberct."

Was that a flash of fear in Hengist's eyes?

Hengist leaned on his shield, using all of his bulk and strength to try to force Beobrand backwards. Then, all of a sudden, the pressure left his shield and Beobrand staggered forward. He caught himself and prepared to parry or deflect the attack that he knew would come. It was a slicing cut aimed at his unprotected shins, but Beobrand skipped backwards, the weight of the armour forgotten, and Hengist's blade sliced through air.

The battle fury was upon Beobrand now. His senses acute to every nuance of his enemy's movements. Hengist made a feint at his head, but Beobrand recognised it and was ready with his shield to block the low cut that followed it. A thrust at his midriff was easily turned away on the rim of his shield. When Hengist made to lunge forward with his shield boss, Beobrand soaked up the blow on his own shield, twisted his body and delivered a slicing cut to Hengist's forearm.

The two warriors pulled back, each now breathing heavily.

All along the line men were grunting and shouting abuse. Screams of the injured and dying mingled with the mad laughter of warriors wallowing in the glory of battle. All was accented by the clash and crash of metal on metal.

Hengist was wary now. Beobrand had drawn first blood. The cut to his arm was superficial and not long, having been partially stopped by the leather wrist guard he wore. He could hardly feel it, but he could see the blood oozing from the wound.

It was Beobrand who now pushed the attack. He sprang forward. He was certain of the outcome of the attack. He would catch Hengist off guard and find his mark again with his fine blade. Taking Hengist's head from his shoulders.

But the gods laugh at men who believe themselves free from danger. In his overconfidence and pride, he lifted his shield away from his body, swinging Hrunting with his right hand in a sweeping arc aimed at Hengist's neck.

Hengist timed his reaction perfectly. He had survived many battles and had the instincts of a cornered animal. He dropped to one knee, raising his shield to protect his head and swiping with his sword upwards. His blade caught Beobrand squarely in the stomach. Beobrand was glad of the iron-knit shirt then. It turned Hengist's blade and rather than being disembowelled, he was merely winded and bruised. The sword was deflected upwards and to the side where it completed its arc by hitting the inside of Beobrand's shield. There it caught his left hand, severing his little finger and the tip of the next.

Beobrand staggered back. Blood streamed from his hand. He could feel his arm growing weak.

Hengist stood, his face once more a gruesome smile. He sensed victory. "I will feed you to the ravens," he spat. "I will kill you like I killed Octa, and then Hrunting will be mine once more."

Beobrand was pale under his helm. He looked at his mutilated hand, unable to understand fully what had happened. Pain began to throb in his hand with each heartbeat. His grip slipped on his shield, the blood slicking inside the iron boss.

At that instant, both shieldwalls seemed to reach some unspoken agreement for respite and they pulled apart. They took several paces back and gulped in the early morning air.

All except for Hengist and Beobrand. They remained where they were and stared into each other's eyes with hatred. Beobrand could think of nothing but vengeance. He shook his head to clear it.

"No," he said. "Hrunting was never yours. It was gifted to my brother, Octa, son of Grimgundi, and I am his last kin. And I am sworn to avenge his murder." With that, he leapt forward again, Hrunting held out before him. Hengist laughed aloud and parried the blow easily.

Despite his brave words, Beobrand could feel his strength waning. His grip was weakening on his shield as the injury to his hand took its toll. He would get ever slower. And then Hengist would kill him.

All along both shieldwalls, the men stood and watched in awe as these two huge men, resplendent in war gear, fought out their blood feud. It was the stuff of songs and none dared interfere.

Hengist sent a flurry of blows resounding off of Beobrand's shield. Beobrand stepped back quickly, leading Hengist on towards him. Hengist came on, smiling, scenting Beobrand's weakness as a wolf sniffs out a lamb. With no warning Beobrand sidestepped and aimed a desperate strike at Hengist's thigh. It was a clumsy attack, and Hengist saw it coming. He parried with his blade and then, quick as a snake, he flicked out the point and raked Beobrand's forearm.

More pain, and more blood. Beobrand retreated, just avoiding a follow-up blow aimed at his face.

This must end now. He was injured badly. He was almost dropping his shield, he would not be able to grip the boss much longer and now his sword arm was cut deeply, the blood running freely. Had it all come to this? Despair's icy fingers ran down his spine. In the end, Hengist was stronger and more experienced in battle. Beobrand could not defeat him.

"Beobrand, look out!" shouted Acennan, breaking the silence that had descended on the battlefield.

Hengist had seen his opportunity to finish this once and for all. Beobrand looked spent, dazed; blood-splattered and weary. Hengist seized his chance and lashed out his sword at Beobrand's face.

But Acennan's warning penetrated Beobrand's despondency and instinctively he threw his shield up and forward to deflect the thrust. His hand, weak and blood-slick could no longer hold the weight of the linden board. The handle of the iron boss at the shield's centre slipped through his fingers and the circular shield flew forwards, catching Hengist's blade and turning it away, but then moving on, through the air, straight at Hengist's face.

Hengist swayed sideways, dodging the flying shield, which narrowly missed him before it embedded into the soft ground. There it remained, sunk at an angle into the marshy turf.

Hengist began to smile broadly, his scarred face hideous with glee at his opponent's loss of the shield.

But the moment of distraction had provided Beobrand with his own chance and channelling all the anguish, pain, loss and despair of the last months, he grasped that chance fiercely. He had no shield now. He was badly injured and Hengist was stronger, rested and deadly. Beobrand realised that he would die, but he was sworn to avenge Octa, Cathryn and Strang. Hengist must not live.

So, in that moment of Hengist's triumph, while his attention was still on the shield in the earth, Beobrand leapt forward, all thoughts of defence gone. He would die, but Hengist would join him this day. Beobrand let out a scream of such unearthly rage that men involuntarily stepped back, touching holy amulets. He flung himself at his kin's slayer.

Hrunting's blade slid into Hengist's unarmoured throat. Such was the force of the attack that Beobrand felt no resistance. Octa's sword travelled through Hengist's neck, splitting flesh, sinew and bone. The blade's full length sank into him and Beobrand came to a halt with the hand on Hrunting's hilt rubbing against Hengist's black beard.

The smile left Hengist's face. His eyes burnt with a fury and hatred to rival Beobrand's. For a moment they stood, as close as lovers. Hengist, in a last effort to take Beobrand with him to the afterlife, tried to swing his own blade into Beobrand's body. But Beobrand sensed the movement and reached out with his mutilated left hand and grasped Hengist's wrist. For a heartbeat they struggled. Beobrand's bloody hand slipped on the thick leather of Hengist's wrist guard. Hengist's power was shocking, even in the throes of death. Yet his struggles grew weaker with each passing moment.

Hengist dropped his sword and opened his mouth to speak. He mouthed angry words, but no sound emerged. Beobrand could smell the last sour breath gush from him. Hengist slumped and slid from Hrunting's blade, a great gout of crimson gushing from the wound as he fell.

Beobrand looked down upon his foe. Hengist's throat bubbled and spouted. He was still clinging to life. His hand was searching the ground to his side, flopping and flapping like an injured bird. Beobrand saw that he wished to hold his sword as he left this life. Only then could he be sure Woden would see his death and take him to his corpse hall.

Beobrand took a step and kicked Hengist's blade out of his reach. He then stepped on his wrist, crushing it savagely beneath his foot. Hengist looked up at him, his eyes imploring. Just as Cathryn had begged for help.

"You killed without honour," said Beobrand, his words carrying over all of the warriors amassed on both sides. "You stole and murdered in darkness. You are craven and do not deserve to dine at Woden's table. I curse you, Hengist." Hengist's eyes widened into a final bright instant of abject terror. Beobrand spat into his face and held his gaze until the light had left his adversary's eyes.

Only then did he stagger back to the Bernician shieldwall.

Acennan gripped his shoulder and, casting a worried glance at his friend's left hand and bloody right arm he leaned in close to Beobrand. "How bad is it?" he asked.

"I'll live," he said and turned back to look at Hengist's corpse, lying on the earth. Beobrand had forgotten to reclaim his shield, and it still stood there like a leaning grave marker at Hengist's head. "Which is more than can be said for him."

Despite the glory of young Beobrand's victory over the evil-looking warrior, Scand was rapidly losing hope. It had been briefly rekindled, but there had been too much fighting. Coupled with the sleepless night of fast-paced marching, the strength sapped from him by moments. He could feel the energy leaving his men, like lifeblood pumping with each beat of a dying heart. He looked up and down the line and saw exhaustion, injury and death on either side. The line had held the first onslaught and despite the tiredness wracking his body, and the despair that threatened to engulf him, he felt a surge of pride. These men were worthy companions. They would be remembered for their valour. They would die with honour and the Waelisc would suffer before the end.

The ending of Beobrand's feud before all of them sent a ripple throughout the gathered warriors. It was as if a spell had been broken and now, having witnessed the duel to the death, both Bernicians and Waelisc were ready to resume their battle-play.

He swiped his forearm across his brow to clear it of sweat. All he managed to do was smear blood from cuts on his arm over his face. He turned to the men closest to him. He forced a smile.

"Well, my friends. Beobrand has once more reminded us of who we are. Let us take up shield and spear one more time and send some more of these bastards to the afterlife before we have another rest."

A burly warrior next to him returned his grin. "A rest, is it? I think the next time we lie down we won't be getting up again. It's been an honour. You have been the best of lords."

Others of his retinue heard the exchange and voiced their approval of their lord. He had given rings and served plentiful mead in the halls they had shared. He was worthy of their deaths. They lifted their weapons one more time and prepared for the end.

A horn sounded far off in the east. The note was long and drifted to them on the soft breeze. Both groups of warriors hushed, listening, unsure that they had heard the sound.

It came again. Clearer now. A strong blast from a hunting horn. Long and plaintive.

The Waelisc pulled back from the Bernicians and turned to look towards Bebbanburg.

Scand and the Bernicians could not see past the Waelisc shieldwall. But they began to wonder at the turn of events. Could they be spared defeat? Again seizing victory when all appeared hopeless?

The Waelisc retreated further. The horn sounded again, closer now.

Shouted orders rang out in the musical tongue of the Waelisc. Then their shieldwall broke up and they ran to their horses.

From the gates of the fortress of Bebbanburg streamed several dozen armed men. They were shadowed by the crag but they could be clearly made out.

They came in a tight group; a bristling hedge of spears.

The Bernicians let out a ragged cheer.

Beobrand watched as the Waelisc moved away towards the tethered horses. Behind them they left several dead and dying. He looked again at the still form of Hengist, his tormentor, the man who had slain Octa and so many others. He could hardly believe Hengist was dead or that he had survived. His left hand felt as if it had been dipped into boiling water and his right arm stung as if plunged it into a bees' nest. The pain rose up both arms, making him weak. He did not feel the elation he had hoped for upon Hengist's death. He felt empty and bone tired. All around him men cheered and rejoiced at being saved from certain death.

He stumbled, a wave of dizziness hitting him, and Acennan put his arm around his shoulders, holding him upright.

"Looks like we live. And that ugly whoreson won't be troubling you again. Not a bad day's work, eh?"

They watched as the Waelisc mounted and galloped away to the north. Men moved through the bodies left in the wake of the Waelisc looking for loot. Any enemy found alive was quickly dispatched.

Beobrand and Acennan watched as the warband from Bebbanburg approached. The mounted Waelisc were distant now, receding into the haze of the early morning.

At the head of the warriors strode a tall, thin man. His face was serious beneath a fine helm that was girded with silver. He was clothed in a polished byrnie and a sumptuous cloak of red wool draped his shoulders. To his left a man held aloft a starkly plain wooden cross. It seemed to be in place of the more gaudy banners usually chosen by warlords.

Scand, battle-weary and smeared with gore and grime, stepped forward and knelt at the feet of the imperious lord.

"I give you thanks, Oswald, son of Æthelfrith, son of Aethelric. You have saved us."

"Praise the one true God, Scand, son of Scaend. I am merely his messenger." Oswald looked around at the wounded and broken men. "What news of my brother?"

"We come with ill news. Eanfrith is killed and Gefrin has fallen to Cadwallon."

A strange expression passed over Oswald's features, as if many emotions vied for supremacy. After a moment, his face settled on a scowl.

"Come, let us retreat behind the walls of Bebbanburg. There, you and your men can rest and you can tell me how my brother fell."

23

Sunniva dipped the cloth again into the bowl of water. She wiped Beobrand's brow, trying to soothe his fever. His body trembled at her touch. He was wrapped in blankets and yet he seemed to be cold, his body racked with shivering.

The hall where he lay was filled with other men who had arrived injured from Gefrin. The sound of coughing could be frequently heard. The coarse retching of someone vomiting was less frequent, but still quite common. Three men had died from their wounds, or the fever that set in soon after, in the week since they had arrived.

As they had entered the fortress, Sunniva had been overjoyed to see Beobrand still alive. He was exhausted and wounded, but he was still living. She had flung herself into his arms and wept with joy. He had held her tightly, crushing her to his muscular frame. They had stood that way in the courtyard for a long time.

Later, she had cleaned and bound his hand and forearm. The stumps of his fingers had been raw and inflamed, but he had appeared well enough. Well enough to make love to her. She remembered the passion of that afternoon's reunion.

They had found an unoccupied stall in the stables and coupled frantically. He had lifted her with ease despite his injuries, his strength and vigour intoxicating to her.

Now she looked at him and wondered how such energy could dissipate so fast. His skin was sallow. Sweat drenched his hair. He had lost weight, making his cheeks more prominent. Dark, bruised-looking skin ringed his eyes.

He had fallen ill the day after arriving. He had complained that his hand was hurting during the feast that evening, but the drink had dulled the pain and it was not till the following morning that it became clear that elf-shot fever had entered into the wounded fingers. He had rapidly grown worse and soon he could not recall who she was. He spoke with the strong dialect of his homeland, but she could easily pick out words and phrases as she tended him. He spoke of his brother, Octa, and he sometimes mistook her for his mother. He would fall into a fitful sleep and then awake with a start screaming the name of Hengist. At times he would cry, cowering from some shade only he could see. It was difficult to understand all he said, but it sounded like he begged his father to stop. To stop what, she could only imagine.

Seeing him in this diminished state, vulnerable and powerless, made her love him all the more. And fear more keenly that he might be about to leave her for ever.

She stayed with him day and night, as if her presence could stop the unthinkable from happening. She would not allow him to die. She prayed to the old gods and even asked one of King Oswald's Christ priests to come and say his magical words over Beobrand.

An old woman boiled up a wild garlic and bread poultice and helped her to wrap the stumps of his fingers. "It will draw out the fever, if the gods are smiling and the sisters of Wyrd are not set to cut his thread," she said. Sunniva had thanked her, but the words filled her with dread. The three sisters, who spin the strands of the lives of everyone on middle earth, appeared to have decided to kill all of her loved ones.

"Don't look so afraid, girl. He is young and strong and he has you and those fine hips of yours to come back to." She had offered Sunniva a toothless grin, patted her arm and moved on to help others amongst the wounded.

Sunniva had been surprised when Acennan had come to Beobrand's sickbed the day after he had fallen ill. When she had seen them last, they had been enemies and she stiffened as he approached, ready to drive him away. But he had knelt gently at her side and taken Beobrand's hand in his.

"You need to rest, Sunniva," he had said in a quiet voice. "I will sit with him a while." He had seen the look on her face and said, "Things have changed between us now. We have stood side by side in the shieldwall. We are brothers in arms. I will not let anyone do him harm. I will watch over him. I'll send word for you should anything change."

She had looked at his face for a long time, before finally nodding and seeking a place to sleep for a time.

When she had returned, he was still sitting there. Straight-backed and proud, like a door ward protecting his lord's hall.

Each day had seen the same pattern. Sunniva would sit with Beobrand during the night and for much of the day, but Acennan came each afternoon and allowed her some respite from her vigil. She came to appreciate the stocky warrior and was gladdened by his faithfulness towards Beobrand.

The fever broke after the seventh night. Sunniva had been prepared for the worst. Beobrand had looked truly terrible during the dark marches of the night. His face shone, pallid in the gloom.

Sunniva drifted into a doze but was awoken with a start when Beobrand reached out and stroked her hair. Outside drizzle was falling and a dim, watery light filtered into the hall from the small windows. Despite the grey morning light Sunniva could see straight away that his cheeks had more colour. His eyes were open and focused on her. He smiled and her heart leapt in her chest.

"You look lovely," he said, his voice cracking from the dryness of his throat. She helped him to sit and offered him some ale to sip. He could feel the liquid running down inside his body, being soaked up like a dry summer field soaks up the first rain after a drought.

"You look awful," she replied, smiling. He returned the smile and started to laugh. The laughter quickly turned into coughing and he fell back onto the pallet.

"Gods, I'm exhausted," he said. "And starving. How long have I been ill?"

"A sennight. We feared you would leave this world." Her voice broke. "I thought you would leave me."

"You made me promise I'd come back, remember? I don't break my oaths."

She brought him some broth and they talked for a long while.

They talked of the past. Of the battle of Gefrin ford and Leofwine's death at the hands of Hengist. They spoke of the stand with Scand before Bebbanburg, the slaying of Hengist, the loss of his fingers and then the arrival of Oswald.

Beobrand removed the bandage and poultice from his hand and looked at the damage Hengist's blade had done. The swelling had subsided and the wounds were scabbed and healing well. The old woman's poultices had done their job and drawn out the evil from the wound. He flexed the fingers of his right hand. His forearm was stiff and sore, but it was much better.

"I thought I would feel joy at Hengist's death. That I would be satisfied with vengeance for all the lives he took from me." He looked at Sunniva, thinking of her father. "From us," he corrected.

"And what do you feel?" she asked.

"I don't know. Relief perhaps. He is gone now. For too long he has been a shadow over my life. But he taught me much."

"Such as?"

"That you cannot know the mind of those around you. You must judge them on their actions, not on what they say."

She smoothed his hair and kissed him lightly. "When you are strong enough, I will show you how I feel with actions." She gave him a mischievous smile. She had had enough of killing and death. She wanted to talk and think of other things.

"What has happened while I slept?" asked Beobrand.

"Oswald, Eanfrith's younger brother, has declared himself king of Bernicia," she said.

"And what did Scand think of that?"

"Scand and all of the men from Gefrin have sworn oaths to Oswald."

Beobrand nodded. It seemed like a good decision. "And what of Cadwallon?" he said.

"News reached us that the king of Gwynedd is still ill. He has been struck down with a fever following his injury at Gefrin."

"Is he still at Gefrin?"

"No. He has returned south to his camp near the great Wall. But his men still maraud throughout the land, destroying homesteads, slaughtering men and taking women and children into slavery. Bernicia is at war. King Oswald has started preparations to lead a force south to face Cadwallon in battle. He has said he means to eradicate Cadwallon and his warhost from the land."

They talked until Beobrand's eyelids began to droop. He was keen to go and talk to Acennan and Scand. To understand Oswald's plans. But his body was as weak as a newborn's.

"Rest now," Sunniva said, placing a soft kiss on his lips. "Acennan will come to see you in the afternoon, as he has every day."

That afternoon Acennan rejoiced to find Beobrand much restored. He had eaten some more and was even strong enough to stand.

"Help me to walk outside," said Beobrand. "I would see the sky and breathe air that is not foetid with the breath of the sick and dying."

And so it was that they made their way out into the courtyard. From there, Beobrand wished to climb up to the palisade.

"I haven't seen the sea in nearly a year," he mused. The afternoon was warm, but the breeze from the sea was chill, so Acennan, fearing for his friend's health, placed his own cloak about his shoulders. Beobrand struggled with the ladder, unable to grasp well with his left hand. The bandage, the pain and the unfamiliarity of the missing fingers, made it hard going, but Acennan was close behind, ready with a steadying hand.

At last they reached the platform, Beobrand feeling lightheaded and breathless, trembling slightly at the exertion as much as the cool wind.

Acennan was concerned. "We should go back down before you faint and I have to carry you," he said, putting a smile in his voice that he did not feel.

"I have been abed too long, Acennan. It is as if I had died and now I am reborn." He looked out over the slate-grey sea. The Whale Road, sailors called it. Gannets and guillemots and other sea birds cavorted in the sky, relishing the zephyrs that wafted over the water and up the cliffs. The rain had blown over and now the sky was dotted with clouds that cast shadows on the water. In the distance they could see a small group of islands and a little way to the north lay a larger island, closer to the land. It was high tide now, the waves rolling in to the cliffs below Bebbanburg, but at low tide it would be possible to ride a horse over to that island.

"We thought you would die," said Acennan quietly. "I'm glad you didn't."

Beobrand smiled. This gruff assertion was all he could expect from Acennan, and he needed no more.

They stood in silence for a while, watching the birds and feeling the wind on their faces.

"You know," said Beobrand, "this is where I arrived in Bernicia. It was less than a year ago. It seems like a lifetime. In that time I have learnt of my brother's death, killed men and fought in battles worthy of song." He thought of Leofwine, lying dead in his arms. Tata sprawled on the altar at Engelmynster. Cathryn's pleading face. Strang's mutilated body. "And I've seen too many good people die."

He would have to return to Engelmynster and inform Alric and Wilda of their son's death. They deserved that at least. They had been so kind to him. He would see Coenred too and his spirits lifted at the prospect of seeing the young monk again.

They turned as someone else climbed the ladder and joined them on the platform. It was Scand. He looked refreshed, but older than he had only a couple of weeks before.

"But you've learnt to fight as well as any warrior I've known, Beobrand," he said, clearly having overheard the conversation. "Your defeat of Hengist has already become legendary on the mead benches of Bebbanburg. Slaying your brother's murderer and avenging Strang is a thing to be proud of."

Scand looked at Beobrand and Acennan. "And you have made good friends. That is something any man can be content with. True friends are as rare as gold, and more valuable. You also have a beautiful woman who dotes on you. Life can be harsh, it is true. But you must learn to dwell on the now and the future."

"And what does the future hold for me?" asked Beobrand.

"Who can say? But if you will still follow me, we will march soon to crush Cadwallon in battle once and for all."

"I've heard that before. Last time I was here, I swore fealty to Edwin and we marched to Elmet."

"As I said, do not dwell on the past. Much has changed. Penda no longer stands with Cadwallon. The Waelisc king is weakened. Now is Oswald's time."

"Why did he not respond to the beacons?" Beobrand asked the question that had troubled him.

"Ours is not to question the ways of kings," replied Scand.

Beobrand thought that it surely benefited Oswald to have his brother killed by Cadwallon. He wondered what the Christ god's priests preached on the subject of brother-slaying, but he held his tongue. He was sure the Christ god would not smile on all of his actions this past year. Grimgundi's face came into his mind, peering through smoke, then his mother's voice: "You... are... not... your... father's... son..." What had she meant? He pushed thoughts of his parents away. He should take Scand's advice and think of the present and the future, not the past.

"So you have sworn fealty to Oswald?"

"I have."

"Is he a good man?" asked Beobrand.

"He is a king of the royal line of Aethelric, descended from Woden himself. That is good enough for me. We are but warriors, Beobrand. We need a lord to follow, and to protect us."

"I gave my oath to you, lord Scand. If you now follow Oswald, then my oath is already his too."

Scand clapped him on the shoulder. "I am glad to hear it. You are a formidable addition to any warband. It is good to see you back on your feet too. We will be marching soon. You must regain your strength." Scand turned to leave.

"When I last stood here I had only a boy's dreams of being a warrior and seeing the glory of battle. I wept for the death of my brother and hoped that if I became a shield-bearer I would find happiness. Now I have a fine sword, helm, shield and iron-knit shirt. And I have killed many men."

Scand paused at the top of the ladder. "And have you found happiness?"

"I don't know what happiness is anymore."

"You were born to fight. I have seen you wield the sword. But the way of the sword is not rife with happiness. The sword is like a serpent. You can try to tame it, but it is venomous and will often bite the hand that holds it." The old lord descended the ladder and was gone from view.

Beobrand turned back to look out to sea. Far away on the horizon beyond the sun-dappled waves of the Whale Road storm clouds were brewing.

Acennan placed a hand on his shoulder. "We should go back down. It is cold and you need more rest."

Beobrand nodded and made his way awkwardly down the ladder. Towards the good woman who loved him.

His limbs quivered with weakness when he reached the ground. He did need rest. And time alone with Sunniva. Scand was right. He should not dwell on the past.

Tomorrow would come soon enough.

Historical Note

The first half of the seventh century is situated deep in what is traditionally called the Dark Ages. The period is dark in many ways. It was a violent time, where races clashed and kingdoms were created and destroyed by the sword.

Men with ambition ruled kingdoms with small numbers of warriors – their gesithas, or retinue of companions. Although they professed kingship tracing back their claim through ancestors all the way to the gods themselves, I imagine them to be more akin to gangsters, or the cattle barons of the American West of the nineteenth century. Each vied for dominance over the land, clashing with other kings in battles which were little more than turf wars. They exacted payment in tribute from their ceorls, or churls – the peasants that lived on their land. This was basically protection money to keep the king and his retinue stocked up with weapons, food and luxuries, so that they would be at hand to defend the populace against the dangers of a largely lawless land.

Throw into this mix racial tensions and the expansion of the Angles, Saxons and Jutes from the east of Britain, enslaving and subjugating the older inhabitants of the island

– the Waelisc, as the continental invaders called all foreigners (and the word that spawned the modern name for Wales, Welsh and Cornwall), and you have a situation not unlike the American "Wild West". Invaders from the east, with superior fighting power destroying a proud culture that inhabited the land long before they came. As the Saxons pushed further westward, there would inevitably have been a frontier where any semblance of control from the different power factions was weak at best and at worst totally absent. As in the Wild West of cowboys and Native Americans, men and women who wished to live outside of the laws laid down by their societies would have gravitated into these vacuums of power.

As if that wasn't enough, there is also the clash at this time of several major religions. Many of the native Britons would worship the same gods they had believed in for centuries while many others worshipped Christ; the Angelfolc (the name used by Bede and adopted in the novel to describe the people who would eventually become known as the English) were just beginning to be converted to Christianity, but many still worshipped the old pantheon of Woden and Thunor (more commonly known by modern-day readers by the Norse names of Odin and Thor). Christianity itself was being spread from two main power bases: the island of Hii (Iona), where the Irish tradition had taken root, and Rome, from where Italian priests, such as Paulinus had been sent. Christianity would eventually sweep all other religions away before it, and the disagreements on the finer points of theology would later be settled at the Synod of Whitby (but that is for another book).

Above all else, the Dark Ages is an apt name for this period, due to the lack of first-hand written accounts. Much of what we know comes from writings that were penned many years later. Two principal sources are Bede's *A History of the*

English Church and People and the *Anglo-Saxon Chronicle*, which was written by many nameless scribes over centuries. Earlier accounts of Germanic and Celtic tribes by Tacitus, a Roman historian, are also useful for inferring what the early Anglo-Saxon cultures were like.

The fact that it is a time seen as "through a glass, darkly" makes it a perfect time to write about. An author does not have a free hand, but there are certainly more areas of uncertainty than with many other periods, allowing a level of flexibility to tell an exciting tale against a backdrop of turmoil and conflict.

Many of the characters, places and events in the book existed. Edwin was the king of Northumbria (and declared by Bede and the *Anglo-Saxon Chronicle* as Bretwalda, or king of the whole of Britain) until 633 when he was killed in the battle of Elmet (also known as Hatfield Chase, or Haethfeld) at the hands of Cadwallon ap Cadfan (or Cadwalla) of Gwynedd and Penda of Mercia.

Following the battle, which took place about eight miles north-east of modern Doncaster, his wife, Ethelburga, and remaining children fled to Kent (Cantware) with Paulinus and Bassus. Bassus is mentioned by Bede and described as a "gallant thegn of King Edwin", so he must have been a character of some standing. The rest of Bassus' exploits are my invention.

The land of Northumbria descended into a period of barbarous lawlessness, in which Cadwallon wreaked havoc on the people. Bede describes how he ravaged "them with ghastly slaughter" and that "this year is looked upon by all good men as despicable and shameful".

Eanfrith and Osric took control of Bernicia and Deira respectively, but were both killed within the year by the implacable Cadwallon. It seems incredible that Eanfrith would travel to speak with Cadwallon with only twelve of his thegns, allowing himself to be dispatched easily. However, this is what is told in the written accounts. Having Eanfrith believe Cadwallon was an ally (as suggested by D. P. Kirby in the book, *The Earliest English Kings*) seemed to provide a plausible background to that event.

Beobrand recalls the atmosphere of the Thrimilci celebrations. This May Day festival (also known as Beltane by the Celts) literally meant "three-milk month". It was a festival of spring and fecundity when, after the long months of winter, cows could be milked three times a day.

The royal villa of Gefrin was destroyed by fire around 633, so it seems likely it was burnt by Cadwallon's forces as they ransacked the land. Again, Eanfrith's naive acceptance of a pact with Cadwallon gave me an excuse to have the king and his retinue there, rather than at the more defensible Bebbanburg.

I have taken some liberties with the location of the river at the site of Gefrin. The River Glen actually runs to the north of the site, not the south. However, there is a stream to the south-west, which I have decided was a larger waterway in the seventh century.

Eanfrith's son, Talorcan, becomes a historical figure of some importance. The name of his mother, a Pictish princess, is unknown, but I have given her the name Finola (a simplified form of the name Fionnguala).

The tale of Eanfrith's brother, Oswald, will be told in subsequent stories, so I will not go into detail here, but I took the decision to have him already present in Bernicia at the time of his brother's demise, ready to pick up the pieces; to seize the moment and the throne.

At this time, many small monastic orders appeared. Some flourished and grew into great medieval monasteries, others faded away or were destroyed. The fate of Engelmynster is yet to be seen, but it is a purely fictional place.

Battles are often portrayed in fiction as huge affairs of thousands of well-armoured men. It is much more likely that battles in this period were between relatively small groups of warriors. There were very few professional soldiers and in a time when the whole of Great Britain had a population of about one million people, it is unlikely that even the largest battles had more than a few hundred people on either side. When kings called upon the fyrd, when each ealdorman would bring his people to war, it is probable that only a small proportion would have had armour and highly-specialised and expensive weapons like swords. Most would have had no armour save for a shield, and would only have carried a spear, which was the mainstay of infantry weaponry. The most common bladed weapon was the seax, a single-edged knife, which gave the Germanic tribes the name native Britons used to describe them: Seaxon.

I took the liberty of adding some langseaxes (a longer seax) into the novel, despite them not appearing until later in history.

It was common practice for the members of a lord's comitatus, his closest gesithas, to give up their lives in battle when their lord fell in battle. At least, that is what is recounted in the sagas and poems from the period. I have taken a slightly more pragmatic stance where that course of action would be the ideal, but an ideal that many would struggle to fulfil and that some would see as wasteful of well-trained warriors.

Swords were very rare. Their blades, pattern-welded out of several strands of iron, were things of great beauty and the ultimate symbol of the elite warrior class. They would also be extremely expensive. Like sports cars today, they would be coveted by many, but owned by few. I am sure that some unscrupulous men, especially men of war, would be more than willing to kill to possess one.

I have used the term thegn to describe a professional warrior or minor noble, despite the term not really being used until later.

The concept of "wyrd" recurs throughout the story. It is similar to fate or destiny. The Anglo-Saxons believed that the paths of their lives were woven in threads by the three sisters of wyrd. Thus, everything could be considered predestined. But it is never that simple, and men still believed that it was possible to face one's wyrd well or poorly. Your wyrd would place obstacles in your path, but you could choose how you would react to them.

I have sought to create a believable world and characters that are true to the time. Any mistakes I may have made are mine alone and I hope they do not detract from the telling of the story.

Beobrand's tale will continue long into the seventh century, as he battles alongside saints and sinners, Christians and pagans. His wyrd will lead him to suffer more losses and maybe even find greater loves, but that is for another day and other stories.

Acknowledgements

I hope you, dear reader, have enjoyed this book. Let me offer you my heartfelt thanks for buying it and taking the time to read it. If you can manage a few extra minutes to leave a review online, or to tweet about it, or sing its praises on Facebook, then I will be eternally grateful.

I would like to express my sincere thanks to the following people for their support and help in the writing of this novel:

Firstly, the test readers who provided great feedback and helped me to hone the final draft: Derek and Jacqui "proofreader extraordinaire" Surgey, Soelwin Oo, Emmett Carter, Naomi Harffy and Carry Crets.

Shane Smart and Richard Ward for the stimulating conversations about the book. Hearing their thoughts each day on the latest section they'd read made going into work even more fun than usual!

Simon Blunsdon, for being such a great sport and providing excellent suggestions about the structure of the novel.

Special thanks to my dad, Clive Harffy, whose detailed feedback really improved the book. Thanks also to my mum, Angela Harffy, not only for reading it, but for liking it too and putting up with dad spending hours reviewing it for me!

The incredibly talented and generous, Matt Bunker, from the amazing re-enactment group, Wulfheodenas, for the cover photograph.

It has taken years to get this book to the point of publication and many other writers, most of whom I have only "met" online, have provided encouragement, advice and support. There are too many to list them all here, but special mention must go to Steven A. McKay, Justin Hill, Angus Donald, Paul Fraser Collard, Carol McGrath, Manda Scott, Elaine Moxon, Derek Birks and E. M. Powell.

Robin Wade, my agent, for believing in me, giving me a great insight into the workings of the publishing industry, and for the pep talks. We got there in the end!

Thanks to Caroline Ridding and all the great team of professionals at Aria/Head of Zeus for taking what I was already proud of and making it even better.

Extra special thanks to Gareth Jones for the friendship, in-depth discussions and unwavering encouragement.

My great friend, Alex Forbes, who read the first few chapters years ago and told me I had to tell Beobrand's story. Without his belief in me, there would be no book in your hand.

Finally, to my wife, Maite and our daughters, Elora and Iona, for being there always, understanding and supporting me every step of the way. They make me strive to be a better version of me and I love them completely.